Selina Penaluna

www.**rbooks**.co.uk

Selina Penaluna

JAN PAGE

DOUBLEDAY

SELINA PENALUNA
A DOUBLEDAY BOOK 978 0 385 61372 9

Published in Great Britain by Doubleday,
an imprint of Random House Children's Books
A Random House Group Company

This edition published 2008

1 3 5 7 9 10 8 6 4 2

Copyright © Jan Page, 2008

The Random House Group Limited supports the Forest Stewardship Council (FSC),
the leading international forest certification organization. All our titles that are p
rinted on Greenpeace-approved FSC-certified paper carry the FSC logo. Our paper
procurement policy can be found at www.rbooks.co.uk/environment.

Set in Caxton

RANDOM HOUSE CHILDREN'S BOOKS
61–63 Uxbridge Road, London W5 5SA

www.**kids**at**randomhouse**.co.uk
www.**rbooks**.co.uk

Addresses for companies within The Random House Group Limited can be found at:
www.randomhouse.co.uk/offices.htm

THE RANDOM HOUSE GROUP Limited Reg. No. 954009

A CIP catalogue record for this book is available from the British Library.

Printed in the UK by
CPI Mackays, Chatham, ME5 8TD

For Renny

PROLOGUE

Selina sits on the black rock, her wild wet hair slapping across her face; her fish tail flaps in the darkness. She's singing a strange ethereal song that hangs in the wind, an underwater tongue so beautiful that it hurts his ears, its high pitch drilling deep into his soul. I want the young man to turn back or strap himself to the mast but instead he sets the tiller for the jagged edge of the rock. The sea rises up as he flings the tiny boat towards her; it cracks and splinters, the icy water floods round his feet, fishing nets tangle. Selina is watching him with her violet eyes – she's calm, poised, her sea-blood runs cold. She dives and vanishes with a flick of her silvery tail.

The sailor is hurled across the broken deck, smashing his ribs against the side. He stares down into the deep, rolling blackness, calling out her name. Suddenly she springs out of the water like a flying fish and she's right next to the boat, one hand stretched out towards him. There's danger in her gaze, but he takes her cold fingers, smiling. He lets himself be pulled into the water. She lifts a lock of wet hair from his eyes and embraces him, kissing the last air from his bow-shaped mouth as they sink beneath the waves.

ONE

'Remember it yet?'

My granddaughter looks from left to right, small white bungalows on one side, green fields of toffee-coloured cows on the other.

'Not really, but I'm sure I will when we get to the house.'

We continue down the steep narrow hill towards the sea, pausing in the bent elbow of the lane to let a car pass, laden with surfboards, bikes and windswept children. She looks up at the post office, now also a general store, off licence, tearoom and mini art gallery. 'Has that always been there?'

'Yes, in one form or another. It's very fancy these days – all ciabatta bread and pain au chocolat.'

'Doesn't sound very Cornish,' she laughs.

'Don't worry – it's still the same old place.'

Cassie last came to Spindrift when she was eight, the summer before my son Michael took his family to live in Australia. Now she's nineteen. I have only seen her once in the intervening years, when Richard and I went over one Christmas. She was thirteen then and more interested in boys than long-lost grandparents. I had remembered her as fidgety and rather rude and was totally unprepared for the tanned vision of loveliness that greeted me at the airport. She's 'doing Europe' for a few months. Her plan had been to stay with me in London and she has already hinted that she could manage quite happily in my flat by herself. Although it is beautiful here, I realize that the freezing Atlantic Ocean and three foot of surf is no lure for an Aussie, but I have a job to do and I need her help.

We turn another corner, taking the narrow unmade path, barely wide enough for a car, to Spindrift, looking its best in the fierce afternoon sunshine – its smooth slate tiles glistening, the roof furry with moss and mustard-coloured lichen. The house has what the estate agents will no doubt describe as a stunning location, sitting on a small promontory that juts out like a witch's nose between a sandy bay and a vast expanse of rocks. It's so worn and weather-beaten, so much part of the landscape, that you could paint the entire scene with a simple colour palette of grey, blue, white, yellow and brown.

The lock resists as I open the front door. I sniff, holding the smell in my nose to commit it to memory – dust, sand, salt, dry wood. A few envelopes lie on the mat. Bending down carefully, I pick them up, shuffling them between my mottled hands like a giant pack of cards. As I linger in the hallway I can hear the sounds of the distant past: the whole family arriving at once, heaving suitcases noisily up the stairs, calling to each other as they unpacked and made up the beds. They were the best summers, when the grandchildren were young.

'Yes,' Cassie whispers, 'I remember it now . . . It hasn't changed one bit.'

She sighs and drops her huge rucksack on the floor as if she has been carrying it for miles although it's been in the back of my car since I picked her up at the airport five hours ago. She removes the band from her hair, shakes out her blonde curls and restrains them again, a little higher up her head.

'Where am I sleeping?'

'In your old room. See if you can find it.'

She bounds up the stairs two at a time and suddenly I see a lively, tomboyish six-year-old, leapfrogging over the bollards in Padstow harbour or clambering up the rocks in her pink plastic sandals, a bucket of shrimps swinging from her arm. Cassandra with the tousled hair, bleached almost white in the summer sun, who always looked as if she were about to run a race, bouncing around at some imaginary starting line, her eager young legs on springs.

'The big one, overlooking the beach, isn't it?' She leans over the banisters. 'I remember the big fireplace, the wind whistling down it at night. Used to scare the pants off us.'

Spindrift . . . What will the viewers think when they step inside? I expect they will find the place tired and old-fashioned, imagining – quite wrongly – that because there is no tasteful colour scheme, no careful arrangement of furniture, it has been unloved. My uncle's old leather arm-chair and two sagging sofas take up most of the sitting room – grains of last summer's sand still clinging to the lumpy cushions. The oak bookcase is stuffed with battered novels; dozens of old newspapers are yellowing in a wicker basket next to the slate fireplace – their articles read long ago, their crosswords partially completed. A piece of gnarled driftwood suns itself like a lizard on the coffee table and a green bottle of shells holds back the open door. On the walls are water-colour seascapes, charcoal sketches of wild flowers and Cornish birds. Only the mantelpiece remains uncluttered – at its centre sits a plain grey stone in the perfect shape of a heart.

The house has become a cross between a second-hand emporium and a huge nature table, heaving with objects that once lay on the beach. Every shell and pebble, every oily feather, each lump of driftwood and piece of slate was once singled out for being beautiful or strange. Somebody (over the years I've forgotten exactly who found what) picked it up, turned it over in their hands and held it up to the sunlight, put it in a bucket or a trouser pocket and took it back to the house. This act of bringing the outside in is a family compulsion and I feel the house gradually sinking into its surroundings – the rocks, the sand, maybe even the sea itself.

The green velvet curtains, sun-faded between their folds, rattle on their brass rings as I draw them back. I wrench open the window, and the sea roars into the room so loudly that I step back as if to avoid an incoming wave. The tide is right up – the ocean's foamy fingers touching the watermark on the sea wall like a swimmer racing to the finishing line. But it will only be a short while before the sea tumble-turns and makes its way back, revealing a landscape of glassy rock pools where translucent shrimps dart through an underwater forest of pungent brown seaweed.

I join Cassie in the master bedroom with the views of the sandy bay and the large round blow-hole on the cliff top. It's a jumble of mismatched furniture – a huge mahogany wardrobe, my aunt's oak dressing table with the three mirrors, a large white chest of drawers, deep red curtains that don't go with the yellow bedspread, a creaky iron-framed double bed.

'Didn't we have bunks?' she says, sitting down to unlace her traveller's walking boots.

I nod. 'We always put all the cousins in together.'

'Yeah, we had some great holidays here . . .' She sighs. 'Do you see Kim and Billie much?'

'Not any more. After the divorce it all went very sour . . . Your uncle's in South America, you know, and the children have gone to live in France. I'm the only one left in this country now.'

'Well, I'm here – for a few weeks, at least.'

'Yes, and it's wonderful to see you.' I give her a brief hug.

She walks over to the window and sighs at the view. 'This is such a fantastic house. How can you bear to sell it?'

'I have no choice. It's too much to look after and—'

'Oh, I forgot,' she interrupts. 'I brought you a present.'

'You shouldn't have.'

'Hey, Gran, I haven't sent you so much as a birthday card for the last five years. It's downstairs, in my rucksack.'

Cassie gives me a beautiful hardback book, the kind you might find lingering on a coffee table. Its title is picked out in glittery swirls over a deep blue background – *A Symphony of Mermaids*.

'Thank you, dear,' I say, removing the plastic film wrapper. 'But you shouldn't have spent all this money. I'm sure this was very expensive.'

'Don't worry about it.' She leans over me eagerly as I turn the pages – glossy coloured illustrations of long-haired top-less maidens draped around their lovers, perched on a rock out at sea or reclining by the shore.

'The illustrations are beautiful,' I reply. 'I'll take it to bed tonight, have a proper read.'

'I've got a bit of a thing about mermaids,' Cassie continues. 'Not sure why. Ever since I was little they've really fascinated me. Mum used to read me that Hans Christian Andersen story, about the Little Mermaid. It always made me cry.'

'Yes, it's very sad . . .' I murmur quietly, although in truth I have never felt much sympathy for mermaids.

'When she gives up her tail and walks on land for the first time – remember that bit? It feels like she's walking on broken glass, but she carries on.' Cassie stops, seeing the expression on my face.

I am staring at the illustration on the page opposite, entitled *Lost at Sea*. A handsome young sailor is battling through a storm in a tiny fishing boat, leaning over the side as a beautiful mermaid with violet eyes and long golden hair tries to pull him into the water.

'Are you OK, Gran? Only you've gone ever so pale.'

'What? Oh no, dear, it's nothing. Just feeling a little tired, that's all.'

'Can I get you something? A glass of water?'

'No, no, I'm fine. Absolutely fine.' I shut the book firmly and put it on the table. 'I expect you're hungry,' I announce, keeping my voice as steady as possible. 'Shall I start the supper?'

After we've eaten, Cassie decides to go and see 'what's happening in the village', a remark which mildly amuses me. I offer to take her to the pub and introduce her to the locals, but she shakes her head.

'Thanks, but I don't want to be forced on anyone just because I'm your granddaughter.'

The front door slams heavily behind her in the evening breeze. I take a few seconds to absorb the silence, to accept that the only sounds I'll hear in the house this evening will be the ones I make – a boiling kettle, the flush of the toilet, a knife scraping a dirty plate. But I am a widow now, almost used to that.

I pour myself a gin and tonic, pick up the mermaid book and go upstairs to my room. It's the smallest bedroom, tucked away at the back with a view just of the ocean, not even a glimpse of the cliffs that embrace the house on either side. It was the room I was given when we first arrived and I have always slept here, not even moving into the master bedroom after my aunt died. Perhaps it's because I still feel like a guest, or simply because I have always felt closest to Jack here. I used to stand by the open window and imagine I was on the deck of a ship, cast adrift, the safety and comfort of dry land a hundred miles away. I would sway slightly from side to side as if I were sailing through a vast graveyard, searching for him.

I take off my sandals and sit with my legs up on the bedspread, the book resting on my lap. I stare at the cover nervously – it's no good, I must steel myself to look at the picture again. As I open the book the pages flutter as if turned by an invisible hand and it's no surprise where they finally come to rest.

I stare at the painting: the colours blur and it seems to flicker like a movie on an old cinema screen. The glossy paper shines in the lamplight and as I trace my finger along the white tip of a wave it feels cold, almost wet. I am pulled into the boat as it battles its way through the storm. I touch the soaked white shirt of the sailor as he clings to the side, feel the cold terror on his skin. The black ocean heaves, knives of rain stab the surface, water on water, darkness above and beneath.

The mermaid's face stares out at me brazenly, challenging me to recognize her. Our eyes meet.

Yes, Selina, I know it's you . . .

TWO

I came out of a pool so deep no man has ever touched the bottom of it.

That's what the woman I called my mother told me. If my father was hearing me he'd slam his fist down on the table and swear the story is nothing but mad nonsense. But this is what Morva told me word for word, as best I remember it.

It's summertime and she's out walking on the cliffs with her first born in her arms – a small pink slippery girl no more than a few months old. She's looking over the edge, down into the rocky cove beneath, when she comes over with a fierce longing to feel the cold of the sea on her skin. So Morva do make a cradle out of her shawl and tie it round her neck, tucking her baby inside it. She starts going down the steep path to the cove, shuffling on her arse over the sharp rocks, the baby wriggling like an angleditch.

She's on the beach now – the tide's out and the black slate's drying grey in the sun – and she's picking her way across the rocks with the child bouncing on her chest, squealing and kicking her bare feet. Morva finds this deep, dark pool – in the shape of a near circle, like somebody's hewn it out of the rock. She do sit herself down on the edge and dips her toes in. The water's so cold and tingly it makes her gasp and want more. There's nobody else on the beach to see so she lifts her dress and tucks it into her drawers, shifts herself forward and dangles her legs in up to her white thighs. But the sides of the pool are slimy with bright green weed and she can't keep hold. In goes Morva, can't stop herself, and her little writhing worm of a baby slides out of the shawl and shoots into the water, sinking straight down without a splash or a cry. The child is gone and not so much as a bubble of breath rises to the surface.

Now Morva's flapping and flailing about, gulping in seawater, squalling and screaming to the heavens for help for she can't swim, but only the gulls can hear her. She takes hold of a straggly bunch of seaweed and hauls her body back onto the rocks and kneels there, shaking with shock, her dress dripping, her shoes lost and her wet hair wrapped cold about her face. She glazes down into the deep black pool, the surface all still now, not moving a ripple, and she knows in that moment that her child has gone for ever. And she lets up a roar of pain and is ready to fling herself back in the water and drown with grief when suddenly the strangest thing do happen.

A child bobs up in the water afore her very eyes – smiling, laughing and gurgling, swimming like a seal. And thinking that it's her own baby, Morva screams out for joy and grabs her and clasps her tight against her chest, thanking God for a miracle. When she's done cuddling and kissing and crying she do lay her down on the warm slate to look at her closer and check she still has all her toes and fingers, and it's only then she sees it's not her child at all, but another baby girl she's never clept eyes on before! For her daughter's skin was pink and this baby is white as marble, her eyes were grey-blue but these are deep violet, her hair wispy brown but this head has dried to golden curls.

Morva is so afeard she nearly throws me back in the water! Yet I do laugh and smile so and look up at the sun like it's a thing of wonder and am such an odd little creature that she cannot bring herself to do it. She's in such a shock she stays on the beach until the sun goes down, sobbing in the darkness for her own dear girl, wondering what kind of creature I might be. But being afeard of getting the blame for her daughter's drowning, she do choose to keep me, wraps me up in her shawl and takes me home to her husband. And him being a man what understands nothing about babies, he never sees the difference.

THREE

The morning sun eventually wakes me – my skin is hot and damp, my head hurts, the sheets smell of stale sweat and talcum powder. I feel groggy, as if after a heavy night's drinking – I can't remember how or when I got back into bed. The mermaid book is lying face down on the other pillow, still open at the picture of Selina. I shut it quickly, careful not to catch her eye.

I hurriedly shower, put on yesterday's blouse and skirt and go down to the kitchen, but I feel nervous, as if she's following me. My hands shake as I fill the kettle. I jump when the bread pops out of the toaster. Every sound I make seems amplified, every action exaggerated. The toast is brittle and snaps between my fingers; a corner falls into my lap, jam side down. What I need is activity, a task to occupy my mind, focus my energies.

Today I will empty the attic and sort its contents into three piles – one to take to the dump, one to keep and one for the charity shop. Nobody has been up there for about twenty years and I have to admit that the prospect scares me. I know there are some things up there that will be hard to deal with, that should have been thrown out long ago. But there can be no more excuses: I must make myself do this.

'You can't sell Spindrift, it's always belonged in the family,' my son Michael protested when I rang to say I was putting the house on the market. He is wrong on both counts. I do not come from a line of homeowners, but poor tenants who often had to pawn their belongings to pay the weekly rent. And although my name is on all the papers, I have never felt that I truly own the place. I came here with my brother, Jack, over sixty years ago and nobody expected us to stay more than a few weeks. It's the house that owns *me* now.

I'm not going to find it easy to open cupboards and drawers, to sort and discard, to remove carpets and furniture, to listen to my shoes on bare floorboards, to gaze at empty walls, remembering what once hung in the spaces. Every sight, sound and smell will be conspiring against me, joining forces to test my resolve. Even my aunt's paintings will have to go; I have no room for them at home. I look across at a watercolour of the bay that hangs over the fireplace, still searching for Jack on the crowded beach – hoping to find him as a brown flick on the pale wash of yellow, a coloured dot bobbing in the unpainted white of the waves . . .

Luckily the ceilings in the house are low and I can easily reach the loft hatch by standing on a stepladder. But the door is stiff and I have to push with all my strength to release it. A square of musty darkness opens up above me. I climb a little higher and shine my torch through the hole, sweeping the beam backwards and forwards like a searchlight, not daring to look at what I might be illuminating. I pause for several seconds to give any inhabitants a chance to hide, but I hear nothing. There is no life up there, only the possessions of the dead.

Cassie stumbles across me two hours later on her way to the bathroom. I'm sitting on the landing surrounded by cardboard boxes, dusty plastic bags and old leather suitcases. My hair is sticky with cobwebs, my hands black with old dirt. I smile at her triumphantly.

'Where's it come from?' Cassie raises her eyebrows.

I point upwards at the open hatch. 'There's a lot more – books, china, ornaments, bits of furniture – you wouldn't believe how much is up there. I've got to be brave – ruthless – but I don't know where to start.'

Cassie doesn't share my fear of the past. She plonks herself down on the carpet and reaches for the oldest-looking box, peeling off the yellowing tape. Inside is a jumble of art materials – squashed tubes of watercolours, brushes of several sizes, a dirty cloth torn from an old vest, a box of brittle charcoal sticks, some chalk, three soft drawing pencils sharpened by a knife.

'My aunt's,' I explain.

'Oh, right . . . So she did all the paintings?' Cassie glances up at three small seascapes hanging on the wall above us.

'Yes. I don't know what I'm going to do with them all. Some of them are quite good, but . . . I can't keep everything.'

'Could I have these brushes? They're real sable.'

'Of course. Do you paint?'

'Didn't Dad tell you, I'm going to do art at uni – well, more like mixed media. Fine art's boring.'

Cassie chatters on while she plunders the boxes, un-wrapping china and reading aloud from the bits of crumpled newspaper thirty or forty years old, laughing at the adverts for corsets or laundry aids. She tries on a cardigan of my uncle's and makes faces in the mirror. She builds a wall out of damp hardback novels and sorts through a box of dog-eared piano music – all the time marvelling why anyone would want to keep so much junk.

'Most of this stuff doesn't belong to me,' I confess, looking bewildered at the mess. 'I suppose I never felt entitled to throw it out.'

'Well, you've got no choice now.' She grins.

Cassie passes down yet another heavy cardboard box – 'More books, I think.' But when I open it up I find an assort-ment of memorabilia – photographs, theatre and concert programmes, old postcards and letters.

My brain stirs with remembering as I take out a cream leather photo album, decorated with an ornate gold design, much of which has rubbed off with handling. Inside the pages are smooth and black. The prints have been carefully slipped into transparent triangles at the corners; white clay pencil writing underneath gave the date, location and the names of those pictured: *Jack and Ellen, by the Round Hole, 12th April, 1940; The twins on a walk to the lighthouse, 10th May*.

Cassie looks from one small, fuzzy face to the other – 'You don't look like twins.' I sense what she is thinking – that God had only one set of good looks to donate to the family and unfairly allocated them all to Jack. His nose is fine and straight, whereas mine leans slightly to one side, and his mouth is shaped in a perfect bow in contrast to my lopsided blob. I am the factory second and he the finished article, taller, stronger, his brown hair a little wavier. But our legs look identical, long, thin, knees a little knobbly, as if they belong to one four-legged animal. Or is it just the way we're standing, both with our weight on the right foot, the left knee slightly bent? We're looking at the camera in the same way too, wanting to please and yet a little embarrassed, unused to having our picture taken. Yes, it's not our features that identify us as twins – it's our stance, our attitude, the unified gaze.

'Your brother – wasn't he killed in the war?'

'Yes, but not fighting . . . He was too young to fight.'

'How old was he then?'

'Sixteen . . . All his things must be up there, somewhere.' I look up at the dark hole of the loft hatch. 'After he died my uncle emptied his room, packed all his clothes and belongings into cardboard boxes and hid them away.'

'Why?'

'My aunt was ill and he felt all the reminders were making her worse. We had to carry on as if Jack had never existed. I wasn't happy about it but my uncle ruled the roost.'

'Sounds a bit weird to me . . .'

I return to the photograph album and turn the page. 'Here he is. Charles Algernon Augustive Rosewarne.' We are looking at a tall, thin man in his late forties, standing on the rocks, a few strands of hair pasted across a balding head, round spectacles, white shirt, trousers rolled halfway up his calves.

'He wasn't our real uncle, you see, that's just how he liked us to address him . . . We weren't related at all.'

'So Rosewarne isn't your real name?' Cassie sounds shocked.

'It's not the name on my birth certificate, if that's what you mean. We were evacuees.'

I turn the pages until I find the other photograph I've been looking for – Aunt Clara, about thirty years younger than I am now. She's standing with her back to the sea, her dark, shoulder-length hair blown back by the wind, her eyes screwed up against the sun. She's wearing a floral dress, impossible to tell from the black and white picture which colour, but I remember it was sage-green with a small white collar, a chunky brooch pinned in the centre of her chest. Her coat is unbuttoned and a square box hangs from her shoulder on a thin strap – it is this object that pins the picture down to within a few years. She is no longer just a woman smiling on the beach, but a part of history, scooped up in the butterfly net of time.

FOUR

Jack and I were twelve years old before we saw the sea, and yet we were born on an island. We lived in North Woolwich in the East End of London – a crisscross of mean, narrow streets that were bound by the docks to the north and the winding river Thames to the south and east. We must have known that the huge freight vessels that steamed past eventually reached the open sea, but to us the Thames was no more than an enormous bath, frothy with effluent that left a dirty ring of green slime around its banks at low tide.

Ours was the last house of a terraced row that came to a halt outside the King George V Dock, its high concrete wall topped with black timber fencing. A ditch ran alongside our stretch of wall, a filthy stagnant trench full of empty bottles and old rags, so encrusted with algae that when the sun shone on its bright green surface the water looked solid. But in the spring it bubbled with frogs like a witch's cauldron and we spent hours there, our legs dangling over the side, trying to fish them out. The ditch was too wide to jump over and our only bridge was an old scaffolding plank borrowed from the builder's yard at the back of our house. On the other side was

Granddad's allotment, a narrow strip of poor ground that ran against the dock wall, where he grew a few vegetables – potatoes, carrots, cabbages and beetroot.

If I had known when we marched out of the playground on that warm September morning that we would never return to North Woolwich, perhaps I would have tried harder to store up the memories of those early years. Now just a few images rise randomly to the surface, like scum foaming in a pot of boiling bones. Domestic scenes mostly – my father warming up his jug of beer with a red-hot poker, plucking a freshly killed chicken, its feathers flying across the yard. My mother scrubbing the scullery floor, wiping soot from the window-sills, polishing the pavement outside the front door until it shone like a white half-moon. But my strongest image is of my grandfather laid out in his coffin on the dining table – suit, white shirt, scrubbed fingernails, his big labourer's hands folded across his chest – the back room full of his mates eating pie and mash while they waited for the hearse to arrive, Jack and I huddled together tearfully in the corner. From that day I could never stand the smell of green eel liquor – to me it was the stink of death.

Mum insisted that Jack and I stayed together when we went out, much to his annoyance because he liked to hang around with the boys at the dock gates, begging for cigarette cards. After school we'd sneak round the side of the locks and run across the yards – usually chased by a dock policeman – to what we called the 'skinny bridge'. On the other side was a small inlet bustling with all kinds of interesting river craft.

We'd wander up and down the quay looking at the boats and picking out which one we'd buy if we had the money. Jack had a passion for the river and talked of becoming a bargee when he grew up.

One Sunday afternoon he persuaded Shonny Sullivan, who was a couple of years older and the local 'bad boy', to take us to his older brother's barge, which was moored offshore opposite the park. We scrambled over the slippery pebble beach and took our places in a tiny rowing boat. Shonny stood up like a proper waterman, pushing off from the bank and sculling with a single oar as we set out to cross one of the busiest waterways in the world.

The Thames was teeming with tugboats, dredgers, police launches and merchant vessels, ploughing back and forth to the Pool of London along the deep water lanes, but we were taking the shorter, but far more perilous route from north to south. Our little boat was rocking furiously across the grey furrows of dirty water, our bottoms involuntarily rising from the hard wooden seat as we bounced along, cutting across the channel. I clung onto Jack, terrified, watching Shonny's thin, bony legs swaying from side to side as he tried to keep his balance. He was wearing heavy black boots and long shorts, his calves were covered in scratches and bruises, and dirty grey socks gathered at his ankles.

'We can't swim!' I screamed.

Shonny laughed. 'Nor can I!' he shouted back wildly, a manic look in his eyes. Jack was whooping and cheering, but as he gripped the bench I could see that his knuckles were white.

'Turn round!' I cried. 'You'll get us killed!'

'Don't take no notice, Shonny!' called Jack, cruelly trying to wrench me free from his arm. I looked back in desperation to the park behind us. It was full of people taking their Sunday afternoon stroll through the cool avenue of trees that overlooked the river – courting couples walking out, soldiers from the Artillery Depot in their heavy, high-buttoned tunics, families trooping along in large cumbersome groups, the children lagging behind, itching in their Sunday best. The Royal Artillery Band was playing on the bandstand, their cheerful brassy music wafting over the bright flowerbeds, drowning out my cries for help as Shonny rowed us further and further away, the middle channel of the river looming before us, beckoning certain death. Then I saw a woman standing on the causeway, shouting and waving her arms furiously. It was Mum. Even from a distance I could see that she was shaking, her face red with anger.

'Look!' I shouted. 'She's seen us!'

Jack groaned. 'We're in for a right hiding now,' he said ruefully. 'Sorry, mate. Better turn back.'

'What the hell did you think you was doing?' Mum screamed, dragging us out of the boat as soon as Shonny pulled up on the pebbly beach. I looked down at my white canvas shoes, bought new for the summer – they were green with slime. 'You stupid idiots,' she cried. 'You could 'a' drowned!'

She grabbed us by the wrists and hauled us up Barge House Road, gripping us tightly as if we were two balloons that might float away. Neither of us spoke, but I knew what we were both thinking. How on earth could Mum have known what we were up to? Later she told me she'd been sitting on a chair outside the front door and had fallen asleep in the afternoon sunshine. She'd had a dream that Jack was up to his chin in deep, swirling water. His head was sinking and rising, sinking and rising; each time he came up it was for a few seconds less. Something was dragging him under and he was losing the struggle, gulping in water, gasping for every breath. The vision was so strong that she'd woken up screaming and run all the way from our house to the water, knowing she'd find him there.

It was summer and all the talk was of some German chap called Herr Hitler, who apparently had designs on our country and wanted to gas us all to death. We were sent back to school in the holidays to practise for evacuation. Our headmaster, Mr Coleman, made us march around the playground in the hot sunshine, a small suitcase in our hands or a haversack slung across our backs, our newly issued gas masks in cardboard boxes swinging round our necks. He led the dummy parade, a small banner held before his waist bearing the name of our school.

On Friday September 1st we did it for real. Where we were going or for how long nobody seemed to know, but it was almost certainly going to be 'in the country'. Living so close to the docks would make us a certain target for the bombs, and we all believed that Hitler was going to drop them on our heads the very moment war was officially declared. We were led to the big station where the platforms were packed with children, some sad and bewildered, but most behaving as if they were off on some holiday jaunt. Mr Coleman had great difficulty keeping us all together despite his banner, which rose by the minute until he was waving it frantically above his head.

I spotted a small group of sailors standing by the wall of the railway café, chatting and smoking. Mum had once told me that if you touched a sailor's collar it would bring you luck, so I crept forward and tapped one of them lightly on the shoulder. If he felt it he didn't bother to turn round and I ran back to Jack, triumphant. He told me I was barmy, but I felt we needed all the luck we could get that day, travelling alone with one small case and a label pinned to our coats, not knowing where we were going or who might take us in.

Even now, I can remember the journey, sitting on my cardboard suitcase in the packed, sweaty corridor, its hard covering chafing the back of my legs. Two or three teachers were standing by the window and every so often one of them would shift to one side to let us look at the view. The harvest was in and huge bales were stacked in the shorn fields. We shouted out whenever we passed cows or sheep and the adults laughed at our excitement. As we travelled further west the railway embankments turned from dull brown to a deep rusty red.

'Where are all the houses?' I whispered to Jack, wondering if this was how London would look once Hitler had finished bombing – the buildings flattened, the grass growing through the concrete, the city reduced to large empty fields. There was so little sign of human life, so few roads or bridges or shops, that I was starting to lose all sense of scale.

We arrived at the station in the middle of a small town, hungry and exhausted, all pushing past each other in a desperate rush for the toilet. We were led to the bus depot, where some Girl Guides pressed slices of cake and glasses of lemonade into our dirty, sweaty hands before we were put on a charabanc. As we drove through the winding streets of the town dozens of local people gathered on the pavements, gawping at us as if we'd just landed from outer space. After no more than a few minutes we arrived at the Friends' Meeting House, where fussy ladies in floral dresses gave us a paper carrier bag each. Inside were tins of beef and milk, a packet of biscuits and even a small bar of chocolate.

Once we'd been signed in we were taken into a hall and paraded round in a big circle for the local people to take their pick. Tall strapping lads were the first to go, chosen by farmers to work in the fields. Then the neatly dressed children with tidy haircuts and better luggage were led away. I felt myself burning with embarrassment as we walked round and round while strangers stared and pointed, mumbling to each other and shaking their heads. By early evening the final sticky trainload had arrived and over four hundred children had been dispatched to their billets. But nobody wanted us. There were only nine children left, including two groups of brothers who, like us, were refusing to be split up.

Eventually a smartly dressed couple several years older than our parents walked into the room and looked us all up and down, talking in muffled whispers to each other. Then the man beckoned Jack over and asked him his age and name. Jack told him straight away that we came as a pair so I was called over too.

'And what's your name, dear?' asked the lady.

'Ellen,' I mumbled.

'But we all call her Nellie,' added Jack.

'Well, I shall call you Ellen. It's such a lovely name.'

The tall elegant gentleman with deep blue eyes and thin silvery hair held out his hand. 'I am Charles Rosewarne and this is my wife, Clara.'

'Welcome to Cornwall.' She smiled at us reassuringly.

Mr Rosewarne lifted my label and frowned at the message – *Twins* – *not to be sepperated*, it read.

'Who wrote that?' he asked abruptly. 'Not your teacher, I hope.'

'No, mister, my mum done it,' Jack replied stiffly. I instantly felt ashamed. I knew that she'd spelled it wrongly, but hadn't liked to correct it. It was just like her to throw in an extra 'p' for good measure, as if it were an extra dollop of mashed potato.

'Well, I think they're just perfect,' Mrs Rosewarne said, tugging at her husband's sleeve. Perfect for what? I thought. But we didn't say anything, just smiled a little and nodded when they told us to gather our things and make our way to the car.

We drove out of the town and were soon jolting along narrow lanes, twisting deeper into the darkness. With the headlamps covered it was almost impossible to see where we were going. We followed a horse and cart for a few miles – not daring to overtake – and narrowly missed a man trembling on an unlit bicycle. I instinctively moved closer to Jack, gripping his arm, our thoughts hanging in the silence. As we passed the grey shapes of farmhouses, pubs and isolated rows of small cottages, not one friendly chink of light twinkled at us in the blackout.

'Our house is called Spindrift,' Mrs Rosewarne whispered. 'That's the spray that blows off the top of the waves. We live right on the cliffs, you see.' We turned left into the village. The car hurtled down the steep, curving hill and Mr Rosewarne drew up safely at the edge of the path. I could smell the sea, but the tide must have been right out because all I could glimpse was the sharp black shapes of the rocks.

Jack and I were taken straight indoors and put in separate rooms, a cup of Ovaltine and a malted biscuit at the side of our beds. I spent a restless night tossing about in the crisp linen sheets, my head under the pillow as I tried to cut out the heavy snores of the ocean. It felt as if I were living next to a railway track, only worse because the waves never once stopped as they rumbled towards the shore. I worried that I would have to stay awake for the rest of the war, but eventually the rhythm of the waves must have soothed me to sleep because when I woke it was already morning.

The sun was shining through the floral curtains, turning

the fabric into folds of golden light, and I spent several minutes gazing at the luminous pink and yellow roses before remembering that there was more to see beyond. I drew back the curtains and gasped at the great expanse of glittering water – an intense petrol-blue flecked with white beneath a bold stripe of clearest sky. The simplicity of it astounded me. Water and air, two elements neatly divided by the long, uninterrupted line of the horizon, so straight that God must have drawn it with a ruler. Suddenly I understood that the earth was just a planet and the sky nothing but endless space. I wanted to swim out to the horizon and peer over the edge of the world.

That first morning we were taken on a two-hour walk over the cliffs and up the Camel estuary to Padstow harbour. Mr Rosewarne lectured us the whole way, giving us the history of the area as we climbed over stiles and stumbled up and down the stony paths.

We stopped at the Daymark, a tall stone tower on the cliff top, built a hundred years earlier to warn ships that they were near the treacherous Stepper Point. Now it was a playground for dozens of brown rabbits, running round the foot of the tower and hiding in the gorse. Jack and I stood inside and stared up at the circle of sky until we felt dizzy. The cold sea breeze cut through the open windows and boxed our aching ears.

'*From Padstow Point to Lundy Light, Is a sailor's grave by day or night*,' Mr Rosewarne recited solemnly.

We carried on past fields and farms whose strange names

spoke of ancient, vanished cultures until we came to Mussel Cove, a steep row of cottages and a large shed where the lifeboats were kept. Two leather-faced coastguards were sitting on the steps of the fisherman's store, making crab pots. Although the tide was right out there was still water off the cove and a group of boys were diving off a wobbly landing stage.

'I wish I could do that,' Jack said.

Before us stretched the Doom Bar – a vast bank of glistening wet sand, dotted with feeding gulls. In the distance we could see a lone figure walking across the strand, a young girl with golden hair, the shallow water around her bare feet shimmering like a sheet of glass.

'Many hundreds of years ago a fisherman accidentally wounded a mermaid that lived in this estuary,' said Mr Rosewarne. 'She swept up that bank of sand in her fury and cursed all sailors that might pass. Since then hundreds of ships have come to grief on the Doom Bar.'

'Of course it's just a myth,' his wife added. 'Something the locals like to tell the visitors.'

'You forget, I am a local boy.' He twinkled. 'Come along.'

FIVE

Morva carries on with her life, pretending to all the world that I am her own child, feeding and clothing me and calling me Selina, same as her that was lost in the pool. And nobody ever thinks I'm anything but her daughter. People stop us in the street and say how I'm the fairest child they ever did see, such beautiful eyes and hair like an angel . . . But Morva doesn't care how pretty I am or how sweet my nature is, she cannot love me. I might only be a tiddler but I know there's a sorrow hanging between us, for I can't please this woman no matter how hard I try.

'You'm a merrymaid, Selina,' she says. 'One day you'll grow a fish tail and live for ever in the sea.'

'But I don't want to live in the sea,' I answer. 'I want to live at home in our cottage, with you and Dad.'

'I know, my love, but it cannot be. You'm not like the rest of us.'

I cannot believe her. 'I must be your own child,' I say. 'Everybody says I'm the ashes of 'ee. Our noses are just the same and though my hair is brighter than yours it still curls the way yours do.'

'You'm not mine, I tell 'ee. You came out of that water, not my own body,' Morva says, getting angry now. 'My own lovely girl has gone. The Mer people took her and sent you in her place.'

So now I'm some puzzled and I don't know what is true. Am I a Penaluna or do I belong to the Mer people? If my mother is right and I am a merrymaid, when will the changes happen? And if I grow a fish tail will I have to live in the sea or can I shift shape and stay on the land as long as I please? I can't stop thinking about it and soon I'm dreaming of merrymaids every night. Sometimes they're good dreams – me swimming about with my shiny fish tail, dipping in and out of the sea like one of they basking sharks or bathing in the shallows of a sandy cove, sitting on a rock combing my hair and laughing up at the sky. And I feel free and glad in my heart, for when all's said and done, don't we all want to live for ever?

But other times the dreams turn nightmares. I'm on my own, far out in the ocean – I don't know where zackly but a long way from dry land. The water's deep and some freezing and I don't know how to swim. I just sink down and down to the bottom. I'm lying on the sea bed, with crabs and lobsters crawling all over me, nipping at my skin. I can't breathe and I can't move for I have no fish tail, just two useless legs. I'm not a merrymaid at all, only a human girl. I try screaming for help but no sound comes out my mouth, just bubbles of air. When I wake up my nightdress is soaking and I've wet the bed.

The nightmares are so bad sometimes I'm afeard to sleep. So I creep downstairs and sit on my father's lap by the fire. 'I don't want to be a merrymaid,' I cry. 'Please, Dad, don't let the Mer people take me away.' And this is how my father finds out what's been said to me and he do go straight off into a boiling rage. He turns on Morva and says he'll have her locked up in a mad house for filling my head with such wicked lies, for there's no such thing as merrymaids and even if there were, I'm not one and never will be neither. And she do shout back at him that he's an ignorant pig and not my real father anyways and he clots her across the face and calls her a whore. He swears I am his own true flesh and blood, born upstairs in his bed in this very house, and not one inch of me will ever turn fish.

We live at Mussel Cove, in one of the old pilot's cottages, a couple of miles or so out of town as you follow the estuary towards the Point. Ma wanted to stay in Padsta but it's better fit we stay here for this is where Father keeps his fishing boat, the *Louisa May* – unless there's a storm blewing up, when he takes her up town to safe harbour. Our cottage sits in the middle of a row that climbs the steep hill up to the cliff top. The front gardens are long and full of flowers, but the backs face north, looking out to sea – that's where I sleep, in the coldest room of the house. Even in summer bitter draughts creep through the gap under the windowsill where the wood has shrunk, for the winds blow some fierce in this part of the world.

We've no electric yet in Cove and we have to get our water

from the stone trough – it's clean when it comes down the chute from the stream in the field above but folks out walking will wash their boots in it, and we're forever picking out clumps of mud and grass. The lavvies are at the top of the row, next to the pig houses; they do make you heave with the smell of warm shit and Jeyes fluid – it goes right up your nose. We have to do our business in the bucket and then empty it over the cliffs – I say it's disgusting, but Dad only laughs – food for fishes, he says . . .

Morva hates living here, for it's some lonely with only the one row of cottages and the boathouse where they keep the lifeboat. It's a long walk to Padsta if you run out of something and she don't care for the neighbours so she won't ask nobody to lend her so much as a cup of flour. But I love being so close to the shore, to lie in bed at night and listen to the sea grinding over the shingle – even when there's no wind and the tide's right out you can catch the trickle of the stream that runs down the field behind. So I'm never without the sound of water in my ears.

We don't have much in the way of decent furniture brought up from the old place, just our beds, a few chairs that don't match proper and a table covered in scratches. The only thing Morva cares about is this small gramophone that somebody gave her backalong times, before she was married. She only has three records, and when she listens to them she smiles and then starts crying. Dad hates that gramophone, I don't know why zackly, but he won't let her play it when he's in the house. He says if he hears one note of music coming out of that bloody box he's going to throw it off the cliff. He tells Morva to sell it and buy me some new clothes with the money, for I'm growing like a fern out of my dresses and my toes are packed tight as pilchards in my shoes, but she won't hear of letting it go.

Sometimes she carries the gramophone out of the house under a blanket and puts it in the punt. Off she goes by herself, sculling down the estuary to some small beach you can only reach by boat. I always beg her to take me with her and let me do the winding up, for I love to listen to the music, but she never do say yes. I have to stay in the house or stand on the slipway to wait for Dad to come back from his fishing. If he gets home and there's nothing on the table for his tea he flies into a temper and clots me one round the ear. It's not my fault though, if his wife won't cook for him.

My father's up every morning before dawn to go fishing. Since we moved to Cove Morva's taken to staying in bed till long after he's gone off in the boat. Some days she don't get up till it's dark, and once I came back from school and found her sitting on the beach in just her nightshift. She floats about the house like she's been wisht by the piskies, with a faraway look in her eyes and letting out these deep long sighs. I know folks gossip about her, saying she's not right in the head. She don't bother herself about me, scarce notices if I'm in the house, never reminds me to wash my face in the morning or tells me to get ready to go school.

She's a strange one, Morva – only takes a bath and puts on a clean dress when her friend the Corona Man delivers once a fortnight. He gives me a bottle of fizzy orange and tells me to go down to the beach and watch the tide come in, and if I see my father's boat I'm to run back up and let them know of it. They go inside and my mother bolts the door – she won't let me in even if it's raining. I don't care. If I need shelter I go to the pig house. Other times I stand on the edge of the jetty and drink the fizz slow as I can, washing it round my mouth and sticking out my tongue to see how orange it is. Then I bend down and fill the empty bottle with seawater so I can stare at what tiny creatures are swimming in it. Or I do scoop up tiny pieces of broken shell and shake the bottle so it makes patterns like one of they kaleidoscopes.

After an hour or so the Corona Man creeps out of the house by the back door and walks all the way up the hill and back down to the front garden like he's only just got here. My mother opens the door and makes a great fuss of giving him the empties back, but I never give him my bottle even though he says I can keep the deposit money.

'It's gone,' I tell him. 'I put a secret message in it and sent it out to sea.'

'What sort of secret might that be, then?' says my mother, giving me a dark look. Her ears are all red and her eyes shine as bright as a cat in the dark. But I say nothing. Truth is, I hide the old bottles in the tamarisk hedge – thirteen of them so far – that's how I know how many times the Corona Man has been to our house.

SIX

Jack and I were as wild as the flowers that grew in the hedgerows – traveller's joy, red campion, bindweed, tufted vetch. Mr Rosewarne led us down the lanes and along the cliff paths, stopping every few yards to bend down and take a flowery stem in his hand. Every flower had not one name, but three – English, Cornish and Latin. He made us repeat them after him and tested our memories on the way back. Jack showed little interest, mumbling his answers and complaining to me later that it was all 'sissy stuff'. But I soaked up the knowledge like a thirsty tomato plant, growing and ripening in the late summer sun. At night I lay in bed, unable to sleep, my brain excited by unpronounceable words – *Silene dioica*, *Lonicera periclymenum*, *Pulicaria dysenterica*.

Mr Rosewarne carried a long stick like an ancient wizard. He knew which leaves could stem the flow of blood, help soothe a burn, make a wart vanish or sprout new hairs on a bald head. In the same solemn voice he informed us that the rosebay willowherb (Herb of Heaven, *Chamerion angustifolium*) was sacred and should never be picked, while the hollow stem of the cow parsley (Queen Anne's Lace,

Anthriscus sylvestris) made a perfect pea-shooter. I stared at him open-mouthed, drawing in his Celtic wisdom with great gulps of fresh air.

The weather was unusually warm for September, grey skies clearing by mid-morning to a clear blue canopy, speckled with screaming seabirds. We roamed over the shingle picking up pinky-brown periwinkles and creamy cockleshells until Jack's trouser pockets sagged beneath their weight. We gathered up armfuls of olive-brown seaweed and sat on the rocks, laughing as we popped their gassy bladders. In the afternoons we hurtled down to the empty beach like greyhounds out of the slips – tripping over the soft crumpled sand at the top of the bay as we ran towards the sea, smacking our bare feet along the flat, water-logged shoreline, jumping over the mysterious spirals of worm casts, leaping across the trickling channels of clear, cold water that ran between the rocks.

Mr Rosewarne was never far away. He would roll up his trouser legs and stand in the shallows, watching us with a knowing smile as we jumped over the waves, our faces turning browner every day, our hair bleached and sticky with salt. Wherever he took us he never missed an opportunity to name and explain, compare and distinguish – the whole world was his open-air classroom and we the only pupils. In the two weeks before the start of school – delayed by the onset of war – I learned more than I had in the last seven years.

And our education continued inside the house. There were books everywhere – encyclopaedias, dictionaries, novels and poetry, biographies, histories, books in foreign languages, even in foreign alphabets. They were neatly stacked in subject sections on polished wooden shelves in the alcoves on either side of the fireplace, ranged up the side of the staircase and in a bookcase on the landing. In the study – a small room at the back, which looked out over the sea – there was another bookcase with locked glass doors where Mr Rosewarne kept what he called his 'first editions'.

Some evenings he would take a book from the shelf and read aloud to us – extracts from Chaucer's *Canterbury Tales* and Shakespeare's *Complete Works*. Most of all we loved to hear him read from the foreign books, listening to the strange sounds transporting us to mysterious lands far away. We discovered that French was full of extravagant 'r's and thin, nasal sneers while the heavy Russian made us think of people with fur hats stamping in the snow, their mouths full of liquid honey. But the Arabic was our favourite – we laughed as Mr Rosewarne waved his arms and rolled his eyes to the ceiling. He might have been pleading for his life or driving a hard bargain – we neither knew nor cared. We just wanted him to crackle and spit, coughing up the words as if trying to clear phlegm from his throat.

'More! Please, mister, do some more!' Jack would say as the two of us broke into spontaneous applause. 'Do some German now. We never heard no German before.'

But Mr Rosewarne shook his head. 'When the war is over,' he promised dramatically. 'But until that happy day, not one German word will cross my lips.'

'Excuse me asking, but how come you know all them languages?' I said as politely as I could.

'My mother, God rest her soul, was French,' Mr Rosewarne replied. 'The daughter of a Breton with a successful fishing business; he came across the Channel and settled in Cornwall. My father was a highly educated man, Cornish to the bone. I went up to Cambridge, and then took up the law. In nineteen nineteen I went to work for the League of Nations Secretariat and they sent me to Syria.' We both looked at him blankly. 'That's where I picked up the Arabic.'

'We don't even have one book in our house,' I said quietly. 'You must have hundreds.'

'And you may read as many as you wish while you're here,' said Mrs Rosewarne kindly. 'Isn't that right, Charles?'

'Indeed. I will look out some novels for you to start with. *Wuthering Heights* for you, Ellen, and perhaps *Great Expectations* for Jack. Yes, I'll start a list.'

'What did you have to go and say that for?' Jack whispered to me later as we climbed the stairs to go to our rooms. 'I don't want to read a load of boring old books.'

'Well, I do,' I said firmly. 'I want to learn things. This is our chance, don't you see?'

Jack shrugged. 'What's the point? We'll be off home soon. Soon as we leave school I'll go to the docks and you'll work in a factory – maybe a shop if you're lucky. Book-learning's not for the likes of us, Nellie.'

* * *

One afternoon when the tide was out Mr Rosewarne took us across the rocks to a natural swimming pool in the middle of Rocky Beach. It was a rough rectangle, about thirty foot long and fifteen across, the edges draped with strong-smelling seaweed, studded with limpets and blue-black mussels. Mrs Rosewarne had made me an elasticated costume out of an old summer dress and Jack was wearing a pair of baggy green shorts.

'Ladies first,' Mr Rosewarne said, looking expectantly at me.

I stared into the still, dark water. 'What, in there?'

'Well, you can't learn to swim on dry land,' he replied smartly. 'Come on, in you get . . . Don't worry, I'm right behind you.'

I sat on the edge and gently eased myself in, gasping at the icy water as it lapped around my waist, slicing me in two. Within moments, the tips of my fingers were white and bloodless and my trembling lips had turned a purplish blue.

'I can't do it,' I said. 'I've got to get out.'

'Just get your shoulders under.' He jumped in briskly beside me with a large splash. I bent my knees and felt the painful coldness creep up my body. He put his hands gently under my stomach and told me to take my feet off the stony bottom. I bent forward and let my full weight sink into his large hands. 'Keep your legs straight and kick with your feet,' he commanded. 'Good . . . Now stretch out your arms and paddle like a dog.' I screwed up my face, splashing and grabbing at the water, while Jack sat on a rock, laughing.

'Your turn next,' warned Mr Rosewarne. He moved his hand away from my tummy, holding it an inch or so beneath. 'That's it, my girl, keep going,' he urged as I reached out to grasp the threads of green moss that lined the pool's sides. But the slimy strands slipped through my fingers and my head went under. Mr Rosewarne immediately clutched my waist and pulled me up. I was coughing and spluttering, my eyes stinging with salt.

'Bravo! You did it!' he cried triumphantly. Three more trips across the length of the pool and I could swim a few yards unaided. The only reason I learned so quickly was because I was desperate to get out of the freezing water. He bundled me up in a large rough towel and sent me back to the house, where Mrs Rosewarne gave me a mug of hot chocolate and put me in a hot bath.

I was expecting Jack to come back soon after me, but he and Mr Rosewarne were gone for hours. I wondered how Jack was faring – secretly hoping that he had turned out to be a slower learner than me – but when they finally came back to the house Mr Rosewarne declared that Jack was 'a natural' and would be a champion swimmer once he had better-fitting shorts. He got out his camera and Mrs Rosewarne took a photo of the two of them, Mr Rosewarne's face beaming, his arm clapped round Jack's shoulder. Later, Mrs Rosewarne put the photo in the album with the title, *The day Jack learned to swim*. Both of them seemed to have forgotten that it was the day I had learned too.

Mr Rosewarne started taking Jack on fishing trips.

Sometimes he'd take a boat out and they'd be gone for the whole day, returning like weary explorers from an expedition, their booty a string of shining mackerel. Or he would take Jack onto the rocks to fish for sea bass at high tide. In the evenings, after we'd eaten what we children knew as 'tea' but were now told to call 'dinner', Mr Rosewarne would change out of his suit and summon Jack to the beach for cricket practice. I would stand in the garden and watch them bowling at three sticks sunk into the flat, wet sand – or see Mr Rosewarne standing close behind Jack, his hands around the neck of the bat, directing the swing. From a distance it was an idyllic picture: anyone would have assumed they were father and son. But Jack didn't much care for cricket and started making excuses for not playing. When Mr Rosewarne tried to get him interested in rugby he drew the line, saying it was a 'toff's game'. The only sport Jack liked was football, and he longed to be back at home, playing on the cinder pitch or in the streets with his mates.

Of course, nobody even thought of including me in such activities, and for the most part I didn't mind, happy to stay at home with Mrs Rosewarne. The County Regiment was apparently in need of mufflers, socks and gloves, and she had immediately dragooned her neighbours into forming a knitting circle. I was taught to knit – 'in-over-through-off, in-over-through-off' – and spent many evenings making socks for giant soldiers with odd-sized feet, the tension far too loose, the wool twisting itself mischievously into knots. But I wasn't really interested in knitting, or looking after the new hens, or digging the vegetable plot – I wanted to read. Every evening the books stared down at me from the shelves – Emily Brontë, Charles Dickens, Daphne Du Maurier – their names etched in gold on red leather spines. 'Hadn't you better get started?' they seemed to say. 'You won't be here for much longer.'

How much longer, exactly? Nobody seemed to know. Jack was constantly enthusing about what we were going to do once we were 'back 'ome', while the Rosewarnes behaved as if we were going to be in Cornwall for the rest of our lives. I hovered in between, trying to keep the distance of a perfect guest and yet desperate to belong. It was like being caught in an early morning dream, drifting deliciously in and out of reality, trying to reach the end of the fairy tale before I was woken up. But I knew one day that alarm clock was going to ring and I would be sent back to London, my new clothes turned to rags and no glass slipper to leave behind me.

SEVEN

I've made a den for myself in the tamarisk hedge with an old blanket and a pink satin cushion Missus Tabb gave me. It's the best place for watching folks without them knowing. You can peek through the leaves and see the whole beach, and if you look out to one side you can see the comings and goings by the Mission Church or keep watch on the track that leads up to the farm. If I look ahead I can see straight down the wooden landing stage that takes you out to the deeper water. The lads dive off the end all summer – they do love to push each other in and shout they heads off.

I was hiding in the tamarisk when I saw the butcher drown himself. His name was Benson. I'd never seen him out of his shop before, nor without his long white apron on, for he usually sent the errand boy on the bicycle to fetch the orders and deliver the meat. He must have thought Cove was empty – I'm sure he wouldn't have done it if he'd known someone was watching. I kept wondering why he was standing there on the very edge, wearing his best suit on a weekday, not moving, just staring down into the water. After a good while he takes his hat off and lays it down careful on the planking.

Then he do straighten up and stare at the water for another few minutes, leaning his body more and more forward till he loses his balance and drops off, stiff as a pole, barely making a splash as he hits the water. His head only comes up once, his eyes roll and he opens his mouth wide before going back under.

I wait a bit, then I creep out of the hedge and walk onto the landing stage to see where he's got to but there's not a sign of him. Just his hat, lying on the dark wet planks, brown felt with a dark ribbon round the brim. I took a fancy to that hat. I know I shouldn't have, but I snatched it up and hid it under the tamarisk to keep my shells and bits of coloured glass in.

People said Benson's death must have been an accident, but I know it wasn't. I never told nobody what I saw, not even my mother or father. I often wonder what was so bad about the butcher's life that he wanted to end it. I still dream about him dropping into the water wearing his best suit, his boots on and all . . .

One night there's a right terrible storm – the wind screeches down the chimney and the waves hammer the rocks at the foot of the house. The rain beats against the windows and the dead pear tree in next door's front garden snaps in two. I'm lying in bed counting the slates as they slide off the roof and smash to the ground. And then I hear an odd tinkling sound – I sit up and listen, can't work out what's making the noise at first, then I realize it's my Corona bottles rolling out of the tamarisk hedge and clinking into each other. Then there's another gust of wind and they tumble off the edge of the rocks, smashing on the shingle below.

Next morning my father is untying the punt when he sees the pile of broken glass. He seems to know straight away what it means, for he picks up a jagged piece and takes it back to the house, shouting for Morva. He runs into their room and slams the door behind him. I'm lying in bed with my head under the covers listening to the sounds of them fighting – things being knocked over, him cursing and shouting, throwing her against the wall, her screaming at him to leave her be. Then it all stops for a minute or so and all I can hear is her sobbing. After that my father storms out the house and goes off in his boat – he don't come back for three days.

I wait a while, then crawl out of bed and tiptoe into their room. Morva's lying on the bed – there's blood on the sheet and she's not moving so at first I'm thinking she's dead. But she turns slowly towards me . . .

'Happy now?' she mutters. Her mouth is cut and swollen up, she's got a black eye and a nasty slash across her cheek. I fetch some water and a cloth and try to wash the blood off her face, but she shoves me away and tells me to go school, saying I mustn't tell anyone what's been going on. She looks so awful I think maybe I should fetch the doctor or ask next door for help but I'm afeard they'll call the police and then my father will go to prison. I get dressed but don't go school, just take a crust of bread and a lump of cheese and hide in the tamarisk hedge. I feel some bad now for holding onto the bottles. I wish I'd handed them over and taken the pennies. Or at least I should have hid them somewhere safer. And this makes me worry my father will search the tamarisk hedge and find Benson's hat and then there'll be even more trouble. The police might think I murdered the butcher and then I'd be hanged.

I'm thinking what's best to do next when our front door opens and Morva steps out, wearing her coat and hat, a green scarf tied round her neck, pulled up as far as she can to hide her battered face. She's carrying a small case tied up with a belt and her gramophone player wedged under her arm. She don't so much as look at me, just starts walking up the back of the houses towards the lavvies. I leap up and chase after her, snapping at her heels like a dog.

'Where 'ee goin', Ma?'

'Nowhere.'

'Padsta?'

She shakes her head and makes a scoffing sound. 'A lot further than that. And don't bother waitin' for me, for I'm not comin' back.' She slurs like a drunk through her thick lip.

'Not coming back? What, not never?'

'And tell 'im not to come lookin' for me neither – he won't find me.' She crosses the field, making for the gap in the wall where the farm road starts.

'Can't I come with 'ee, Ma?'

'No. Nick won't like it if I turn up with 'ee in tow . . .' I don't know who this Nick is but I reckon he must be the Corona Man.

'Let me carry the gramophone for 'ee, it's some heavy,'

I say, but she shakes her head, gripping it all the tighter.
'Go on, I'll be no bother, I don't eat much.'

'I can't take 'ee, that's all there is to it.'

'Please, don't leave me, Ma . . .'

'You'll be all right – just keep out of your father's way.'

'Will 'ee come back and fetch me later then?'

'Maybe, I don't know . . . Please, go back to the 'owse,
Selina!' She don't even give me a hug or kiss goodbye, just
hurries away from me up the road, stumbling over the stones
with her gramophone. How is it she can take that stupid thing
and leave me behind? I stand there squalling, the tears rolling
down to the corners of my mouth, watching her grow smaller
and smaller as she reaches the top of the hill. She doesn't
even look back before she turns the corner, not even for a last
glimpse of the sea. Then she's gone. And that's the last I see
of the woman I called my mother.

For the next three days I'm on my own in the house. I don't
go school, just wander along the beach or stand on the edge
of the jetty throwing stones in the water, wondering what will
become of me if my father don't ever come back. When it gets
dark I go indoors and bolt the door, but I don't bother lighting
a fire, just pile all the blankets onto my bed and creep under.
I get all the candles and put them in my room and keep them
all burning till I go to sleep. I've finished off a bit of meat and
the loaf and a whole packet of arrowroot biscuits, but by the
morning there's nothing left save a bit of old cabbage and I
can't go shops because Morva's took the housekeeping tin.
The neighbours seem to know there's something up, for

Missus Tabb knocks on the door and asks me if I'm all right and why I've been left on my own with nobody to tend me. I make up a story about my ma having to go visit an aunt who's sick and Dad being out on a trawler. She feels some sorry for me then and takes me into her kitchen and gives me a cup of sweet tea and two chunks of marble cake.

On the third night Dad do come back, banging on the door and shouting for Morva to let him in. I go downstairs and open up.

'Why's the door bolted? Where's tha' ma?' he shouts, pushing past me. He stinks of whisky and rotten fish, like he's been sleeping on his boat.

'Gone,' I say.

'She might 'ave left us some dinner . . .' He starts opening and slamming cupboards, looking for something to eat. 'I'm some leary . . . What's been goin' on 'ere? There's not a scrap of food in the 'owse!'

'She's gone . . .' I say again, resting one foot upon the bottom stair in case I have to make a dash for it if he goes to clot me.

'Gone where?' He stops and turns to me, gripping me by the shoulders. 'What tha' sayin'? Don't stare at me like a sticked pig. Go on, spit it out . . . Where's she gone?'

'Don't know zackly, she went Monday . . .' I lower my voice to a whisper. 'Said to tell 'ee she's not comin' back . . .'

'Did her say where her was goin'?' I shake my head. 'I see then . . . It's come to that, 'as it? Gone to her fancy man, 'as she? Stupid bitch . . . He can 'ave 'er – she's no use to me – never been raight, not since the day you was born . . .'

'I'm sorry . . .' I murmur.

'A pretty beauty she turned out to be . . . Goes off with her fancy man and leaves 'ee on yer own to starve . . . There's a mother's love for 'ee . . .'

'I was all right. Next door's gave me some dinner.'

'What am I to do with 'ee now, eh?' He slams his fist against the wall, making me flinch. I can't tell what's making him the more angry – Morva going off with another man, or her not taking me with her.

'Please, Dad, I'm sorry, I never meant to cause no trouble,' I plead.

'Stop snivellin'!' He paces about the tiny room, breathing hard, his fist still clenched, his arms pinned straight to his side like two heavy hammers – any moment I think he's going to start swinging them and smash the whole place to pieces. 'I knew somethin' was goin' on . . .' he fumes. 'Under my own roof too. If she shows her face again I'll kill 'er . . .'

My legs start to shake and I sink down on the stair, wrap my arms round my knees, tucking my head in tight, squeezing into the dark hole of myself. I feel like I'm falling away: my tummy's so light and empty I think I might be sick and the tips of my fingers start to tingle, like when you come in from the bitter cold and put them before the fire. I want to take deep breaths, but the air won't go all the way down and I've never felt so alone in my whole life . . .

Later Dad goes upstairs and takes the sheets off the bed, still stained with my mother's blood. He rips them into rags and puts them on the fire, as if he's murdered her and is destroying the proof. He don't say anything, just stares at the flames and chews on his pipe. I suppose he's thinking how will he manage without a woman in the house to cook and clean and stream the clothes? But he never mentions her name again and nor do I, for I'm too afeard that he'll strike me.

It's late October, two months since Morva left, and no word from her. I think she must have found her Corona Man because he never turns up again neither. The fishing is all but over for the winter so Dad takes all the pots out of the sea and stores them in the boathouse. He pulls the *Louisa May* out the water and gives her hull a proper scraping, cuts out the rotted planking and caulks the joints. He uncoils the fathoms of rope and repairs the frays; he mends the withy pots and cleans the marking buoys. He makes me stand on the slipway, steeved with cold, and never says a word to me save to ask me to fetch this and that or make him a mug of hot tea. He takes the engine out and oils the workings. He gives her body a good scrub, then re-paints her white with dark red trim lines. By the time he finishes she's a right beauty again, all gleaming in the winter sunshine. Father spends so much time and care on that boat I know he do love her more than me.

In the evening he brings his stinking nets inside and ties them to the leg of the kitchen table to mend them. He boils up crabs' legs or burns a few tatties and a bit of greasy meat and we spend the whole meal time in silence for he will not have talking while we eat. He won't bother to light a fire in the front room so we sit by the stove in the lamplight while he carries on with the nets. He lights his pipe and smoke fills the tiny room and makes me cough. Then he tells me to go up and get straight into bed and not waste a candle for he has to go out on some fishing business. But my father tells lies faster than an 'oss can gallop and I know he's only sitting in The Ship, for he comes back at midnight drunk as a mattress, stumbling about in the dark and cursing at the top of his voice. And I'm in bed listening to the sea and wishing I had a mother to sing me to sleep and comb the wind out of my curls. I keep thinking of Morva and the Corona Man, driving around the county in his lorry full of jangling bottles with the gramophone on her lap. I can hear her laughing and singing along to her three records and I wonder if she's happy now she's away from the both of us.

For it's some lonely here in the winter – nobody calls and my father won't take me with him when he rows up Padsta to fetch the groceries. I go down to the beach and hunt for strange-shaped stones, or I cut mussels off the rocks beneath the house. When it's gluthening up the sky falls into the water and everything turns a soft greeny grey. And I can't help wishing the storm had saved just one of they empty Corona bottles for me, then I could write a message to the Mer people and ask them to come fetch me. For if I am one of their kind, surely they must be missing me now and wanting me home . . .

Since Morva left us I've been having awful nightmares and

Dad tells me I sleepwalk. I get out of bed and wander around the house in the dark, bumping into things and knocking chairs over. It wakes him up and he has to come down and take me back to bed but I have no memory of ever doing such things, although I do find strange bruises on my body and don't know how they came there. Once, he says, I went down the stairs, opened the door and left the cottage, I walked down the path and onto the beach, all without waking up. My father found me standing on the very edge of the jetty in the dead of night, wearing just my shift and no shoes on my feet, staring into the black water as if I was about to throw myself in. Like Benson, I thought, but I didn't say nothing.

So now he bolts the door at night to keep me from drowning. And he makes me share his bed so he can keep watch over me. We lie there in the darkness and he puts his arms tight round me, nuzzling into my neck like a snorting 'oss and running his fingers through my hair. His hands smell of mackerel and cold tar soap and his breath reeks of the tot of whisky he takes before he comes upstairs. I keep my back to him, my legs shut tight together, for he likes to pull my shift up and run his rough hands over my thighs. It's to comfort me, he says, and help me sleep, but I hate it. He gets all hot and presses himself hard against the back of my legs and I keep moving away from him till I'm hanging over the edge of the bed. Soon as I hear him snoring I wriggle out and crawl back to my room. Sometimes I do think I'd be safer walking the cliffs all night than lying in his baissly arms.

I wish I was a small grey pebble lying on the beach, just

one little stone amongst hundreds of thousands. Nobody
would have to tend me for I'd never have need of food or drink
or fresh clothes, never have to do chores or go school. I'd just
lie there with the waves washing over me or drying out in the
sun. I'd never move, save a few inches back and forth with the
tide. I could stay there for ever, without a name, minding my
own business, nobody even knowing I'm there. But maybe
one day a nice boy would wander onto the beach, looking for
shells or driftwood. He'd bend down and pick me up, hold me
in his hand for a moment or two, feel how small and smooth
I am. Then he'd stand up and throw me with all his might. I'd
fly through the air and glance across the surface of the water
before I sank. I'd like that – to be a small grey pebble lost for
ever at the bottom of the sea . . .

EIGHT

The village was one steep hill with narrow lanes threading off on either side like veins on a leaf, and it didn't take us long to know most of the people who lived there. Aunt Clara tried her best to make us feel part of the community, introducing us as 'our dear London friends'. Soon I was chatting politely with the spinsterish Walters sisters, who ran the Laurels Guest House, laughing at Mr Dobbin's obscure jokes when he sold me stamps at the post office and smiling with the appropriate level of thinness when I met 'the Ghastly Mrs Pascoe', a forceful woman who battled daily with Mrs Rosewarne for control of the Women's Institute.

The locals were used to mixing with holidaymakers and most treated us like out-of-season visitors – with a superficial friendliness and a wary eye. But the local newspapers that had so warmly greeted us poor Cockney darlings were now reporting thefts from sweetshops, raided jewellery boxes and 'borrowed' bicycles that ended up in the harbour. 'We know you're not like that,' Mrs Rosewarne would say kindly, deliberately leaving her purse on the dining table when she went upstairs for her afternoon rest.

We had become separated from our East London school-mates on the first day we arrived in Cornwall, and although there was another group of evacuees in our class they all came from the same school in Plymouth and stuck to each other like glue. We were expected to strike up relationships with local children, but it wasn't easy. Jack refused point-blank to join the Scouts but I was willingly enrolled into the Girl Guides, pleased when Mrs Rosewarne introduced me as Ellen rather than Nellie. I began a tentative friendship with a couple of girls in my patrol – pretty Violet Merrion, whose parents ran the Seaview Hotel, and mousy Mary Trengrouse, who came from the next bay.

Then we met Jory Nancarrow, the farmer's son who lived at Clifftop Farm. He was a hefty lad, a couple of years older than us, blue-eyed and freckle-faced with an untidy thatch of blond hair, pale as corn. His clothes were old and roughly mended, and when he stood in the middle of the field he looked like an overstuffed scarecrow. We started going up to the farm almost every day, fascinated by the animals. We'd chase the hens or stroke the horse – sometimes riding on the cart with Jory's mother to deliver the milk round the village, watching her ladle it out of the churns without spilling one drop. Some of the farmhands had joined the army so Jory always had plenty of chores to do. After school we'd go up there and hang about until he'd finished. I'd sit on the gate swinging my legs while Jack scuffed a football across the yard as we waited for Jory to 'meat' the pigs or coax the last cow into the milking shed.

'How are 'ee, my handsome?' Jory would say to me every

morning as he pushed his rusty old bike past us up the hill on the way to school.

'Fine, thank you,' I'd reply, not knowing why I was blushing. Then off he'd rattle into the distance, his tin of mid-morning crib tied onto the back with an old leather belt, pedalling fast enough to turn his bottle of milk to cream.

Jory was never going to be anything but a farmer. He showed us over his land, the brown stubble as dry as a Rich Tea biscuit, the smoking fertilizer wafting over the cliff tops. Behind the farmhouse the cows pottered about the pasture, chewing the last of the grass before it was ploughed up for potatoes.

'They fields will all belong t' me some day,' he told us proudly. He spoke warmly of dredge corn and barley, late savoys and turnip-rooted beet, potash and copper lime dust. 'My dad do want me to pack in school,' he said. 'I might as well – I'm shakin' up fourteen anyhow.'

We went to church for the Thanksgiving Harvest and for the first time I understood what it meant to sing, '*We plough the fields and scatter*'. But our celebrations were overtaken by the news of the village's first war casualty, a young seaman who had gone down with the minesweeper, HMS *Courageous*. There were sniffs and white hankies in the pews, and I found my own eyes watering, even though I didn't even know what the chap had looked like. At last the war seemed real.

'The world has sown bad crops,' boomed the vicar, deftly bringing us back to the purpose of his service, 'and who can say what harvest we will reap in the months and years to come? But sow the seeds of God's goodness and you will receive the rewards of your toil.'

But what rewards should I expect? I was working hard for the war effort, and at school I was the most conscientious pupil in my class. I practised my times tables and managed to write neatly with an ink pen. At home, I even did some of Jack's chores so the Rosewarnes would have nothing to complain about. When the Billeting Officer came to check how we were faring, I told him we'd been treated as if we their very own kids, only better. I saw Mr and Mrs Rosewarne exchange a satisfied nod and my heart swelled with pride. The Rosewarnes had no children and never explained why, but I couldn't believe they were childless by choice. I saw Aunt Clara as a tragic figure – her maternal instincts cruelly deprived by nature – and decided it was our moral duty to fill the gaping hole in her heart. It also helped to make me feel less guilty about preferring the Rosewarnes' home to my own.

Aunt Clara loved mothering us, and undeniably had a particularly soft spot for Jack. If he uttered one nice comment about a meal it would become 'Jack's favourite' and she'd make it again the following week. He was always turning up late for dinner but she never once reprimanded him and seemed genuinely delighted when he tore the knees of his trousers or lost a shirt button. She warmed our beds, made us mugs of Ovaltine before we went to sleep, and laid out our clean, ironed clothes for the next day. She sent us to school with delicious home-baked pasties for our lunch and we often found sweets mysteriously slipped into our pockets. I loved

the care and attention and was always thanking her, but Jack
behaved as if he didn't notice, and certainly never showed any
gratitude for her kindnesses.

We were playing a game of Mummies and Daddies – they
were the loving, doting parents and we their neat,
symmetrical family, a boy for Charles and a girl for Clara. I
played my role with passion and commitment, as if there were
some prize at stake – the Best Evacuee in Britain, the Perfect
Pretend Daughter. But Jack was always spoiling the game. If
the four of us were picnicking on the beach or playing a
friendly round of cards after dinner he would start talking
about our real mum and dad, deliberately dragging them into
the conversation – 'Do you think Dad has killed any Germans
yet?' or 'What you goin' to buy with that postal order Mum
sent you, Nellie?'

Mr and Mrs Rosewarne kept trying to pull Jack into our
fold, offering him treats and incentives – he was given his
own fishing rod, Mrs Rosewarne knitted him a cricket jumper,
Mr Rosewarne even gave up his campaign to convert Jack to
rugby and bought him a smart leather football. Jack took the
bribes, but resolutely retained his position. He kept insisting
that there was something odd about them – he couldn't put
his finger on it. Whenever we went out together he made sure
everybody knew he was not their son.

One Friday evening the spring tides reached their highest
level of the year. As the sun went down so the seawater rose,
spilling over the harbour walls and washing through the

streets. The shopkeepers and publicans in the Market Place had already boarded up their premises, but were soon wading two feet deep.

'If the wind had been south-westerly it would have been worse,' Mr Rosewarne informed us as we stood at the top of the street, an outing to the Padstow Cinedrome cancelled by the emergency below. People rushed past us in Wellingtons and waders, struggling with heavy sandbags and shouting orders in the splashing darkness.

'This is absurd,' complained Mrs Rosewarne. 'Surely they can turn some lights on. They haven't even started bombing London, let alone here. I don't think Hitler dares to invade us,' she continued imperiously. 'I'm sick of this phoney war. Why can't we stop all this nonsense and get on with our lives as before?'

'Yeah, you're right. Me and Nellie should go 'ome,' said Jack.

'Oh no, that's not what I meant,' replied Mrs Rosewarne anxiously. 'We don't ever want you to go home . . .' She faltered. 'I mean, not until the war's over.'

'Other kids 'ave gone back, why shouldn't we?' Jack persisted. It was true that some of the evacuees had already returned to London, unhappy with their billets, missed by their mothers or simply believing it had all been a false alarm.

'There's no question of your going back, Jack, no question at all,' said Mr Rosewarne firmly, as if to signal that no further discussion was necessary. He gave Mrs Rosewarne a furious glare and went to offer his services to the ARP

Warden, but was told he was inappropriately dressed and there was nothing he could do.

We walked home in silence, taking the shorter and more direct route along the lanes, feeling in the darkness for the sudden bends, muddy ditches and ankle-twisting potholes. Bats swooped in front of us, owls hooted and the hedgerows rustled, but for once Mr Rosewarne didn't make a single reference to the nocturnal wildlife. He and Mrs Rosewarne walked side by side, almost deliberately out of step – tight-lipped and seething.

Jack grabbed hold of me, dragging me back. 'I knew there was something fishy about them two,' he whispered. 'They want to keep us! That's what all the presents are about. They're trying to get us over to their side.'

'Don't be daft,' I whispered back. 'They're just being kind.'

'They've got their hooks into you, but I'm not fooled. The way they look at me sometimes, makes my flesh creep. Especially her . . .' He nodded in the Rosewarnes' direction. They were pulling away from us now, their shadowy shapes looking almost sinister in the monochrome distance.

'You're just being stupid,' I hissed.

'It's all right for you – she doesn't come into your room every night.'

'Yes she does, to tuck me in.'

'But she stands by my bed and stares at me – for ages! I pretend to be asleep, but she still doesn't go away. What's that all about, eh?'

'You're probably just imagining it,' I replied irritably,

reminding myself to stay awake that night to see if I got the same special treatment.

'I'm goin' to send Mum a card, tell 'er to come and fetch us.'

'You can't do that,' I hissed. 'It's not allowed.'

'Who says? I'll do what I want . . . Don't go tellin' them two, mind . . .'

I wrenched myself away from Jack and ran after them, a sick feeling burning in my stomach. I ran up and put my hand on Mr Rosewarne's sleeve, feeling the roughness of his tweed jacket. He smelled comfortingly of his pipe tobacco.

'Where's Jack?' he asked. 'Not stolen by the piskies, I hope.'

Jack lagged behind us the rest of the way, kicking at stones, while Mr and Mrs Rosewarne and I walked back to the house, me wedged determinedly between them. Mr Rosewarne stood by the open door and waited patiently for Jack to enter the house before he drew the blackout curtain. Then Mrs Rosewarne switched on the light and the colour instantly returned to their clothes and features – brown trousers, blue eyes, green dress, pink cheeks. They looked like their normal selves – a warm-hearted, generous couple with not a speck of harm in them.

'We would like you to call us Uncle Charles and Aunt Clara from now on,' Mr Rosewarne announced the next evening over dinner.

Jack looked up from his plate of kidneys, cabbage and boiled potatoes and frowned. 'Why? We ain't family.'

'No, but we wish you to think of us as such,' Mr Rosewarne replied, 'and besides, you may be here for some time.'

'What about you, Ellen?' Mrs Rosewarne turned to me. 'Do you think you could learn to call me Aunt?'

'Yes, Mrs Rosewarne,' I mumbled, trying to scoop the gravy off my plate.

'Good.' She gave me a warm smile. 'Don't lick your knife, dear, there's a good girl.'

'So . . . Aunt and Uncle now, is it? What's all that about?' Jack muttered as we went upstairs to bed.

'Nothing. They're just trying to make us feel more at home.'

Jack scoffed. 'Not a chance! Soon as we can, we're going back to London, that's where home is.' I didn't answer, but I knew he could read my thoughts. 'Both of us, Nellie,' he added warningly. 'Not to be separated, remember?'

That night I drew the blanket over my head and cried silently into the pillow. My emotions were as extreme as the spring tide, suddenly overflowing and then withdrawing to a dull empty pain. What was wrong with me? Didn't I love my own parents any more? I tried to picture them – my father in his collarless work shirt, a silk scarf round his neck, his dark trousers dusty, his heavy boots caked in dirt; my mother's smiling face, the small, neat features, wavy hair tied back in a low bun. I tried to remember the smell and touch of her as she'd hugged me goodbye on the doorstep, the sound of her voice as she made us promise to keep in touch. *Of course I miss them*, I told myself. *Of course I do*. And chanting those words like a mantra, I let the sea rock me gently to sleep.

At the beginning of December Mum replied to Jack's letter saying she thought it best we stayed in Cornwall for the holiday. Dad had joined the army and was stationed somewhere up north – he wasn't allowed to say exactly where, and had no idea when he might be back. With nobody at home to look after, Mum had taken a job in a munitions factory. The boss was making them work all the hours God sent and she didn't think it was worth us making the journey when she'd hardly have time to see us. Jack was very upset. 'You'd think she'd want to spend Christmas Day with us at least,' he said miserably.

'She just doesn't want the expense of it,' I replied, knowing that Mum would have already counted the cost of our train fares, a few treats for our stockings and Christmas dinner.

'S'pose so . . .' Jack gave me suspicious look. 'Still, you got what you wanted. Bet you're happy now.'

'That's not fair!' I protested. 'I wanted to see Mum as much as you did.'

Uncle Charles and Aunt Clara were delighted when we asked if we could stay for Christmas. They bought a large tree that touched the ceiling and decked the halls – not to mention the sitting room, dining room and even the kitchen – with boughs of holly.

'It's going to be a real family celebration,' Aunt Clara declared, her eyes shining.

A few days before Christmas, Uncle Charles took the

Austin 8 out of storage, put back the rotor arm and drove off to Newquay on a 'secret mission'. I was making mince pies for a whist drive that Aunt Clara was hosting in aid of men working on the minesweepers. I stood in the kitchen rubbing the fat and flour into sweaty crumbs, my face hot with effort and the heat of the range, and imagined the seamen somewhere out there, scanning the depths of the cold dark sea. The weather was bitter: a strong gale was whipping round the house and snow was reported to be on the way. Aunt Clara was boiling a joint of ham for what she called 'the cold table' and a plump goose hung in the outhouse. Rationing was about to start but the Rosewarnes always seemed to have plenty of everything.

'We may be at war,' said Aunt Clara, 'but I think this is going to be our best Christmas ever.'

I thought of Mum on her own in the house with nobody to cook for, or standing behind some noisy machine in the factory, smudges of oil and grease on her face; I pictured Dad marching around a freezing parade ground in his army uniform, or squeezed round a long thin table, eating chicken in congealed gravy off a tin plate.

Two hours later Uncle Charles popped his head round the kitchen door, his eyes sparkling with childish excitement. 'Where's Jack?' he said.

'He's up at the farm with Jory Nancarrow,' I replied.

'You're not to step outside until I say so. And from now on, the potting shed is strictly out of bounds.' He gave Aunt Clara a playful wink and disappeared again. A few minutes later we could hear him rummaging in the cupboard under the stairs and then he tried to sneak past me with a pot of paint behind his back.

'You can't do it now!' Aunt Clara protested. 'I need you to receive our guests. I have to see to the wassail cup.'

'Ellen can do that,' he replied airily. So I had to watch over the strange brew of red wine and brandy that bubbled on the stove, bobbing with shiny red apples and slices of orange. It was the Rosewarne Christmas in a saucepan – warm, sugary and full of intoxicating forgetfulness.

On Christmas morning I woke to find a bulging stocking sitting at the foot of my bed. Inside there was a box of Cornish fudge, oranges, nuts, a shiny half-crown, a book of poetry and my own copy of *Wuthering Heights*. After an enormous lunch we sat at the foot of the tree while Aunt Clara and Uncle Charles opened their presents to each other. He had bought her a set of watercolour paints and a sketchbook, while she'd bought him a bottle of his favourite malt whisky and an expensive-looking checked shirt folded neatly into its own box. I had painstakingly knitted a dishcloth for Aunt Clara and a maroon silk tie for Uncle Charles.

'The presents are from both of us,' I announced, knowing full well that Jack hadn't bothered to give them anything.

'Now, I want you both to close your eyes and don't open them until I say so.' Uncle Charles took us by the hand and led us outside into the cobbled courtyard. There, propped up against the wall, were two brand-new bicycles, their mud-guards carefully painted white.

'It was my idea,' he explained proudly. 'So that you can be seen more clearly in the blackout.'

'Cor! I've never rode a bike before,' said Jack, grinning.

'They must have been ever so expensive,' I added worriedly.

They smiled at each other and Aunt Clara squeezed Uncle Charles's arm.

'We decided that you needed them for school,' she said.

For the first and the only time I can remember, Jack threw his arms round her neck. 'Best present I ever had!' he cried.

It was the ultimate bribe.

NINE

You can see how I'm glad when spring comes and the fishing starts up again, for my father is some busy laying the new pots and leaves me well alone. He goes out soon as the sun is up and I have to take myself off to school in Padsta. It's a long walk round the cliffs and across the dunes, dodging the waves when the tide's up, and most days I arrive there soaking wet and my legs splattered with mud. The teacher makes me take my socks off; once she even made me strip down to my vest and knickers and put my dress over the back of my chair to dry. The other children laugh at me for my hair is so long and tangled and my clothes full of stains I can't wash out no matter how hard I scrub. The girls say bad things about my mother and won't let me join in their games. They make me sit by myself when we eat our dinner.

Now we're at war the school's full to bursting with foreign kids, come down from London to escape the bombings, here all by they selves without they mothers or fathers, the lucky buggers. I wish the Germans would drop a few on town, then I could be sent away too. We're told we have to welcome them and make them feel at home, but we don't mix much. They go about together in groups, clinging to the sides of the play-ground like great clumps of seaweed, whispering in funny accents and gaking at the rest of us. There's a teacher with them – she's from up-country too, a big whale of a woman called Miss Smelt – it's the funniest name I ever did hear but nobody dare laugh at it. She takes most of Class Two's lessons now. I do hate her – she's old and some ugly and forever giving out punishments.

The other day she's going on about something, I can't call home what – history or geography or some such thing I don't care to learn about – and she catches me staring out the window.

'You, girl!' her bawls. 'Stand up!' I'm so far away in my head I don't realize she's speaking to me, and the maid sitting in the next desk has to give me a kick. 'Yes – you, with the hair!'

She makes me come up to the front of the class and read out loud from this book. The truth is I've never gone in much for reading or writing, and I can't make head nor tail of the words.

'Speak up, girl!' Her's standing right up close to me, shout-ing right in my face. There's grease at the sides of her mouth, her chin wobbles and her hot breath stinks of the pasty she had for dinner.

'I can't do it, miss,' I whisper.

'Don't be ridiculous!' she snaps. She makes me hold out my hand and do whack me three times with the ruler on my palm. It stings but I don't so much as flinch, just stare right into her piggy little eyes with all the hate I can summon up. 'Now read!' she shouts. 'So the whole class can hear.'

'It don't matter how many times 'ee clot me, miss, if I don't know the words I can't speak 'em.' She calls me 'insolent' then and sends me to the headmaster. And he do give me the cane across the back of my legs.

It's a waste of time me going school, and what with the classrooms being so crowded I don't reckon I'll be missed, so I start minching it. Every morning, soon as Dad goes off to fetch his boat, I get out of bed and make up my dinner bag. I dress proper and do leave zackly the time I ought – in case Missus Tabb next door sees and tells him. I do set off down the path alongside the estuary like for all the world I'm going school, but when I get to the beach I slip down and hide in the dunes and wait till everyone's passed. When I'm sure it's safe I climb out and set off the other way, across the cliffs, walking a mile or so till I'm west of the Point. And I choose one of they small coves nobody believes you can get to save by boat, and slide down on my arse. I'm not a bit afeard 'cos anything beats sitting in class and getting the ruler just for not being able to read.

Soon as I touch the sand I throw off my shoes, lift my skirt right up fork and run into the sea till it's up by my thighs. Or I do skeer stones, or make pictures from shells, or jump in and out of the pools and chase crabs under rocks. And by now I'm raunish so I find a sand bunker out of the wind and make a nest to sit and eat my pasty in. I spend all day in my own company, only sometime a wrecker do come on the beach and ask whose maid I am and how I'm not at my lessons. I tell her I've been bad and teacher has told me not to show my face for a few days. I keep expecting a letter to turn up, telling my father I've not been going school, but it never does. Months go by but Mrs Smelt don't report it. I reckon if you looked in her register book there'd be a tick next to my name every day of the week. I don't want to go and she don't want me there, so it suits the both of us.

Why should I sit in a stuffy old classroom reading books when I can lie on my back listening to the waves roaring, or watch the gulls circling above me in the sky? I belong in the outdoor world. My mother used to say there was salt water gushing through my veins instead of blood – my skin is pale as death and my cheeks never flush red, not even when I'm running. I'm a cage of bones, as scraggy as a starving seabird, so light the wind could lift me into the sky and carry me away. What do I care? I'd like to be a bird, free to roam the air. Missus Tabb reckons I've been wisht by the piskies, for there's a faraway look in my eyes and her says their colour's not natural – purple like irises growing on a riverbank. She's always going on at my father to take a pair of shears to my hair. It's grown so long and full of tangles you can't pass a comb through it no more. That's all there is to me, hair and eyes – the rest of me is nothing but water.

Maybe that's why nobody had to teach me to swim, not as I remember anyhow. I love swimming – don't care how cold the weather is, I'll bathe right through the winter if I want. I've not got a costume so I go strip down to my knickers, and if I'm on my own and there's nobody around to gake at me I take all my clothes off and swim naked, let the sea soak through every part of my body. I don't swim about, just lie still with my face in the water and blow bubbles, my arms down by my sides like fins, my legs straight and close together like a long tail. If I'm in a shallow pool where the water's clear I open my eyes and watch the shrimps and tiny crabs crawling between the rocks and ore-weed – grass-green, sludge-yellow, deep browny purple, like plants in a garden. And my hair spreads out behind me, floats on the surface of the pool like golden fern.

Even in the summer it don't take long to make my whole body shiver with the cold. My skin turns icy blue, my toes and the tips of my fingers go white and stiff, my nipples tighten like pink walnuts, so small and hard they ache. Everything inside me slows down, even my heartbeat, and I can hardly move. But I don't mind for it's the cold I'm wanting: the colder it gets the less I can think. And all the bad things in my life, all my loneliness and longing, they just float out of my head. It's so cold I can't feel any pain no more, I'm numb to the very heart of me. I can forget being human, I'm a sea creature with no more feelings than a lobster.

I do believe there are merrymaids out there, like the one that's supposed to live on the Doom Bar. I'm dagging to meet her and ask questions. Like how do it feel to breathe under the water and never come up for air, and how do she stand the cold when she's diving so deep? Is it true a merrymaid can wish her tail away and live among folk as a maid, even marry a man and bear his children – and if so, have I seen her walking around the harbour and not known her? But most I want to know if she was born with her tail or if it crept up on her – for I lie in bed at night touching my thighs, all soft and warm like dough, and I tremble to think of them joined together and covered in slimy scales. I'm burning up with questions only a merrymaid can answer so I go onto the bar every day when the tide's out. I run through the gulls, calling and begging her to come and talk with me, but she never do.

I keep thinking of what Morva said about the strange way I came into this world and I beg my father to tell me what he knows. He laughs and says if I believe one word of the nonsense my stupid bitch of a mother told me I'm as daft as a carrot half scraped. For even though he's a fisherman he don't believe there are such things as merrymaids, not living on the Doom Bar, nor in any other part of Cornwall for that matter. So I go next door to Missus Tabb and ask her to tell me about merrymaids, and she says I'm as pretty as any of them in the storybooks and will be sure to break a few hearts one day.

So now I see that asking help from humans is no use for they cannot understand. The longing to talk with a merrymaid takes hold of me so I start going out in the boat with my father, searching for them. He's thinking I want to be with him and learn his craft, but that's a long way from truth for it don't feel right any more to catch fish. A long time ago my grandmother – God rest her poor soul – would make stargazy pie with the mackerels' heads poking out the top, and I would lick my lips and ask for the biggest piece, but now I can't stomach fish, for it makes me think of eating my own flesh.

My father do take the punt off its moorings and sculls out to the *Louisa May*. I wait while he brings her to the beach and runs her aground so he can load the new pots. The sun's just up and it's a clear spring morning, and he tells me we're going to Gull Island, two mile out to sea. I'm glad that's where we're heading for it's my belief the Doom Bar merrymaid has her home there, tucked away deep in they underwater caverns where the lobsters and crayfish do live.

We set out into the estuary and I'm hanging over the side of the boat staring down, hoping to see a streak of her rainbow body darting through the waves or a flick of her tail as she turns, but there's nothing but dark green water. Father tells me to stop leaning out so far, for if I fall in and drown my death will be of my own making. Then I do cry out for I see a glint of silver moving beneath the surface, and he tells me to hush my bal or I'll scare away the fish, which he reckons is just herring fry. I don't argue and say maybe it were a merrymaid, for I know he'll give me tongue pie and clot me.

We cross the bar and reach the open sea, and I taste salt in the wind. The boat dips and rises in the swell and Father tells me it's mostly sand beneath us now, but if we go further away from the run of the river, the floor will be rocky and thick with kelp and it's there, he says, that the best fishing is. I pretend to mark what he's saying but fact is I'm gaking at the island ahead of us and my heart's jumping in my boots for I can see a grey shape lying on the rocks. But when we get closer I see it's just a baby seal dozing in the sunshine and my father spots it too and frowns, for fishermen don't care for them.

So now we're at the island, which I do love for it's all peace and quietness save the gulls screeching and the waves smashing against the black rocks. Cormorants and shags are nesting on the ledges, white foam is pouring down the sides like cream off a pudding, and I make myself a promise that if I ever turn into a merrymaid I shall come and live in this place, for it already feels more like home than my own poor house.

My father knows there are caverns beneath us, though we can't see them for the water's so deep, and he tells me it's here we'll lay the string of pots. He takes the boat in a full wide circle and throws the end dan over the side. The line and weights fall in after and I watch the rope uncoil, slipping fast into the water. Then the first pot starts to move, so Father do pick it up and steady it on the gunwale, ready to push it in. As it drops overboard and sinks down I wonder how it do feel to be a merrymaid hiding in the weed and hearing the clatter of pots overhead. And I tell myself that if I lived in they rocky caverns I'd break the pots and let the lobsters and crabs scuttle free, so the fishermen would learn to stop coming here and leave us in peace. Course Father would never know it was the maid he calls his own daughter that was spoiling his fishing, for I'd vanish one day and he'd never know what became of me. He'd think I drowned and that'd be an easy trick to play for folks are forever sinking round here and their bodies never turning up on the shore.

So I'm sitting in the boat dreaming of how it will be when

I have my fish tail. I shall take off my dress and lie on that flat slab of rock, where the seal is now, with the sky blue as a cornflower and the sun cracking the edges. My hair will grow to my ankles and I'll comb out the tangles with a jagged shell. I'll learn to sing and let my voice dance on the wind. I'll feed off kelp and steal birds' eggs from their nests. And when I see a boat heading this way I'll slither off the rock and hide in my cavern so the fishermen won't hear my song and follow, for there are enough wrecks in these waters and I won't make matters worse.

TEN

By the end of the following April the fishing season was in full swing. The trawlers went out for about a week at a time and there was always a welcoming party on the quayside waiting hopefully, sometimes anxiously, for their return. Sole, slips, butts, brill, roker, whiting and 'lemons' lay like shimmering jewels in wooden boxes, whisked off the boats and thrown onto the freight trains that took them to Billingsgate market. Jack joked that he was going to hide in a crate of mackerel and stow away to London.

'I don't care how much it stinks,' he said. 'I just want to see our mum.'

But she came to see us instead, arriving late one Friday evening, tired and grey-faced, on an unlit train packed with airmen. We hadn't seen her for nearly eight months and we hardly recognized each other. She'd lost weight, her hair was loose instead of in the usual bun at the nape of her neck, and she had red lipstick on. Mum burst into tears when she finally realized that we were right there on the platform – two chubby-faced, neatly dressed children standing either side of a distinguished man in a tweed jacket.

'Just look at you!' she cried, peering into our faces. 'I've never seen you lookin' so healthy. Haven't you grown!'

Jack gave her a tight, long hug. 'I've missed you, Mum,' he said.

'Yeah, well, there's no need to suffocate me . . . Come on, Nellie, give us a cuddle.'

'Did you have a good journey?' I asked.

'No, bloody awful, if you must know. I'm bushed!' I felt myself wince and shot a glance at Uncle Charles but his face didn't flicker.

'It's just a short drive to the house,' he said, taking her small case. 'Shall we go?'

She settled herself into the passenger seat of Uncle Charles's Austin 8, marvelling at the smart leather seats and the highly polished dashboard.

'A ride in a motor car,' she laughed. 'This is a treat I never expected!'

They gave her the guest room at the side of the house, which had a spectacular view across Rocky Beach. Aunt Clara showed her the bathroom and Mum exclaimed appreciatively at every luxury and convenience. 'It's like staying in some swanky hotel up West,' she said, sniffing the bar of soap. 'You wait till I tell the girls at the factory. They'll be green.'

'I'll leave you to unpack. No doubt you'd like an early night,' said Aunt Clara. 'If there's anything you need, please ask. I do hope you sleep well.'

'Don't worry, I'll be out like a light,' Mum assured her. But an hour later she crept into my room and squeezed in bed beside me.

'This is a turn-up for the books,' she said. 'You said they was rich in your letters, but, well, I never imagined anything like this . . .'

'Not so loud,' I hissed, moving my feet away from her cold toes. 'Mum, hadn't you better go back to bed?'

'I can't sleep with that racket going on,' she whispered.

'It's only the sea. Please, Mum, they've given you your own room, you should at least use it.'

'I only wanted a cuddle,' she said, clasping me tightly. 'What with you and your dad away, I get lonely . . . Some new people have moved in upstairs, a young couple – he's just been called up. Jenny, that's the wife, I got her a job at the factory. She's ever so nice, you'll like her.'

'Tell me in the morning, Mum,' I said sleepily.

The next day Jack and I took her for a walk along the headland towards Stepper Point. The air was fresh and the sun bright. We stopped at the Round Hole on the cliff top – a deep basin of soft red earth, its rocky floor scattered with fallen rubble, the sea running round in circles beneath, desperately looking for a way to escape. Uncle Charles had told us the hole had been caused by soil erosion, but I had other theories – falling meteorites from outer space, or perhaps a Cornish ogre jumping up and down in anger. All Mum could say was that it looked 'bloody dangerous' and made us promise never to climb down there.

We walked on past Jory's farm, the ploughed fields dotted

with birds, leading her up and down the steep rocky paths that wound round the coastline. I pointed out a cormorant on the ledge drying his outstretched wings, a small fishing boat chugging picturesquely towards Gull Island, but the surroundings seemed to make no impact on her at all. She chatted on about her boss and her new friends – people we'd never heard of nor met – giggling as she caught the strap of her gas mask on the edge of a gate, protesting as we helped her clamber over a stile. She recounted funny stories about Granddad's old boss, Mr Banks, who'd become an ARP Warden, and told us jokes about Hitler that she'd learned at work. Jack took her arm and they trudged along the cliff path as if it were Barge House Road, singing the latest war song at the tops of their voices – *'We'll meet again, don't know where, don't know wh-e-n!'*

'What's wrong, Nellie?' Mum shouted. 'Cat got your tongue?'

'She's gone all snooty since she's been 'ere,' said Jack snidely.

'No, I haven't,' I insisted. 'I just don't feel like singing, that's all.'

I left the stony path and marched towards the cliff edge. The earth here was crumbly; clumps of heather gripped the silvery grey slate and the wiry grass shivered in the wind. I edged myself forward and looked down. Far beneath me the waves were pounding an outcrop of black rocks that stood like petrified giants, their granite legs drenched in spray, foam swirling round their feet. The sea was viridian green.

'Careful, Nellie!' called Mum. 'You'll fall.' I heard her footsteps running towards me, stopping just short. 'Come away from the edge,' she said breathlessly.

'Look below, Mum,' I said. 'Just stop and look. It's so beautiful.'

'Yes,' she agreed, without moving a step. 'It's lovely. Bit breezy, mind you. Come on, I promised Jack we'd go to the pictures. Edward G. Robinson – you like him.'

That afternoon we went to the Padstow Cinedrome and watched *Confessions of a Nazi Spy*.

'Uncle can speak German,' said Jack in a loud voice. 'Perhaps *he's* a spy.'

'Don't say things like that,' Mum retorted. 'Not even as a joke.'

'It's not a joke,' replied Jack defensively. 'Everyone says you have to watch out for 'em. Where does he get all his money from, eh? He hardly ever goes to his office. Perhaps the Germans are paying 'im to spy on us.'

Somebody behind us let out a loud 'Shush!'

'His family are just rich, that's all,' I whispered. 'Anyway, what would be the point of spying in Cornwall? There's nothing going on here.'

'There's nothing going on in London neither,' said Mum. 'That's why I've come to take you home.' Jack let out a loud cheer.

'Hush your bal, will 'ee?' grunted an old chap, leaning forward and tapping him sharply on the shoulder.

I don't remember what happened in the rest of the film. My

eyes clouded with tears and the picture went out of focus. I sat in the flickering darkness, my world seemingly at an end. I didn't want to go home. I wanted to stay with Auntie and Uncle – at that moment I didn't care even if he *was* a Nazi spy.

'This is foolish,' said Uncle Charles when Mum announced the news over dinner. 'If you take the twins back now you are putting them in grave danger. Bombing raids on London are inevitable – it's simply a matter of time.'

'We're very happy to look after them,' added Aunt Clara. 'They're no trouble.'

'Well, I'm glad to hear that,' said Mum, finishing off her sago pudding. 'But hundreds of kids have already come back to the city – it don't feel right them still being away.'

'It's not possible to say exactly when the attacks will begin, but I have it on good authority that it will be soon,' said Uncle Charles dramatically. 'Hitler doesn't want to destroy our Empire unless he has to – he would rather Britain surrender without a fight so he can take it over in good shape. But we are not going to capitulate! He will lose patience and then we will feel the full force of his considerable military power. London will be the prime target, especially the docks.'

'I don't want to go back if we're going to be bombed,' I said quietly.

'Don't be soft,' muttered Jack. 'A few Germans don't scare me.'

'But I miss 'em!' my mother implored. 'What with their father being away in the forces too . . . I get lonely.'

Uncle Charles turned to Mum. 'Mrs Morrison, we are at war. This is not the time to be selfish. Don't think of your own needs – think of the children! They should stay here with us, where it's safe. You must not take them back to the East End.' He lowered his voice, as if about to reveal a secret. 'I can assure you, their lives are at risk.'

'Really? You think so?' Mum frowned.

'And there's your job at the munitions factory,' added Aunt Clara. 'It's vital work for the war effort. Surely it will be difficult to devote time to the children when you're working such long hours.'

'I suppose that's true,' Mum faltered. 'But I expect we'd manage—'

'No, it's too dangerous! I simply can't allow it,' said Uncle Charles emphatically, as if the decision were solely his to make. 'Ellen and Jack will stay here until the war is over. You can visit them whenever you like, Mrs Morrison, but you cannot take them away now.'

My mother stared at him open-mouthed, shocked into silence. Charles had struck her with the superior force of class, wealth and education and she had no ammunition to fire back. Mum returned to her sago pudding and carried on eating without another word of protest. Jack put down his spoon and looked grimly at the tablecloth. I tried to hide a smile.

'It's not fair. Please take me back, Mum!' begged Jack as she said goodbye to us at the station the following day.

'Next time, eh?' she said, hugging us both warmly. I can see her face still – framed with brown hair, her mouth a small red blob, the arm of her thin navy-blue coat leaning on the edge of the open window. She dabbed the tears from her eyes. 'Now you be good for Mr and Mrs Rosewarne, and work hard at school.'

'Yes, Mum, don't worry about us,' I said.

As the train pulled away in a dirty blanket of steam she ducked back into the carriage, her shouts of goodbye fading. All that remained of my mother was a waving handkerchief. She had surrendered.

Afterwards Jack was angry with me for having been so standoffish with Mum. He said it was my fault that she'd agreed to leave us behind – if we'd both pleaded she would have taken us. He accused me of feeling embarrassed by her – which was true, although I denied it fiercely – and said I was a traitor to the family. He barely spoke to me for weeks, spending all his free time up at the farm with Jory, or playing football with a few of the lads from school. Emotions were always simple for Jack – love, hate, jealousy, fear – he could tell you in an instant where he stood on a matter. But my feelings were as tangled as my knitting and no amount of soul-searching could unravel the knots in my heart.

ELEVEN

It's morning. The ocean's a dull, nondescript colour like an artist's dirty paint jar, a random mix of green, blue and grey. My kitchen window is spattered with fine drops of rain – a soft persistent drizzle that feels light to the touch, but soaks you through just as easily as a downpour. In the holiday bungalows, parents will be looking out of the window and wondering how to amuse the children, flicking through leaflets for wet weather amusements – trips to the magical land of smugglers, pirates and bouncy castles.

Cassie will not surface for another few hours. She has been here for ten days but we're in different time zones, as if we're still living thousands of miles away from each other. Currently she is about four hours behind, which means break-fast at noon, lunch late in the afternoon, and who knows when she has supper, if she has it at all – I've only managed to cook for her twice. She goes out every evening without a word of explanation and creeps back in at about three a.m. I can't for the life of me imagine what she finds to do all night. When I ask she mumbles something about hanging about on the beach with her new friends or going clubbing in Newquay.

She spends hours in the bathroom before she goes out, titivating her hair, applying her make-up. And the way she dresses – so provocatively. Too-small T-shirts that stop short of her waist, tight jeans deliberately ripped at the knees. And in her bellybutton she wears a silver stud that gleams against her tanned, toned skin, tight as a drum. I could blame age or childbirth but the truth is my tummy was never as flat as Cassie's. Or Selina's. She would have pierced her bellybutton for sure, with a jewel perhaps, deep blue or sea-green. Selina would have loved the chance to draw attention to her taut young flesh – forcing the old and flabby amongst us to stare for a moment and admit defeat. But I'm trying not to think about Selina.

Cassie seems to have joined Scott Nancarrow's crowd – I'm glad she's made friends so easily but I suppose I'd hoped she'd want to spend more time with me. To be frank I could do with the help. There is so much to do – getting rid of the junk, tidying up, giving the house a thorough clean before it goes up for sale. But when I mention any of this to Cassie she changes the subject or actively tries to put me off – 'All in good time, Gran. Why don't you just enjoy the summer?'

The truth is I have done very little about the house these past few days. My mind just won't apply itself. I have been buried in the archives of memory, reliving the past until it becomes more vivid and tangible than the present. It's not just wading through boxes of memorabilia that I'm finding difficult – I came upon Jack's tatty old schoolbooks yesterday and wept for half an hour. It's that mermaid picture.

I couldn't bear the book being in my room so I took it downstairs and hid it amongst the books in the alcove next to the fireplace, its spine facing the wall. But Cassie found it straight away and pulled it out. 'You don't mind if I have a borrow?' she asked. It was impossible to refuse. Now she treats the book like a doll, carrying it from room to room, giving it spurts of attention and then abandoning it in strange places. The wretched thing lies in wait for me, hoping to catch me off guard. I find it next to the fridge, on the floor of the downstairs cloakroom, behind a cushion on the sofa – sometimes closed but very often open, falling as naturally as a hair-parting at the page where Selina lives.

I can't go on like this, it's ridiculous.

I put the book in a plastic carrier bag and leave the house, trying my best to feel normal. I'm going to immerse myself in the present, think only about the future. As I walk up the hill towards the post office I feel determination growing with every step.

The shop smells of warm bread and melting chocolate. The jars, tins and packets are still stacked on the shelves behind the counter, so there's a long queue of people waiting to be served. Sally spends all day in the kitchen baking Cornish pasties and currant scones while her husband Geoff scurries between the post office booth and shop counter, paying out pensions and benefits with one hand and taking the money back at the till with the other. As I wait for a half-dressed woman in a sarong to decide how many pasties she needs for lunch my resolve to stay in the present weakens.

I can see my aunt standing in front of me. She's wearing the sage-green dress from the photograph, and has a wicker basket on her arm. The shopkeeper asks her if she thinks the weather will stay fine for the weekend. There's no rationing yet, so my aunt buys a loaf of bread, some bacon, a pat of butter and a quarter of boiled sweets, which she gives to Jack and me. It's a warm day, mid-September, and by the time we get back to the house the sweets have softened and stuck to the bag. I carefully peel off the thin white paper, but Jack tears it, putting the sweets straight into his mouth, paper and all.

I eventually manage to buy my newspaper and continue up the hill. Clifftop Farm is on my left, down a driveway bearing a large hand-painted sign to the farm shop. I tell myself that I want a lettuce, but the truth is, I need to see Jory. He's the only person still living in this village who was here during the war – probably the only person in the world who can remember Nellie Morrison before she became Ellen Rosewarne. He is simply my oldest – although not my closest – friend. We went to each other's weddings, the christenings, the funerals . . . I was there when Jory's wife died of cancer at only thirty-six. When the boys were little I'd always bring them up to the farm and Jory would let them feed the pigs or scatter grain for the hens. Michael and Peter used to be very close to Jory's son, Philip, but as they grew up they lost touch. Jory has never visited me in London – says he doesn't care for the place, although he's never been – but I always go to see him when I'm in Cornwall. I send him birthday cards, not minding that he never remembers mine, and we have a sherry or two at Christmas. In all the many years we've been friends Jory hasn't changed one bit. He said he would never leave the farm and so far he's managed to keep his word, although the last I heard his family were trying to move him into an old people's home nearby. I'm not too concerned about Jory; he won't go down without a fight.

To my right is the farmhouse – dirty white walls, black paint peeling off the window frames, the front door slightly ajar. A dog is tied up in the yard; he barks at me, pulling away from his chain until his front legs are stiff, his paws off the ground. Nobody comes out to see why he's making such a noise. A tatty Land Rover is parked further down towards the fields – I can see distant rows of cabbages and carrots, bunches of floppy green leaves, maybe spinach or lettuce – it's hard to tell. Odd pieces of rusty machinery lean against a large wooden shed; its corrugated iron roof shines hot in the sun. A long hose screwed to a tap on the wall winds like a bright green worm across my path. The hedge buzzes, the dog keeps barking, the shed doors are open and I can hear the sound of chomping animals, the rustle of hooves in the straw. There is evidence of activity everywhere and yet the farm has a deserted air – too much work and not enough people to do it.

In my memory I can see young Jory Nancarrow pushing the pigs around the pen, shaking a bucket of potato peelings in their soggy snouts. He has a name for each of them, even though his father has warned him not to get too fond, and he shouts at them to take their turn. 'They can't understand you!' laughs Jack, who is standing in the doorway, a football fidgeting in his hands, as a brown and shiny as a conker, the hard leather unscuffed, the mustard-yellow lace clean and taut. Our new bicycles are leaning against the wall of the shed, their white mudguards gleaming.

'When do you finish?' I ask Jory shyly.

'A lot sooner if 'ee give me hand.' He grins.

His grandson Scott is walking up the track from the far cornfields that run almost to the edge of the cliff. It's just a couple of weeks till the harvest. If he'd been wearing a checked shirt and corduroy trousers instead of jeans and a T-shirt I could have thought it was young Jory walking towards me, raising his hand in a casual wave. Scott has the Nancarrow hair – wayward and straw-coloured – and the same bridge of freckles running across his nose.

'Hello, Scott. Is your granddad about?'

'He's in the upper field. Shall I get him for you?'

'Only if he can spare the time . . . I'll be in the shop.'

The shed is warm and smells of freshly dug earth. There's nobody serving at a till, just a plastic box on the table to leave your money in. The produce varies according to what has just been picked and today there are punnets of late strawberries, misshapen marrows, limp lettuces, dusty new potatoes and carrots encrusted with dry mud. I am hesitating over the strawberries, trying to decide whether to buy some for tea, when Jory walks in, carrying a box of runner beans.

'Ellen!' he calls. 'How are 'ee, me handsome?' I laugh. 'I was wondering when you was going to turn up. How's it going then? All right?'

'Yes, Jory . . .' I sigh. 'Yes, thank you.' I watch as he grabs handfuls of beans, weighing them roughly on some rusty scales before shoving them into plastic bags. His hands are large and callused and he's tanned in that weather-beaten way that most of the local men are. His thick hair has almost gone and what little remains is pale silvery grey.

'I heard 'ee was selling up.'

'News travels fast.'

Jory whistles. 'It'll go for top whack. 'Ee should see the prices some of them do fetch. More second homers, I suppose, down from London.'

'It's my second home,' I remind him, a little defensively.

'Nah, 'ee don't count.' He finds a grubby sheet of labels and writes *50p* on a dozen of them. 'So, what you'm doin' with the cash? Buyin' a villa in Spain?'

'No, I don't think so.' I choose a lettuce and a bag of pale tomatoes, putting a two-pound coin in the box.

'Your granddaughter's been here a few times.' His eyes start to twinkle mischievously. 'Reckon there's some romance brewin' between 'er and Scott.'

'Really? I know they've made friends, but . . . She's only staying for a few weeks.'

'Who knows, eh?' He chuckles. 'Here, give me a hand, stick these on for me, will 'ee? I can't peel 'em off, me nails are too short.' He hands me a sheet of labels.

'Something really strange has happened, Jory. I need to talk to you.'

Just then a man enters the shop. He's tall, tanned, blond, not a hair on his bare chest. He lingers over the fruit and veg, picking items up and then putting them back. He reads the ageing adverts for riding lessons and clotted cream on the notice board, in no hurry to leave the time-warp, enjoying the musty coolness of the shed.

Jory gestures at me to step outside. 'Let's go somewhere we can get some peace and quiet.'

He takes me down the track that leads towards the cliff edge. We used to run along this path together, grit rattling in our sandals, or race along on our bikes, bumping over the pebbles, skidding through the dust. Now we carefully place each step to avoid protruding stones and jagged pieces of slate, mindful of weak ankles and unreliable hip joints. The landscape has hardly changed, but we have become two elderly people, the years gently wrapping themselves around us like rings on a tree.

'Well . . .' says Jory. 'Are 'ee going to tell me or not?'

I take a deep breath, unsure where or how to start. 'Cassie gave me this book. It's a coffee-table book – you know the kind of thing, mainly illustrations. It's all about mermaids . . . Not the sort of book I'd ever buy, to be honest.' I realize I am waffling horribly.

'And?'

'There's this painting. When I saw it, I tell you, Jory, it made my blood run cold. It's of this mermaid in the sea, pulling a young man off a fishing boat . . . She looks exactly like Selina Penaluna.'

Jory turns and looks at me, surprised. 'How many years must it be since you've mentioned 'er name?'

I shrug. 'I've done my best to forget her.'

'Selina Penaluna . . . Now there was a rare beauty. If she were alive now she'd be one of them supermodels.'

'If she were alive now she'd be seventy-seven,' I snap.

'True . . . Better fit she died young, before the decaying process set in.' He laughs grimly. 'So where was it you saw her, in a photo?'

'No, Jory – a painting, a photograph of a painting. She's a mermaid – I mean, it's her face . . .' I tail off, faltering with embarrassment, starting to wish I'd never brought the subject up.

'I never saw Selina with a tail, but she were as slippery as a fish, that's for sure. Had all of us wrapped round 'er little finger.'

'You maybe; I never fell for it.'

'I felt sorry for the girl – she was one of them lost souls . . .'

'She was a menace.'

'She wasn't the type you brought home to your mother, but there was no real harm in 'er.'

'She once told me she thought she was a mermaid.'

'Oh yes, she used to give me that story too: it was 'er "dark secret". How far she actually believed it, I don't know. She were a bit loopy, mind. How does Scott put it – two slices short of a sandwich!' He chuckles. 'But 'ee can see how she got the idea, with that hair an' all . . . She did have a mermaid look about 'er.'

'Yes . . . I suppose so. It's just that the resemblance to her in the picture is unnerving.'

'Come on, mermaids all look the same, don't they?'

'Look for yourself.' I take out the book and hand it over.

Jory slowly turns the pages with his rough, yellow-tipped fingers – passing his eye over the sumptuous drawings. When he reaches the painting of Selina I look away.

'Yes, I see what 'ee mean,' he says after what feels like an age of waiting. 'It do look like her . . .'

'I don't know why, but it's really upset me, brought everything back. I keep thinking about Jack . . .' I pause. 'I wish we could have made our peace.'

'I understand that . . . But what's the use of getting worked up over it? It was all so long ago.'

'Then why does it feel as if it happened only yesterday?'

' 'Ee've 'ad a lot to cope with recently . . .' He puts his arm round my shoulders and we walk on a few yards. 'I'm, er, sorry I couldn't make Richard's funeral.'

'Don't be silly, I never expected you to come, not all that way.' I lean against a mossy wall that separates the farm from the common land, crushing a tuft of small pink flowers – Herb Robert, Bachelor's Buttons, *Geranium robertianum*. I feel hot and weary, unable to explain myself properly. Jory gently turns me round and leads me to the end of the lane. I'm red in the face and short of breath; I feel as if my heart might burst through my cotton blouse.

'It's a big thing for anyone to go through, moving house,' he says. 'Doin' it on your own too.'

'I've got Cassie . . . Although I don't think this was quite what she bargained for.'

'Can't one of the boys come over and give 'ee a hand?'

'They're not boys any more, Jory, they're in their forties . . . Anyway, they both live on the other side of the world.'

'They can get on a plane, can't they? It don't seem fair to me . . . Family's family.'

'Peter's always been hopeless at keeping in touch; since his divorce he's been worse. He didn't even come over for his father's funeral. And Michael's not offering to help because he doesn't want me to sell. He thinks I should rent the house out and make a fortune. All the more for him to inherit,' I add bitterly.

'I see. So he's sent young Cassie over to make 'ee change your mind, has he?'

'I don't know, maybe . . . But it's not going to work. I'll be all right, I just need to get through it, that's all. Spindrift holds a lot of memories for me . . .'

'True, but there's no need to go upsetting y'self over a load of old nonsense. Selina is long dead and gone.'

'I know, you're right, I'm just being pathetic . . .'

'Here, let me take this,' he says, tucking the mermaid book under his arm. 'I'll get Scott to take it to the charity shop.'

TWELVE

It was early summer 1940 when Churchill broadcast a special message asking for volunteers to form a local defence force. He'd hardly finished speaking before Uncle Charles had run out of the door to sign up at the police station. Soon he was taking part in evening training exercises, and was put in charge of a platoon. It took ages for anything resembling a proper uniform to arrive and there wasn't enough fighting equipment, but Uncle Charles still polished his boots before every drill and moaned continuously about others' lack of commitment. He was particularly cross with Ted Nancarrow, Jory's father, who had eagerly volunteered but consistently failed to turn up to parades – blaming his absence on the increased workload at the farm. They had a nasty argument outside the post office during which Uncle Charles called him a bungling amateur and was accused of being 'a foreigner' in return.

The Cornish called anyone who came from outside the county a foreigner, but Ted Nancarrow's objection to Charles was on account of his being half French. This didn't make sense to me, for surely the French were on our side? My uncle was distraught when France fell to the Germans – although his mother was dead he still had relatives in Brittany and was worried for their safety. He started to fret about the useless-ness of the Home Guard and said patrolling the north coast was pointless when it was obvious any invasion would come from the south.

But at the beginning of August he received a letter from an old Cambridge friend that raised his spirits hugely, although he wouldn't say what the letter was about and even burned it in the sink. He went straight to London, returning a few days later full of secret excitement.

'I'm afraid I have to go away for a short while,' he informed us. 'It's a business matter, a legal case that I cannot deal with here, nothing more. Aunt Clara will be holding the fort in my absence and will need your full co-operation and help. I'm sure I can count on you both to provide it.'

Uncle Charles's 'legal case' lasted for several weeks, and during that time we had no communication from him, although a couple of times a letter came addressed to my aunt, which she eagerly took to her room and then mysteri-ously threw on the fire. Jack found a corner of one in the grate. We couldn't read more than a couple of words, but it definitely wasn't my uncle's handwriting. Clara started read-ing the papers more closely and listened avidly to the radio, particularly to any mention of France. I speculated that Charles was doing something heroic and top secret for the war effort, but Jack was less convinced. He could just as easily be working for the Nazis, he said, and we had a huge row.

It was the peak of the holiday season but the beaches were virtually empty. Buckets and spades were used to fill sandbags and the only strangers who arrived at the railway station were servicemen. After the long wait, things were starting to happen. An emergency first-aid post was opened in the Deep Sea Fishermen Mission Hall – six empty beds lay in eerie waiting for casualties; rolls of bandages lined the cupboards, ready to stem the flow of blood. The council bought an air-raid siren and, after much arguing, hung it on the wall of a shopkeeper's shed. One Sunday a man from the Ministry of Information addressed a meeting on the quayside in Padstow. 'Cast your eyes over things that matter and do whatever you can in the great task that confronts you,' he cried fervently. 'We must repel the threat of invasion by the enemy!' There was loud applause and cries of 'God save the King!'

Jack and I did our bit by helping with the harvest, standing on the soft, unruly stacks and lifting forkfuls of hay off the cart. The weather was blazing hot and there was no shade in the fields. The thirsty horses dragged their hooves and the workers snapped at each other in the unrelenting sunshine. The newspapers were soon full of reports of a record crop – 'The nation will feed itself,' they declared triumphantly. But the Nancarrows were too tired to rejoice. A couple of Land Army girls were brought in to help but Ted complained they were too weak, worse than useless, and barked at them until they cried. He had been ordered to build smaller haystacks this year, to space them out and dig a trench around their base – all in case of incendiary attacks. Ted Nancarrow was furious, claiming that it involved too much extra work and was in any case an unnecessary precaution. The Germans weren't going to attack here. And he was right. The small, scattered stacks lay unscathed in the fields as monuments to our safety, while in September the German bombers began the Blitzkrieg with a direct attack on our street.

'Thank goodness we didn't let your mother take you back,' said Aunt Clara every time she opened the morning paper.

But not being there didn't make me any less scared – if anything, it made me feel even guiltier for allowing Mum to be left on her own. Jack's response was to draw pictures of British fighter planes repelling the enemy on butcher's paper, muttering sound effects under his breath – '*Akk-akk-akk, eee-yow . . . pfuuuh!*' – as Messerschmitts plunged to the ground in an explosion of heavy pencil. Hitler seemed to have pin-pointed North Woolwich as his main target. Every photograph in the paper looked as if it had been taken in our street; all the victims looked like people I knew. Those were our neigh-bours being carried out on stretchers, my school friends with heads swathed in bloody bandages. I saw pictures of men picking their way through a bomb site and was convinced they were standing in the ruins of our house – wasn't that our copper, our dining table, Dad's easy chair? And who was that woman being lifted out of the rubble? Our mother had a white blouse and a straight skirt just like that.

Uncle Charles returned home without any warning – I don't think even my aunt was expecting him. We came back from school one afternoon and found him sitting by the fire, smoking his pipe and reading *The Times* as if he'd never been away. But as I came closer I saw that his cheeks were hollow and his eyes dull with exhaustion.

'Children!' he cried. 'My dear children.' He rose slowly and held out his arms. He looked thinner, taller, swamped in the new grey cardigan Aunt Clara had knitted during his absence. As I hugged him I could feel the hard ridges of his ribs.

'Where have you been?' I cried. 'What have you been doing?'

'I've been working in London on a legal case, as I said.'

'We thought you were up to something. How come you never got in touch?' asked Jack suspiciously.

Charles exchanged a quick glance with Aunt Clara, who was sitting on the other side of the fireplace, her face taken over by an enormous smile. 'I was very busy,' he replied. 'I'm afraid I can't say any more. Ask no questions and I'll tell you no lies.'

'What's it like in London?' I said, trying to change the subject. 'Is it bombed to bits?'

'No, not at all,' Charles replied cagily. 'Have you heard from your parents? Are they bearing up?'

'We don't know where Dad is, but Mum's OK,' I answered. 'We got a letter last week. Says she's spending every night in the Underground.'

'Good. It's the safest place to be.'

As soon as he returned, Charles resigned from the village platoon and joined another Home Guard unit, based a few miles away, although he never explained exactly where. This new unit seemed far better organized. They had proper uniforms, all sorts of interesting equipment, and Charles was issued with a smart rifle with a long bayonet. From that moment on he was constantly going away on training exercises, sometimes lasting the whole weekend, and he'd frequently stay out all night. Early in the morning I would find my uncle slumped exhausted over the kitchen table, still in his uniform, his boots thick with mud and his face blackened. Sometimes we'd hear muffled voices talking in the kitchen during the middle of the night or a car would turn up outside the house and drive my uncle away.

Charles started spending time with three particular men from his unit – a carpenter called John Dyer, Michael Legge, who ran a garage near Padstow, and George Langham, who farmed land alongside the estuary near Mussel Cove. They were often at our house having meetings or cleaning equipment; once John Dyer turned up with a nasty cut on his hand and my aunt had to put a dressing on it. The men were always polite but never spoke much. Jack and I thought it all very peculiar – they seemed very unlikely friends for my uncle.

Then something else very odd happened – a telephone was installed in the house, the only one in the entire village, although we were absolutely forbidden to answer it and were threatened with all manner of punishments if we dared to listen in on any conversations. This seemed to us to be the final proof that Charles was involved in something rather secret and exciting, but he insisted he was just on normal

Home Guard duties. He made it very clear that we were not to ask questions, nor to say a word to anyone else. 'Careless talk costs lives' was the government motto, although it didn't stop the village gossip about the new telephone – 'Such an extravagance in these times of hardship' – or Charles's defection to the new unit – 'So we'm not good enough for 'im, is that it?' Members of his old platoon snubbed him in the street, complaining bitterly that he'd deserted them as their leader – though most of them had resented his leadership in the first place.

Despite such antagonism from the neighbours and rumblings in the WI, Aunt Clara went about her fundraising activities with her head held defiantly high. She hosted hot suppers and whist drives, organized sales of vegetables and handiwork exhibitions of 'useful and attractive' items made entirely from scrap paper and old rags. She knocked on doors asking for aluminium and was a founding member of the local Spitfire Fund committee. As the weeks went by she looked more and more exhausted, but was determined to fill every minute of the day.

Christmas took us by surprise that year, sneaking up and tapping us on the shoulder in mid-December. We were sent – Jack somewhat reluctantly – to the WI's children's fancy dress party. Jack refused to dress up but I went as a Red Cross nurse. We played hoopla, marly up, tailed the donkey and threw beanbags at a Hitler shy. Despite all the food shortages, we sat down to a fine spread – jam and paste sandwiches,

lemon squash, fairy cakes and strawberry jelly. We were waiting patiently for the present-giving to begin – Mr Dobbin
dressed up in his wife's red dressing gown as Father
Christmas hovering in the doorway with a sack – when Uncle
Charles pushed past him and came into the hall. His face was
serious and pale, his voice quivering as he spoke.

'Jack, Ellen – I need a word. Now please.'

Aunt Clara hurriedly wiped her hands on her apron and
ushered us out. 'Whatever is it, Charles?' she whispered, but
he gave her a fixed, don't-ask-me-now look.

'Mr Palmer, the Billeting Officer, is here,' he explained.
'He'd like to talk to you straight away.'

'But we're just getting to the best bit!' protested Jack.

'He's not going to send us somewhere else, is he?' I said.

'No, my dear,' Uncle Charles replied. 'You must have no
fear of that . . . Get your coats, quickly please. He's waiting
for you.'

'Do they want their presents now then?' asked Mr Dobbin,
rummaging in his sack, but Uncle Charles shook his head and
led us away.

We heard the news from a stranger in a tweed coat. He stood
nervously in front of the blazing fire, twisting the rim of his
black felt hat, hesitant, deferential, twitching with apology, as
if our parents' death were his fault. In the following weeks Mr
Palmer appeared in most of my nightmares – the undertaker
walking before the coffins, the German pilot looking gleefully
out of the cockpit as he released the bomb, or, most

frighteningly, as himself – a dark, sorrowful man surrounded in flames.

'They must have made a mistake. Dad's away in the army,' insisted Jack twenty times that evening, when all that remained of Mr Palmer was a cold cup of tea resting on the mantelpiece. I buried myself in Aunt Clara's lap and sobbed until her dress was soaked with tears. But Jack just sat there with his fists clenched, telling me to shut up, saying over and over again that it couldn't be true. Charles reached out to comfort him, but he shoved him away. 'They're lying!' he shouted. 'You're all lying!' running upstairs to his room.

But the next day a letter arrived from Mum's friend Jenny. *'Your dad had just come home on leave. The siren sounded and I ran out to the shelter, but your mum and dad stayed indoors,'* she wrote. *'They hadn't seen each other for so long I suppose they decided to risk it. There's nothing left of the house, I'm afraid. I grabbed what was worth taking, but it don't amount to much.'*

Jack couldn't deny it any longer. Now we were not only evacuees, but homeless orphans too.

Yet this was war. We weren't the only sufferers – we were expected to bear our losses bravely or, if that wasn't possible, to bear them silently at least. To submit to despair, I was told, was to submit to Hitler. But even so, I cried almost continually for seven days, curled up on the sofa with my fist stuffed into my mouth like a baby thrown out of the womb. I couldn't understand why the world had so little trouble carrying on without my parents. They were not the most beautiful people

you could ever hope to meet, nor the cleverest, nor bravest –
I wouldn't even pretend they were the kindest souls on earth
– but why had the firemen fought to save St Paul's Cathedral
and left my mum and dad to burn?

I never saw Jack shed a tear. He had converted all his grief
to anger – with Hitler, with Mum and Dad for getting themselves killed, but most of all with the Rosewarnes – as if it
had all been their doing, part of some devious plot to get rid
of our parents so that they could keep us for ever. He glared
at them across the table, fidgeting with his food, refusing to
speak, and went to his room straight after dinner, thumping
up the stairs as a signal of his fury. Clara tried to bring him
round but he wasn't interested, just shouted at her that she
didn't understand, shrugged off all her attempts to give him
hugs. Once Charles insisted they went out for a stroll, hoping
to have a man-to-man chat, I suppose, but they were soon
back – Jack grim-faced and resolutely silent, my uncle
shaking his head in defeat as he hung up his jacket.

Nothing had been said officially about where we would go
or who would look after us, but it was clear that the
Rosewarnes had no plans for us to leave. They showed us
nothing but kindness and sympathy, but sometimes Clara
forgot herself and became rather excited – sensing the
probability that we might now stay for good. The way she
looked at Jack in particular was a little unnerving – her eyes
full of soft maternal love, as if some dream she'd been
nursing for many years had finally come true. I'm sure he
noticed it. Or she would start talking about the future –

sending us to new schools, taking us away for a holiday when the war was over – and Jack would instantly storm out of the room, slamming the door behind him.

'He'll come back to us, don't worry,' soothed Aunt Clara optimistically. 'Just give him time.'

Jack was angry with me too of course, knowing that there had been moments when I'd wished that Charles and Clara were our real parents – maybe he suspected that I was secretly rejoicing. After all, I seemed to have got what I wanted. This thought lay between us like a drawn sword. I longed to defend myself, to tell him that he was mistaken, but he refused to talk. I was the only family he had left and yet he seemed to want to pull away from me, ever further. 'Just leave me be, Nellie,' he kept saying when I knocked on his bedroom door. He even left for school by himself, rising earlier each morning to make sure he missed me.

But time passed. The hours became days, the days inevitably turned to weeks; finally I got to the end of a day and realized I hadn't cried once. Life returned to a superficial normality. I fed the hens, ate my porridge, took my bike from the shed and wheeled it down the path. I went back to school, did my lessons and cycled home again. I helped prepare the evening meal and laid the table. After dinner I went to my room and read a book. At night I lay in the darkness and fought off sleep, fearful of my dreams, waking each morning surprised to find that the sun had risen on yet another day.

What is death but an absence? I told myself it was simple

– things that had happened hundreds, maybe thousands of times would never happen again. I would no longer hear my mother's voice calling me in to tea, nor see my father's familiar shape rolling down the street. Never again would I experience that unique combination of smell and touch and sound that set those two people apart from all the other millions in the world. My parents. I hadn't seen my father for over sixteen months, my mother for more than eight. In many ways they had already turned a corner in my life and disappeared from view. I hadn't felt deserted by them before – on the contrary, I had relished my new existence. But now the realization that they *weren't* somewhere out there, breathing, moving, eating, sleeping – loving us – terrified me.

My memories took on new, symbolic meanings – my mother's visit, her embarrassing red lipstick, the disembodied hand desperately waving a white handkerchief, that last hug I should have returned more warmly – that I *would* have returned more warmly if only I had known. It was less painful to think about my father, but I couldn't remember how I'd last seen him. I had no problem picturing him sitting by the fire rolling a cigarette or taking a chair onto the pavement to drink his beer. I hung these portraits on the wall of my memory, but the painting of our last moment together was still missing. I tried to invent the scene, imagining his clothes, his stance, a gesture, that final look, but every element eluded me.

While I lived in the art gallery of my mind, Jack turned to real pencil and paper. He no longer drew fighter planes, exploding buildings, or battles in the sky but sought refuge in natural objects – dry seaweed, stones, pieces of driftwood. There were thousands of shells on Rocky Beach, but he spent hours selecting ones to draw, turning them over reverently in his hand as if remembering that they were once living things. He took Aunt Clara's sketchbooks, charcoal and watercolour paints and sat silently at the dining table every evening. I watched him following the spiralling whorls of the whelk, recording every warty scar of the common limpet, smudging his finger into the shady bowl of the periwinkle, tracing the five rigid arms of the sandstar.

One day he found a dead seahorse clinging to a frond of seaweed and brought it home, tenderly wrapped in his handkerchief, sharpening his pencil to its finest point to capture the compassionate angle of its head, its thin fragile body tapering to a simple, perfect curl. And when he tired of me standing behind him, casting a shadow over the page, he left the house and began to sketch the landscape. I would look out of the window and see him sitting on the headland, bent over a large sketchbook, looking up every now and then to check the shape of the cliff, the sweep of the bay, holding his stick of charcoal before him to measure the height of the lighthouse or the distance between the rocky island and the shore. But as a source of comfort it was short-lived: he gave it all up after a few weeks, handing the sketchbooks and pens back to my aunt with a silent shrug.

The Rosewarnes set about the task of adopting us. I suppose there must have been some discussion about it, but

I don't remember actually being asked. The authorities considered it an act of extreme generosity on their part and we had no choice unless we wanted to end up in some children's home. We only had one relative that we knew – Aunt Edie, our father's sister, who lived in North London. She was a sharp, mean-spirited woman; she had never got on with Dad and had openly disliked Mum – if she appeared upset by their death it was only because she assumed we would be foisted upon her. Mum had two younger half-brothers, but they had emigrated to Australia after the First World War and all contact had been lost. All our grandparents were dead. With no competition, Uncle Charles used all his legal skills to push the adoption ahead and within a couple of months the process was complete. Jack didn't openly protest but he behaved as if nothing had happened, refusing to use the Rosewarne name.

Naturally I was grateful to Charles and Clara, but their desire to adopt us puzzled me. We were no longer the sunny, innocent children that had jumped in the surf or rattled down the hill with our feet swinging off our bicycle pedals, behaving as if we were on some holiday lark. I did everything I could to please them, frightened perhaps that they might change their mind and turf us out onto the streets. I tried to compensate for Jack's hostility, yet he remained their favourite. It was a little hurtful at times but I told myself there must be a good reason – perhaps they had always wanted a boy.

Now we were officially part of the family the local schools

were no longer good enough for us, so I was sent to Hawthorne House, a private establishment for young ladies situated several miles inland at the end of a long tree-lined drive. I was kitted out in a navy pleated skirt and blazer, gabardine raincoat and felt hat with a maroon ribbon around the crown. Specially embroidered nametapes were sewn onto every waistband and collar, confirming that I was no longer the East End evacuee Nellie Morrison but the refined, elegant Miss E. Rosewarne. Just reading my name on the inside of my coat or the front of my schoolbooks sent a thrill through my veins.

Every day I arrived eagerly at school, my brain as freshly washed and ironed as my crisp white blouse. I read and studied and studied and read, far beyond anybody's expectations or requirements. Not only was I a model pupil in the academic subjects, I threw my heart and soul into mastering the skills of a successful housewife – needlework, laundry and cookery. In class I sat with a firm straight back, remembered never to cross my legs and was duly awarded a Posture Stripe – a slim rectangle of pale blue ribbon that I proudly sewed onto the lapel of my blazer. I was in gymslip heaven.

Jack meanwhile was rotting in a private schoolboy hell by the name of Babbington's – where the other pupils laughed at his Cockney accent and the teachers were appalled by his ineptitude at maths. He'd only been accepted because the headmaster was an old chum of Uncle Charles, and he was always being reminded of the fact. Jack played truant, refused to do his homework, started fights in the playground and was sullen with the teachers. In return they gave him detentions, rapped his knuckles and beat him with the slipper. Only the art teacher showed any liking or sympathy for Jack. He had a small studio in a hut behind the main school building and he'd let Jack hide there in the lunch hour on the pretext that he needed to finish a drawing or a sculpture. We'd meet on the homeward train and I'd prattle on about French and needlework, while Jack stared furiously out of the window at the bleak estuary landscape, picking red modelling clay from his fingernails and flicking it across the carriage floor.

'They can't make me stay,' he kept saying. 'All I need is a bit of cash, then I'm going back 'ome.'

'But this *is* our home now, Jack,' I replied primly. 'There's nothing left of our old house.'

'I know that. I meant the East End, stupid – what's left of it. We're fourteen: we can leave school this summer, get shot of the bloody Rosewarnes. I reckon if we're both working we could afford to rent a couple of rooms, share a landing or something.'

'I don't think that's what Uncle Charles has in mind,' I murmured. 'He wants us to stay on into the sixth form, even go on to university.'

'I've told you before, that's not for the likes of us, Nellie.'

'But surely Mother and Father would want us to better ourselves, if we have the chance.'

'It's my life, I'll do what I want with it,' Jack fumed. 'I don't care how many bits of paper they've got – the Rosewarnes don't own me. Soon as I've got a bit of cash together, I'm off. You'll come with me, won't you?' he said.

'Of course,' I replied. I felt my heart skip half a beat – was it a sudden surge of happiness that he wanted to be with me or because I'd just lied?

With my false promise safe in his heart, Jack moved closer to me for a while. At weekends he'd ask me to go on cycle rides with him – we'd pack a lunch and a flask of hot tea and take to the lanes. Sometimes we had a firm destination in mind – the larger town of Wadebridge or the remote lighthouse at Trevose Head. At other times we'd take a random route inland – setting our sights on a distant church spire or following a stream as far as it would take us. When we came to a junction Jack always chose the narrower path in the hope that it would lead to adventure, but more often than not we'd find ourselves pedalling through a muddy farmyard, skirting round hissing geese and flapping ducks, chased by suspicious dogs snapping at our wheels.

I loved those outings despite the harsh winter. By the end of the day my fingers ached with cold, my lips were cracked and my nose was a red button, but I didn't care. The two of us were together again and for a brief time I felt optimistic that I would eventually win Jack round to my point of view. But I had no idea what, or indeed who, was waiting for us round the corner.

One grey Saturday afternoon in March we strayed slightly from the path of the Camel estuary and came across a small area of isolated marshland that we'd never seen before. A sharp wind was blowing across the flats, threading in and out of the reeds. White snowdrops lifted their drooping heads out of the murky water like survivors from a shipwreck. A solitary figure was standing in the middle of the marsh, slim bare legs in rubber boots, a large sack of sticks on her back. She was wearing a thin sea-green dress that clung round her thighs in the wind and her long golden hair fluttered behind her like a tattered flag. Every so often she bent down to cut off a stem with a small knife, slinging the stick over her shoulder and into the sack in one flowing gesture.

'What's she doing?' whispered Jack, laying his bike on the ground.

'I don't know.' I shrugged. 'Collecting firewood?'

'You can't burn that stuff, it's soaking wet.'

'We shouldn't be staring,' I said. 'Let's go.' But Jack walked to the edge of the marsh. He took one step forward and the mud oozed up his boots. 'You'll get stuck,' I warned, but he wasn't listening.

'Hello!' His voice dropped like a stone into the water.

The figure calmly finished cutting off a stick, then straightened up and turned round slowly. I will never forget Jack's gasp the first time he saw her face. She had a kind of beauty I'd never seen before – it was unearthly – small perfect features, intense violet eyes, pale bloodless lips, a mass of bright hair that fell in tangles to her waist, skin so white it was almost translucent. Angelic features and yet . . .

'Wait there,' she ordered, wading towards us between the

reeds, fixing us with a fierce stare, defying us to move. She stood before us and we let her look us up and down, first Jack and then me, measuring us to the last inch. She had ripped out my heart and was weighing it in her hands.

'You'm twins,' she announced finally.

'That's right, how did you guess? I'm Jack and this is Nellie.'

'Ellen,' I corrected sharply.

'What are you doing?' Jack asked.

'Collectin' willow for the withy pots, course.'

'What's a withy pot?'

She laughed. ''Ee from up-country then?' We both nodded. 'Thought so . . . For catchin' lobsters.' She stepped onto the path, her boots squelching, her long slender legs lightly spattered with mud.

'Want help with that?' Jack asked, gesturing towards the heavy, dripping sack. 'I could put it on my bike, if you like.'

'No need. It's not far.'

'Live round here, do you?'

'Might do.' The springy sticks of willow looked like a collection of magic wands and I briefly wondered whether she was a witch's daughter – given a beauty potion by her ugly hag of a mother to enchant young men and put them in her thrall. Because that was exactly how Jack was behaving – as if he had been put under some bewitching spell.

'So, what's your name then?' he said urgently. 'You haven't told us your name.'

She paused and we waited, Jack's gaze fixed on her

wickedly beautiful face. I realized that even I was holding my breath.

'Selina Penaluna,' she replied at last. Then she suddenly turned away from us and ran down an overgrown path, canopied with trees. The twisted branches seemed to close behind her and she vanished into the landscape.

'Selina Penaluna,' murmured Jack, tasting the sounds in his mouth. 'Selina Penaluna . . .'

THIRTEEN

If I had one wish right now it would be for this here Churchill to send my father away to the war and for him to not come back. But he's too old to be called up, and besides, they need him for the lifeboat. There are few 'ansum enough young men in Padsta and now they'm off getting themselves killed, soon nobody will be left to make us husbands. I can't see any good in this stupid war – men dying, women digging up flowers and planting tatties, and Missus Tabb keep telling me to get off my arse and do something useful, like be a Land Girl. So now I have to keep going fishing to make sure nobody'll send me off to work on some bloody farm, for I'd rather be out at sea than micking out pigsties, even if I have to spend my days with the bastard that calls himself my father.

He's got me for a labbet, that's all, making me cook and clean the house for him and not giving me one kind word back, save when he's drunk and then it's worse, for he grabs hold of me and kisses me straight on my mouth, mumbling 'Sorry,' in my ear while he puts his baissly fingers inside my blouse and searches for my tits. His hands are some rough and his stubbly chin scratches my cheeks and I daren't fight him off for I'm afeard to make him angry. I know it'll go further if I'm not mindful, so now I make sure to be in my room when he comes home from The Ship and I do stick a chair under the door handle so he can't force his way in. I may be old enough to give my body to a man, but I'll die sooner than it be him. It sets me thinking I can't be his flesh and blood – for why would any man want to do such things to his own daughter? Perhaps he knows in his heart that my true father lives in the sea, and that I do belong to the Mer people.

We do leave the house at five every morning to go check the pots and he makes me wear rubber boots and a barble round my waist like a proper fishwife. He turns the boat and we sets off out of the estuary to the open sea. I sit in the stern, as far away from him as I can be, and fix my eyes on the coast, for I will not speak to him lest I have to. We get to my island soon enough – I call it mine now for it's where I fancy I'd live if I was a merrymaid – and he pulls up alongside the flag dan. He drags up the lines and heaves the pots on board and it's my job to swing them onto the thwart and deal with what we've caught.

He says I bring him bad fortune, for when I'm with him the catch is always poor, but that's because I throw a crab or lobster back when he's not looking. I untie the old bait and fling it overboard for the gulls who come flocking round, screaming and fighting for the rotten bits of fish, and if Dad's busy hauling in I don't put in the fresh bait, or I tie it on so loose it'll come off soon as the pot hits the water again. I'll do what I can to get my own back on that bastard, for I cannot abide the way he gakes at me when we're out at sea just the two of us, like he hates me and wants me at the same time. It's not my fault my mother went off with the Corona Man and left him without a woman to poke. If he lunges at me I tell you I'll stab him with a spinner and gut him like a mackerel, or I'll jump right off the boat and into the sea and I don't care how big the waves are or how deep the water. If it comes to it, I'll sink to the bottom and breathe like a fish, for I feel that power's inside me if I ever have to call upon it.

There are other men too that would touch me if they had the chance. I know by the way they look at me when I walk round the harbour, wishing they could see straight through my dress. I see their wives and sweethearts narrow their eyes when I come towards them, gripping their men by the arm and leading them out of my way like I've got danger writ across my forehead. I've no maid friends to call my own, but that's of my own making for I never did spend much time at school and never got to know nobody. I'm eaten up now to see girls from my class chatting away together, housing or going off on their bikes. They know full well who I am but they act like I'm a foreigner from up-country, for they stop talking when I pass by and their eyes burn into my back like pokers. I used to be happy enough spending so much time by myself, but these days I feel as lonely as an 'oss hitched to a post.

I'm in my fifteens now and no longer a child – I've shape in my hips and breasts like two ripe peaches, my hair is grown so long I can sit on it. Every month my belly aches like something gnawing at my insides and I do imagine it's the stirrings of a fish tail growing, but of course it's only the curse. Still, it sets me wondering what has to happen before a human girl can turn merrymaid. Maybe, I think, her tail can't grow till she opens her legs and lets a man inside her, like it's the breaking of a spell. For though they're called merry*maids* they're none of them virgins. It's said that many of them are wives and mothers living amongst human folk – but that life wouldn't be for me. I'd not stay on land like a tame creature. I'd be one of those merrymaids you see in picture books, spending my days by the sea, sitting on rocks combing out my hair, waiting for some 'ansum strong fisherman to pass by and be my lover. And if he didn't please me I'd throw him back into the water like a tiddler and find another.

I don't know what's wrong with me these days, but I cannot put the thought of merrymaids out of my head. Sometimes I think I must be going mad, for who in their right minds would spend their days imagining what it must be like to be half fish and live in the sea, and dream about it every single night? There's nobody in the world I can talk to about it – they'd only laugh at me and tell me not to be so daft. We're allowed to believe in such things when we're babies – everyone knows stories of witches, piskies, giants, fairies, even Father Christmas . . . But I should have grown out of it like a pair of shoes.

Why can't I stop it? Sometimes it makes me so mazzed, I even shout at myself out loud, like I'm speaking to another maid who's inside me, a mean, wicked girl that's forcing me to imagine such stupid things. But it don't make a spot of difference. The same strange thoughts and strong feelings keep flooding into my mind – no, not into my mind so much, more like into my body. Or rather, it's as if some dark horrible truth always lives deep inside of me, at the bottom of my stomach, where my womb lies. It rises up to my throat like bile and makes my heart beat some fast. And then I get this urge to run out the house and jump off the end of the jetty or fling myself over the cliff. I want to escape myself, to be nothing. I want to be in the water, right deep under the water, where it's dark and cold . . . I hate it. It frightens me to death.

There's a looking glass on the dressing table in my father's bedroom and when he's out of the house I go in there and gake at my reflection. I do take all my clothes off and stand naked on the bed so I can study my body from top to toe. I turn this way and that, raising my arms, bending over, then standing with my back to the glass and look over my shoulder, or lift my leg and rest my foot on the corner of the bedstead. I go up close and glaze right into my eyes, then step back as far as I can to take in the whole picture.

I make myself touch every part of me, head first, working my way down to my feet. I comb my hair with stretched fingers, measure the length of my nose, brush against my eyelashes, stroke my soft cheeks, feel my tongue flick away from me, alive in my mouth. I press the bones beneath my white skin, the tiny gaps between my ribs, I take the weight of each breast in my hand, poke into my navel, wrap my arms around my waist, feel down to the opening between my legs – touch the secret folds of damp flesh like the insides of an oyster . . . I know I am all over beautiful, I cannot find fault with any part of me. But the more I stare at myself the less I know who, or what, I am.

Sometimes in my dreams I go to the deep pool where Morva said I first came into this human world, and I find my real Mer father. He knows at first glance I'm his long-lost daughter and tears of joy trickle down his golden beard. He calls down for my merrymaid mother to come see for herself. She springs out of the water and do let out a cry of surprise when she sees me. She laughs and holds me in her warm, wet arms and begs forgiveness that she ever swapped me for a human chield. Then they take my hands and we dive into the pool to meet my brothers and sisters who've been waiting for me these long years. These are the good dreams, yet they still make me shout out in my sleep and wake with tears running down my face. I feel that I cannot take much more of it, so I decide to go back to that cove and see once and for all where the truth of the story lies.

I wait till the sun has nearly gone down, for I'm thinking that if by some chance there are Mer people there they will not show themselves in broad daylight. Besides, I don't want no one to see me going down there in case I don't come back again and they try to search for me.

The beach is covered in slabs of loose slate and the sand's damp and gritty. I'm shivering already so I do put a blanket round my shoulders and walk towards the sea. The tide's ebbing, pulling itself back like a cloth, uncovering the rocks inch by inch, and I know the pool's hiding there somewhere though I can't see it. I climb over the wet rocks, slippery as a glass bottle, and I nearly lose my footing two or three times. Then I see a large black shape ahead and know that's where I must go, but the light's fading fast and I have to hurry, picking my way between the rocks and shallow pools. As I get there the sun drops into the sea like a thrown stone and there's nothing but darkness all around me. I've brought a candle and a box of matches but every time I light it the wind blows it out. So there's nothing to do now but sit on the edge and wait.

The sea's roaring and the gulls are screeching but it's other sounds I'm listening out for – I lie on my belly and lean right over the pool, letting my hair dip and float in the water. I'm trying to hear the Mer folk down there – maybe fish tails flapping, my sisters laughing and playing, my mother singing a sweet song . . . But the water's black and still; there's not a murmur coming from its depths and I never felt more alone in all my life. I don't know how long it is I'm waiting, but hours must pass for I see the tide is on its way back in and I must move myself or drown. So I stand up and shout above the waves, telling my folks that their daughter's come back, that I'm ready to join them again, but they do not hear me. And I wonder, should I take off all my clothes and dive in to search for them under the water, but my fingers are so cold I can't undo the buttons of my blouse.

I feel hopeless then and I do pitch crying and calling out to Morva, cursing her for telling me she was never my real mother and filling my head with this stupid talk of merrymaids. I scream to the wind how I hate her for leaving me to suffer Penaluna with his baissly hands, and I tell the sea to come and swallow me up in the darkness. But as soon as I feel it creeping icy over my toes I'm up and going like a skeiner, jumping over the rocks, tripping over bunches of weed and falling in the puddles, running fast as I can to get away from it. I scramble up the cliff and hurl myself onto the cold grass, lying there catching my breath, my face dabbered with mud and my heart racing. And I run back home, hoping to make it afore my father, but I'm too late for he's sitting by the fire with a face like a thunderstorm, waiting for me.

'Where d'ee think you'm bin?' he bawls, grabbing my hair and pulling me towards him. I can feel the flames warming the backs of my legs, smell the beer and tobacco on his foul breath. 'Who you'm bin with, hussy? What's 'is name?'

'Nobody,' I whisper. 'Bin by meself, out walkin', that's all.'

'Tell the truth or I'll clot 'ee!'

I tell him it *is* the truth, that the only man that's ever touched me is him, my own father, and he slaps me round the face and makes my cheek burn. I try to run out the room, but he grabs my wrist and grips it so tightly I think my hand will come off. And I'm crying and begging him to leave me be and let me go to bed. Then he comes over all sorry for 'isself and starts hugging me and leaning into me till I almost fall into the fire. I know what's coming next but I've no strength left to fight him.

'You'm makin' me do this, Selina,' he murmurs. 'You'm makin' me.' He kisses me with his fat slobbering mouth and pushes me down on the rug. He starts pulling at my skirt and I try to stop his hand, then all at sudden he falls on me like he's been shot in the back and breaks out sobbing. He's lying on me so heavy I can hardly breathe and I try to lift him off me but he won't budge, just weeps like a child, and I can feel his hot tears dripping onto my neck. And I'm lying so close to the fire I think my hair might catch and set us both alight, but I can't move.

I don't know how long he lays on me like this, wailing and saying how it's all my fault for tempting him into sin, and how he knows I go with other men to mock him, but at last I manage to shift him off me. I roll out from under him and he crumples up on the rug. I leave him there and go up to my room, putting the chair under the door handle in case he wants to try finishing what he started.

FOURTEEN

The estate agent will be here soon and Cassie is still in bed. I told her yesterday that he would be here at 11 a.m., and she promised faithfully to be up and about by then. I've been listening out for signs of life from within her room, but so far nothing. It's irritating. She's nineteen, for God's sake. I shouldn't have to march in there and turf her out of bed.

I have hoovered and tidied as best I can, but I'm unable to shake off the feeling that Spindrift is looking tired and in need of 'a makeover'. But it's the location that will sell this place, not its shabby interior.

I can't wait for Cassie to rouse herself a moment longer and knock quietly on her bedroom door. There's no reply so I knock again. Wondering whether maybe she hasn't come home at all, I squeeze the handle and put my head round the door. The curtains are still drawn and the room is a tip, clothes strewn all over the floor. Two pairs of bare feet stick out from beneath the covers – *two* pairs of feet . . .

Cassie is lying on her side away from the man, who is on his front. His muscular left arm hangs over the edge of the bed and he's starting to stir. I gasp and withdraw, banging the door shut behind me. I am flushed with embarrassment, or is it more like shock? Annoyance perhaps – I can't exactly describe the feeling but it's very unpleasant. I can't believe that Cassie would have the nerve to bring a man she must hardly know back to my house, where she is after all just a guest. They must have arrived in the early hours of this morning. Did they have sex in that bed? Suddenly images from the past push themselves forward to the front of my brain – Jack, Selina . . . But I don't want to think about that, not now, not ever. I must stay in the present, cling to the simple facts. There's a man lying in bed with my granddaughter and the estate agent is about to ring the doorbell. What on earth am I going to do?

Cassie's door opens and the man emerges. It's Scott Nancarrow, bare-chested and wearing just his jeans, his blond hair tousled, a tattoo round his upper arm like a black bangle. He starts when he sees me, and rubs his eyes. 'Hi . . .' he mumbles sheepishly. 'Where's the bathroom?' I point at the door and he staggers across the landing. I am speechless.

Walking into the room, I shake Cassie gently by the shoulders. 'Wake up,' I say urgently. She shifts luxuriously in her sleep. I am embarrassed by her nakedness beneath the sheets. 'Please, wake up, Cassie. I need to talk to you.'

'Whaa?' She lifts her head and pushes back a strand of hair.

'You need to get up – immediately. The estate agent is coming to value the house – I'll need to show him the room.'

'Oh, right . . . yeah, OK . . . sorry, I forgot.'

'And I'd like Scott to leave straight away, please.'

I rush out of the room before she can reply, and go downstairs. I fuss about with the cushions, pick a feather off the rug, adjust a picture, all the time listening for signs of movement above. After a few minutes I hear them coming down the stairs, exchanging a few muffled words at the front door, then it opening and closing again. Cassie comes in and sits on the sofa. She's wearing khaki shorts and a white sleeveless top; her belly button gleams . . .

'Sorry about that,' she says eventually.

'Well, it was rather a shock.'

'I should have told you.'

'You should have *asked* me,' I correct stiffly. 'I want you to feel at home here, but . . .'

'It kind of happened out of the blue. I wasn't expecting to meet anybody, not down here anyway.'

'Yes, well, it all seems very sudden to me – you hardly know him. But then, I'm old-fashioned . . .'

'He's a really sweet guy.'

'I don't doubt it. I've known Scott since he was a baby. His grandfather and I are very old friends.'

'Yeah, Jory, he was telling me . . .' There is a long, heavy silence.

'Is your room tidy? Only, the estate agent . . .'

'I'll fix it.' She rises and pads out of the room, turning at the doorway. 'And please don't worry about Scott – I know what I'm doing. I can take care of myself.'

'But I *do* worry, Cassie. I wouldn't like your parents to think I was condoning anything.'

'I'm nineteen, Gran.'

'Sorry, Cassie, but I don't want him staying the night again.'

The estate agent is mercifully twenty minutes late, sweaty with apologies for having been stuck behind a tractor. His short clipped hair, white shirt and grey trousers make him look like a sixth former.

'I've always wondered what it was like inside this house,' he says brightly.

'It will probably be a disappointment then,' I reply, still smarting from the awkward exchange with Cassie. 'Where do you want to start?'

As we go from room to room he scribbles excitedly on his notepad. 'It's great that you've kept so many of the original features,' he enthuses, as if it had been a deliberate act on my part. When we reach the bedrooms he goes to the windows and marvels at the views. 'Of course it needs a complete refurb – new windows, kitchen, bathrooms ... But the location, well, Mrs Kingston, you can't put too high a price on it.'

'Oh, everything has its price,' I say.

When we get to Cassie's room she's sitting with her feet up on the bed, flicking through a magazine. The room, although not spotless, is a lot tidier and thankfully the underwear has gone. She looks up and smiles sweetly as 'Gareth' introduces himself while trying not to stare at her bare midriff and her long brown legs.

As soon as he's gone Cassie comes downstairs and wanders around the sitting room, looking out of the window, flicking through the agent's publicity details while I busy myself in the kitchen, washing up the cups.

'Shall we talk?' I say eventually, drying my soapy hands on a towel and sitting beside her.

'I'm sorry,' Cassie begins, 'but I don't see why you won't allow me to sleep with Scott.'

'I'm not comfortable with it, that's all.'

'His parents don't mind me staying at the farm.'

'Then what's the problem?'

'Well, if I stay there every night I won't see you much.'

'We hardly spend any time together as it is,' I reply sharply. 'You were supposed to be helping me, but you've hardly lifted a finger.' There is a long awkward pause.

'Why did you give my present away?' Cassie's tone accuses me in return. 'The mermaid book – I saw it at the farm.'

'Oh, I'm sorry – I didn't give it away as such. I, er . . .' I falter, feeling myself blush. 'It's a bit hard to explain.'

'No need.' She shrugs. 'It's your book, you can do what you like with it.'

'Please don't be offended . . . It wasn't like that. I showed the book to Jory and he just took it off me. I shouldn't have let him.'

'He said one of the pictures upset you.'

'Well, yes – it did a little. It reminded me of someone I once knew. But it's nothing. I'm sorry, dear, it sounds really stupid now.' I can feel myself reddening by the second.

'Selina Penaluna.' Cassie utters the words slowly and deliberately, as if it's an incantation. I look around nervously, half expecting her ghost to appear in the doorway, leaning idly against the frame. 'Selina Penaluna . . . it sounds so beautiful, really unusual.'

'Do you think so? Penaluna is quite a common name in Cornwall.'

Cassie shoots me an arch look. 'What was she like?'

'Oh, I don't know.' I sigh. 'Very strange . . . Difficult . . . I never really knew what to make of her.'

'Sounds as if you didn't like her much.'

'If it wasn't for Selina Penaluna my brother might still be alive.'

'Yeah, I know . . .' Cassie frowns. 'Jory told me what happened.'

'Did he? Then you'll understand why I don't really want to talk about it.' I stand up and irritably smooth the creases of my skirt. 'Now if you'll excuse me, I've got to go into Padstow. I've a few chores to see to.'

'I've got to go out too,' she counter-attacks. 'I said I'd meet Scott at the café.'

I decide not to rise to the bait, but walk out of the room to pick up my jacket. Cassie manages to make her exit first, shoving her feet into her sandals and pulling the door perhaps a little too firmly behind her.

'Satisfied now, Selina?' I whisper to the void. I can see her again, quite clearly – she's lying casually across the sofa, her long white arms draped over the back, her naked breasts barely covered by her long wavy hair. She smiles and says nothing, just winds a golden tress between her fingers, flaps her wet fish tail insolently on the cushions.

As soon as I go out she will change shape and wander through the house like a mischievous sprite, picking up ornaments from the dresser and putting them back in the wrong place, stealing biscuits from the larder, rifling through the drawers of my desk. She'll bounce on the chairs and scribble over my crossword puzzle, or sit on the window seat and write her name on the misty glass. She'll run up the stairs and go into my room, opening my wardrobe and taking out my dresses; she'll hold a blouse to herself in the mirror, grimacing at the insipid colour, the lack of shape. I can see her falling back on my bed, resting her head on my orthopaedic neck pillow. The mattress is too hard and she leaps off – she is Goldilocks in the bedroom of the Three Bears. Selina sits at my dressing table and pokes her fingers into my wrinkle cream, sprays her wrists with my eau de cologne. She removes a strand of grey hair from my brush and holds it against her young, flawless face.

It's only a short journey to Padstow, up the hill and then along the coast road, but I'm in no fit state to drive. The roads seem too narrow, the bends too sharp. As I chug along close to the hedgerows I note my hands tightly gripping the wheel, my shoulders hunched with tension. I'm so distracted by the visions in my head that I drive right past the turning to the town centre and screech to a halt in the bus lay-by, my heart pounding as strongly as if I'd narrowly avoided a collision. This is ridiculous.

I take my foot off the pedals and take a few deep breaths, lift my head to look in the mirror and try to relax the stress lines at the corner of my eyes. 'You are just a silly old woman,' I say out loud. 'Now pull yourself together.' I restart the engine and turn the car round, only this time I drive past the Padstow turning deliberately, continuing for a quarter of a mile in the direction of home and parking outside the cemetery. I am in need of some reality – the reality of death.

I wish Jack could have been buried in the beautiful grave-yard of St Petroc's Church, nestling amongst the fishermen's cottages in the heart of the town, but it was full up by the turn of the last century. There is no chapel or church here, nothing to inspire the feeling of God's presence. The cemetery has the atmosphere of an overspill car park, isolated and windswept, surrounded by fields of green pasture. It looks as if some farmer simply dug up a field and started planting crops of dead people.

The graves are arranged by date, with the most recent ones nearest to the road. The 1940s, where Jack lies, can be found on the left-hand side, while my aunt and uncle are buried together further down on the right. For years I regularly brought fresh flowers and wiped over their tombstones with a damp cloth, but eventually came to the conclusion that although their bodies might still be there in some form, their souls were not. I haven't been here for a very long time, longer than I care to remember. But I have no trouble finding Jack's grave; the headstone made of smooth grey slate, the inscription as clear to read as the day it was carved.

JACK ROSEWARNE

UNFORTUNATELY DROWNED AT SEA, MARCH 15, 1944, AGED 16

March 15 1944 – that's the date on his death certificate. It's a vague, inconclusive document, the time of death unknown, the location uncertain, the date itself no more than a presumption. It assumes that he drowned that evening, blind in the darkness of the storm, but he may have survived until the morning, clinging to a plank of wreckage, his numb fingers giving way to hopelessness, sliding into the depths as the sun rose into a mackerel sky. Nobody will ever know exactly what took place.

The local paper described it as a tragic accident – a young lad and his girlfriend drowned in a violent storm. At his funeral service several weeks later we sang '*For those in peril on the sea*' and blamed the elements. But there were other mutterings in the pews and shop doorways. What on earth did the two of them think they were doing? Taking a boat out in such weather was reckless, not to say illegal after sunset. Jack was not a local boy – they could understand his lack of respect for the sea – but Selina was a fisherman's daughter and should have known better. Now Tom Penaluna had lost his livelihood as well as his only child – it was a sad state of affairs and there was the truth of it. But then the country was at war and people were losing their loved ones every day of the week.

March 15 was a Wednesday.

How unremarkably that date used to dawn before Jack's death, how easily it slipped by unnoticed. Now March 15 is as familiar to me as my own birthday – our birthday. So much so that I have come to think of it as the date of my death also, for symmetry's sake.

> 'He hath all the storms outrode,
> Found the rest we toil to find,
> Landed in the arms of God.'

But there was no such rest for you, was there, Selina? How I longed for them to find your body, to prove beyond all doubt that you were really dead and out of my life for ever. But typically, you would not give me even that satisfaction. No, you are still very much alive in my mind. There are brief glimpses, echoes of you everywhere – a bobbing head in the middle of the crowd, the back of a girl standing in a queue. I hear the sound of your mocking laughter behind me on the bus, but when I turn round you've just gone down the stairs. You close doors behind me, rush past me in the crowded street, tiptoe into my peripheral vision then dart away. You run across the distant darkness, disappear round corners. I can never catch up with you, never pin you down. You turn up when I least expect it; when I think I've finally got you out of my head you make a sudden appearance, just to knock me off balance. Anywhere that smells faintly of damp firewood betrays your recent presence. Almost anyone with long bright hair is you.

I want us to come face to face, you and I, Selina. Let me see you as you would look if you were still alive, an old woman in your late seventies – deep creases around your eyes and mouth, your fair skin freckled with age spots, your gold hair turned white and cut short into a neat, modern style. Surely you look like me, with full hips and sagging breasts, swollen ankles, arthritic hands . . . my equal at last. But the image will not form. It flies away like sparks off a bonfire, spinning into the night, disintegrating into nothingness. No, you are for ever beautiful in my mind, ageless and immortal – maybe that's why I hated you from the first moment we met.

FIFTEEN

The 'Obby 'Oss celebrations came round again – a festival so dear to the people of Padstow that not even a German invasion would have stopped it taking place. While men waded through mud and killed strangers, we danced and sang in the streets. No longer the quiet, sober community that stood in neat rows in the church and prayed to God, we turned pagan for a day and worshipped the horse-god Epona. We decked the streets with flowers and greenery – bluebells, lily-of-the-valley, forget-me-nots, hazel branches bobbing with sticky catkins, quivering twigs of sycamore – and embraced the coming of summer. Young girls entwined the colourful ribbons of the female goddess around the maypole of the male god and made a dance of their own fertility. This was Beltane, May Day, Walpurgis – when mortals mixed unknowingly with fairy folk, when spells were woven and dark promises were made. We were exposing ourselves to dangers far more perilous than war. Our guard was lowered, our good sense distracted; today we would let the doors of our hearts swing open.

And yet the 'Obby 'Oss was also something completely

opposite. It was a community get-together, a day off school, an unofficial bank holiday, a laugh, a jaunt, a spree, and above all a celebration of being 'Padsta'. Excited children hopped from one foot to another, laughing and licking toffee apples, cheap-jacks stood on the quayside shouting their wares, normally serious men ran around dressed in white with coloured sashes and flowers pinned to their shirts. Accordions played their brash, jaunty music and drums pounded as the people endlessly sang the ancient May Day song with its mysterious words, the tune ringing in our ears for days after. They sang of wishful virgins strewing their chambers with roses, lusty young men with swords at their side and steeds waiting impatiently in the stables. The year before we had been astonished by the oddity of it all and struggled to join in, but we were fourteen now and understood what we were singing. Be lusty but practical, we urged each other – find yourself a bride and make a good bargain.

Everyone shoved and pushed to get to the front of the crowd as we waited for the 'Osses to emerge from their stables. The blue Peace 'Oss came out first, a large black disc decked in long skirts, two white feet beneath, a tall pointed mask tied to its head that looked both comic and fierce. A lolloping red tongue hung clownishly out of its mouth, yet at a second look it became a flame of monstrous breath. It pranced like a clumsy circus horse, swaying from side to side, spinning its skirts, snapping its wooden jaws and flicking its long feathery tail. We clapped and shouted as it lumbered towards us, spinning and hopping, momentarily losing its balance as it rounded the corner by the bandstand. Before it danced the Teazer – a local man dressed in a white shirt and trousers, a white beret on his head and blue ribbons round his waist. He led the 'Oss round the harbour and we followed it, the women shouting, ''Oss, 'Oss, wee 'Oss!' as if it were a battle cry.

Aunt Clara walked sedately behind, determined not to let herself get caught in the undertow of the atmosphere. She was wearing her Sunday clothes even though it was Thursday – a straight coat and navy felt hat with a trim of white squares around the crown. It made her look geometric and a little disapproving. 'I'll never make a Cornishwoman out of her,' laughed Uncle Charles. 'She's Buckinghamshire through and through.'

Suddenly the crowd ahead of us began screaming and whooping, the accordion crashed, the drummer increased his pace. We pressed forward to see what was going on. The 'Oss had grabbed someone from the front of the crowd – a girl by the sound of her – and was holding her beneath his long black skirt. She was laughing and struggling while the people clapped and urged the monster on.

'What's he doing?' I asked, jumping up to see between two tall shoulders.

'If the 'Oss manages to capture a young woman it's said she'll fall pregnant and bear a child by next May Day,' explained Uncle Charles. I started to edge backwards in case I might be next. 'It's just an old ritual,' he added, smiling at my startled face.

A few seconds later the girl emerged, a fresh smudge of soot across her flushed cheek, excited and breathless, her dark eyes shining with success. She took the Teazer by the hand and skipped down the centre of the street; her golden hair rippled with flowers and red ribbons, her white skirt swirling around her long bare legs. She laughed and danced and looked every man in the eye. She was the first day of summer.

'It's Selina Penaluna,' said Jack. 'Remember, Nellie, that day at the marsh?'

I nodded quickly – of course I remembered – hers was not a face you could easily forget. The Old 'Oss shook its mane, snapped its jaws and reclaimed centre-stage. The party turned and made its way up a side street, the singers carried on to the next verse, the accordion faded and Selina's bright head sank into the crowds.

'Well, I think I deserve a drink after all that,' said Uncle Charles, taking Aunt Clara by the arm and leading her towards the pub. I turned to talk to Jack, but he'd gone.

After that, scarcely a day went by when Jack didn't see Selina. He would meet her by the harbour, or she would be waiting for him near the house, standing barefoot on the rocks, her canvas shoes dangling from one hand by the laces. He would fling his bicycle down in the courtyard and rush out to see her, hurriedly pulling off his socks, turning up the bottoms of his trousers. They would walk out as far as the tide would let them, or climb over the rocks that surrounded the house. I

could see them from my bedroom window, their legs outstretched on the hard, warm stone as they watched the waves
perform, laughing every time they were hit by their spray.

Sometimes I'd follow them when they walked along the
cliff path to the next bay, lingering by the cornfields, stopping
every now and then to point something out, vanishing from
sight for a few minutes to follow the track as it curved
inwards. They seemed to take for ever to reappear and I'd
start to think they'd taken a path inland, just to spite me. But
then they'd suddenly walk back into vision and I'd leap to my
feet, trailing behind them again as if I were on some long,
invisible lead. They never looked back, but I was sure they
knew I was there. I got to know the shape of their backs –
Selina's bright coat of hair, the way her dress fell effortlessly
over her narrow hips, the slim calves, the womanly ease of
her walk contrasting with Jack's boyish shuffle, his right foot
kicking at stones, his head continually turned to one side to
look at her, drinking her in like she was his first glass of beer.

Watching them became an obsession. They choreographed
my every movement, tapped out the rhythm of my days. It
was ruining my summer, but I couldn't leave them alone.
I was desperately jealous of Selina, furious with her for taking
Jack away from me. But I tried to justify my behaviour, telling
myself it was my duty to stay with my brother – hadn't Mum
always insisted that I stick close to him, make sure he didn't
do anything stupid? This girl was more dangerous than any
sea current or crumbling cliff edge; he needed protecting.
Besides, I could go where I liked – it was still a free country,

wasn't it? It wasn't my fault that we always seemed to be walking in the same direction, or that I needed to stop at the very moment they decided to rest. They didn't own the beach or the Atlantic Ocean, even though they acted as if they did. But of course I was spying on them, nothing more.

I knew Jack wanted to confront me over it – I could feel his irritation simmering inside him, about to boil over. But Selina dealt with the problem in her own, cleverer way. To Jack's horror she invited me to join them, pretending that she wanted to get to know me better, that she wanted to be my friend. It was a masterful stroke. If I refused with some excuse then I couldn't follow them around, but if I went along with them I would be humiliated – forced to recognize myself as the gooseberry, the outsider, third place, last in line, bottom of the list. I should have kept my dignity and walked away; I should have called on Violet Merrion or Mary Trengrouse, or just stayed at home and knitted mufflers with Aunt Clara. But I couldn't.

So we became an awkward trio, an unfinished sum, two plus one. The path was always too narrow to go three abreast, the rock only big enough for two to lie on. And it was always Jack and Selina that made the pair – Jack and Selina, then me. My place was just in front, close behind, or out to one side, as if I were some lady-in-waiting. We never arranged ourselves by gender – Ellen and Selina, then Jack, or by blood – Jack and Ellen, then Selina. It was as if Jack and I had never lain in the womb side by side, floating in the same fluid, our fingers lightly touching, his feet brushing my head. We were two separate people who happened to share a surname, although even that was no longer true because Jack refused to be called Rosewarne.

Selina consolidated her triumph by being nice to me. If she had excluded me from the conversations – as Jack tried to – then I would have had good reason to hate her. Of course she wanted me to go away, but I had to jump, I must not be pushed. So she admired my hair, which was dull and straight, and said she wished her skin would tan like mine. She asked after my feelings – did I miss my parents? How did I feel about living in Cornwall? She talked about her own mother, who had run off with another man when she was small, and she hadn't a good word to say about her father, whom she called 'the drunken bastard'.

Whenever there was a strong onshore breeze Selina would take us wrecking – combing the cliffs and beaches for flotsam that had been washed up on the beach. She kept her father's fire burning with scavenged wood, and once she'd spotted a piece beyond the reef she had a real skill for working out where it would come ashore. With her help, we were often the first to get to a find, coaxing the stuff in with a stone tied to the end of a rope. If that failed, she would tuck her dress into her knickers and wade into the water, even in the middle of winter, and pull the wood in with her bare hands. If there was too much of it to carry back to the cottage we'd drag the planks up beyond the high-water mark and leave a rock on them, which meant they had already been claimed and could not be taken by any other wrecker. Then, later,

Tom Penaluna would come down with a cart and take it away.

I wasn't sure what to make of Tom Penaluna: that he drank too much was obvious, but he was part of the lifeboat crew so I reasoned that he couldn't be all bad. He encouraged Jack and Selina's relationship, maybe because he had his eye on the Rosewarnes' inheritance. I always felt uncomfortable in that house, perched on the cliffs above the beach at Mussel Cove. It was narrow and stuffy, gloomy even on the brightest day – the fire choking with damp unseasoned wood, the air thick with tobacco smoke, the table littered with crumbs and empty beer bottles. Jack would sit in a tatty armchair by the fireplace and Selina would nestle at his feet, tucking herself between his knees, leaning her head back so that he could work his fingers through her hair. Jack drank beer and learned how to roll cigarettes. Tom talked about Spindrift as if he'd been inside many times, although I couldn't see how. He said that smugglers had used it 'in the olden days' for hiding booty – that there were clever hiding places in the house which he knew of, but which we'd never manage to find. Tom Penaluna said a lot of stupid things when he was full of drink. I think Selina was scared of him but he made Jack cry with laughter. I could never understand what was so funny. I'd sit prim and proper at the table, desperate to find a cloth and wipe it clean, feeling totally out of place and yet unable to leave them to it. To this day, I don't know why I didn't just go back home.

Once Selina took us to an isolated bay just this side of the lighthouse. The weather was warm with barely a breeze and it was a long trudge along the cliff path. Selina dictated the pace as usual. She grabbed Jack's arm and propelled him forward, skipping over stones, swerving round the swing gates, running up and down the slopes. If he'd been walking behind her, I thought, he would have wondered at this delicate creature, so quick and light on her feet, so cool in the hot sunshine. She made me feel flat-footed and leaden. The buckles on my new leather sandals rattled as I tried to keep up with them, my armpits damp with sweat.

'Can't we slow down a bit?' I puffed.

'Got to get there 'fore the tide comes in,' Selina answered as she climbed down a bank of sand dunes and led us across the beach. 'We'll cut across, it'll be quicker.'

'What's so special about this place, anyway?'

'There's somethin' I want to show 'ee,' she answered mysteriously. 'Come on, stop sludgin' tha' feet!'

It was about three o'clock in the afternoon when she finally stopped without warning in the middle of the path. We didn't seem to have arrived anywhere in particular. To our left were cornfields, to our right the edge fell to a sheer drop, thin layers of jagged slate piled on top of each other like an uneven stack of trays. Below us the pale sand glistened like a newly painted canvas, an unmarked expanse of creamy yellow – begging to be walked upon.

'That's where we'm goin',' she announced.

'And how are we supposed to get down there?' I said sceptically.

'There's a path, I'll show 'ee.' She led us a few paces on

until we came to a steep, narrow ladder of crumbling earth with tufts of dry grass and the odd stone for rungs. 'Don't look down and 'old on tight.'

We shuffled down on our bottoms – for once in single file, one plus one plus one, Selina first, then Jack, then me. The back of the beach was all rock and pebbles, fallen slate, gritty, speckled sand. Jack and I crunched our way over the cockleshells, idly picking up bits of driftwood and snagged fishing net, wondering at an old bottle, dirtying our hands on a piece of oily rag. Now we were down here, it seemed like any other cove. Selina had already climbed halfway round a large rock to the left of the beach; she shouted at us urgently to follow.

She was standing next to a small pool surrounded by tall, looming rocks that hid it from outside view and kept the water in eternal shadow. I felt as if I were staring into a well of green-black ink and dabbled my fingers in, half expecting the liquid to stain my skin. The surface rippled briefly and then was still. The water was stinging cold, heavy with salt.

'My ma loved comin' down 'ere. She brought her baby 'ere when it were first born,' Selina said. I looked back up at the steep incline – it seemed unlikely. 'She was sittin' right 'ere, dangling her legs in the pool, when she slipped and the chield wriggled off 'er lap and slid into the water. Her just disappeared, sinkin' down and down into the blackness.'

'Your mother lost her baby in that pool?' I said, horrified.

'Just listen, will 'ee?' She shot me a contemptuous look. 'She couldn't swim or nothin'. She managed to get out and started cryin' and screamin' for help, but no one were about. Minutes passed, many minutes. She was desperate. Then all of a sudden I bob up to the surface, eyes wide open, laughin', paddlin' my little feet, wavin' my arms, and I'm swimmin'. She can't believe her eyes! But she reaches out and grabs me, brings me back on dry land.'

'What? You mean you were the baby?' said Jack, confused.

'You can't have been minutes under the water,' I added. 'You'd never survive. It just *felt* like you were under the water for ages because your mother was in a panic. I expect it was actually no more than a few seconds.'

'Maybe, yes, maybe. I'd never thought of it that way,' Selina replied softly. 'But my mother always said that the baby who came up was a different child.'

'How can that be?' Jack frowned. 'It's not possible.'

'That's what Morva – the woman I called my mother – told me.'

'Perhaps people look peculiar when they're half drowned,' said Jack helpfully. 'Especially babies.'

'But 'er said that – that . . .' She faltered. Her face washed paler than ever, her skin bluish, almost transparent.

'Are you all right, Selina?' said Jack. 'You've gone a bit strange.'

'What on earth are you trying to say?' I gave her one of my withering glances.

'If I tell 'ee something will you promise to keep it secret?'

'Of course!' Jack squeezed her hand and I smiled limply.

' 'Ee won't laugh?'

'No, you can trust us.'

She took a deep breath. 'When I came up out of this pool my ma took me in her arms and hugged me close, but when she laid me down on the rock she saw I wasn't 'er own baby, but a different chield altogether.'

'Yes, that's the third time you've explained it and it still doesn't make any sense.' I sighed irritably.

'Go on, Selina . . .'

'She reckoned the Mer people stole 'er baby and sent a merrymaid in 'er place.'

'I think you mean a *mer*maid, don't you?' I let out a scoffing laugh. 'Is this some kind of joke?'

'No . . .'

Jack looked shocked but he didn't say a word: his eyes were fixed on Selina, leaning over the edge, gazing down into the still black water as if the truth lay at the bottom, hidden under a large, heavy rock.

'Do you think it could be true?' she whispered. 'That I'm a merrymaid?'

'Don't be ridiculous,' I retorted. 'There's no such thing.'

'Cornish folk still believe in 'em . . .'

'I'm sure my uncle doesn't.'

'I don't think there's any such thing as mermaids,' said Jack gently. 'Your mum felt guilty for nearly drowning you, that's all.'

'Yes, I suppose that's it.' Selina stopped looking into the pool and gazed wistfully out to sea. 'I just wonder sometimes, that's all . . .'

SIXTEEN

I've been courting Jack for a whole year now and my father do mostly leave me alone – unless he's pissed as a newt and forgets himself. I've learned to stay out on a Saturday night and not come home till he's back from The Ship and has fallen asleep in front of the stove. But these days, even if I wake him when I creep in he doesn't always follow me up the stairs, and if I fight him off he knows not to hit me where Jack might see the bruises.

I reckon my dad's a bit afeard of Jack, for the Rosewarnes is bettermost folk and Mr Rosewarne's the town's law man, which must be only one down from being a judge. If he found out what were going on he could put my father in jail. But I've not said anything to Jack, for it's shameful to tell a lad your own father's already had his hands up your skirt. The poor boy thinks I'm just an ignorant maid who knows nothing about what men do and he treats me respectful.

Me and Jack see each other almost every day – when I come back from fishing we go wrecking, looking for firewood mostly, though one time we found three boxes of butter – none of it spoiled – and a case of firelighters, but they were wet and no use. We climb up the cliffs and steal gulls' eggs from the ledges or we just lie in the dunes and gaze up at the sky. Jack tells me funny stories about London – the house where he used to live and playing round the docks – but he gets upset when he talks about his mum and dad, who got killed by the Germans. He says I am the only good thing that's happened to him since the war broke out.

I can talk to Jack about almost anything. I tell him about the mermaid dreams and the sleepwalking, and how I am afeard of what I might do.

'I'm worried about you,' he says. 'You should see the doctor.'

'Oh yes, and with what money?' I answer. 'Anyhow, I don't see how no doctor could 'elp. I bet you all he'd do is 'ave me carted off and then 'ee'd never see me again.'

'No he wouldn't. And even if he tried, I wouldn't let them take you. You belong to me, Selina. I'll never let you go.'

And we do kiss then and he holds me close like he thinks the wind's going to grab hold of me and blow me out to sea. He tucks me right under his arm like I'm a nestling bird and strokes my hair, and I never felt so safe in my whole life. 'I need you, we need each other,' he whispers. 'I got nobody else but you.'

'What 'bout Ellen?' I say, but he just frowns and says she's gone over to the Enemy – that's what he calls the Rosewarnes; anyone would think they were as bad as the Nazis the way he goes on. Why he hates them so much I can't understand for they are some rich and treat him like their own son, paying for his schooling and not making him work for his living. I would like to live in that fine house and have a motor car to drive me about, but Jack says they can stick the lot of it.

He won't call his sister Ellen neither – only Nellie. She gets so mazzed with him over it we can't help but laugh. First I thought Ellen was going to be my friend, and I was so happy for I've never had a maid to share my secrets with, but now I'm not so sure of her. I wish I hadn't taken her to the pool and told her the one thing I'd sworn to myself I would never tell another soul. I don't know why I did that, it was some stupid . . . The way Ellen talks and uses long words, she do think well of herself, all puffed up like a bladder of lard. I have to say she looks some smart in her school uniform with her hat and shiny shoes and her leather satchel swinging over her shoulder. And there's me, going out on the boat in a rubber apron and woolly hat, my hands red raw and covered in scratches . . .

Jack always has his bicycle with him and he sits me on the handlebars and we go shooting down the hill into Cove fast as lightning, screaming our heads off. Once we only just missed crashing into the boathouse – that was a near thing, I can tell you; for a second I thought my life was going to end there and then. He's teaching me now how to ride for myself, so we can have a borrow of Ellen's cycle – she hardly uses it these days – then we'll go for a trip, see how far we can get in a day. I'd like to go to one of they big towns like Newquay or Truro and see the sights, walk along the prom arm-in-arm with Jack, and take tea in a café like we're a proper courting couple, taking a holiday. Not that anyone's taking a holiday now the war's on.

This stupid war's taking over everything, you can't escape from it. Padsta's full of soldiers and airmen, billeted in the hotels and guesthouses, drinking in the pubs, hanging around the harbour after hours – getting thrown in too sometimes. Come Sunday there's nearly always a parade in the streets: a band plays hymns and prayers are said on the quayside. Women go round collecting money in a bucket for the Red Cross and such like, but I don't join in with any of that stuff. At night you can hear the planes taking off from the nearby airfields; there are lookout posts on the cliff tops and even some of the fishing boats have machine guns on them now. I don't know of anyone who's had cause to use them yet. We've only had one bomb fall on Padsta and they say that was a mistake. I expect it's a lot worse in the rest of the county and I cannot imagine how frightening London must be.

Some days, after I've dropped off the catch I go to railway station and watch the comings and goings. I like the airmen the most – they have nicer uniforms than the soldiers. The trains are packed tight as fish crates with them, hanging out the windows, smoking and looking all about them with wide eyes like they've no idea where they've come to. They jump out onto the platform, shouting and swinging their kit bags. Sometimes the men do call out to me and whistle, so I smile and give them back a wave – we're not supposed to but I don't see how it hurts to show a bit of friendliness. I like to hear the men make nice remarks about my hair and my shape. They tell me I'm pretty enough to be a film star and some of them ask what I'm doing Saturday night and if I've got any sisters for their mates. They do make me laugh. If I didn't already have Jack for my sweetheart I'd let them take me out, I would, just for a walk round town or maybe to the Cinedrome. I'd take the tallest, strongest, 'ansumest airman I could find and bring him home to meet my father. That'd give him something to chew on his pipe about.

Ellen reads the newspapers and knows all about what's going on in France and Africa, but it don't mean much to me – not that I don't care about Padsta folk getting killed for I do, but I cannot find tears for strangers dying in places I never even heard of. She tells me I'm being unpatriotic because I won't knit and I know she blames me for Jack minching school. There's been a couple of letters sent home and Mr Rosewarne's threatened Jack he must finish his education or there'll be 'dire consequences' but he never says what those consequences might be. Jack's not bothered; he wants to leave anyway and go lowster at the farm. He might as well too – it's honest labour and the Nancarrows are desperate for help now they lost two more stand-ta-works to the war.

I used to think I'd hate land work but I don't mind it at the farm – Jack takes me up there some days to see Jory and we help out in the fields a bit. Ellen even joins us sometimes at the weekends when she's not got her head stuck inside a book. We watch the lads skidding dung or tealing or shifting hay and Jory lets us maids meat the pigs or take water to the horses. I like Jory: he's comfortable and we do have a giggle, the four of us.

After he's done working we walk along the top and throw stones into the coves or dare each other to stand at the cliff edge. We lean forward till we feel dizzy and gake down at the beach below, and sometimes I imagine how free it would feel just to jump right off and hang in the sky with nothing below or above me. I'd be a white gull, stretching out my wings – I'd skate on the breeze, I'd spin and turn and flutter like a snowflake, I'd glide on the air currents and let them carry me far out to sea. And Jack always seems to know what's in my mind for he pulls me back sharply and says, 'Come on, let's walk,' and he grips my hand like he's afeard I might jump off for real.

I reckon Ellen has feelings for Jory, but she's such a dark horse she won't open up her heart to anyone. If I dared ask her straight out she'd deny it, but she do stare like a stoat at him while he's working the soil, in particular when it's hot and he takes his shirt off. She sits close by him to eat her crib and is forever picking bits of straw out of his hair or telling him there's a crumb of pasty on his chin, laughing at all his jokes and pretending to understand them – all sure signs of fondness. Yet she's holding herself back – probably thinks she could do better for herself than marry a farmer's son. I wish I could be like Ellen. She's got her head screwed on tight as a pickle jar and won't be a fool for any man; she'll not end up with a child in her belly and no husband to tend her. But I'm not strong-minded and clever like her, I'm too soft and willing. I've no mother to put me on the right path and make me stick to it.

I don't know if Jory has worked out Ellen's got a fancy for him for he spends his whole time glazing at me. Sometimes it feels like I'm courting two lads, Jory do make such a fuss of me, always remarking on how well I look in my clothes, or noticing if I've just washed my hair. He's forever finding ways to brush up against my body, and when he helps me off the cart he holds my waist just that bit longer than he needs to. I know he would like me to be his girl and thinks himself a better match for me, for Jack is a foreigner and always talking of going back home to London. And though I love Jack I don't think I could go up-country with him, for I cannot be so far from the sea. He tells me the river in London is big and wide enough for great ships to pass through, so how can there not be water enough for me there? And I tell him a merrymaid could never be happy swimming in such foul, baissly stuff, surrounded by factories and warehouses instead of rocks and sand.

Jack always makes light of it when I start talking of merrymaids. He says I'm pretty enough to be one with my long gold hair but he don't fancy the idea of me having a scaly tail and says he never could marry a woman that reeked of mackerel. Jack says the day he leaves for London he will tie me up in a sack and put me in the mail coach and have me delivered to his door. Or if I've turned merrymaid by then he'll pack me in ice and send me on the overnight train to

Billingsgate fish market, and when they open up the crates and find me I'll be the talk of the town. We do laugh then, and he chases me about the beach.

Jory's different, see – he's a Cornishman and knows that there are so many tales of merrymaids living in these waters, there must be a drop of truth in them. Sometimes when Jack has to show his face at school to keep the peace, I go up farm by myself – I take Jory a bit of crib and talk to him while he works. Before I know it, I'm telling him the story of how I came into this world. His blue eyes do sparkle and he lets out a long, low whistle.

'That don't surprise me one bit,' he says, setting down his pitchfork. 'I've always thought you'm too beautiful to belong to this ugly old world.'

'Jory Nancarrow, you'm a poet or somethin'?' I do tease him something rotten for coming over so romantic and his face colours up like a beetroot.

After that he starts asking me all kinds of questions about merrymaids – like, do I know for certain that's what I am, and when will my tail grow, and will I keep it for ever or shift my shape as it pleases me? – all the same questions I used to want to ask when I was a girl. I tell him I still don't have the answers to them, but I promise that if I ever do become a merrymaid he can visit me on my island and it will be a secret betwixt the two of us.

'Won't Jack be jealous?' laughs Jory. 'Surely 'ee'll be wantin' to visit too?'

'Maybe he won't get the chance! I'm not sure Jack believes

me yet . . . says he's goin' to wait for it to 'appen for real.'

'Well, they do say seein' is believin' . . .' and Jory gives me one of they funny looks I don't quite understand the meaning of.

The next day I find myself going to farm again, and we're alone, just the two of us. There's a strange feeling hanging in the air like a mist; we both have an idea what's going on but don't want to put it into words. After an hour or so, mucking out the stable and scrubbing down the yard, we go to the barn to fetch hay for the horses. Jory sits me down on a pook and do take off my shoes. He holds my bare feet gently in his hands and tickles my soles, turning them this way and that, like he's a doctor, examining me all over. So I ask him what he's doing.

'Lookin' for a sign of 'em turnin' into flippers,' he says, and the look on his face is so serious I know he's not making fun of me. Then he slowly lifts my skirt over my knees and strokes my legs up and down; his hands are rough like my father's but his touch is more loving.

'Tha' skin's too soft and smooth for scales,' he tells me. 'And tha' blood runs too warm for a fish. I can't see 'ee lastin' in the water for long.' He reaches up and catches his fingers in the tangles of my hair, leans right forward and sniffs me, nibbles my ear and whispers that I smell of honey and roses. Merrymaid or no, he says, I'm the prettiest thing he ever clept eyes on.

He kneels down and kisses me on the lips, and I can't help but open my mouth and let him feel the insides with his tongue. He nuzzles his face into my neck, and sighs and murmurs my name, puts his large farmer's hand round my left breast and squeezes it gently. I want to stop him, but I don't know how. He pushes me back into the hay then and climbs on top of me. He parts my blouse and pulls up my vest, pausing to take his fill of my bare flesh, then puts his mouth over my nipple and sucks it till it stands up, hard. I do want him to stop for it's Jack I love, not Jory, but there's no power in me to shake him off. The barn's warm and the hay smells some sweet, and motes of dust hang like faeries in the shafts of sunlight over my head. And I feel like I'm drunk on beer or cider, my limbs soft and heavy, my body asleep and my mind dreaming.

But then he reaches down and starts fumbling with the buttons of his fly. 'I'll go careful,' he says. 'Done it before, 'aven't 'ee?'

'No, no! Stop,' I shout, coming to my senses at last. I try to sit up and cover myself, but he's looming over me, his hand on the large bulge under his trousers.

'What's wrong? We both want it, 'ee as much as me . . .'

'No, no, I don't . . . It's not right. I'm Jack's girl, and you'm 'is best pal. Think 'ow hurt he'd be if he ever found out.'

He pulls away then and stands up, his brackety face all red and sweaty, shifts from one foot to the other, looking awkward. 'Why d'ee let me go so far?'

'I don't know. One minute we're talkin' and then you'm right on top of me.'

'It's your fault,' he says, anger now in his voice. 'It's 'ee

what keeps comin' to see me, not t'other way round . . .
Followin' me about the farm, sitting there flashin' yer bare
legs, getting' me all worked up with talk of merrymaids –
what d'ee expect?'

'I'm sorry, I didn't mean—'

Jory walks off and flings open the barn door, letting the
daylight flood in. 'Don't come round on yer own again.'

'No, no, I won't . . . Promise not to say a word to Jack—'

'Go 'ome, Selina!' He stands at the door and watches me
run down the field, my shoes in my hand, my blouse half
undone and my hair flying.

Jory's right, it's my fault these things do happen. Maybe
it's because I'm a merrymaid that I'm so weak and wicked, for
now I feel black and bad in my heart, ashamed of what I just
let him do. But when a man looks at me that way and says
such soft things, I just can't stop myself.

SEVENTEEN

Violet Merrion, whose parents ran the Seaview Hotel, hit upon the idea to form a Junior Salvage Club. Jack and I were dragooned by Aunt Clara to join up, although we were fifteen years old now and hardly 'juniors'. I in turn persuaded Jory to take part. We were to work in pairs, patrolling the streets with wheelbarrows or wooden trucks to collect scrap paper from the houses. Then all of it was to be taken back to Violet's father's garage, where it could be sorted – newspapers, periodicals, cartons, cardboard, white paper, etc. – before the council collected it fortnightly in a truck.

The children of the village, some as young as five or six, embarked on this enterprise with great gusto and people were soon complaining that they were being pestered – some doors were being knocked several times a day. So a meeting was held and it was decided that each pair would have their own beat, so as to avoid duplication. Also, every householder would be given a piece of card with 'S' for Salvage written on it which they were to hang on their gate whenever they had some paper in need of collection. The latter was Jack's idea and Violet thought it marvellous. She clapped her hands with delight and reached for her wax crayons, but to my astonishment Jack insisted that he would make all the cards – saying it would be a pleasure to do it for the cause.

And so the village became decked with beautifully drawn and decorated signs, which in Jack's mind did not say 'S' for Salvage at all, but for Selina. He was like Shakespeare's Orlando carving Rosalind's initials on every tree in the forest – besotted, passionate, a little foolish. He took Selina on a tour of the streets to show her all the signs he had made for her sake. She laughed and told him he was an idiot, and then stole her favourite, which she put on the mantelpiece at home. Her flippant attitude towards the war effort made me seethe.

I was supposed to be working in a pair with Jack, but once he'd made his joke he lost interest and went off with Selina, so most evenings I found myself pushing the wheelbarrow on my own. What had started out as fun soon became a tedious duty, but I didn't want to be accused of not pulling my weight. So instead of wandering the streets, I searched Spindrift for all the scrap paper I could find. I virtually snatched *The Times* out of Uncle Charles's hands as soon as he finished reading it; I rummaged in cupboards for magazines and knitting patterns and begged my aunt for any old letters or postcards. Even drawer liners were sacrificed so that I could keep my end up with Violet.

One afternoon after school, when everyone else was out, I had the brilliant idea of raiding the sheet music in the old piano stool in the spare bedroom and came across an old farming catalogue, right at the bottom. I was absolutely certain that it had been put there by mistake and long since forgotten. So I triumphantly took it straight to the garage and put it in the periodical pile, making sure that Violet saw me. Jack was meant to be helping with the sorting but was just riding idly up and down the back lane on his bike. Jory was in the garage, breaking down some cartons with his hobnailed boots.

'What's that?' he asked.

'Just some farming thing,' I said. 'Highworth's Fertilizers.'

'Highworth's Fertilizers?' Jory frowned. 'Never heard of 'em. Let's 'ave a look.' He sat down on a pile of newspapers and started flicking through the book. The first pages were just what you'd expect from a farming catalogue – spades, hoes, attachments for a tractor, all kinds of things I'd never heard of – and long lists of prices. But when he got towards the back of the book, Jory's eyes started to widen.

'Eh, Jack! Come take a look at this!' he called. Jack swung round and rode up to the garage. He flung his bike against a wheelbarrow and took the book off Jory.

'Bloody hell!' said Jack, his eyes skimming the pages. 'Where did this come from?'

'From the house,' I answered.

'What? *Our* house?' Jack looked at me, incredulous. 'You sure?'

'Yes. It was at the bottom of a piano stool. Why, what's wrong?'

'I knew it!' said Jack. 'I bloody knew it.'

'What are you talking about?' I demanded, trying to snatch

the book back, but Jack swerved it out of my grasp. 'What is it? Tell me!'

'There's stuff in 'ere about makin' bombs,' Jory said, his voice sunk to a hoarse whisper.

'Bombs? Don't be silly, there can't be,' said Violet haughtily.

'Look for 'eeself if 'ee don't believe us.' Jory spread the book on the ground before us. We gazed at diagrams showing wires and fuses, lists of ingredients and equipment which, the book assured the reader, could 'easily be obtained without arousing suspicion'.

'We must report it,' said Violet. 'Report it to the police.'

'But – but – I can't,' I stammered. 'It's my uncle's . . . at least, I think it is.'

'Why would he want to know about makin' bombs?' asked Jory.

'I don't know, but there must be a good reason . . .' I replied, rather lamely.

'I've always thought there was something funny about him,' said Jack, looking at the catalogue more closely. 'Like when he went away for all those months, he said he was working in London, but I bet he wasn't. Now he keeps disappearing off for days on end, or goes out at night and doesn't come back till dawn. And he speaks German, you know,' he added with a flourish.

'He's a Nazi spy!' cried Violet, holding her hand against her mouth in a dramatic gesture that made me want to slap her round the face.

'No he's not! You can't say that!' I shouted furiously. 'Just because he can speak German doesn't mean he's a spy. That's stupid!'

Jack shoved the book towards me. 'OK, so why would anyone want to make bombs if they weren't working for the Nazis?'

'I-I don't know . . .' My bottom lip started to tremble, tears were pricking behind my eyes and I felt dizzy. How could Charles possibly be a traitor? I couldn't believe it – I refused to believe it. 'I'm sure there's a simple explanation,' I said stiffly.

'Trust you to stick up for him.' Jack gave me a vicious look. 'He's got you in his power.'

'Anyway, there's no point in asking Mr Rosewarne – if he's a spy he'll just lie.' Violet flicked her hair knowledgeably behind her shoulder.

'That's true,' said Jack. 'Spies always have some story ready. And they're always the people you least expect. That's why you have to watch out for them.' Jory looked down uncomfortably at his boots, but Violet nodded in sage agreement.

'He's not a spy!' I insisted.

'The police will decide that,' pronounced Violet. 'This book is evidence. It's our duty to show them.'

'No, you can't!' I screamed. 'It's mine, I want it back.'

'Too late! It belongs to my salvage club,' she said imperiously.

'It's not your salvage club . . .' Jory grumbled.

'Well, it's my garage, so there. Come along, Jack. We'll show it to my father – he'll know what to do.'

Jack stood up, solemnly clutching the book to his chest. He shot me a defiant look as if to say, *I told you so*, and marched into the back of the hotel with Violet.

I burst into uncontrollable tears. 'What have I done, Jory?' I wailed. 'Now they'll arrest him and it's all my fault.'

'I'm sorry,' he said, taking me in his arms and holding me tightly. My wet face was pressed hard against his shirt: his body smelled of earth and hay. He gently stroked the back of my head with his large hands. 'There, there,' he said softly, as if soothing an animal.

'Uncle Charles loves England – and France!' I sniffed loudly. 'He would never do anything to betray us.'

'I know, I believe 'ee. It'll just be some misunderstanding.' He lifted my face and wiped away the tears with his crumpled hankie. We stared into each other's eyes and for a moment I thought he was going to kiss me. If he had I probably would have kissed him back.

I ran back home and up to my room, where I cried noisily into my pillow until I had no more tears left in me. Aunt Clara was at a committee meeting and Uncle Charles was away 'on business', although now the thought of what that business might be made me feel sick. Could the others be right? I racked my brains trying to think of plausible reasons why Charles might have a bomb-making book in his possession and why it had been disguised as a farming catalogue. They only led to one conclusion – he was planning acts of sabotage

– and only the Nazis could possibly be behind that. And what about Clara? Was she innocent or were they both spies, in the plot together?

Yet it seemed impossible, the stuff of melodrama. None of it squared with the people I had come to love, to think of as my own parents. The Rosewarnes had treated us with extraordinary kindness and generosity, fed and clothed us, paid for us to go to expensive schools. Legally we were now their children, part of the family. But then again, if Charles *was* guilty, where did that leave us?

As darkness fell I crept downstairs and drew all the blackout curtains. I couldn't eat the meal that had been left out for me, didn't even attempt to start my homework. I sat by the fire, listening nervously for the sound of cars drawing up outside, a knock on the door, shouts through the letterbox, police officers storming the house. But nobody came. My aunt arrived home at about ten o'clock, full of complaints about the other committee members, and didn't notice my distress. Jack crept in about an hour later, looking flushed and excited, smelling of tobacco, his eyes as bright as if the stars still shone in them. I guessed he'd been with Selina, boasting of his triumph. I glared at him, trying to read his thoughts, but he just grinned back mischievously, giving nothing away.

Jack went straight up to his room – I wanted to go and confront him but didn't dare. That night I hardly slept, shifting restlessly in my bed, wrestling with the sheets. I was angry with myself for taking the book – if only I had looked in it properly first. At least I could have spoken to Charles about it, given him a chance to explain himself. I was furious with Jack too, for immediately siding with Violet and going off to the police. Where was his loyalty? If he didn't feel he owed anything to the Rosewarnes, at least he owed it to me. But now wheels had been set in motion and there was nothing I could do to stop them. I just had to wait.

But the days and weeks passed and nothing happened. When I asked Jack what he'd done with the book he told me he'd passed it over to Violet's father, who'd said he would take it straight to the police. But if that was so, why hadn't Charles been arrested? It didn't make any sense. Jack was clearly disappointed, but expounded various theories for the lack of action. He reckoned my uncle was being watched in the hope he would eventually lead the police to some bigger prize – perhaps even the British controller of Nazi spies. Although I told Jack this was nonsense, I started looking out for strangers in dark coats lurking round corners, expecting to see binoculars sticking out of the hedge, trained on our front door. Whenever I went out with Uncle Charles I was constantly turning round to check if somebody was following us, my feelings an uncomfortable mixture of guilt and disloyalty.

Jack enjoyed playing detective, eavesdropping on phone calls and Charles's conversations with Clara, running downstairs as soon as the post arrived and holding the envelopes up to the light. Once he even tried to break into the locked drawers in Charles's desk. I was worried that my uncle would catch him, but Jack said he didn't care if he did – it was his duty to report anything suspicious. I maintained that the reason the police hadn't done anything was because they knew Charles was innocent. But Jack laughed and said I was a fool if I really believed that.

The truth was I didn't know what I believed. But the weeks became months and the police failed to appear. The house wasn't being watched, nobody was following us, it had clearly all been a big misunderstanding. I tidied the matter away neatly in the back of my mind, feeling hugely relieved and rather superior towards Jack, having been proved right. Of course, I had no idea what was really going on . . .

EIGHTEEN

We're coming to the end of the fishing now, just making our last few trips to fetch the pots home. Winter's on its way, there's a hag hanging over the sea in the mornings and it's growing colder by the day. Soon we'll be taking the *Louisa May* out the water, and start scraping the barnacles off her hull. Dad will strip the engine and take out the rotten planking and I'll help give her a new lick of paint. I don't know how it's come about but I've grown fond of that little boat and want to tend her, keep her safe. I may be a skinny-ribs but I'm some powerful in the arms and can take the wheel, I know how to handle her and weave her through the narrow channels at low tide. I can take her over the bar, turn her and even bring back her into harbour.

I used to hate the life, but truth is now I want to be out at sea and don't look forward to the winter rest as I used to. I've a raw hunger for the salt, the swell heaving under me, the slap of the water against the sides of the boat. If a day passes and I don't go in the sea, wade out to the punt, or at least feel the spindrift spraying onto my face, I feel wrong, in some kilter. I need the water – without it I'm floundering about on the shore, gasping for breath, my skin drying up, the taste of me sharp as a kipper. No, I'm a proper fisherman's daughter now, can't see me doing anything else – but there's one thing still troubles me. I still do hate killing fish, specially crabs and lobsters. If I had the choice I'd not eat them, but I can't just live off cabbage and tatties – I'd starve.

One morning we're up and about early, just back from Gull Island where we've been bringing up the last of our pots to store in the boathouse at Cove. The poor old *Louisa May*'s overloaded with the dripping, stinking cages – too many for one journey – and I'm wedged between them in the stern. It's high tide so we can tie up at the jetty to unload. Dad jumps off quick and starts lifting the pots off; he's shouting at me to hurry for the weather's coming up dirty and he wants to take the boat into safe harbour before the storm breaks. But I'm feeling sluggish: the curse has just come on and I'm as taisy as a snake.

'Come on, pass 'em along,' he shouts.

'They'm too heavy. And I need the lavvy!' I grasp my belly, hoping he'll catch my meaning.

''Ee'll 'ave to wait!' he says.

'Well I can't.' I try to climb out the boat but he pushes me roughly and I topple back over a basket full of crabs.

'Want me to break my neck, do 'ee?' I snap. 'I'll not be much use to 'ee then.'

'Enough of tha' cheek. Do as I tell 'ee or I'll give 'ee a good collupin'!'

'But I 'ave to go,' I plead. 'I'm bad . . . women's trouble!'

He looks awkward then and helps me off. 'Be quick about it!' he shouts after me. 'Come right back!'

So I do nip into the house to fetch a bit of cloth and then run up to the lavvies. I'm steeved with cold and aching in my belly. I feel like death warmed up and daggin' to get in front of the fire. Anyway, I finish and come out, and I'm emptying out the bucket when I see four soldiers hurtling down the field towards the pig houses, carrying something in sacks. Soon as they see me gaking up at them they stop in their tracks. Their faces are blacked up so I don't recognize them at first, but then I see one of them is Mr Harrow, which is no surprise as it's his fields, but the other is Mr Rosewarne. I know it's him though he's never met me and I reckon he knows who I am too for he looks me up and down for a moment and nearly says something.

'Morning!' I call out, as if everything's as normal as washday.

'Morning,' mutters Mr Harrow out the side of his mouth. He nudges at the others to come, and the four of them march off towards the farmhouse without another word; only Mr Rosewarne looks over his shoulder once before they go round the bend.

When I see Jack later I ask him questions about his uncle and why he should be running about the fields like a wild rabbit with his face all dabbered.

'Like I told you, Selina, he's a spy,' is his reply. 'I reckon the others are in on it too. They pretend they're training for the Home Guard but actually they're making bombs and stuff, preparing the way for the Nazis.'

'Don't think so,' I laugh. 'They were just playin' at soldiers
. . . Anyway, if they know they'm traitors, why don't they just
arrest 'em?'

Jack bites his lip. 'I don't know – biding their time, I
suppose, waiting to catch the bigger fish.'

After that I keep asking Jack to take me home to meet his
uncle, and his aunt too, for I've only ever seen her in the
queue for the butcher's in Padsta. I'd like to find out for
myself if they're really as snotty as he says, and I'm dagging
to look inside that fine house they've got. I can see how many
rooms there must be just from counting the windows. But he
won't let me go anywhere near them.

' 'Ee don't 'ave to worry,' I tell him. 'I may be 'andy with a
penknife but I do know 'ow to use cutlery proper.' We're in the
boathouse, tidying up, scrubbing the weed and bits of rotted
bait off the pots and stacking them in the corner so as to
make room for the fathoms of ropes. 'Tell 'em we're courtin'
and I bet you a pound they ask me over this Sunday.'

'You haven't got a pound,' Jack mutters.

'Come on, they do think the sun shines out of yer arse,
they'd not turn me away.'

'I'm not taking you home and that's that.'

But I've got the bit betwixt my teeth now and I'm not
giving up. 'They've got manners, I'm sure they'd give me a
leak o' tea,' I say. 'Who can say, I might get a slab of cake too
if they like me.'

'They don't like you,' he barks. 'That's the point.'

'Giss on! How can they not like me? They don't know me.'

'They know you're the reason I've been skiving off school, that's enough.'

'You never told 'em that, did 'ee?'

'No, it was Nellie of course – went and opened her big mouth, didn't she?' Jack sits down heavily on a withy pot and takes off his cap. 'If you must know, Uncle took me to one side and said I wasn't to see you any more . . . We had a bad row over it, nearly came to blows . . .'

That do bring me up short, the thought of Jack fighting with his uncle. 'What – just 'cos I keep 'ee from goin' school?'

'No, not exactly.' Jack sighs irritably. 'He says you're not "suitable" for me.'

'What do he mean by that?'

'Look, it doesn't matter. Whatever he says he's not going to stop us.'

'But I want to know why I'm not suitable!'

'Come on, Selina, you already know the answer to that . . .' He gets up and starts pacing the shed. 'You've got a reputation. People say things about you . . . bad things, about you and men.'

'Sounds like you believe 'em,' I answer.

'I don't, you know I don't . . .' He tries to put his arm round me then and I do shake it off. And that's how our first falling-out starts.

'It's not my fault men go after me. Just because I'm pretty they think I'm there for the takin'.'

'But sometimes, the way you act, you come across too

friendly – it gives people the wrong idea. Makes a fool out of me too.'

'Is that's all 'ee care about, lookin' a fool?' I shout. ' 'Ee don't know the 'alf of what I've 'ad to put up with over the years . . . Still, there's plenty of others who'll take me off tha' 'ands if that's what you want. Jory's one fer a start.' Well, that gets Jack's tail up and he grabs hold of me by the arm.

'What do you mean? What's been going on with Jory then?'

'None of tha' business, go to hell!'

We set to, screaming at each other and hurling insults. I tell him all men are the same and not to be trusted, to get out and never come back, and he shouts that suits him very well for he's off to London soon and he'll be happy if he never clep eyes on me again. I'm so mazzed I throw a bucket of stinking bait at his head: it hits him full on his chin and filthy water splashes all over his trousers. Then I run at him and pound my fists against his chest. I want to hurt him so bad for saying he's leaving me, I want to make him sorrier than he's ever been. So I tell him how there's others who've gone further with me than he has – not that he should care less for he don't love me. Nobody loves me, not one soul in the world . . .

He starts squalling then and thrashing about the room, throwing the pots, smashing them to pieces, like he's taken leave of his senses. I try to stop him but he grabs my hands and pins them down at my sides, shoves me back against the wall and holds me still. He puts his face up close and glazes right into my eyes, just stares as if he can see deep into the heart of me. Like he knows me for what I am. We're both of us shaking and there's tears streaming down his cheeks, but neither of us utters a word. Then he do start kissing me all over my face and neck, pulling at my hair. He presses tight on my mouth, stronger than he's ever done before, like he wants to suck the very life out of me. And we slide down the wall and roll about the wet, baissly floor, gripping each other and tugging at our clothes.

'Tell me,' I gasp when he lets me catch my breath. 'Tell me. Am I suitable for 'ee now?'

NINETEEN

What happened to Violet Merrion? I wonder. Her family left
the village a few years after the end of the war to run a hotel
in Torbay. We weren't proper friends; we just went to the same
events – Sunday school, the Girl Guides, the WI children's
parties – and the Junior Salvage Company of course. After the
Highworth's Fertilizers incident I stopped collecting waste
paper and Violet and I carefully avoided each other. I don't
think we spoke again until Jack's funeral. 'Sorry,' was all she
said, but I didn't know what she was apologizing for.

I'm standing in the narrow lane outside the garage of the
Seaview Hotel, long since extended and renamed 'Tamarisk'.
I can see Violet now, full of self-importance, bending over the
boxes of paper with the sleeves of her cardigan rolled up, her
calves a little heavy, her blouse tight across her generous
young breasts. She has a pretty face – a small snub nose, full
red lips. I can't remember the colour of her eyes but I'm guess-
ing that they're brown. Her hair is thick and dark, pinned
back at the sides and fastened with a tortoiseshell comb. She
puts a maternal hand on the shoulder of a girl half her age –
navy-blue pinafore with straps crisscrossed over her back,

short puffy sleeves, her name lost to me now – and tells her to put the newspapers into the tatty carton that once held Quaker Oats.

A thin layer of sand covers the pavement, muffling my footsteps as I pass behind a row of large Victorian houses, now separated into holiday flats. The charred, fruity smell of barbecues wafts out from their tiny paved gardens; wetsuits and coloured towels hang over the washing lines. People are chatting and clinking glasses, huddling round the last patch of sunshine on the patio. I can hear somebody playing an acoustic guitar. A small child runs into the lane in his pyjamas to retrieve a ball and nobody shouts at him to mind the cars.

Maybe I should just abandon Spindrift, walk out of the door and throw the key into the sea. Let the dust settle, the roof leak, the pipes burst in the winter, the ceilings fall in, the floorboards rot, let the walls crumble into the ocean and sink beneath the waves. But then I turn the corner and the house swings into view. The tide is up, swirling around the building like a moat; the slate roof gleams in the early evening sun like polished metal and I am struck by its solid greyness, its oneness with the landscape. It sits there as naturally as if it has been carved out of the rock, a grand sculpture that promises to endure long after my death. I am just passing through. The new owners will remove all traces of me, of the Rosewarnes and their ancestors; they will scrape us off like layers of old paint.

I decide not to go inside just yet. I must practise walking

past the door, teach my fingers not to rummage for the keys, look up at unfamiliar curtains at the windows, note with indifference the new car in the driveway, the sound of strangers' voices in the garden . . . I will learn to be a visitor, although I have no intention of ever returning to this place.

I need to rid myself of all these memories, these random, useless visions of the past. What does it matter that those flat patches of grass in the car park are all that's left of the tennis courts? Or that you could once take a packet of sugar to the ladies who lived above the tearooms and they would turn it into soft, sweet fudge? The young don't care; they don't need to know how things were or what they used to look like. I am part of the dying generation, watching my last years trickle through the hourglass. I cannot simply flip it over and live my life again.

I step onto the beach and am instantly confronted by the tide, thundering in with a vengeance, the rocks drowning in a thick soup of boiling foam. I venture onto the crunching shells and tuck myself against the west wall of the house, easing myself down onto a low natural seat of slate. The waves are at their highest, their underbellies threaded with white like pale green marble – a solid wall of curved water stretching across the bay. Spirals of swirling spindrift form a misty curtain, lit here and there by scattered rainbows where the sun catches the spray. Gulls are circling and swooping overhead, or bobbing on the surface of the exhausted water as it comes to rest at the shore's ever-changing edge. The sea is finding its way into the valleys and crevices, seeping and creeping in between the rocks. The shallow pools tremble, as if there are movements deep below in the earth, but it's the sharp breeze that's making the water shiver – I can feel it stroking my face.

I could sit here all day, spellbound by the awesome power of the ocean. I could follow the sea as it withdraws, make the first new footprints on the drenched beach, pick my way across the gleaming black rocks before the sun returns them to matt greyness, and stand enchanted at the farthest limits of the shore, only the horizon before me – sea and sky, two simple stripes of green and blue. It's so easy to lose myself here, to forget about the minutiae of life, the petty irritations, the difficult issues I should face – like my awkward relationship with Cassie and my annoyance with Jory for telling her about Selina Penaluna.

I don't know what to do about Cassie – she's in the uneasy position of being a close relative and yet a stranger, both of us even more unsure of her status now I have refused to allow Scott to stay the night. Am I doing the right thing? I can't stop them having sex, and anyway, why should I be trying? It's none of my business what they do, although they've only known each other a few weeks and it feels too early to me – I'm worried that somebody will get hurt, although I suspect it won't be my sassy, independent granddaughter. To be fair, Cassie's behaviour has been apologetic, and although she's not sleeping here at the moment, she is spending more time with me during the day. I'm not sure whether she is simply trying to win me round and make me change my mind or whether she has decided to get to know me at last, remembering that I am her grandmother and not just a seaside landlady.

Cassie pops in to see me most mornings, drowsy from last night's passion, and sits with me in the garden – idly passing the time while Scott labours at the farm, bringing the harvest in. She is in a state of suspended animation, no longer interested in surfing or exploring the coastline, just happy to watch the sun's journey from east to west, waiting to begin her bodily preparations to meet her lover, retiring to the house to shower and change earlier each day. I try to remember how I felt when I first met Richard – light-headedness, a vague longing, the seeming pointlessness of any activity that wasn't connected to him. But we didn't have sex until we were married – it was all so different then, I can't really put myself in Cassie's place.

Just as I'm thinking about her, Cassie emerges at the top of the stone steps and waves. I wave back and she comes down onto the narrow strip of remaining beach to meet me. She is dressed all in white like some hippy bride – a long frilled cotton skirt and a camisole top, cut short above the waist. Her skin has a soft even brownness and the sun is dancing in the highlights of her blonde hair. A green cotton bag hangs over her shoulder.

'There you are,' she says.

'Hello, dear. What a lovely skirt.'

'Thanks, I bought it in Wadebridge yesterday. I went to the art shop to get some watercolour paper and a box of paints.'

She slides down next to me and perches companionably on another slab of slate. 'It's cosy here, out of the wind,' she says, taking the art materials out of the bag and laying them on the shingle. I reach for a pebble and place it on top of the book of paper.

'I want to paint the waves,' she says, 'but it's so hard.'

'My aunt never could get them right,' I reply. 'She gave up trying seascapes in the end and stuck to wild flowers.'

'I don't blame her . . .' Cassie laughs. She takes a soft pencil from a tin box and starts to sketch the rocks. I watch her work in silence for a few minutes, her head on one side as she considers her effort, flicking the pencil over to rub out her mistakes.

'There's this story Dad tells,' Cassie says, holding the paper before her at arm's length. 'I was five or six and we were here on this beach, fishing in the rock pools. I had a square bucket shaped like a sand castle, you know, and a yellow net. And Dad used to slice mussels off the rocks with a penknife, scooping their insides out to use as bait.'

'My uncle taught me to how to do that . . . then I taught your father.'

'Yeah, well, apparently I was really upset about this – I suppose I thought it was cruel . . . But you could catch loads of fish with it. Anyway, we must have been somewhere right out there' – she gestures at the furthest outcrop of rocks, the tips of them just visible above the waves – 'and my bucket was full of the fish we'd caught – shrimps, crabs, whatever. Then Dad said, quite casually, that the tide had turned and was on its way in. But I thought he meant it would be coming in immediately and, like, really fast, so I panicked.

'I dropped my net and the bucket, and all the shrimps escaped, and I started to run back, as if the sea was chasing after me. I shouted at him to run too, because I was frightened he was going to drown. But he just laughed and told me to come back. I didn't believe him, so I kept on running and jumping across the rocks, but it was really slimy and stuff and I fell into this pool and hurt myself quite badly, and I was bleeding and I couldn't walk. So I was screaming and crying, absolutely terrified – according to Dad anyway. He came and found me and picked me up and carried me back to the house and Mum put my leg in a bandage . . .' Cassie pauses, thinking. 'I don't actually remember any of that – I don't think so anyway. It's just that I've heard Dad tell the story so many times that it's kind of become one of my memories – do you know what I mean?'

'Of course . . . Photographs have the same effect – they distort the memory. You remember the photo rather than the moment it captured. It can be very confusing.'

'You must have thousands of memories.'

'Yes . . . The further back I go the stronger they are. That's what happens when you get old, I'm afraid. I can remember all sorts of things that happened when I was a girl, but I haven't a clue what I did last Thursday . . .'

'I don't think you're quite that bad yet, Gran.' Cassie laughs. She roots around in the cotton bag and brings out a small paintbox, a paper cup and one of Clara's sable brushes.

She stands up and walks to the water's edge, no more than a few yards in front of us, and fills the cup with salty, fizzing water.

'Jory's asked me to find out about the picture of Selina,' she says casually, returning to my side and adjusting the watercolour pad on her lap.

I feel my whole body stiffen. 'What do you mean, find out about it?'

'He wants to know about the artist that painted it.'

'Why?'

'I don't know. He's just interested . . . His name's Paul Blanchard.'

'Is it? I've never heard of him, have you?'

'No, but I did a search for him on the Net and a couple of things came up. He's an American, lives in California,' Cassie explains. 'He's got a real thing about mermaids, paints almost nothing else. *Lost at Sea* was painted in the nineteen fifties – it's an early work apparently.'

'How old is he?'

'Born in nineteen twenty-four, so that makes him well into his eighties – if he's still alive. I haven't found that out yet.' She mixes the palest of greys and starts to block in the rocks. 'When I told Jory he got really excited about it.'

'Well, there were hundreds of Americans stationed here in nineteen forty-three, getting ready for D-Day. Believe it or not, they were all crammed into Ocean Terrace.' I gesture to the six elegant white houses behind us, these days all holiday lets, accommodating no more than ten guests each.

'Was Selina friendly with any of them?' Cassie asks.

'With several, I believe,' I reply disapprovingly.

'Maybe one of them was an artist.'

'I suppose it's possible. Men buzzed round her like flies but she seemed to like it, encourage them even. Somehow she couldn't see that they were only after one thing . . .'

'Sounds like a case of low self-esteem,' ponders Cassie, rinsing the brush, 'which is strange, given how attractive she was.'

'That's a very generous way to look at it,' I admit. 'My brother was very much under her spell. But everyone else, well, they just thought she was a tart.'

'You should talk to Jory.' Cassie looks up. 'I'm sure he'd appreciate a visit.'

'If he wants to talk about it, he can come and see me.'

'Didn't you know he's got a heart condition? He hasn't left the farm for months.'

'No, I had no idea.' I feel myself blush. 'He never said . . .'

'Yeah, well, Tina and Phil are really worried – he's refusing to give up smoking.'

'You sound like you're part of the family already.'

'They've been great – really welcoming . . .' Cassie bites her lip, aware of the implication of what she's just said.

'They're lovely people, the Nancarrows – very close,' I say. 'Three generations living and working together like that.'

'Yeah . . . I hope they won't mind Scott leaving.' Cassie lets the words hang in the air. She is mixing blue and green now as a base for the sea, her hand trembling a little as she holds the brush.

'Leaving?'

'Yeah. He's decided to come travelling with me.'

'I see . . .' I stop for a few seconds to work out what I should say next, pick up a shell, run my fingers over its contours, then return it to the beach. 'I don't want to interfere, Cassie, but are you sure this is a good idea? It's all so sudden, this relationship . . . . I mean, wouldn't it be better—'

'I can't stay here,' she cuts in. 'I'll go mad . . . I mean, it's really beautiful and all that, but I'm meant to be going round the world! Scott's twenty-three – he doesn't want to spend the rest of his life as a farmer. He's been wanting to get out for ages, it's not just because of me . . .'

'They'll miss him at the farm. Especially now Jory can't do anything. I can't see how Phil and Tina will manage by themselves.'

'I don't know, I expect they'll hire people. They can't make Scott stay there for the rest of his life, it's not fair.'

'Has he told them yet?'

She shakes her head. 'He wants to wait till after the harvest . . . So it looks like you'll be stuck with me for another few weeks . . .' She laughs. 'If that's all right?'

'Of course. I don't think anything's going to happen with the house immediately.'

'Thanks . . .' She leans over and gives me a light peck on the cheek. 'Why don't you come up to the farm with me now, see Jory?'

'Yes, perhaps I should . . .'

*　*　*

Half an hour later and I'm sitting in Jory's smoky living room, drinking tea while the dog shuffles about uncomfortably on the rug, put out because I'm sitting in his usual armchair. Theoretically Jory lives by himself in the tatty old farmhouse – Phil and Tina built a brand-new bungalow for themselves in the back field a few years ago. I feel as if I'm on the television set of some rural drama – the dirt and clutter seem deliberately arranged: newspapers, piles of old clothes (for the wash or to be ironed?), a stack of papers and unpaid bills, broken clocks, screwdrivers, an old tap, the inner tube from a bicycle tyre, clumps of dog hair, lumps of dry mud from Wellington boots . . .

'You told me you were taking the mermaid book to the charity shop,' I say ruefully. 'You knew it was a present from Cassie – it made me feel very embarrassed.'

'What? Oh, I told Scott to take it, but he's not had the time.' Jory taps the dog roughly on the behind. 'Sit still or go out.'

'Why did you ask her to find out about the artist?'

'No particular reason.' Jory's veined cheeks redden. 'I just said how the picture was the very ashes of Selina and I wondered who painted it, that's all.'

'Well, I wish you hadn't. Now Cassie wants me to tell her all about what happened. You know I hate thinking about Selina – it just stirs everything up again and there's no point.'

Jory leans forward and offers me a biscuit from a tin – it's the nearest to an apology I'm going to get so I take a ginger snap. It's soft and stale but I have to eat it because there's no plate to leave it on. A large crumb falls onto my lap and I brush it onto the floor for Blackie to lick up.

'More importantly, I don't want her to tell Michael,' I continue. 'If he hears I've been working myself into a state over a stupid picture in a book he'll think I'm going funny. He's already told me I'm mad to be selling the house.'

'Thinks 'ee've gone off tha' rocker, do he?' Jory laughs grimly. He drags over a ratty footstool and rests his leg. 'He'll 'ave you in the old folks' home before 'ee know it. That's what they'm tryin' to do with me. They want me to sign the farm over so they can dig up my fields and build holiday bungalows.'

'You won't let them push you about.'

'That's easier said than done . . . I won't be around much longer and once I'm dead they can do what they bloody well like.' He reaches into his pocket and fetches out a battered packet of cigarettes. His fingertips are nicotine-stained, his knuckles cracked and raw, his yellowing nails thick and solid as hooves. I watch him light up and throw the spent match into the grate. He sucks on the cigarette and blows the smoke heavily through his nose.

There's a long pause. Jory stares out of the window at the framed rectangle of darkening sky, a slash of deep pink above the black silhouettes of trees. We must have spent hundreds of hours chatting in this room over the years, exchanging family news – births, marriages, deaths . . . For a long time all we have had in common is the past, but it hasn't stopped us being friends. Today, however, I sense he's finding my presence uncomfortable.

'So this Paul Blanchard that painted the picture . . .' I say, breaking the silence. 'You think he might have been billeted in the village and met Selina?'

'Somethin' like that . . .' he replies vaguely.

'Well, it's not impossible. I mean, we all know what she was like. But I very much doubt the painting's actually of her, don't you?'

'Yes, like I said, all mermaids look the same. Anyway, what does it matter? Don't think any more about it, Ellen. She's dead and gone.' He stubs his cigarette out in a battered tin ashtray and sighs wistfully. 'Pity though . . . she was the prettiest thing I ever clept eyes on . . .'

'You should give those up,' I mutter sharply.

'Too late for that, m'dear.' Jory smiles. 'Far too late for that.'

Paul Blanchard. I can imagine him in 1944, twenty, lean and tanned, smart in his GI uniform. He's leaning against a truck that's parked up on the gravel path outside Ocean Terrace. Lieutenant Blanchard – he pronounces his name with a soft drawl – flicks open a fresh pack of cigarettes and lights up. 'She's there again,' he says, pointing to a distant figure perched on a rock, staring out to sea. 'Who the hell is she waiting for?'

'Not you, Paul, you can bet on that,' the guy standing next to him laughs.

Three weeks ago he'd never heard of Cornwall, never even been out of his state. What he's seen so far of England hasn't exactly impressed. The roads are narrow and meandering, the trees too small, the houses damp and poky, the beer lousy, the accents incomprehensible. Only the kids seem pleased to see them and that's because they crave the gum and Hershey bars. Oh, the folks are polite enough, but they don't like the way the Yanks crowd into the pubs, singing unfamiliar songs at the tops of their voices, drinking the place dry. They find them loud and brash, too full of themselves. They won't let them take their daughters out – not that they're much to write home about, but it's not easy to get to the larger towns where they say girls will lie down for a pair of nylons. And everybody's feeling so nervous . . . Any day they could be out of here and on their way to France. These could be their last days on earth, damn it – why did they have to spend them in this godforsaken hell hole, with one half-empty shop and a two-mile walk to the nearest bar?

But Paul likes it here. While the others are frying dough-nuts or teaching the boys to play baseball he's on Rocky Beach collecting shells, hunting for starfish. He makes draw-ings in a small leather-bound sketchbook – seabirds, dead crabs, tresses of greeny-brown seaweed . . . His pencil follows the zigzagging coast to his left, fields ploughed right up to the edge, black rocks, the distant lighthouse. He sits on the pebbles with his back against the concrete capstan and draws the large grey house that stands like a fort between the two bays – broken lines for the uneven hanging slates, scribbled tufts of lichen, a wisp of smoke rising from the chimney. He dips his finger in a rock pool and sends smudged pencil clouds scudding across the page . . .

The girl is there so often he can't help but draw her – she is flora and fauna, part of the seascape. She's aware of him staring of course; Paul knows by the way she positions herself and arranges her hair. She keeps her head quite still, like a model, knowing that his artist's eye is tracing the line of her profile, the perfect curve of her breasts. Sometimes she hangs around the beach café, perched on the wall, swinging her legs, or climbs to the top of the large rock in the middle of the sandy beach and lets the sea rush in around her – he thinks of her as a princess trapped in a tower and would like to wade out and rescue her.

Selina draws up her thin cotton dress of deep sea-green and bares her long legs. She slips off her shoes and dips her feet in the icy water of a rock pool, startling the shrimps. She has been sitting there for over an hour, barely moving, her skin damp with spray, her gaze fixed on the receding ocean. She's waiting for some lucky guy. He's late, but she knows he will come eventually; he hasn't failed her yet.

Paul Blanchard finishes his cigarette and steps onto the shingle in his large polished boots. He cannot take his eyes off the girl in the distance, the colour of her dress merging with the sea, bare white arms, golden hair rippling in the wind like a flame, lighting a fuse in his body. And the longer he stares the more she looks like a mermaid, sunning herself on the rock. Never before has he seen such a rare specimen, this beautiful, wild creature at ease in her own watery world. And when he blocks out the shout and clatter of the men, the whirr of the generator, the grinding of the trucks as they bump along the cliff path, he's sure he can hear the faint sounds of her strange ethereal song. He wants to take off his boots and tiptoe barefoot over the rocks, to creep up behind her and catch a glimpse of her wet naked breasts, to touch her shiny, slippery fish tail before she senses his presence and dives into the sea.

Maybe that's how it was . . . just maybe . . .

TWENTY

It was 1944 and we had just turned sixteen. I could hardly believe how many years had slipped by since we had first come to Cornwall. I was in the sixth form, studying hard for public exams and contemplating university. Clara was still beavering away on her fundraising committees and I assisted her as any loving, dutiful daughter would. There was Knitting for Victory, Salute the Soldier Week, and the latest imperative was to collect books to send to the armed forces or to the libraries in the cities that had been blitzed – to hoard books was to help Hitler, we were told. By February our area had collected a staggering fourteen thousand, but only a couple came from Spindrift. After the horrible experience with Highworth's Fertilizers I was reluctant to search the house for any printed material, and in any case, there were very few books that Charles was prepared to part with.

When I wasn't knocking on doors, pestering our neighbours, I was at the WI hall rehearsing a song and dance routine as a member of the Sandy Bay Glamour Girls: our first performances were planned for the end of March at the Padstow Variety Club Concert. Clara helped me sew my costume, a ridiculously short black pleated skirt and a red gingham puffed-sleeve blouse. None of us had proper dancing shoes so we practised in bare feet, forming an uneven chorus line – different heights, sizes and ages – hands on each other's shoulders, smiling to our imagined audience while Mrs Pascoe thumped out a tune on the piano. It was all good clean fun, as my aunt put it – although the tragedy meant I never performed in the concert itself.

The war had become a normal way of life – waste not, want not, make do and mend, learning how to amuse oneself in patriotic ways, enduring modest amounts of self-sacrifice. I was happy to tolerate its privations because the war was an essential part of my new identity as a burgeoning blue stocking. I started to worry that when the war ended I would be sent back to North Woolwich as plain, working-class Nellie Morrison to scavenge amongst the ruins that had once been Claremont Street and find work in a factory. I knew rationally that this was extremely unlikely to happen, but when people began to talk about the invasion of France, the Beginning of the End instead of the End of the Beginning, I found it hard to react with the required enthusiasm. The war, quite simply, had been good for me. How could I know what peace might bring?

But there was no prospect of peace at Spindrift. Jack was constantly falling out with Charles and Clara. He and Selina had been inseparable for more than two years and the Rosewarnes hated the influence she had over him. She was never once invited to meet them and they always sneeringly referred to her as 'that girl'. Jack had left school the previous summer after flunking his school certificate and had gone to be a labourer at Clifftop Farm. With so many able-bodied young men away in the services, there was little casual help to be found and all the farmers were exhausted, working from dawn till gone eight at night and then expected to turn up for Home Guard parades twice a week. Morale was low – it had been one of the worst harvests in living memory: months of rain had almost destroyed the oat crop and farmers were worried about feeding their stock. Jack's help was sorely needed, but that didn't make Charles any less annoyed – 'I will not have a son of mine a labourer,' he raved. Jack's main reason for working at the farm was because he was good friends with Jory, but Charles felt that he'd taken the job to spite him.

During those last months there were terrible scenes – Jack swearing and slamming doors, my uncle shouting and pounding his fist on the table, my aunt trying to calm them down only to be screamed at by both of them, fleeing in tears to her room. But to my amazement, Charles never so much as threatened to turn Jack out. He was holding onto Jack as if he were hanging off the edge of a perilous cliff, determined to drag him to safety. He would not release his grip and let him fall. He believed that Jack would eventually come to his senses, grow out of his infatuation with Selina and embark on a proper career. I didn't share his optimism or strength of faith.

Why were the Rosewarnes so determined to win Jack over?

They had more than fulfilled their duty as part of the war effort by taking us into their home. Even if this relationship had been an experiment in social engineering – a thought that often occurred to me – surely they already had their results: one success, one failure. Why couldn't they concentrate on celebrating my transformation and just accept defeat with Jack? He was abusive and deceitful, accepting their generosity without a word of thanks. He said he hated them, that they had ruined his life, but whenever he stormed out of the house he always returned. He would disappear for several days, sleeping on the Nancarrows' sofa or maybe even at Selina's place – I never knew for sure where he went – but the Rosewarnes took him back every time without a word of reproach, more forgiving than any natural parents.

Meanwhile I, the perfect, obedient daughter, stood bewildered on the sidelines, witness to a love I could not compete with, of a strength and depth that I could neither offer nor ever hope to receive. There is no point in blaming the Rosewarnes for the inequality of their feelings towards us – they couldn't help it. They always treated me with nothing but kindness and affection, but I know that had God given them the choice between us on March 15, they would have surrendered me without a second thought.

The village was full to bursting with allied soldiers and airmen – squeezed into every hotel and guesthouse, even sleeping in garages and garden sheds. The houses in Ocean Terrace were commandeered and five hundred GIs moved in, but strangely nobody was billeted with us, although we had a spare bedroom and plenty of space downstairs. While other houses entertained their exotic guests with impromptu parties, trips out to dances and sing-songs around the piano, Spindrift remained quiet, the atmosphere increasingly icy. I longed for visitors – not for their lively conversation or their gifts of tinned fruit and spam, but because their presence might relieve the tension in the house.

Although nobody ever confronted us about this apparent unfairness I knew there was gossip – people thought we were selfish and unpatriotic; it was said that Charles had high-up military connections, that he could 'pull strings'. But I took it as more evidence that he was involved in secret operations, deducing that security could have been compromised by having servicemen billeted in the house. I'd long suspected that the Home Guard platoon to which he devoted so much energy was just a cover for more serious activities – there only seemed to be three other members for a start and the so-called training exercises they went on were unusually challenging.

In recent months there had definitely been a momentum gathering: Charles was in an excited mood and going away more than ever. The telephone would ring or a telegram would arrive and he'd be out of the door within minutes; he might only be gone for the afternoon, or he might not be back for a week. The consistent story was that he was away on 'legal business' – if my aunt had any idea of his true whereabouts she never shared them with me. In my imagination my uncle was engaged in dangerous and rather glamorous missions, bravely risking his life for his country on a daily basis. I longed for the truth of his heroism to be revealed, to show our doubting neighbours that the Rosewarnes were more patriotic than the rest of the village put together.

Our everyday lives were increasingly dominated by the presence of the Americans. They fascinated me, although I was absolutely forbidden to mix with them – 'fraternization', Charles called it – and had to be content with spying on them from the window. I liked their uniforms, smooth green khaki, the angle of their caps. I enjoyed listening to the muffled thump of their rubber-soled boots as they marched up and down the lanes. I watched them firing bazookas down the beach, playing volleyball on the lawn in front of the terrace, handing out freshly fried doughnuts to hordes of clamouring kids. Some of them played cards, others wrote letters, a few read books. It was as if they were trapped in a large waiting room, with no idea of when they would be leaving or where they were going. I wanted to know these men who were apparently prepared to lay down their lives on my behalf but I wasn't even allowed to say hello.

It was a chilly February afternoon, the day was fading and everything was bathed in a deep blue light. I was walking down the hill on my way home from school, reciting the table of irregular French verbs in my head, fitting them to the rhythm of our dance routine, nodding my head in time to the imagined piano music. We had seen a lot of rain recently and the lane was muddy with tyre tracks from the GIs' jeeps, which roared past me every so often, forcing me to press myself against the wet, sweet-smelling hedge.

I turned the corner just after the post office and stopped for a moment, as I nearly always did, to look at the sea. Large rolls of barbed wire stretched out across the sandy beach and a few GIs were battling to launch a boat into the waves. Several trucks – gleaming olive-green giants decked with all manner of winches and towing equipment – were parked up on the grass between the two bays, now a churned-up muddy mess. Their engines were turning over, and some of the GIs were polishing the paintwork. A small group of about six men was huddled around a jeep, like bees round a honeypot – they were jostling for territory, laughing in that false jocular fashion that men do when they want to impress. I thought they must be gambling or looking at some risqué magazine, but then I heard a woman's laugh rise into the air – I'd know that voice anywhere, I said to myself. It was Selina, of course.

I don't know how she knew I was walking past; she couldn't possibly have seen me, surrounded by all those men – she had such an acute instinct, like an animal picking up the smell of the enemy. Or maybe it was just coincidence. Either way, she jumped out of the jeep, pushed the GIs aside and came striding towards me, hands on hips.

'Look, it's one of the Sandy Bay Glamour Girls!' she taunted, her eyes sparkling as she wound a thick lock of gold hair round her fingers.

'It's for the Red Cross,' I blurted back, as if that explained everything. The men walked towards me and stood in a

pathetic, doting huddle behind her. I blushed as I saw them
look me up and down, taking in my plain features and boring
hairstyle, my gabardine school coat, my childish felt hat.

'Want some gum?' Selina held out a packet but I shook my
head fiercely. 'Why not? Won't Mr Rosewarne let 'ee 'ave it?'

'I don't like it, that's all.'

'Bet 'ee never even tried it.' She popped a strip into her
mouth.

'What are you doing here?' I said accusingly, trying to get
back some ground. 'Jack won't finish work for another couple
of hours.' I emphasized the word 'Jack' as heavily as I could
and looked pointedly at the cluster of GIs.

'I do know,' Selina replied. 'I've been getting to know the
lads, that's all. They'm goin' to take me for a ride in the jeep.
Want to come?'

'It's not allowed, is it?'

'It's OK, we're only going to do a couple of circuits,' said
one of the guys, dark-haired, heavy eyebrows, Italian-looking.

'No thank you,' I mumbled.

'Don't 'ee dare?' Selina gave me one of her piercing,
challenging looks.

'It's not that . . .' I hesitated. 'I don't think you should go.
Jack wouldn't be very happy if he saw you with these men.'

'Don't 'ee tell me what I can or can't do!' She flounced off,
turning her back on me to face the GIs, who were clearly
amused by our ridiculous and embarrassing confrontation.
'So, who's goin' to take me for this ride?' she said flirtatiously.
The men all offered at once. 'I think I'm goin' to choose . . .

You!' Selina pointed at the best-looking chap and he gave her a mock salute.

'Yes, ma'm!' he shouted. They all laughed, but I just stood there, glowering.

'You wait till I tell Jack!' I shouted, and stormed off, my heavy satchel banging against my back as I marched back to the house.

And tell him I did, that evening over supper. We were tucking into grilled mackerel and boiled potatoes – Clara always served the fish whole with the head still on and I remember its glassy eye staring up at me as I picked away at its flesh as if telling me, *Go on then, say it*, but I was struggling for a way to bring the subject up. The atmosphere round the table was as awkward as ever, the clatter of our knives and forks punctuated with stilted, intermittent conversation. Charles enquired about my day at school and Clara told the story of a GI who had fallen into the inner harbour at Padstow and had been rescued by Harry Lanyon, the baker. As usual, Jack had not contributed a single word to the meal, save for a mumbled 'thanks' when Clara put his plate before him. Supper was nearly over and I knew that if I didn't say something now I never would.

'I saw Selina today, Jack,' I began, my voice trembling very slightly.

Jack looked up, surprised. 'Did you? When was that?'

'This afternoon. I saw her on my way home. She was with some soldiers.'

Charles and Clara briefly exchanged a glance and Jack's face reddened.

'So?'

'She had her arm round one of them, a young, nice-looking chap. She asked him to take her for a ride in his jeep. I don't know where they went exactly . . . I'm surprised she didn't turn up to meet you – perhaps she's still with him.'

Jack immediately rose from the table. 'Lying bitch,' he muttered under his breath. The three of us sat there, knives and forks raised in shock, as if frozen in time.

'Language, Jack,' protested Charles.

'I hope that wasn't directed at Ellen,' Clara added.

'Bitch!' he repeated right in my face, and pushed his chair over.

'Jack! This will not do!' roared Charles. 'I will not have a son of mine behaving in this despicable manner.'

'How many more times – I am *not* your son!' screamed Jack. 'I'd be ashamed to be your son!'

'Stop it, dear, please!' begged Clara. 'You mustn't say such things '

'Ssh, Clara, let me handle this.'

'But, Charles—'

'Jack, put that chair back and sit down! Ellen is only trying to warn you – she can see you making a fool of yourself.'

'She doesn't care a shit about me,' shouted Jack. 'She's just jealous!'

'Of a little fisherman's daughter?' scoffed Charles. 'How ridiculous! No, Ellen has your best interests at heart. We all do.'

'Well, I don't care what you think. Selina and I are going

to be married and there's nothing you can do to stop us.'

'There's plenty I can do,' snapped Charles. 'As your adoptive father, you need my permission until you come of age. And you can rest assured that I'm not going to give it to you, no matter what tricks she gets up to.' He looked at Jack darkly. 'You know my meaning . . . She'll think she can force us by getting herself into trouble and you probably won't even be the father.'

'How dare you!' screamed Jack. 'How dare you say that about my Selina!'

'She's not just *your* Selina, though, is she?' he tutted. 'She's little more than a whore—'

Immediately Jack swung out his fist, connecting with Charles's chin. He reeled back towards the wall. Clara screamed and grabbed my arm, but Charles calmly took out his hankie and wiped the blood from his bottom lip. Jack lurched at him again and tried to land another punch but not before Charles swiftly moved to one side and dodged out of the way.

'Like it or not, son, it's the truth,' he said quietly. Jack screamed words of abuse and threw himself forward, falling onto Charles with his whole weight. They staggered about in a desperate embrace, like two boxers in the ring, Charles trying to break free and Jack flailing his arms about wildly.

'Stop it!' I cried. 'Stop it!'

Jack stepped back, breathing hard, then launched himself at Charles's stomach, pummelling into him. Here was all Jack's pain, his grief, humiliation, loss, uncertainty, frustration – every ounce of suffering that he'd borne for nearly five years compressed into his fists. Charles didn't strike back once; just stood there, taking the punishment. Tears were streaming down Jack's face as he sobbed and punched, each strike weaker than the last, until he was pawing at Charles's shirt like a puppy. Then he let out a long groan and collapsed onto his knees, burying his head in his hands.

Charles stared down at him, slightly bent over with pain, clutching his stomach. His balding head was sweating, he was fighting for breath. 'For God's sake, stand up,' he gasped. 'Get a grip of yourself.'

'I've finished with you!' Jack got to his feet and staggered towards the door. 'And with you too, Nellie, the lot of you . . . Selina and I love each other. We're getting out of here and never coming back.'

'Don't say that, Jack,' begged Clara. 'Please don't say that.' She reached out desperately to touch him, but he backed away.

'Get your hands off me!' Jack ran out of the house, slamming the front door behind him. Charles sat down heavily and mopped his brow; Clara started whimpering into her napkin.

'I'm sorry,' I said. 'It was my fault. I shouldn't have said anything.'

Charles shook his head. 'No, no, Ellen, you were right . . . We have to find a way to stop this disastrous relationship or that girl will ruin his life.'

I cried myself to sleep that night, like a small child punished for a terrible wrongdoing, banished from the warm circle of brotherly love. The glue that had held me and Jack together for sixteen years had finally come unstuck – no amount of making do or mending could put us back together. After a few days Jack turned up again at the house and sat down for his dinner as if nothing had happened. I suppose he had nowhere else to go; perhaps he was simply biding his time until he could leave. He never apologized for attacking Charles and no more was said about it – there seemed to be no limit to the Rosewarnes' patience and forgiveness. I tried to make up with Jack but he refused to have anything to do with me. It's my greatest sadness that we were never reconciled – it was only a few weeks before he drowned . . .

TWENTY-ONE

My father heard a bad storm was on the way: it would be on us tonight – force ten, they reckoned – so he wakes me up before dawn and tells me we've to shift the pots. I don't want to go, for it's cold as a quilkin, but he shakes me and pulls off my blanket, standing over me while I put on my warmest clothes and boots, making me wear his old oilskin, though it's too big for me.

'Stop sludgin' tha' feet!' he shouts as I stumble down the slipway to the beach. He's already sitting in the punt waiting for me, lighting his pipe. We row out to the *Louisa May* and tie the punt astern, then soon as we come afloat he starts the engine. It's not light yet so I sit in the bow and shine the torch in front of us as he takes the boat down the channel towards the mouth of the estuary.

'It'll be low water by the time we've done,' he says, so he unties the punt and lashes it to a mooring stump set in the rocks further down so we can pick it up later. It's quieter than the grave and sets me thinking about all the fishermen and sailors that drowned on the Doom Bar and how these waters must be thick with ghosts.

Long ago they do say a Padsta fisherman was bringing home his catch when he saw a doxy young maid sunning herself on a rock in a small hidden cove along the estuary. Her back was turned to him but he could tell that she was naked and had just been swimming, for her white arms were glistening in the evening sun. She was combing the tangled wet tresses of her yellow hair that reached far beyond her waist. And the girl was singing to herself, a high-pitched eerie song in foreign words he could not understand, but still they filled his soul with longing and sadness.

The young man called out to her but she did not seem to hear him, so he ran his boat gently aground on the shore and started walking boldly towards her. When she heard his boots crunching on the shingle she turned round to face him and suddenly their eyes met. And he was startled, not by the beauty of her face or her wet naked breasts, but by the shiny silver fish tail that stretched from beneath her navel. She smiled at him and reached out her hand to draw him nearer, but he was struck with fear. He took his bow and arrow and shot her through the heart. And as she lay on the ground dying she cursed him and all the young men that ever sailed these waters. She summoned the wind to bring on a terrible storm and that night an enormous bank of sand was swept up in the middle of channel.

We're crossing the Doom Bar now as the estuary opens out to meet the sea, the boat pointing towards my island. A skivvy rain's falling, the swell is making my stomach turn and I'm feeling rough as rats. The dawn's just breaking, framing the clouds with fire; the sky is nothing but streaks of yellow, gold and green, but dark grey clouds are looming to the west.

My father brings us alongside the first string of five pots and we fetch them up – there's two good lobsters in them but no crabs. We stack the pots in the stern and take the boat round to the lee of the island so we can lay them where there's a chance they'll be safe. The boat rolls from side to side like a rocking cradle. My fingers are frozen up with the cold and it's hard to keep my grip on the sodden rope. My father keeps his pipe in his mouth, and as he sucks the bitter smell of his tobacco wafts towards me – we don't speak a word to each other, but work quickly together, almost to a beat, both looking up as a plane passes over our heads, just taken off from one of the nearby airfields.

We do stop for a second to watch it climb slowly into the sky like a large lumbering bird as it heads off out across the black ocean. And I'm idly wondering where it might be heading when all of a sudden we hear this terrifying noise like thunder, only much louder, and the plane explodes in mid-air – just turns into a tiny ball of fire and falls into the sea. I scream and drop the rope and we both fall to the deck, thinking we're caught in the middle of a raid. But we can't hear any other planes and the sky's empty, save for the birds who have taken fright and are circling wildly above our heads, screeching to each other. After a few moments Dad tells me to get up for there's no sign of Germans. We look out across the sea for the plane but we're too far away to see where it came down.

'What d'ee reckon 'appened?' I ask him.

'I dunno. But we'd best get back fast as we can – no doubt they'll be calling out the lifeboat.'

So we do leave off shifting the rest of the pots, which will have to take their chances now if there's a storm, turn the *Louisa May* round and head back towards Padsta. Dad brings us into the estuary and we pick up the punt and put it in tow, chugging up the channel till the boat runs aground on the sand. I'm still shaking with the shock of what we've just seen. I keep looking into the sky and listening for sounds of Germans, but there's nothing up there, just grey soggy clouds.

Dad anchors the *Louisa May* fore and aft, making sure she can't shift. 'I'll come back later and bring her into harbour where she'll be safe,' he says. So we climb into the punt and scull to shore. I take the lobsters and put them in the keep-box while he runs to the coastguard's house to find out what's going on.

It was so early in the morning that very few people actually saw the plane come down – Jory in the upper field, fetching in the cows for milking; two GIs on the cliff path, finishing the night patrol; Mr Dobbin in his dressing gown, looking idly out of the window while he waited for his tea to brew; and Mrs Pascoe walking her dog, unable to sleep since her son had been reported missing in North Africa. I was a witness too of sorts, hearing the dull boom of the explosion in my dreams.

'Quick, Ellen, get up, get up!' cried my aunt, running into my room and shaking me awake.

We rushed into the back garden in our slippers and dressing gowns. Jack was already there, half dressed, buttoning up his shirt.

'Is it one of ours?' I whispered.

'Can't tell from here,' he replied.

The three of us stood and watched the distant wreckage as it burned on the surface of the sea; fire and water in open combat, intense orange flames cutting through the waves. There were no rocket flares shooting into the sky, no distant bobbing figures screaming for help – just the silent dignity of instant death. A sight of extraordinary beauty, like a Viking funeral ship taking its heroes on a final glorious journey across the waters of darkness to the Other World.

'Somebody should raise the alarm,' said Jack. 'Get the lifeboat . . . Shouldn't we use the telephone?'

'I wish your uncle were here,' murmured Clara. 'He would know what to do.'

But there was nothing anybody *could* do. The Air Sea Rescue launch arrived soon after but there were no shivering survivors in need of dry clothes or mugs of hot tea. Villagers and soldiers gathered in small groups on the cliff top and stared helplessly out to sea. Some reckoned it had been shot down, others said there must have been a collision. But Jory insisted that the plane – a Warwick, he thought – had been flying alone and had simply exploded in mid-air.

The crowd watched until the fire consumed itself and the wreckage sank. It was as if we'd been watching some film in the cinema and now it had come to an end. We returned to reality, blinking at the daylight, remembering we'd not yet had breakfast or fed the hens. Jory went back to his cows. My aunt told me that if I didn't get my skates on I would be late for school. Jack fetched his bike and wiped the dew from the saddle.

'Not sure when I'll be back,' he said. I knew without asking that he was going to find Selina.

'Aren't you supposed to be working?' I said.

'Can't you mind your own bleedin' business for a change?' he grunted as he rode off.

My aunt heaved a weary sigh and put her arm round my shoulders. 'He doesn't mean it,' she said. 'Don't take any notice.'

So I went to school and sat through my lessons: French, history, housewifery. It all seemed so trivial reciting irregular verbs, listing the causes of the English Reformation, learning how to hang up washing to ensure the most efficient dry. We stood in the garden behind the kitchens, each holding a man's shirt, the collars and cuffs frayed beyond repair, now only used for practising laundry skills. The shirts were buttoned to the neck and then pegged onto the line by the back bottom edge, letting the front fall loose to create a bag that would trap the air. I tried my best to concentrate on this small, mindless task but I kept drifting away. It was as if a fragment of a dream had broken off and was floating around my head.

I kept thinking about the people on the plane, wondering what their names were and where they had been heading. I imagined them rising before dawn, dressing in the dark, walking across the airfield in the early morning mist, climbing into the waiting aircraft. Did the pilot hesitate before he switched on the engine? Did the passengers look out of the window as the plane trundled down the runway and wonder? And the women – sisters, mothers, wives – waking up this morning, doing ordinary things, brushing their hair, packing the children off to school, sharing a joke with a neighbour as they hung out their washing; unaware that their men were now dead, their bodies lying peacefully on the bottom of the ocean, or churning with the current, bruising over the rocks as they rushed towards the shore. As our thirty white shirts swelled and lifted in the blustering breeze all I could see was a row of drowned headless men, their bodies bloated with seawater. I wept for these women's loved ones. I took their place until the telegrams arrived.

Once I've seen to the lobsters I go back to the cottage and put the kettle on the stove, thinking maybe I'll put a bit of my father's rum in my tea, for the plane crash has rattled my nerves and I'm starting at every noise. I'm gazing out the window when I see Jack riding down the path.

'What 'ee doin' 'ere this time of day?' I say, coming to the door.

He flings his bike down and gives me a rough hug. 'You wouldn't believe what just happened. A Warwick's gone down, just outside our bay.'

'Yes, I know, I saw it. We was out by the island, shiftin' pots. The thing just blew up – terrified the life out of me; thought we was being shot at.'

'No, it was just an accident. No survivors of course.'

'Didn't think there would be, poor buggers.' We're both silent for a moment, thinking of the dead, I suppose. I shiver, like someone's just walked over my grave. 'Come in,' I say. 'I'm just brewin' up.'

Jack sits by the stove in my father's chair and warms his hands on the mug. 'Shakes you up a bit, doesn't it,' he says, 'when something like that happens so close . . . Brings it all home.'

'Yes, I kep thinkin' how the plane could have fallen on top of the *Louisa May* and killed us outright . . . What was it carryin', do you reckon – people or cargo?'

'No idea, but there must have been some stuff on board,' says Jack. 'Useful stuff that might wash up . . .'

We give each other a slow smile, the same idea just popping into our heads. 'We can't get onto the main beaches,' I say, 'they'm swarmin' with soldiers, but we could search a few of the smaller coves.'

'That's what I was thinking. We'll have to be careful, mind – there'll be trouble if we're caught.' Jack frowns.

'We'll only search places where we can't be seen from the cliff top,' I answer. 'But we've got to be quick, before anyone else gets the same idea . . .'

So we down our tea fast and I find Jack a woolly hat to wear to keep his ears warm for it'll be cold down there by the shore. He do leave his bike at the back of the house and we set off along the lane past the farm, taking the path between the fields that cuts off the headland. It's gluthening up and the wind's whipping off the sea. We quicken up our pace and I slip my hand in Jack's pocket to keep warm. He don't say much, seems miles off in a dream. I can sense there's something weighing on his mind but I'm not sure if it's good or bad.

'I love 'ee,' I say, nuzzling my face into his jacket. 'Go on, tell me 'ee love me too.' But he doesn't say anything, just keeps on walking, looking straight ahead. 'What's wrong, Jack? Don't 'ee love me no more?'

'You know I do,' he mumbles. 'But don't make me say it – it doesn't count if I'm forced.'

'Don't sink into a black mood.' I grip his arm tight. ''Ee was all excited when 'ee came by, now 'ee look as glum as a tooth-drawer.'

'Oh, I've been doing some thinking, that's all . . .' He stops for a moment. 'Thinking about you and me.'

'Only nice things, I hope . . .' I say, but again he don't reply. We get to a stile and he helps me over. The path's steep now up to the edge – there's a sharp sting of salt in the air, the spiky gorse starting to come out in deep yellow buds, the long grass leaning over in the wind.

We start our search in the coves that lie just west of the Point; the cliffs are high here and the drop is steep. There are tracks you can get down by, but they're narrow and muddy so you have to go slow. First we lie on our bellies and gake over the edge – it's the best way to get close without being blown over – to see if there's anything washed up that looks worth going down for.

'Well? What do you reckon?' says Jack.

I shake my head. 'Nothin' that I can see from 'ere.' We stand up and brush the mud off our clothes, then walk on past another few coves, all of them empty. 'We need to go somewhere narrow, where there are more rocks than beach,' I tell him, 'where nobody would ever dare to go down. I know the fitty place . . . There's no path and the cliffs hang right over the cove so once we'm on the sand, nobody will be able to see us.'

'But how we will get down to it if there's no path?' says Jack.

'There *is* a path, but it do lead into the cove on the other side, so we'll get down that way, then walk along the beach and wade a short way out into the water. There's a crop of rocks that go into the sea – we can climb over 'em and that'll take us round. 'Ee'll 'ave to watch tha' step, but I've done it before. Just follow me, I know the best way.'

'But if we find anything we'll never be able to bring it back up.'

'There's caves we can hide stuff in, then we can come back in the boat once everyone's forgotten, and pick it up. Trust me,' I say, 'I know what I'm doin'.'

'Hmmm,' grumbles Jack. 'I know who to blame if we break our necks.'

So we get to the place I've set my mind on and try to make our way down. It's a harder climb down than I remember – the slate's crumbling at the edges and it's pitching to rain again. So we do stop on a ledge and look about us from there –

there's a few pieces of driftwood that look as if they've been washed up a while, but nothing else of value.

'Maybe we should turn back,' says Jack.

'We've come so far, we might as well go into the next cove,' I answer boldly. So we slide down the rock onto the sand and run across the short stretch of shingle beach. Then we do take off our shoes, tie the laces together and sling them round our necks. Jack rolls his trousers up to his knees and I tuck my skirt into my drawers. The tide's right out now so we don't have to wade far till we can get onto the large rock that juts out into the sea. The water's some freezing and our feet slip on the wet granite, but Jack tucks in close behind me and we pick our way between the boulders till we reach the other side.

This cove is long and thin, the beach almost all shingle, with overhanging rocks that drip pale muddy water and leave purple streaks in the spongy stone. There are a few good pieces of driftwood lying on the ground, some broken pieces of net, a wrecked withy pot, a few dead crabs, a smashed-up crate and an empty bottle – it's covered in sticky grit but I can see straight away it's a Corona bottle – makes my heart miss a beat. I don't know why but I have to pick it up and roll it over in my hand – old memories spin into my head and I think how it's now nine year since I last saw the woman I called my mother.

'Selina!' I look up to see Jack standing amid the pools on the other side of the beach, waving at me. 'Come here, quick!'

'You found something?' He nods fiercely. 'What?' I throw down the bottle, smashing it to bits on the rocks. 'What is it?' I shout. 'Tell us! Is it worth much?'

He don't reply, so I run down to him at the water's edge.

Jack's staring at a man's body lying face down in the shallows. I gasp and hold onto Jack's arm.

'Is he dead?' I whisper.

'Of course, what do you think? Must be from the plane.'

'So why isn't he in uniform then?' I answer.

'I don't know.' We just stand there, staring at him, looking at him all over. His hair is cropped short like a serviceman but he's wearing dark corduroy trousers and a white shirt, ripped across the back. I notice how he's still wearing his boots – like Benson the butcher.

'Shall we turn him over?' says Jack suddenly.

'No, don't touch 'im!' But he turns him all the same – it's not easy for he's a big man and full of water. I wish he hadn't done it now for as I feared the man's face is all smashed up and his skin's burned black. It makes me urge, my breakfast rises in my mouth and I start to shake. 'We must fetch the police,' I say. 'Leave it to them.' But Jack won't listen – he grabs hold of the body by the ankles and drags it further up the beach, till it's right out of the water. Then he kneels down and starts going through the pockets.

'What 'ee doing? Leave 'im be!' I shout.

'I'm just trying to find out who he is.' He brings out half a packet of wet cigarettes.

'This is wrong, Jack,' I mutter. ''Ee shouldn't touch a dead body. It'll bring bad luck. We should leave it for the police or the lifeboat to find.' But he won't take no notice.

'Hang on, he's got something round his waist.' Jack starts fumbling with the bloke's trousers. He's wearing a strange kind of belt – looks like it's made of silk or something. Anyway, Jack unties it and takes it off him. He holds it up and shakes it. 'There's coins inside,' he says, undoing one of the zipper fastenings and unwrapping a small parcel. 'Blimey, Selina, it's gold!'

'Have 'ee taken leave of tha' senses?'

'Papers too, but they're all wet, can't read them properly . . . and what's this, a hankie?' Jack fetches out a piece of white silk, but it's not a hankie at all – it seems to be a kind of map. I've never seen anything like it before. He lays it out on a flat piece of rock, traces his fingers over the black spidery lines and reads out a few of the names.

'*Roumania . . . Budapest, Varna . . .* These are the Balkan countries. This must be where the plane was heading. What do you make of it, eh?'

'I think 'ee should put it straight back and we should get out of 'ere 'fore anyone finds us, that's what,' I answer sharply. 'We could be in big trouble . . .'

'You must be joking. I'm keeping this, it'll make a great souvenir.'

No matter how I try I can't for the life of me make him put the belt back on the corpse. Soaking wet as it is, he ties it round his own waist and tucks it under his shirt. We go back across the rocks, run up the other beach and climb back to the top fast as we can. It's late afternoon by now, the sky's black with cloud and it's blowing a gale, but Jack's so full of himself, talking about the gold and the silk map and how he reckons the man must have been a spy on a secret mission. I'm begging him not to say nothing to nobody, not even Jory, for if it gets out we stole from a corpse they'll have the police on us and we'll be put in jail or worse.

'If I was in London I could sell this gold,' he says. 'It must be worth a good bit. What we'll do is hide it in your cottage until—'

'Oh no 'ee won't,' I answer. 'I'm not being party to it.'

'You've no choice, you're in this as thick as me now.' He grins. 'We'll take the belt back to Spindrift; I'll find somewhere safe for it . . . Come on, we need to dry off.' He starts striding ahead of me. 'And we need some food. I'm bloody starving . . .'

There's no gainsaying him so we do walk on towards his house, our arms wrapped about each other like two horses harnessed to a cart, moving forward with the same step. There's a guilty secret tucked between us now, drawing us together. We're walking so close to each other I can feel Jack's heart beating in my chest. He's wound up so tight it's as if we murdered the man on the beach, not just found his corpse.

When we reach the big hole in the cliffs we take the short cut round the side of the farm and down the lane into the village. I go onto Rocky Beach and sit on a narrow ledge against the side wall of the house and wait while Jack goes inside to fetch us something to eat.

After only a minute he opens a window and calls down to

me, 'You can come in. Everyone's out – we've got the place to ourselves.' Now this is the first time I've ever been into Jack's house so I'm keen to have a proper look round. He lets me in by a side door that opens onto this sort of courtyard, paved with large slabs of slate. We go into the kitchen and Jack cuts us two chunks of bread and finds a bit of cake in the tin.

'I could do with a leak o' tea,' I say. 'I'm some parched.'

'We can do better than tea,' Jack replies, his dark eyes all shining. He takes me into the parlour. I've never seen such fine furniture – there's a table by the window, polished up so much you can see your face in it, and a big leather chair next to the fire. There are paintings all over the walls and all kinds of ornaments – a black vase painted with roses, a china girl feeding a goose, and a large ticking clock in a glass case. Jack goes to the sideboard and pours out two glasses of whisky from a glass bottle with a stopper like a huge diamond. I take a swig; the liquor burns my throat and makes me cough.

'Can I take a look around?' I ask.

'If you like,' says Jack, pouring himself another glass.

I go back into the corridor and turn the corner. At the end is a small room, all dark and panelled; the walls are painted dark green and there's a beautiful rug on the floor. I'm thinking this must be Mr Rosewarne's room where he does his law work. I sit in his chair at the desk, stroke the smooth leather top, play with a silver inkpot and a small knife on a tray. I never seen so many books and I take one off the shelves to look at the drawings, but Jack do come in then and tell me to leave things be, for he don't want his uncle to know we've been snooping about.

'You're shivering,' he says. 'You should change out of those wet clothes. Let's go and find something of Nellie's.'

'Are you sure she won't mind?' I ask.

'Who cares if she does?' He grins.

So we go upstairs and Jack takes me into her room – the smallest room at the back of the house: pale painted walls, dark wood furniture, a brown marble fireplace, a big bed in the middle with a pink coverlet, and a view of the sea out the window – all grey heaving ocean but for a large ship in the distance and the black shape of my island on the horizon. The dressing table's covered in books and papers, all stacked up to one side. Jack opens up the wardrobe and takes out one of his sister's dresses – silvery grey with a faint dark blue print. I think it must be one she wears to church or for special occasions, for I've never seen her in it before.

'I can't wear this,' I say, 'it's 'er Sunday best,' but Jack still lays it out on the bed, smoothing out the skirt.

'So what?' he replies. 'Anyway, it's only to borrow. I'll fetch you a towel to dry your hair.'

I've been dagging to see inside this house but now I'm here I feel some awkward – standing in Ellen's own bedroom where she sleeps and dresses, brushes her hair, and does her school work by the looks of it . . . It feels as if she's watching me, hiding under the bed or at the back of the wardrobe, about to jump out and tell me off for trespassing. But I do as Jack says and take my wet clothes off and pull Ellen's dress over my head, staring at myself in the glass – it doesn't look like me, but then it doesn't look like her either, just a strange mix of the both of us. The dress feels cold and silky against my bare flesh, makes me shiver.

Jack walks back into the room and starts, like he's seen a ghost. 'It looks loads better on you than her.' He comes up close behind me and presses his body flat against my back. 'You're not wearing anything underneath, are you?' he says. I shake my head. He puts his hand up my skirt and strokes my bare arse.

'What 'ee doing?' I murmur, not stopping him. Jack lays his chin on my shoulder, gaking at my reflection as he takes the hem of Ellen's dress and starts to roll it up. Inch by inch it goes, over my knees and thighs, the grey silky cloth rising like a curtain, up over my navel towards my breasts, till we can see every naked white bit of me. We hold our breaths, staring at my body, both knowing what's going to happen next.

'You're so beautiful,' he says, and he suddenly wrenches the dress over my head and throws it on the floor.

'No, Jack,' I say as he turns my body round to face him and starts kissing me all over. 'We shouldn't be doin' this, not here . . .'

'Why not? We love each other . . .' My legs are feeling weak and I'm shaking. I want him so much but at the same I'm afeard, so afeard of what might happen if I let him go all the way.

'But, Jack, I don't think—'

'It's all right, I know what to do.' He takes off his shirt and pulls down his trousers, kicking them off his ankles and kissing me at the same time.

'It's just that – I can't – please, slow up, will 'ee!' But it's like he can't hear me, he's so lost in the smell and touch of my flesh. He's panting now and making hungry grunting noises, pushing me across the room and onto the bed. Ellen's bed. We do kiss and roll around and I try to take his hand away from between my legs. 'Don't do that,' I say.

'What's wrong?' he says, pulling away. 'You frightened it'll hurt?'

'No, I just don't like it, that's all.'

Jack looks at me, thunderstruck. 'What do you mean, you don't like it?' I turn my head away, biting my lip, cursing myself for letting those stupid words slip out. I try telling him I never said it but that only makes it worse: he's onto it now like a cat smelling a mouse in the wall. 'You know what it's like, do you? Tell me, Selina. Who else have you been with?'

'Nobody. I'm still a maid, I've told you a thousand times. I know nobody else round here believes me, but it's true.'

'You're not answering my question. I want to know what you mean.'

'I didn't mean nothing. Forget I ever said it, will 'ee? For God's sake, just do what you want and get on with it.' I take his hand and shove it back between my legs, but he pulls it away.

'Somebody's been touching you, I want to know who. Is it Jory?'

'No, it ain't.' It's the truth but I feel myself colouring up all the same.

'That GI who won't leave you alone, what's his name? It's him, isn't it? If he's had his hand up you I'll kill him.'

'Stop it, Jack! You'm disgusting!'

'I know you're lying to me, Selina. Don't lie to me!'

'All right then,' I say, getting angry now. 'If you must know it's my dad! He's been doing it to me since I was ten. Is that what 'ee wanted to hear?'

His mouth drops open and his whole face freezes over. 'Tom? Your own father? Oh my God . . . You telling me the truth?'

'It's when he's drunk mostly – he don't mean to hurt me, even tells me he loves me sometimes . . . He hates hisself for doin' it, always comes beggin' for forgiveness after.'

'I'll kill him!' Jack shouts. 'The dirty bastard, how could he? His own daughter!'

'But what if I'm not his daughter? It's not so bad then, is it?'

'Stop kidding yourself. You're his daughter and he damn well knows it!'

'But he says it's my fault for tempting him into sin . . . I reckon he's right too.' Tears are falling down my cheeks, hot wet tears – can't stop them now they've started. I sniff them up but still more come. 'Sometimes I do think I'm wicked inside. Wherever I go I cause trouble. I don't mean to but I do. I give men bad thoughts, I lead 'em astray, make them do things they shouldn't. I'm not like other girls – there's something wrong with me, I'm bad through and through. I'm not natural, Jack, not like other humans. Sometimes I think what my mother told me is true, I'm a merry—'

'Don't start all that again! For God's sake, you're not a mermaid, Selina! You're just a girl, a very pretty girl.'

'Don't shout at me, Jack. I'm just tellin' 'ee how I feel, how it feels bein' me. I'm afeard of myself!'

'It's not your fault, none of this is your fault,' he says, speaking softer now. 'Stop crying . . . Come here, let me hold you.'

He reaches out to me and curls me into a ball, wraps his arms around me and pulls the bedspread over my shoulders. And my whole self do heave and shake, wave upon wave of tears swell up in my throat and break in a sob, gushing out of my eyes and nose. But Jack just grips me tight, rocking me in his arms, drawing me into himself like he's bringing me to safe harbour. I don't know how long we lie together like this, me roaring and squalling and him comforting me, but at last all the shame and sadness is cried out of me. I do lift my head then and look him right in the face, and I see he's been crying too for his eyes are wet, two shiny brown pebbles washed by the tide.

'That settles it,' Jack says, speaking at last. 'It's been in my mind to get out of this place and I'm taking you with me. You're not spending another night under the same roof as that bastard. We're leaving, going home to London. We'll get married, start a new life. We'll go somewhere nobody will ever find us and never tell a soul where we are – not Penaluna, not the Rosewarnes, not even Nellie.'

'Yes, yes, I want it to be just the two of us,' I whisper. 'Nobody but the two of us. For ever.'

He pulls the pink bedspread right over our heads then, like a giant rose petal, and he kisses me again, more soft and gentle this time and twists my hair in his fingers. And I know for certain he's the only man in the world that truly loves me.

When my aunt met me at the station after school we were both in a distracted state. I had completely forgotten that we'd arranged to meet for supper before going to a whist drive at the Deep Sea Fishermen Mission. We sat in a restaurant on the harbour front, picking at our food – my mind still on the plane crash and hers, it would seem, on my uncle. Charles had been expected home the previous night after his 'business trip' but hadn't turned up.

'I do hope nothing's gone wrong,' she said, folding and re-folding her napkin.

I didn't pay her much attention that evening. Her concerns seemed so trivial by comparison to what had happened earlier in the day. My uncle was always going away, never telling us where or why. I was surprised she hadn't grown used to it. Besides, when he *was* at home there was only trouble between him and Jack. What did it matter that he was a little late? At least he hadn't been killed in a plane crash. But I kept such uncharitable thoughts to myself . . .

We sat in the draughty hall and played a few cheerless rounds of whist while outside the rain began to pour in torrents – we couldn't see it but we could hear it well enough, pummelling the windows behind the blackout curtains. My aunt said she hoped it would stop soon as she'd not thought to bring an umbrella and then somebody else said an umbrella would be useless tonight: gales were expected later – storm force ten, the shipping forecast had said. At the break, I stood by the tea urn, sipping my tea slowly, eavesdropping on the various conversations as people filed by. The talk was mainly about the Warwick, the intense search that had gone on all day in the sea around the crash site; they'd even sent divers down to the wreckage. Somebody claimed that the lifeboat crew had been sworn to secrecy as to who, or more importantly what, had been on board. Nobody would tell them how many bodies they were supposed to be searching for but it was certainly more than the two that had turned up so far.

My aunt looked worried although she pretended it was dis-approval. 'All this idle tittle-tattle, it's supposed to be strictly forbidden,' she complained. The organizer clapped for our attention to start the second half. 'This must be exceedingly tedious for you. Why don't you go home now, dear? I'll be back as soon as it's over.'

I left the Mission Hall and walked briskly along the pave-ment. A couple of shopkeepers were piling up sandbags and boarding up their doors. The spring tides were unusually high – in a few hours' time the water would spill over the harbour wall and seep onto the quayside. Protected as we were in the lee of the hills, I could still feel the rising wind against my face, hear it banging distant gates, shaking up the trees. Out on the open sea, squalls of rain were pounding the surface of the water, ripping up the spindrift, the fish diving to the depths while the birds fled inland. The last of the winter trawlers, one of them Belgian, were sheltering in the inner harbour and the quay was crowded with small, empty craft, their anchors sunk deep into the mud, nudging each other as they began to lift with the rising tide.

Afterwards I tried to remember whether I'd noticed Tom Penaluna's boat amongst them, but it was dark and rainy, and besides, I had no reason to look for it. Nor was I thinking about where Jack might be. I was feeling wet and miserable, cross with my aunt because she had made me go on ahead by myself.

It was a two-mile walk along the twisting lane. Within minutes I was soaked through, my shoes sloshing with water. My school bag was heavy and I had a painful stitch in my side. Rain dripped off the brim of my wilting felt hat and trickled down my back. I ran into the house, threw off my wet coat, drew the blackout curtains and switched on the lights. As I entered the sitting room I heard a faint creaking noise coming from the room above.

I wasn't frightened by the sound, assuming it must be Uncle Charles, home from work and changing his clothes. I went into the hallway and called his name, but there was no reply, so I climbed the stairs and stood on the upstairs landing, trying to locate the noise. The creaking was definitely coming from my bedroom, so without a second thought I opened the door and walked right in.

Jack and Selina were lying naked on my bed. I couldn't see her face because Jack was on top of her, but there was no mistaking the long golden hair spread out across the pillow. Her slim white legs were splayed either side of his and her knees were bent, shaking slightly. Neither of them had noticed I was there.

I stood and watched them, horrified yet unable to pull myself away, a sickness welling in my stomach, my mouth running dry. My twin brother and Selina Penaluna were having full, proper sex and I'd never even been kissed.

After a few moments – maybe more, I don't know how long I was standing there – Jack lifted his head and let out a long, deep groan. Selina clutched him tightly to her and he fell on her chest, lying quite still with his head tucked next to hers, his straight dark hair against her waves of gold. I could see her face then: her eyes were closed but she was crying, tears spilling onto her cheeks. I was desperate to leave the room but my legs refused to move.

Jack rolled over onto his back and saw me standing there, staring. I was mesmerized by Selina's naked body, her skin taut and marble white, her stomach flat, hips slender, firm smooth breasts the size of a man's cupped hand. And I realized in that moment that she was utterly perfect. I was so transfixed by her beauty that I didn't hear Jack shouting at me, didn't see him throw the book. It struck me on the arm and I barely flinched.

Selina sat up and pulled the sheet across. 'Was 'ee watching us?' she asked simply. I shook my head fiercely.

'Course she was . . .' said Jack. 'Get out! Get out!'

I staggered out backwards and stood on the landing for a couple of seconds. The walls were spinning round me, I felt sick, thought I was going to faint. I stumbled blindly into my aunt and uncle's room and threw myself face down on their bed, burying my face in the coverlet. My stupid, ridiculously childish school uniform smelled damp, my stockinged feet were soaking wet. I could hear Jack and Selina moving around next door – in *my* bedroom – gathering up their clothes and getting dressed. I was hurt, enraged, revolted. Why were they in my room and not Jack's? What did it mean? How dare that – that whore – come to our house and behave in this despicable way? What if my aunt or uncle had found them? I wanted to confront them, but I couldn't. Besides, I had no right. I had stood and watched them like a Peeping Tom.

A few minutes later I heard them running down the stairs. They left the house by the back door, slamming it heavily behind them. I managed to get up and went over to the side window, just in time to see Jack open the gate. He took Selina's hand and they turned towards the sandy beach, rounding the corner and disappearing into the darkness. Jack didn't look back once. I don't know how but I knew that I'd never see them again.

TWENTY-TWO

My bedroom was the last place in the world I wanted to be after what had happened there. Just the thought of entering 'the scene of the crime' made me feel physically sick but I could not remain in my aunt and uncle's room, still wearing my wet clothes, snivelling in the dark like a forgotten baby. Either of them could come back at any moment and they would expect, or more likely demand, an explanation. What could I possibly say without causing huge embarrassment? I decided it was my sacrificial duty as a loving daughter to protect them from discovering the sordid truth – for their sakes, not for Jack's, and certainly not for Selina's – although I was convinced that she was entirely to blame for this ugly incident and would have loved to see her punished.

I tidied my aunt and uncle's room first, smoothing out the bedspread, and then went downstairs. I didn't know exactly where Jack and Selina had been but I suspected she'd had a good rummage around, so I scurried from room to room, checking that everything was in its normal place, plumping up cushions, putting the cake tin back in the pantry, tucking my uncle's chair back under his desk. My aunt would be home any minute and I had to make sure that I'd removed any evidence of Jack and Selina's presence. I was still in a fractious state and not at all confident that I could hide it from Clara, so I left a note on the kitchen table to say that I had a headache and had retired for the night. Now I had to tackle my bedroom.

I knew it was going to be an unpleasant task, but I was unprepared for the fresh shock that hit me as I entered. It was if the room had undergone some magical transformation: the colours and the furniture were the same yet it looked totally different; it didn't feel as if it belonged to me any more. My neatly made bed with its pretty pink candlewick cover was in complete disarray – the starched white sheet crumpled, its corners pulled free, the blankets tossed to the floor. When I saw the indentation of her head still on the pillow I almost vomited.

I wanted to tear off the sheets and burn them, but I couldn't even change the linen without my aunt noticing. I had no choice but to remake the bed – *their* bed, it seemed now – smoothing out the wrinkles and tucking in the sheets as if I were the maid, covering up my mistress's marital indiscretions. As I shook the feather pillow the smell of their lovemaking wafted across the room like bitter perfume. Their ghosts were everywhere, mocking me.

I could sense Selina standing at my window, rifling through my drawers, looking at my school books. She'd even tried on my clothes by the look of it. My new silk dress that Clara had adapted from one of her own was lying in a crumpled heap on the floor by the wardrobe. As I hung it up again I picked a long golden hair from the shoulder. The thought that it had been on Selina's perfect body made me start to cry again – it was my favourite dress and suited me well. Now I never wanted to wear it again, but of course I would have to, or it would arouse suspicion. Wherever I turned I was completely trapped.

That night, lying on the same sheets, stained with their lovemaking, was pure torture. I turned from side to side, my eyelids heavy but my mind fully awake, going over and over the events of the hours before. I could not get the images of their naked bodies out of my head. I banished them to the recesses of my mind but they came back a few moments later; with each attack the picture became stronger, more vivid. This self-induced assault went on all night, wearing me down until I gave in and wallowed in the pain. I felt nauseous, unable to take full breaths. I sobbed into the pillow till my eyes stung with tears.

Outside, the storm was living up to its promises. Spindrift was under siege, battered by the relentless wind that whipped violently round the house, hurling the slates from the roof, rattling the window frames, shrieking down the chimneys, hammering on the doors . . . The rain poured out of the sky like an emptying bucket, and as the tide rose to its greatest height, so the mountainous waves hurled themselves against the rocks, grinding across the shingle, leaping over the sea wall and flooding the cliff path in hissing, seething foam. For a while we were surrounded by water on all four sides and I imagined the house a fishing boat, breaking adrift from its moorings, tossing about in the furious sea, lifted up by the waves and thrown onto the rocks; the floorboards splintering like deck planks, the curtains tearing like sails.

Why did it hurt so? I can't explain. Somehow I felt as if Jack and Selina had performed this act purely to spite me, engineering me to be a witness to the mockery of my own virginity. I know now that it was a ridiculous, self-dramatizing interpretation – they were simply making love and I happened to walk in on them. Although why they chose to do it in my bedroom I will never understand. I was shocked, embarrassed, and I felt guilty for having stood and watched them, although at the time I wasn't prepared to admit it to myself. I had stumbled into that mysterious dreamlike world that lovers create, that intense chemistry of the senses, where hours pass in seconds, where nobody else matters and every-thing is forgotten. They had been utterly oblivious to my presence, rendering me invisible, irrelevant, reduced to nothingness.

This feeling of insignificance haunted me. I was not and never would be the object of anyone's desire. I was incapable of inciting such passion – too sensible, too clever, too plain . . . Maybe I would find a husband eventually but it would be a staid, practical relationship, without risk or danger. No man would ever love me in the all-consuming way Jack loved Selina – but I craved it beyond all else.

During that long, sleepless night I discovered that jealousy is the most powerful of all human emotions. It devoured my reason. I let it take root, choke all the goodness in me; I fed and watered it long beyond its natural life. But I was only sixteen then, entirely lacking in self-knowledge, with nobody to confide in or give perspective, to guide me out of my torment. In the end it was simply the passing of time that made my jealousy wither. But it's a stubborn weed; you can never completely get rid of it no matter how deeply you dig.

By the morning I had a fever. My aunt put it down to walking home in the rain and not drying off properly. I was sent back to bed with a hot-water bottle and extra blankets to make me 'sweat it out'.

'I've promised to go to a committee meeting for Salute the Soldier week,' she said, closing my curtains. 'Your uncle came home in the early hours this morning and is asleep, so try not to disturb him unless it's absolute necessary.'

'Did Jack come home?' I asked timidly.

'No,' she replied wearily. 'I haven't seen him since yesterday morning. Get some sleep, dear, and I'll be back as soon as I can.'

But sleep was the last thing I wanted to do. I waited for an hour, then got up and dressed. My gabardine coat was still damp, so I put on a woollen jacket and crept out of the house. The storm had subsided but the air was still wet, the sky heavy with grey scudding clouds. The cliff path was a muddy stream, impassable without rubber boots, so I turned left and walked along the front of the sandy bay, weaving in and out of the GIs' gleaming trucks. Before I realized it, I had climbed to the top of the hill and was halfway to Padstow.

I felt light-headed, intoxicated by the fever, first burning hot then shivering cold, but still I walked on, a stranger to myself, not in command of my own body. I had no idea why I was doing it, but one foot went before the other, propelling me forwards, up towards the Daymark, taking the short cut along the lane that led to Langham's farm, then down into town, drawn as if by some magnetic force to take the street that curved down towards the harbour.

The town was heaving with Americans. A small convoy of trucks charged up the hill, the men looking from side to side as if on a frantic sightseeing tour. On the quayside a small group of Belgian fishermen were sitting on the long bench, smoking, gossiping. Today I felt just as much a stranger as any of them, as if I had been carried away by the storm and washed up onto a foreign shore. The streets, the shops, the cafés, the fish sheds – all seemed new to me.

I wandered up and down, dizzy and breathless, not knowing where I was going or why I had come. I suppose I must have been delirious. So much so that I don't remember who first told me about the *Louisa May*. I heard the story in snippets, from different people at different times and all in the wrong order, like trying to do a jigsaw puzzle with the vital pieces missing. Some details I didn't find out until I heard witnesses speak at the inquest, several weeks later. Nobody will ever know exactly what took place.

I was told that a fisherman called Ned Gibson had gone out at daybreak to see what the storm had done to his lobster pots and found the *Louisa May* – or what was left of it – wedged between some rocks just beyond the mouth of the estuary. He hurried back to raise the alarm, and found Penaluna standing on the jetty outside his cottage, sucking angrily on his pipe, in a foul mood because of last night's storm – the tide had been too low when he'd come back from fishing the previous morning and he'd had to leave his boat moored in a cove further along the estuary. There had been such a fuss over the plane crash rescue operation that he'd not had a chance to bring her into safe harbour. He'd got up before dawn to check the boat and discovered his punt missing. To make matters worse his daughter hadn't come home last night and he'd had to make his own breakfast.

'Might Selina have tried to bring her in?' suggested the fisherman.

'Never,' scoffed Penaluna. 'She may be wild, but she's not stupid.'

'Then where is she?' asked the fisherman gently.

The lifeboat was summoned immediately. Penaluna, being part of the normal crew, insisted he go along although everyone said it was a bad idea and he should stay. By the time I arrived at the harbour they had already left. They were out for several hours, searching the bays on either side of the estuary. More pieces of the *Louisa May* were found – the splintered bow, the shattered wheelhouse, an oar, a wooden box of tools. Then the coxswain spotted something on the small beach of a cove to the west of the Point.

I was standing on North Quay when I saw the lifeboat

heading back towards us. I'd been told by then that they were out looking for Selina, and I knew in my heart that Jack would have been with her. The craft shuddered to a halt a hundred yards ahead, and tied up. Two of the crew climbed up the rusty iron ladder and then turned round to take hold of a large, heavy object wrapped in a blanket that was being passed up to them. Everyone knew it was a body. Several people gathered round as it was laid down on the quayside. Tom Penaluna was the last man in the lifeboat – he just sat there, mesmerized, unable to move.

'Looks like they found her,' someone said.

I ran along the quayside, pushing through the growing crowd of onlookers. 'Let me see!' I shouted. 'My brother, he was with Selina . . . Let me see!'

'Give way to the young lady . . . She needs to have a look . . .' The crowd shuffled back, parted to let me through to the front.

It was a man's body sure enough, a little older than Jack, but a young man nonetheless. He was wearing corduroy trousers and a collarless shirt. His face was cut and charred black as if it had been burned, his short hair matted with dried blood. Bile instantly rose up to my throat. I thought I was going to be sick. But I shook my head and swallowed the bitter taste.

'Anyone recognize him?' asked one of the crew.

'Perhaps he's from the plane crash,' someone suggested. There was a murmur of agreement at the back of the crowd.

'What about the girl?'

'No sign yet.'

My body was starting to sway, my legs felt soft and heavy, there was a hissing in my ears and all I could see was a swirling blackness . . . When I came to, I was lying on a bench in the bar of The Ship, being cared for by Ivy Lanyon, the barmaid, the warm taste of brandy on my lips.

'Have they found him yet, Ivy?' I murmured. 'Tell me, is he dead?'

TWENTY-THREE

The lifeboat crew soon abandoned the search for survivors. My aunt and uncle were told that the police would let us know as soon as the bodies turned up: it could take weeks, even months, they said. They might be washed up further west down the coast or east towards the Bristol Channel – it was extraordinary how far they could travel with the currents. Then again, they might never turn up at all.

I relentlessly played out Jack and Selina's death scene in my mind – the wind, pounding rain, darkness, waves sweeping over them like a thick black cloak, the splintering of wood, Selina screaming, her fingers slipping through his grasp, Jack knocked overboard, gulping in water, struggling and then releasing, giving himself up, sinking . . . Someone had told me, years earlier, that drowning was the most peaceful way to go and I tried to find comfort in the thought. I imagined Jack's body gliding effortlessly through the water, the waves his funeral bier, gently carrying him towards us. I prayed that God would deliver him to the shore and that one morning I would look out of the window and see his body laid out on the rocks – clean white shirt, best trousers, arms crossed against his chest, just as I'd seen my grandfather in the front room of our old house. It wasn't that I wanted Jack to be dead – I just wanted him to come home.

On the surface, Clara was in a worse state than me. She withered like a rose in a dry vase; the colour in her lips and cheeks faded, she refused to wash or brush her hair. Every day she appeared in the same crumpled dress – not mourning black but an arbitrary pale brown – I don't think she even took it off to go to bed. Neighbours called round to offer their condolences, to ask if there was anything they could do to help, but Clara just stared at them blankly, wouldn't even ask them in for a cup of tea. Alice Nancarrow, Jory's mother, brought round pasties and vegetables; even Mrs Pascoe turned up with a mutton stew. I was left to cope with the chores and made a few feeble efforts to cook for my uncle. Charles was very impatient with Clara. He shook her by the shoulders and told her to pull herself together.

'There's no death without a corpse,' he said, 'and until such time as they find his body, we shall assume he is alive.' Charles even had a theory that Jack and Selina hadn't take the *Louisa May* out at all, but had eloped and gone to London. He suspected that Selina was pregnant and that they'd run away. 'They'll come back once their money runs out,' he assured us, 'and we'll all be reunited.'

But this did not make sense to me. Why encourage false hopes in my aunt when it was clear that Jack had drowned? Better to let her experience her grief now rather than store it up for later. I thought my uncle cruel and even told him so, but he wasn't really listening. He sat for hours in his study – reading, writing, maybe just staring out of the window at the sea, I don't know what he was doing – the door was always shut and I was forbidden to disturb him. I knew he was desperately upset, but he wouldn't show it – if he gave in to his emotions it would mean that Jack was dead.

Rumour had it that Tom Penaluna had locked himself in his cottage and taken to the bottle, distraught over the loss of his daughter and his boat. I debated whether I should visit him, thinking he might know more about what had happened, but I was too scared to go by myself. I thought he might be blaming Jack for Selina's death and take his anger out on me. I asked Charles to go with me, but he refused – 'I have nothing whatever to say to that fool,' was all he would say on the subject.

Ten days passed and still there was no sign of the bodies. Clara decided to search for Jack herself. One day she would go west, the next east, walking for several hours along the coast path, then turning round and following the same route back. I asked Charles to accompany her, but he wouldn't – he said it was a waste of time because he was sure Jack was still alive, although the air would do Clara good. He didn't seem able to see the danger she was in. So I had to go with her instead.

We climbed to the top of the cliffs and hovered above the beaches like birds of prey looking for carrion. As we reached each sickening curve in the headland Clara would stand on the very edge, her uncombed hair and thin brown dress quivering in the wind like feathers. She would stare down, her eyes darting back and forth across the cove, looking, looking – for a shoe, a piece of clothing, a leg perhaps, poking out between the rocks. All I could do was stand next to her, trembling with fear, watching out for the slightest movement forward, poised to grab her if she began to sway. But even at those moments when I was sure she was about to jump, I could not ignore the overwhelming beauty of what lay below – the water at its darkest, thickest blue, white foam seething on the granite, the sweep of wet virgin sand . . .

After a few minutes she would shake her head and whisper, 'No, he's not there.' On she would go to the next bay and I would follow, standing beside her once more on the brink of madness, thinking that if this went on much longer the only corpses on the beach would be our own.

We were on our way back one afternoon – a westward walk towards the lighthouse, mercifully cut short by a burst of rain – when we saw two black cars parked outside the house and a tall man in a black overcoat standing sentry at the door.

'They've found him,' said Clara. 'They've found my boy.' She ran up to the front door and almost fell on the man. 'Where is he? Tell me, where did you find him?' she begged, tugging at his sleeve. 'Near here? Which bay?'

But the man didn't reply, just nodded in the direction of the hallway.

'I don't think this is about Jack,' I murmured as we stepped inside.

My uncle was in the drawing room, sitting upright in his leather armchair by the fire, his hands cuffed. Another man, older than the one outside and with a heavy moustache, seemed to be guarding him.

'What's the matter?' I asked.

'Have they found the body?' asked my aunt. Charles shook his head and opened his mouth to say something, but the man put a restraining hand on his shoulder.

'Mr Rosewarne has been placed under arrest,' the man said. 'I'm afraid he is not at liberty to talk to you. And I would be obliged if for the moment you would remain in this room. We are undertaking a search of the house.'

'Have they found the body?' repeated Clara, not understanding.

'No, not yet,' I said quietly. 'Let's sit down over here, shall we?' Charles gave me a brief, thankful smile as I led her to the other armchair.

'My aunt is not well,' I explained. 'My brother drowned two weeks ago and—'

'Yes, we know,' interrupted the man gruffly.

'It might help if you could you tell us what my uncle is being accused of.'

'Sorry, miss, but I can't.'

We sat in silence, listening to the house being torn apart. There were at least two more men conducting the search, one in the kitchen, the other in my uncle's study – opening drawers and emptying cupboards, pulling books from the shelves and throwing them to the floor. I imagined them lifting the rugs and looking for loose floorboards, pressing wooden panels, peering up the chimneys. I remembered Tom

Penaluna telling us that Spindrift had once been a smuggler's cottage and was full of secret hiding places. I started to wonder if these men would find them and what my uncle might have hidden there. The memory of Highworth's Fertilizers with its bomb-making instructions loomed large in my mind. Was this all my fault? Or was Charles indeed a Nazi spy?

The ordeal lasted for two hours, during which my aunt became increasingly agitated and confused. Eventually the guard relented and I was allowed into the kitchen to make her a cup of tea – the room looked as if it had been burgled: they'd even emptied the tea caddy all over the counter and I had to scrape the leaves into the pot. Meanwhile my uncle remained silent in his chair, staring down at his cuffed hands. He did not look guilty or ashamed, just slightly indignant, which gave me hope that he was innocent. I desperately needed him to communicate with me, to tell me his side of the story with a flicker of his eyes or a twitch of his mouth, but he would not meet my gaze.

Whether the men found what they were looking for I don't know, but they finally finished their search and told my uncle it was time to leave. He nodded and stood up, walking across the room towards the door, pausing only briefly to take a last fond look at my poor, bewildered aunt. 'Take good care of her,' he whispered to me. I nodded bravely, fighting back the tears.

'Come along now, sir,' said the guard, prodding him forward.

As Charles left the house Clara leaped up from her seat and

charged after him. 'Let me identify him!' she shouted. 'I'm his mother, it should be me.' As the men put Charles into the back of a car Clara tried to get in beside him. She threw herself on top of my uncle and begged him to take her with him. The officers dragged her out, struggling and screaming. They were in no mood for a scene.

'I'm sorry, terribly sorry,' I cried. 'Please, she doesn't understand.'

'Take her indoors!' ordered one of the men who had been searching. He shoved my aunt towards me and she fell sobbing into my arms. I looked across at Charles but he was staring ahead with a blank gaze, lifting both hands to adjust the knot of his tie. The chap with the moustache got in next to him and my uncle flinched slightly as he slammed the door. Then the cars reversed up the cliff path, disappearing round the corner just as Jack and Selina had done two weeks before. It felt as if everyone was retreating from my life. I took my aunt back inside and opened the bottle of whisky Charles had been saving for Christmas. It seemed like the only thing to do.

There was no word from my uncle, or from anyone else for that matter. We still had no idea where he'd been taken or what crime he'd been accused of; when I went to the police station to enquire they said they knew nothing about the case – it was 'not their department'. Unfortunately several people had seen Charles being driven away and gossip was rife. The initial rush of sympathy we'd received after Jack's death quickly evaporated and I felt that the Nancarrows were the only friends I had left. Miss Ravenhead, Charles's secretary at the Padstow office, came to see my aunt, panicking because his clients were asking awkward questions and she didn't know what answer to give them. Clara completely denied that he'd been arrested, insisting he was away on business, as per the usual story. I couldn't work out whether she was deliberately covering up or was still confused.

Without Charles, Clara sank into a deep depression. She stopped walking the cliffs and took to her bed. I would leave in the morning to go to school and find her still there when I returned, lying on her side, staring at the wallpaper. Her body had shut down all but its most essential functions – if Clara had found the physical strength to hang herself or slash her wrists I'm sure she would have done it. As it was she could barely move; even sitting up to sip a glass of water required huge effort. When she rose to use the bathroom she tottered about the room like a woman who had forgotten how to walk. She hardly seemed to know who I was, answering my questions with a shake or nod of the head, speaking only in whispers.

Spindrift was cold and silent, trapped in time. I could not bear so many empty rooms. Charles's study had been completely turned upside down on the day of the arrest – they'd pulled the drawers right out of the desk, thrown all his files and papers onto the floor and forced open the safe. I had immediately started to tidy up, but Clara had made me come out of the room and locked the door – now she was ill in bed I wanted to finish the job, but I couldn't find where she'd hidden the key.

I was wrung out, exhausted by the endless waiting – for news of Charles, for the bodies to be found. There was nothing I could do but sit at home and listen for a knock at the front door. I jumped at every sound, rushed to the window whenever I heard footsteps on the path. Just a few yards away on the other side of the hedge lay the real world of which I no longer felt a part. Hundreds of allied servicemen were preparing for the invasion of France – the village had never been so bustling. Convoys of trucks thundered out of the village in the middle of the night, only to return a few days later with hungry, weary, dirty soldiers. Gunners fired practice rounds from the cliff tops; soldiers in full kit marched back and forth across the sandy beach carrying boats on their shoulders and then tried to launch them into the waves.

The entire country was caught up in a frenzy of anticipation – the invasion was clearly going to happen soon, but when? It could be weeks, maybe days; the order could even come within the next hour. The GIs were nervous and fidgety: the not knowing was driving them crazy. Was this their last game of baseball on the beach, their last pint of English beer? Would they get a chance to say goodbye to the girl they'd fallen in love with, or to thank the family that had squeezed together to offer them a room? Myself, my aunt, the entire allied forces, even the Germans – we were all waiting. Just waiting . . .

TWENTY-FOUR

Hi there Cassie,

Thanks for getting in touch. It's good to know that people are visiting our website and want to know more about our work. Pleased you like my paintings, and yes, I am the Paul Blanchard that did the painting 'Lost at Sea' that's in your mermaid book, though I did that piece way back in the fifties and my work has moved on a lot since then, as you can see from the gallery section on the website. I'm more into impressionism now, in the general sense anyway.

It's true I've always been fascinated by mermaids, tho' in the last ten years or so I seemed to have drifted into other areas — my recent work is not so figurative, I guess. The west coast of England is full of mermaid legends, as I expect you know, but in fact you can find them all over the world. In Brittany they call them the Morgans, the Germans call them Meerfrau, the Danish Maremind; a Livonian folk story reckons they are Pharaoh's children, drowned in the Red Sea. Then of course there are the Sirens, luring sailors onto the rocks by their song . . . There are several books I could recommend if you're interested. There's lots of stuff on the Net too — most of it I don't agree with. But then, I'm from an older generation . . .

So you're an artist too — that's great — I'd love to see some of your work. Do you have any material with you? Can you e-mail me images from where you are? I think it's a really good idea to do some travelling, get some experience of real life and pick up influences from other cultures, but make sure you go home at the end and DO THAT COURSE. When I was your age I didn't have a clue what I wanted to do with my life. I had no proper art training and had to learn the hard way. So you go for it!

All the best, PB

Hi again Paul,
Thanks for getting back to me so fast. Glad I got the right artist, phew! I'm in England at the moment, in a little village by the sea in Cornwall. Actually I was born here (well, in London) but my parents emigrated to Oz when I was a kid. I'm staying with my grandmother in this

amazing house right on the cliff edge — she's moving and I'm helping her sort stuff out. Then I'm off on my travels again with my boyfriend. We're going round Europe for a bit, then across to the States, so maybe we'll get as far as California and can come and see your gallery.

I know this is going to sound like a really weird question, and I feel a bit embarrassed even asking, but is the mermaid in the picture based on anyone you know? It's just that my boyfriend's grandfather thinks he recognizes her. I know this is incredibly unlikely, but he's got it into his head and wants me to ask. His name is Jory Nancarrow and the girl he thinks is in the picture was called Selina Penaluna — my grandmother knew her too. Apparently she had some idea that she was a mermaid!! It's quite a sad story actually because she drowned when she was only sixteen, over sixty years ago. Anyway, Jory wants to know if you were ever stationed near Padstow in North Cornwall during the Second World War cos he thinks you might have known her. Hope you don't mind me asking — please don't think I'm mad!

Thanks,

Cassie

Hi Cassie,

Sorry it's taken a few days to get back to you. We had a new exhibition opening at the gallery and I didn't get a chance to check my e-mail. I'm afraid I don't know this girl you mention, and no, I've never been to Cornwall. I wasn't even in your country during the war. And the mermaid in the painting was just some art student I met years ago. Sounds like a really sad story about the kid that drowned. Sorry again not to be more help.

Best of luck with your travels etc.,
PB

'So much for that then,' I say, handing the e-mail printouts back to Cassie.

'Jory was disappointed – he really thought he was onto something.'

'Silly old fool . . .'

'Well, I suppose it was worth asking.'

'What difference would it make if Paul Blanchard had known her?'

'I don't know, it's just interesting, I suppose.'

I'm reluctant to admit it, but I know what she means – it *is* interesting, although I'm not sure why. Researching Paul Blanchard has been like playing detectives, following clues, amassing facts, trying to make connections . . . Cassie has been busying away on Scott's computer and printed out everything she can find. I think it's helped to occupy her while Scott has been working, and no doubt Jory has enjoyed the attention. Of course it's irrelevant now, but it turns out that Paul Blanchard is the oldest member of a small consortium of painters who run a gallery in Venice, California. Cassie has printed some of his more recent works off the website – wild seascapes featuring some rather over-enthusiastic wielding of the palette knife in my opinion. I can't make out any mermaids peeping between the crude slashes of colour. There's a photo of Blanchard in the biography section – standing by his easel, brush in hand, prodding at the canvas, surrounded by acres of pale untouched sand and a distant smudge of blue sea. The camera is too far away to pick out his features, but he's tanned, grey-haired and bearded, dressed in traditional artist's garb – paint-spattered jeans, baggy jumper, flat cap. He looks like a typical painter: there's an air of anonymity about him, a separateness. His interest lies in what he can see around him, not in his reflection in the mirror. So it surprises me to read that he is married with three daughters and four 'wonderful grandchildren'.

'Isn't the Internet incredible?' I say to Cassie. 'Just type in a name and you get all this.' I know it's just my age, but I am a little uncomfortable with this fast-food approach to gathering information. In only a few seconds we have gone from complete ignorance to knowing far more than we need to about Paul Blanchard. Cassie has even formed an entirely redundant intimacy with the man via e-mail exchanges. We now realize that he's of no use to us so we can discard him, relieved not to have wasted more of our time. In a year's time Cassie will find his e-mail address on her Friends and Family list and won't be able to remember who he is.

'I found this essay on some university website,' says Cassie, interrupting my idle thoughts. 'There's a couple of paragraphs that mention him. It's not very complimentary, makes him sound like a bit of a pervert.' She takes the sheaf of papers from me and flicks through to find the appropriate part. 'Here . . . *In the sixties, Paul Blanchard, known for his obsession with mermaids, moved his studio right onto the beach, where he found himself surrounded by free models, sunbathing half naked in front of his window . . .*'

'Not very charitable . . .'

'You should read the rest of it – a bit wacky, but interesting. I've been thinking, I might do a special project on mermaids for my course.' She gets up and shakes out her hair. 'Anyway, I'm going to have a shower now – the one at the farm has packed up.'

'OK. Don't be too long, dear – I'm expecting some more viewers.'

'No probs, I'll be quick.' She skips up the stairs two at a time.

I take the Internet essay and my coffee and sit on the window seat overlooking Rocky Beach. The morning sun has already warmed the cushion, and I sit with my back leaning against the inside wall of the bay, noting how the paint is already peeling off the woodwork, although I had the outside painted only last year.

Paul Blanchard, or so this article argues, belongs to a species of male artist that has used and abused the mermaid icon. In nineteenth- and twentieth-century art the mermaid was portrayed in either of two ways: the nubile young girl innocently sunbathing naked, or the lustful siren, leading good men to a watery death. But whatever angle the Victorian artists took they were simply using mermaid mythology as an excuse for painting nude women – soft porn in the drawing room. Whereas in fact the mermaid is an ancient feminist symbol, representing the power of female unconscious desire. Through her, women can dive beneath the surface of their emotions and explore the hidden depths of their passion, finding the truth of their inner selves.

I heave a sigh and look out across the bay. There is no wind today and the ocean is a sheet of rippled green glass. The sun catches the jagged shards of water and I imagine diving in, shattering the brittle surface and swimming down to the depths of my unconscious desire. But the bottom of that sea is cold and dark. Even if I found a buried treasure chest and hauled it to the surface, I suspect it would be full of sand.

Cassie comes downstairs twenty minutes later, her bright hair scrunched up at the back of her head, held in place by a red silk flower.

'See, I told you I wouldn't take long,' she chirrups. Her jeans are slung low beneath her waist and she's wearing a white top cut off just above the midriff; her belly button sparkles. She looks so young and full of – what is it, exactly?

I was going to say full of life, but that seems a very poor description. She is in love, yes, and that gives her eyes a certain glimmer, but there's more to it than that. Her whole attitude is different to mine – she is expectant, looking forward, ready to move on, whereas I am standing still and looking behind me. She makes me feel so very old.

'What did you make of it – the essay?' Cassie asks.

'Oh, yes. Interesting.'

'A bit of a feminist rant, don't you think?'

'Why is feminism such a dirty word these days?' I let out a weary sigh.

'Oh, you know, that bit about women needing to take control of female symbols. I don't see what the problem is – we're already in control, aren't we?' She laughs.

'I have a different view of what the mermaid symbolizes,' I venture, after a long thoughtful pause. 'To me, it means a certain kind of woman whom I can't relate to, whom I distrust and ultimately despise.'

'You're talking about Selina.'

'Yes, I suppose so – whenever I see a mermaid I automatically think of Selina. I have met a few others like her over the years, pale imitations but still dangerous. Believe me, they're to be avoided whenever possible.'

'I don't understand. What was so bad about her?' Cassie sits down on the sofa and tucks her feet under her bottom.

'She unnerved me, threw me off balance. I couldn't work out what was going on inside her head. She was not what I'd call a woman's woman.'

'Explain.'

I sit down on the chair opposite, smoothing my skirt over my legs. 'She didn't know how to relate to other females. I was probably the closest she ever came to having a girl friend and yet she knew nothing about me. We were wary, suspicious of each other; there seemed to be no common ground. As if we were from different species . . .'

'Maybe you were. You were human, she was half fish.' Cassie laughs.

'I'm serious,' I retort. 'True female friendship is about sharing, confiding, confessing our mistakes, comforting each other when we fail. Men are more competitive: they don't want to let their guard down by exposing their weaknesses because they never know when their friend might become their enemy. They are essentially rivals, whereas women – and I'm generalizing here of course – are essentially allies.'

'I don't agree. Women are always competing with each other for guys – they might pretend they aren't, but in reality it's all-out war.'

'Why should we compete for men? It's such a waste of our energies,' I retort. 'We already have enormous power over them – I mean sexual power, of course.'

'I thought they were supposed to have sexual power over us.'

'Physical power, economic power – yes, I grant you – but sexual power? Not at all. How many times has an intelligent, successful man thrown away his career for the sake of a bit of casual sex? It's all too easy to defeat men that way. But that absolutely does not mean we should use that power; quite the contrary, I think it demeans us.'

'And that's why you despised Selina? Because she used her sexual power?'

'Yes, although I don't believe she did it consciously. Selina did everything by instinct.'

'Then you can't blame her,' replies Cassie triumphantly. 'It wasn't her fault she was so beautiful. You could say she was a victim, that she didn't have any choice. If that was how men saw her . . .'

'You're right of course, but . . .' I pause. 'She played up to it, that's all.'

'Sounds like you were jealous.'

'Of course I was jealous,' I snap. 'But remember, she also caused my brother's death.'

'I can see why you didn't like her, but how could you be jealous of somebody who drowned when they were sixteen?' Cassie persists. 'Look what happened to you – you went to Cambridge, became a lawyer, had a brilliant career, married, had kids . . .'

'Yes, yes, but I didn't know that at the time. I told myself that what mattered most was studying and going to university, but all I really wanted was to fall in love.'

'But you got both – a degree and Granddad!' Cassie smiles. 'Selina should have been jealous of *you*.'

'Yes, you're right,' I reply, feeling a little flustered. 'Things turned out well for me in the end. I have much to be thankful for.' Cassie raises her eyebrows and I instantly realize how inadequate and lacking in enthusiasm that sounded. I wish I could explain myself properly to her – the words are there somewhere in my brain, but I can't bring them forth.

The truth is, I have always felt there is some gap in my life, some elusive element. I have been haunted by a mild discontent, a vague yet persistent conviction that I have been excluded from something, that the real drama is being played on stage while I am watching from the wings. What is it that I have missed out on? Grand passion maybe, the violence of emotion, the feeling that your heart is breaking, a love worth dying for . . . But that sounds so ridiculously melodramatic. And disloyal to Richard. I don't know what's wrong with me. Do I really not want to be free of Selina Penaluna after all these years? I am seventy-seven, for God's sake – nobody expects me to be slim or beautiful any more. I'm barely required to be sane.

If Richard had still been alive he would have talked all this through with me sensibly, helped me put things into proportion. He was always very good like that, reasonable in arguments, calm in a crisis, steady as a rock . . . We didn't often speak about Jack and Selina, but he knew the story. 'Of course you were angry,' he would say. 'It's perfectly understandable. You'd already lost your parents, Jack was your only relative left. You felt that Selina was taking him away from you, then she took him for ever. But try not to be bitter, darling, it doesn't suit you. After all, it was a very long time ago.' Then he'd give me one of his sardonic smiles and go back to his crossword, signalling that the conversation was over.

Dear old Richard . . . It wasn't that he was uncomfortable talking about feelings; he just refused to let me wallow in them, always on hand to haul me out of the slough of despond. I miss his accountant's steady head – the checks and balances he put on my emotions. I need him to tell me that I'm doing the right thing, or even the wrong thing. I want his opinion although I didn't always follow his advice. I miss his quiet wit, his boring cardigans, his irritating habit of opening all the windows in the middle of winter, his passion for Wagner that I never really shared . . . It's not that I feel stranded, as some women of my generation are, rendered incapable by their husbands. I can reconcile a bank state-ment, understand an insurance policy; I could handle the conveyancing on the house if I chose. I just don't want to be doing these things by myself, that's all. I miss his company. Richard was a sweet, kind man and together we made a good team. But I was never the love of his life – and nor was he mine.

'Have you decided when you're leaving yet?' I ask, after the silence.

'In about a fortnight, I think. Phil's giving Scott a bit of a hard time at the moment – guilt-tripping him into changing his mind. He won't though.'

'The Nancarrows have run that farm for over a hundred years,' I remind her. 'They need to keep it in the family. I don't suppose Phil can afford to pay an outside labourer's wages.'

'Yeah, but that's not Scott's fault. It's up to him if he doesn't want to spend the rest of his life as a farmer. Can you blame him? It's a terrible life. I think his parents are being really mean. They were so nice to me to begin with, but now it's like I've got the plague or something.'

'I'm really sorry to hear that, but I can't say I'm surprised. They're bound to blame you.'

'I don't see why. I'm not making him come with me. It was his idea in the first—'

We are interrupted by a knock at the door. 'That must be the viewers,' I say. 'Gareth can't make it today – he's asked me to show them round myself.'

'Do you want me to stick around?'

'No, I can manage.' I open the door, expecting to be confronted by some ghastly couple and their marauding kids, but it's Sally from the post office, her face red from running.

'Oh, Ellen,' she puffs. 'I was hoping you hadn't gone out.'

'What's the matter? Please come in.' Sally enters and stops in the hallway. 'Sit down.'

'Thanks.'

'Can I get you a glass of water or something?' asks Cassie. Sally shakes her head. 'I don't know whether you already know,' she begins cautiously, 'but I thought I should come and tell you . . .' I look at her blankly. 'It's Jory – he had another heart attack. They called the ambulance – I expect you heard the siren. They were taking him to the General, when . . .' Sally looked down. 'I'm sorry, Ellen . . .'

I sit down heavily on the sofa.

*   *   *

It's not the kind of ending I would have wished for my dear friend, strapped to a stretcher, rattling around the bends of the coastal road, the siren blaring hopelessly. Jory was alone but for a couple of strangers in green overalls, his son and daughter-in-law following in the car behind. The last words he heard were probably, 'You're going to be all right, Mr Nancarrow. We're getting you to the hospital as fast as we can.' What happened then? Did the siren stop, the ambulance slow down? And did Phil realize at that moment that his father must be dead, and grip the wheel a little tighter, his vision smudged with tears?

I escape to Rocky Beach, where I sit on my favourite slab of slate, my back against the uneven stone wall. As the sea withdraws on the ebb tide, so the children gradually appear with nets and buckets in hand, casting their eyes over the rock pools, looking for shrimps. They skim their nets lightly through the water, lifting them gently every now and then to poke amongst the lurid weeds, sometimes emptying the contents into a bucket before dipping the net again. I understand completely every action involved in their task: how to angle the net, how to lean over the pool yet keep one's balance on the slippery rock, how not to knock over the bucket with a careless foot . . . Yet I feel dislocated, watching them mechanically as if they are images on a screen, distant and nameless, separated by glass. I cannot bear this any more – I have been told too many times that somebody I care about is dead.

There must be a reason why I have been saved till last, the

sole survivor of the shipwreck, washed up on the beach, more bewildered than thankful. I close my eyes and test my senses, listen to the distant churning of the sea, feel the breeze buffeting my face, lick away a salty tear as it slides down the side of my nose. Yes, I am still alive. I am right here, but barely in the Now, losing my weak grip on the Present, drifting back in time . . .

I can see Jory as he was when we first met, with his thatch of yellow hair and the bridge of freckles across his nose – 'A brackety chield is a healthy chield,' the Cornish say. He's standing on top of the cart at harvest, pitchfork in hand, his cheeks shiny with sweat, picking a mouse out of the hay by its tail and throwing it towards me, laughing as I shriek and run away.

Now he's rocketing down the lane on his bike on his way home from school, the mudguard rattling, his feet off the pedals, legs outstretched before him, his hobnailed boots encrusted with dry earth. He skids round the bend onto the farm path, scuffing his feet along the ground to bring himself to a halt, shaking up a cloud of dust.

I can hear the splash and thud of a game of football in the yard, the soggy ball heavy with rainwater. Jory and Jack, socks round their ankles, their calves speckled with mud, colliding in puddles, not noticing how the skies have darkened, not feeling the evening cold . . .

It's late autumn, and the four of us are walking across the fields towards Butter Cove. A fierce afternoon sun hangs low in the sky, blinding our paths – Jack and Selina linger behind, their arms wrapped round each other, kissing and whispering secrets. Jory and I exchange superior glances, pretending we don't want to know what they were saying, that we couldn't care less if they're laughing at us, but of course we care more than we can say.

Jory takes my hand to help me over a stile, and keeps hold of it once I'm on the other side. He's never done that before. We walk on for about thirty yards, in silence, not looking at each other. I don't understand why he's doing this; all I know is that his skin feels rough and his grip is as strong as a man's — my hand feels fragile inside his, as if my fingers might break. Then Selina lets out a snort of laughter from behind and he immediately lets go, stuffing his hand back into his pocket. I don't know whether I'm relieved or disappointed. When we reach the same stile on the way back Jory jumps over and strides ahead without waiting for me. The experiment's over: he never holds my hand again.

TWENTY-FIVE

It was twenty-one days since Jack's disappearance, a Friday, the end of another long, anxious week. I had just got home from school and performed the first tasks in what was becoming a daily routine – a cup of tea and a biscuit for Clara, who was still refusing to get out of bed, and then straight back to the kitchen to prepare the vegetables for supper. It was these small, mindless jobs I hated doing most: there wasn't enough mental effort involved to stop my thoughts wandering to Jack. I was standing at the sink scrubbing potatoes, my fingers growing numb in cold muddy water, trying not to imagine him struggling in the freezing Atlantic, when I heard a knock at the door. I knew instantly what it meant.

'I'm here to see a Mr Charles Rosewarne,' said a police officer I'd never seen before.

'I'm sorry,' I said, wiping my wet hands nervously on my apron, 'but he's away. Mrs Rosewarne is here, but she's unwell. Can I help?'

He paused, uncertain what to do next. 'May I come in?' he said. I showed him into the sitting room and invited him to sit down.

'No thank you, I'm quite all right. Would it be possible to see Mrs Rosewarne? Only, I—'

'It's about my brother, isn't it?' I interrupted. 'You've found him.'

I took the news very calmly, realizing in that moment that I'd known he was dead all along. If I felt anything it was a strange kind of relief – the wretched waiting was over, I didn't have to pretend to hope any more. But Clara shrieked and wailed, staggering about, grabbing onto me, calling out angrily for Charles. Where was he? Why wasn't he with us? We needed him so much.

Jack's body had been washed up some thirty miles or so along the coast. Having been in the sea for so long it was not in a good state, the police officer warned us, but it fitted his description. However, he still had to be formally identified.

'My aunt isn't well enough,' I said to the police officer. 'Can't somebody else do it?'

'No, no, I want to.' Clara turned to him defiantly. 'I have to see my boy.'

So on Monday morning I helped her out of bed, bathed and dressed her like a child – she'd lost a lot of weight and her black dress hung loosely off her like a hand-me-down she had yet to grow into. Her hands were shaking so much she could not do up the buttons. A detective collected her by car and drove her to the mortuary. I begged to come with her but Clara refused.

'No, dear, it will upset you too much,' she said. 'I want you to go to school, behave as normal.'

But it was impossible. I sat in an art lesson, a stick of charcoal in my hand, staring vacantly at an arrangement of dried flowers, making vague black marks on the paper. But all I could see was my brother's swollen corpse, stretched out upon a slab. I pictured myself standing next to Clara, gripping her arm to steady myself, nodding in answer to the question, 'Are you ready?', taking a deep breath as they pulled back the sheet. But then, try as I might, I couldn't imagine Jack's features – it was as if I'd already forgotten them – the shape of his nose, the curve of the eyebrows, the turn of his mouth. All I could see was a blackened mask. I started to cry. The tears slowly poured down my cheeks and dripped off my chin onto the paper. I tried to blot them with my hankie, but I just smudged the charcoal drawing till it looked a grey mist rising from the sea. It was all too much. My teacher saw me and led me out of the classroom.

'What's the matter, dear? Bad news, I expect. Would you like to go home?'

I shook my head. 'I can't – not allowed,' I replied, swallowing the sobs. So I was sent to Matron, who made me a cup of sweet tea and told me to wash my face.

Clara was already back when I returned home at the end of the day. She was sitting in my uncle's leather armchair by the fire, still wearing her hat and coat. Her face was ashen, her pale lips set in a straight line, her eyes dulled and glazed over – she looked like an old woman. When I came into the room she didn't react, seemed unable to answer when I spoke her name. I lifted her out of the chair and tried to walk her out of the room to get her into upstairs to bed, but she wouldn't, or couldn't, move.

'Was it him?' I whispered. She nodded. 'Are you sure?'

'It was my boy,' she croaked. 'My darling boy . . .' And then she collapsed in my arms. I staggered backwards and fell onto the sofa, with her half on top of me. We lay there in cold silence, her weight heavy on my chest.

'Please get off,' I begged. 'I can't breathe.' But Clara made no response. She had lost consciousness.

By the time Dr Lewis arrived, my aunt had come round and was lying very still on the sofa, covered in a blanket. He said there was little he could do – it was just nervous exhaustion.

'Mrs Rosewarne must have plenty of rest,' he told me. 'And it's very important that you get some proper food inside her. Small portions are less alarming and be sure to make the food look attractive to the eye. Your aunt is anaemic, so raw liver is the thing. She won't like it but you have to try. Chop it finely and put it a sandwich with some watercress. Fresh fish, milky puddings, beef tea and toast half an hour before to stimulate the appetite.'

'Fish, milky puddings, beef tea . . .' I muttered, taking frantic notes on the front of an old newspaper. He spoke to me as if I were the maid, not involved in the tragedy at all.

'Beef tea, it's the very best thing. Serve it in a red glass to disguise the colour.'

'I'll do my best,' I mumbled. 'But I'm not a very good cook.'

'Is there nobody who can step in? A mother, a sister

perhaps?' I shook my head. He raised his eyebrows. 'And what about Mr Rosewarne?'

'He's away on—' I was about to say 'on business' as Clara kept insisting, but there was no point in lying any more. 'I don't know,' I mumbled. 'We've had no news.' I started to cry again, sniffing noisily and wiping the tears from my face with my hand.

'Ask the neighbours. Don't be too proud, dear. I'm sure they'll rally round.'

But I wasn't at all sure that they would – everyone knew that Charles had been arrested and I suspected that few believed he was innocent of whatever crime they imagined he'd committed. The only possible person who might help was Alice Nancarrow, Jory's mother, but I hadn't been up to the farm since the accident. More mysteriously, Jory hadn't been to see me once. I couldn't understand it. I felt certain he was avoiding me.

I liked Alice Nancarrow – she was a tough, hard-working woman who thought nothing of lifting heavy bales of hay or pushing cows around. She wore men's jumpers and large rubber boots – sometimes even cooking the dinner in them. In contrast to the Rosewarnes, she was a great believer in being open and telling the truth, so it was not surprising that ten minutes after I arrived in her kitchen she put her hands on her hips and said, 'Out with it then, tell us what's on tha mind.'

'They've found Jack,' I said.

Jory was sitting at the table, digging mud out of the soles

of his boots. He turned pale and dropped the knife. 'Where?'
he gulped.

'Near Bude.'

'Oh, Ellen . . .' gasped Alice. She wiped her hands on her
skirt and hugged me to her large, soft bosom. 'Still, now 'ee
can give 'im a proper Christian burial.'

'They'm sure?' stuttered Jory. 'How d'they know it's 'im?'

'My aunt identified the body.'

'Poor woman . . .' Alice sighed.

Jory started pulling on his boots. 'Got to see to the pigs,' he
said, and walked out without even tying up his laces. I stared
after him, open-mouthed.

'Don't take no notice, he's taken it some bad,' said Alice.
'He thought the world of Jack.'

'I'm sorry,' I sniffed. 'I've been trying my hardest not to cry
but—'

'You squall all 'ee like, no matter to me.'

'I can't manage all by myself. It's impossible without my
uncle. We still don't know where he is – nobody will tell us
anything,' I sobbed. 'He could be in prison, or even dead. I
don't think he's ever coming back!'

'Don't 'ee say such things . . .'

'Now Aunt Clara's collapsed, she won't talk and I can't get
her to eat. I'm frightened, Mrs Nancarrow – I think she's
losing her mind.'

'No, no, she's just full of grief, that's all. Time's a great
healer . . . But 'ee can't blame the woman, poor soul, not after
what 'appened to her son.' Alice stopped when she saw the

look of utter shock on my face, and let out a low manly whistle. 'So nobody told 'ee 'bout Henry then?'

'No . . . Who do you mean? I don't understand.'

'Four year old he was when he died – she never forgave 'erself.'

I sat down heavily on the kitchen chair and put my head in my hands. 'They never said anything . . .' I mumbled. 'Tell me what happened . . . Please, you have to tell me.'

Alice poured two mugs of tea and sat opposite. 'It was October time and we were 'avin' a spell of fine weather, I remember, so her let 'im play out with some older lads, fishin' for crabs or some such like. Anyways, they were meant to be givin' eye to the boy but 'ee know what lads is like . . . Well, Henry scoots off by 'isself. The lads thought he'd gone 'ome – least that's they told the police after – so it's not till Clara comes onto the beach to fetch Henry in for 'is tea that they notice he's missin'. Clara was afeard for she knew Henry loved to climb up to the cliffs and look down the Round Hole, so she ran up there, shoutin' for 'im. He's not there, nor lyin' at the bottom of it neither, so they start up a search, down the lanes, along the cliff path, scourin' the beaches . . . Mr Rosewarne stayed out all night in the pitch dark, callin' 'is name so loud I could 'ear it from my bed. But there was no answer – the boy's just vanished into the air . . .'

'Did they ever find him?'

'Oh yes . . . Six weeks later the body washes up on the other side of the estuary. They reckon he fell off the cliff and was swept out to sea, poor soul. So you see, it's the second time her's been put through this, and no Charles there this time, neither . . .'

'How old would Henry be now, if he was still alive?'

'Let me think . . . he was younger than Jory – I reckon 'bout the same age as you.'

'They never told me. Never even mentioned his name . . . I always assumed they couldn't have children.'

'No, well, that don't surprise me . . .' She sighed. 'I'm not one for keepin' secrets, but better fit 'ee don't say I told 'ee. Not just now, anyhow.'

'Yes, of course . . .'

'At least now 'ee understand . . .' I understood more than Alice Nancarrow could imagine.

I walked slowly back to Spindrift and went straight upstairs to Clara's room. She smiled at me vaguely as I drew the curtains and puffed up her pillows. Then I went to the kitchen to make my first attempt at beef tea, following the instructions that Alice had written out for me on the back of an envelope. As I waited for the meat to steep I considered what to do – should I tell Clara that I knew about Henry or pretend that their secret was safe?

I thought back to the first day we met the Rosewarnes in that church hall, when they called Jack over – it was him they wanted, not me. Charles and Clara had always been happy to look after me as well, but I could see now that I had been surplus to requirements, not essential, not part of the plan. Jack must have seemed like a gift from heaven, a boy the same age as their lost son: surely God had given them a second chance. That's why he was always their favourite, why they'd put up with his appalling behaviour, the ingratitude and rebelliousness – they wanted to redeem themselves for Henry's death. But Selina had put paid to that. Now everything was wrecked – Jack dead, my uncle imprisoned or worse, my aunt on the verge of losing her sanity. I was alone, standing in the ruins of what had almost been a family.

I was filled with an overwhelming urge to run away but there was nowhere for me to go. Besides, my aunt needed me, there were duties to perform, doctor's orders to follow. At least I owed them that. I retched with disgust as I strained the beef through the scalded muslin, seasoning it lightly with salt. I was not going to say anything to Clara. From now on I would have my own secrets. I too could learn how best to disguise the unpalatable truth. Decision made, I poured the bloody liquid into a ruby-coloured glass.

Now there was a body there could be an inquest. As the last person to have seen Jack alive I was called as a witness. I was terrified, not knowing what they would ask and, more importantly, how much detail of that last evening I would need to supply. My evidence would be given under oath: if I were too vague then I might be accused of lying by omission. I rehearsed my account over and over in my head, keeping it to the minimum.

I decided I would say that I returned home just before seven and found Jack and Selina in the house. 'Where in the house? What were they doing?' the Coroner might ask. What was I to say? That I'd found them naked in my bed? It was unthinkable. Better to lie and risk damnation – I would say I'd seen them sitting at the kitchen table, drinking tea. It seemed safe enough. The only people who could contradict me were dead.

Charles was still away and Clara too ill to leave her bed, so Alice Nancarrow went with me to the Coroner's Court. Jory refused to come, saying that there was too much work to do on the farm, that he didn't have a decent suit to wear, that he was squeamish and could not bear to hear any description of Jack's injuries. I knew they were just excuses. Jory was grieving like the rest of us but he refused to show it, avoiding any situation that might lead to talking about his feelings or sharing his suffering.

It was mid April and the whole county had been shut off as the final preparations were made for D-Day. A Prohibited Zone for all shipping, extending out ten miles, was set up around the coast. I couldn't help thinking that if they had imposed the restriction just a fortnight earlier, the accident would never have happened. Access to the beaches was strictly forbidden and even the letterboxes were sealed. Although most of the activity was in the south you could still sense the excitement in the air.

Alice and I were on our way to the inquest when our bus drew up behind a convoy of jeeps. The GIs turned and waved and our driver sounded his horn in reply. Everyone else on the bus cheered and made thumbs-up signs out of the window, but I started to cry.

'Chin up,' whispered Alice, squeezing my hand. 'It'll soon be over.'

Tom Penaluna was already there when we arrived, standing on the pavement outside the courtroom, chewing nervously on his pipe. I'd never seen him wearing a suit before – it looked as if he'd had to borrow it, the sleeves too short, the jacket stretched across his chest.

'Hello,' I mumbled as we walked past. He grunted some reply I didn't catch, removing his cap as he followed us through the doorway. There could be no verdict on what had happened to Selina as she had not yet been found – no body, no jurisdiction. But Penaluna was still asked to give his account of how he and his daughter had taken the *Louisa May* out just before dawn that morning to move the lobster pots to a more sheltered spot on the other side of Gull Island. He explained that the tide was at its lowest point on their return and he'd been forced to leave the boat moored in a cove on the seaward side of the bar. It had been his intention to come back when the tide was up and take the *Louisa May* into harbour, but he had been called away urgently to the lifeboat. A plane had gone down in the sea nearby and they were searching for survivors.

'And that took all day?' asked the Coroner, surprised. Penaluna nodded – they had received most particular instructions that the sea surrounding the crashed aircraft should be thoroughly searched. The Coroner raised his eyebrows. 'That seems strange when it must have been immediately clear that all souls had perished in the unfortunate accident.'

'I can't say no more, sir,' answered Penaluna. 'We were just following orders.'

'So the last time you saw your boat, the *Louisa May*, was when you left it that morning?'

'That's right, sir.'

'And you made no attempt to bring her into safe harbour?'

'No. By the time I got back to Padsta it was too late – it was dark and the storm was breakin'. There was nothin' I could do. I reckoned she'd 'ave to take 'er chances.'

'You, an experienced fisherman, calculated that the risk was too high.'

Penaluna nodded. ''Ee'd 'ave to be mad to shift her in that weather.'

'I see . . . Could the boat have broken up in that manner from her mooring position?'

'Yes, to be sure. But the punt was missing. That's how we knew Selina – and Jack, I suppose – must 'ave tried to bring her in. They'd have had to use the punt to get out to the Louisa, see.'

'But nobody saw them attempt this?'

'No . . . Well, not as far as I know.'

'And the punt, could that have also broken free in the storm?'

'S'pose so,' mumbled Penaluna. 'Yes, I suppose it could.'

'So this is all pure speculation.' The Coroner sighed impatiently.

I was next to take the witness stand. As the deceased's sister I was given more gentle treatment, but I was still shaking with fear, my knees almost giving way under me.

'So, Miss Rosewarne, you say you entered the house and found the deceased and his companion, Miss Penaluna, having a cup of tea in the kitchen . . .' I nodded, biting my lip. 'Do you remember the conversation?'

'Not really. We said a few words . . . about the weather, that's all.'

'You talked about the oncoming storm then?'

'I think so, yes. I don't remember exactly, sorry.'

'That's quite all right. So what happened next?'

'I went upstairs to change out of my wet clothes. Jack and Selina left a few minutes later – they didn't say goodbye.'

'Did they say where they were going?'

'No, sir.'

'Did they at any time mention that they were going to take the *Louisa May* out to sea?'

'No. I had no idea what their plans were.'

'Thank you, Miss Rosewarne. I know how difficult this has been for you. You have acquitted yourself very well.'

In other words, I had got away with it.

The Coroner ruled that he was satisfied that the body found at Bude on April the fifth was indeed that of one Jack Rosewarne, formerly known as Jack Morrison, and that the cause of death was 'asphyxiation due to drowning'. The exact circumstances of his death – namely whether he had been involved in the wrecking of the *Louisa May* – could not, however, be verified.

An article appeared in the paper at the end of the week, quoting some of my evidence, including the lies. I tore out the page and burned it in the fire. I had only perjured myself to protect my aunt and uncle from further village gossip. God would forgive me – I knew He would.

The funeral was a bleak affair – I can hardly bear to recall it. Ted and Alice Nancarrow saw to all the arrangements while Jory stayed in the background, only agreeing to be one of the pallbearers after some hefty persuasion by his father. Virtually everyone in the village attended, and although kind words were said and my arm gently patted countless times, I felt that people were there as curious spectators rather than supporters. Clara's appearance was truly shocking – she had lost over a stone in weight and there were dark grey shadows under her eyes, which had no life in them at all, but stared at the other mourners with a blank expression. She hardly spoke – and when she did it was in a whisper; she couldn't walk without me to support her and nearly collapsed completely while the vicar was reading prayers.

But it was Charles's absence that we felt the most. A few people dared to ask after him, but there was no genuine concern in their voice, just prurient interest. I pretended I hadn't heard, sniffing into my handkerchief until they felt uncomfortable and left me in peace.

As we stood in the windswept cemetery on the hill above Padstow and watched the coffin being lowered into the grave I thought I would finally give in to the grief and weep, but the tears wouldn't fall. I felt strangely numb inside. More than anything was the realization that I was alone in the world, that I had no real family of my own. I had paid a high price for my defection to the Rosewarnes. My mother and father, Jack and Selina were all dead, and I was sure Clara would kill herself if Charles did not return. But the past could not be changed; there was nothing else to do now but carry on.

TWENTY-SIX

Henry's painted iron cot sits in the hallway, waiting to be collected by the house clearance company. Yesterday Cassie dragged it from the furthest reaches of the attic, filthy and covered in cobwebs, but now I've cleaned it up it looks almost new. I have no idea how much it is worth – there's probably not much call for that type of thing these days; as window dressing maybe but not for a child to sleep in – I'm sure it doesn't comply with safety regulations, the bars too close together, the paint made with poisonous lead . . .

The cot is packed with old blankets, books and stacks of crockery wrapped in yellowed newspaper but I can still imagine baby Henry, lying on the mattress, gurgling and putting his toes in his mouth. He is a sturdy child, with his father's long body and clear blue eyes; his hair is wispy and fair but will turn brown like his mother's as he grows. I know this because the other day I found an old chocolate box stuffed with photographs I'd never seen before – newborn Henry cradled in Clara's arms; held aloft in front of the window, the sunlight creating a silhouette; then a formal studio pose – Charles standing behind Clara, who is seated with Henry, now about one, wriggling on her lap. But my favourite photograph is just of him, aged about three – it's been tinted by hand in rose-pink and a pale cobalt-blue. Henry is looking solemnly at the camera, slightly bewildered, on the edge of tears. His short chubby arms are folded across his lap as if cuddling an invisible teddy bear. He is a beautiful child.

I never talked to the Rosewarnes about Henry, not even when I was married and had made Clara a grandmother. She never gave me any tips about pregnancy or childbirth, nor sympathized when I was having problems breastfeeding. Clara knew exactly how to fold a nappy and how to bring up her grandson's wind, but she never admitted where she had learned her maternal skills. Sometimes when she walked back and forth across the bedroom floor, rubbing Michael's soft small back and gently singing him to sleep I would catch the sorrow in her eyes, and was sure she was remembering. I longed to ask her about Henry, but couldn't. Clara and Charles had their own reasons for their pact of silence, and although I was disappointed – even offended – that they never chose to confide in me I could not confront them. It would have been embarrassing for both of us to learn that I had known all along.

Cassie cannot comprehend this, labelling my relationship with the Rosewarnes as 'dysfunctional'. I tell her they came from a different generation and, perhaps even more importantly, a different class. It was normal for them to keep secrets, to put unpleasant things in the back of their minds, coating themselves with a protective layer of silence. Clara and Charles suffered deeply, that's beyond question, but who am I to judge how they dealt with the pain? Now we are appalled by such suppression of emotion, convinced that it is unhealthy and will lead to cancer or a nervous breakdown; we insist on taking the covers off, letting it all out in the open. We talk to counsellors and psychiatrists, our television screens are full of tearful people confessing their sins, baring the agony of their souls before millions. 'I just want to know the truth,' people say time and time again, believing that knowledge will heal them. But the truth is not always followed by understanding or forgiveness. Sometimes it just breaks your heart.

It's a week since Jory's death – a dry, windy Thursday afternoon, too bright and cheerful for a funeral. It should be dull and wet, the skies dressed in mourning, the windscreen spattered with tears, wipers on full speed. But the sun is shining gloriously, making the colours around us seem unusually bright – the fields are a patchwork of green and yellow squares, the sky's a matt cornflower-blue, even the tarmac on the road glistens. I change down a gear to climb one of those long steep hills, its crown topped by a wind farm, a forest of white whirring sticks that look like a modern-art installation. I feel as though I'm driving through a virtual landscape – everything's too boldly drawn, too clear and crisp to be real. It adds to my sense that none of this is actually happening – how can it be that Jory is dead? Will I really never be able to walk up to the farm and find him pottering about the shop or hosing down the yard?

Jory left precise instructions about his funeral, written out on a small sheet of Basildon Bond, three weeks before he died. Phil found the document in an old biscuit tin in the top drawer of his bedside cabinet. To everyone's astonishment, Jory has asked for a non-religious ceremony and has insisted that he must not be buried. You'd think a man who had spent all his life with dirt under his fingernails would feel comfortable with the thought of being laid in the soil like a seed potato, but not Jory. He always had a fear of being underground, hated caves and tunnels, couldn't bear to be somewhere without a view of the sky. Maybe he believed that his spirit, with phobias intact, would live beyond his mortal remains, or maybe he just had trouble imagining himself dead. Jory was not the most logical man I ever met, but I like to think he hadn't completely given up hope of the afterlife.

Phil is determined to carry out Jory's last requests to the letter – after the cremation his ashes are to be taken back to Clifftop Farm and scattered on the lower field, nearest the cliff edge. I think it helps him feel less guilty about going against his father in every other respect. The irony that Jory's ashes will eventually become part of the foundations for the new holiday bungalows seems to have eluded Phil, but it's not my place to say anything.

We draw up outside and I park the car halfway up the grass verge. We walk down the central path, past the neat rows of tombstones, and find the crematorium, tucked discreetly behind the stone chapel – a low, modern, wood-clad building with large glass doors at the entrance. A few other mourners are there, standing in small groups, talking quietly. We nod hello to each other. It's a warm day and the men look hot in their dark suits and shirts buttoned up to the neck, our black clothes absorbing the sun.

A cortege of three black cars turns into the cemetery. As I see the coffin in the back of the hearse, decked with white and gold flowers, my legs weaken and I hold onto Cassie's arm. 'He's here,' I whisper.

The non-religious ceremony is restrained and emotionless, despite the celebrant's valiant efforts to celebrate the life of a man she'd never even met. I would have liked to be able to say a few words about Jory – to recall a few scenes from our childhood, raise an affectionate laugh. But nobody in the family was willing to read so much as a poem. Phil is clearly embarrassed by the lack of prayers or hymns, and I must confess I miss the traditional droning rendition of 'The Lord Is My Shepherd' – it's such a dreary tune, yet strangely comforting.

After the ceremony we go to stare at the flowers, which the undertakers have laid out on the grass, and make subdued, idle conversation. Scott takes Cassie's hand and they walk down the path away from the family, their heads close together. I see his mum, Tina, looking after them curiously. She sees me watching her and gives me a brief, sad smile.

'Coming back to the house?'

'Of course,' I reply.

'Good . . . It's only sandwiches, cup of tea . . .'

'That's all you want at a time like this.'

'Yes . . . Nobody's got much of an appetite at the moment.'

There is a long pause. I bend down to read the cards attached to the wreaths, wondering why most of the messages are addressed to Jory as if he were standing here, reading them – *Missing you always*, *From your loving son* . . . I look around, half expecting to see his ghost at my side dressed all in white – cord trousers, padded waistcoat, flat cap, pristine rubber boots, holding a spade instead of a harp perhaps . . .

'He's not going, you know,' says Tina suddenly.

'Sorry?' I reply. 'Who?'

'Scott – he's decided he's not going travelling with Cassie.'

'Oh. I see . . .' I look across to the two of them, instantly reading from their body language that he's telling her now. They are no longer holding hands and Cassie is walking slowly between the graves, running her fingers along the top of the headstones. Scott is standing still, his head bowed like a disgraced schoolboy.

'It's not that we have anything against Cassie,' Tina assures me. 'She's a lovely girl. It's just that – his dad needs him.'

'Yes.'

'There's so much to do.'

'And I gather you're planning big changes . . . the bungalows?'

Tina shrugs and looks across to Phil, who's talking to some neighbours. 'Who knows what'll happen. We can't go on as we are, that's for sure.'

*　*　*

The funeral tea is being held in the garden of Tina and Phil's bungalow on the very edge of the farm. Cassie has decided she can't face it and I don't blame her. As we wind along the coast road, she wriggles out of her dark stockings and removes the smart linen jacket I bought her especially for the occasion.

'I don't see what difference it makes now that Jory is dead,' she complains. 'He'd already given up all the heavy work as it was, and they're talking about selling the cows. It's just an excuse to put pressure on Scott to stay . . . I don't know why he doesn't stand up to them. He's such a wimp.'

'I told you before, the Nancarrows are a very close family. I don't think Jory ever went abroad; he might never even have left Cornwall. They're tied to the land.'

'No they're not, they're selling it.'

'Well, yes, that's true . . . I'm sorry, Cassie, I don't know what to say.'

'It's OK,' she mutters. 'I didn't come here looking for a boyfriend. I can travel by myself, it's no problem. I just wished I hadn't hung around waiting for him. I could have been in France or Spain by now.'

'Well, I'm glad you did. It's given us a chance to get to know each other.'

'I guess . . .' She leans her elbow on the edge of the open window and cups her head in her hand. 'I just liked him, that's all. I thought we had something . . .'

'Yes, it seemed pretty serious. So, it's over, is it?'

'Kind of. He says he wants me to stay here, but what's the point? I'm starting uni in the New Year: I'm supposed to be seeing the world. Anyway, where would I live? I'm not staying with *them*, that's for sure.'

'I could delay the sale, if you really wanted to stay.'

Cassie shakes her head. 'No thanks, Gran. I'm going to move on, soon as I can . . . Another one bites the dust, eh?' She laughs briefly.

'You'll survive.'

'Course I will.'

Of course she will.

I drop Cassie off at Spindrift and walk up to the farm, passing the scantily clad holidaymakers gingerly picking their barefoot way across the stony car park. A young woman is serving behind the counter at the beach shop, scooping dollops of rich Cornish ice cream into thin wafer cones – strawberry, chocolate chip, rum 'n' raisin, caramel toffee and bright yellow vanilla. We smile at each other with vague recognition as she hands a cornet to a shivering boy.

I walk past the block of public toilets, which by now will be clogged with sand and soggy streams of loo paper, mothers squeezing into the tiny cubicles with screaming toddlers, wrenching wet swimming costumes down, bribing, cajoling, and finally losing their temper. There's a strong breeze and the surf's up – the sea is crowded with hopeful wave-riders, the flat wet sand the pitch for at least six cricket matches and two games of volleyball. I must look strange in my black dress and smart jacket because children keep giving me a second glance – I'm glad I left my hat at the house.

By the time I arrive, the gathering has spread into the garden – about twenty people standing around looking hot and bothered, balancing cups of tea in their hands, soggy half-eaten sandwiches perched on the rims of their saucers. Some of the women have kicked off their shoes; the men have removed their jackets and loosened their ties. Every so often a small group briefly bursts into spontaneous laughter, then people remember the occasion and straighten their faces. I'm not in the mood for conversation, finding myself a wicker chair in the shade from where I can watch proceedings. But I'm not cloaked in invisibility for long – Phil pulls up another chair and joins me.

'Thanks for coming,' he says. I see he has started on the beer. 'I've been sorting out Dad's things. He hasn't got much and most of it's junk, but I thought you might like to have something – as a reminder.'

'Yes, thank you. I'd appreciate that.'

'Come inside and I'll show you. You can choose what you like.'

He leads me through the dining room and into the spare bedroom. Tina and Phil have already been through Jory's cottage and removed the small amount of stuff that's worth keeping. On the bed are a small carton and two black bin liners: the box contains a few books and ornaments, the bags are soft with clothes. On the dressing table are three small piles of what are normally described as 'personal effects'. It's not much for a man of Jory's age – the simplicity, the paucity of it bring tears to my eyes. Not because Jory lived the life of an impoverished farmer but because most of these few 'valuables' I never saw him wear or use. He was a man who needed very little.

The 'jewellery collection' consists of an old watch, some gold cufflinks, a dented cigarette case and a shiny hip flask that looks like an unused gift. There are three spectacle cases, presumably containing three pairs of glasses, although I only ever saw him in one, and some black and white photographs. Ted and Alice feature in one of them, standing outside the front door of the old farmhouse, both wearing their ubiquitous rubber boots. I pick it up and let my eyes linger over the image. It's tempting to ask for this, but I have already thrown away so many old photos: there is no point – I would only put it into a drawer.

'And there's this. It was by his bed,' says Phil, taking the dreaded mermaid book out of the carton. I shudder involuntarily. 'Scott said you gave it to him.'

'Not exactly,' I reply. 'He was meant to be chucking it out for me.'

'Very interested in it, he was. Got very worked up about it – can't think why. Not normally the kind of thing he would read. Didn't read much at all . . .'

'He was a traditional old Cornishman,' I say, trying to keep the conversation light. 'He liked the old myths and legends.'

'You don't want it back then?'

'Not really.'

'There's something else,' says Phil. 'I found this tucked

between the pages.' He hands me an old brown envelope. 'Thought it was just a bookmark. I nearly threw it away.'

'What is it? A letter?' I ask.

'No, much more interesting than that. Take a look.' The envelope is blank and unsealed, but worn, at least thirty years old. The look of anticipation on Phil's face is making me feel nervous, as if some horrible truth is about to revealed. But all that's inside is a small white silk cloth.

'I thought it was just a handkerchief at first,' says Phil. 'Then I realized that it's actually a map.'

'Oh yes, I know what it is. I've seen one of these in a museum.' I spread the cloth out on the dressing table, smoothing the wrinkles. 'It's an escape map. They gave them to parachutists and SOE operatives in the war. The silk was more durable than paper, and it was easier to hide.'

The map is printed in faded black ink, entitled *Bulgaria and Roumania* on one side and *Greece* on the other. Familiar places are marked – *Odessa*, *Bucharest*, *Varna* – but the most important feature seems to be the road system: dozens of thin black lines entwining across the silk like a badly formed spider's web.

'I suppose Dad was wrecking and found it on the beach,' says Phil.

'Yes, they did a lot of that,' I reply, still studying the names of the towns and cities, the harder lines marking the borders between countries that were soon not to exist, the jagged edge of the Black Sea coast . . . 'All the boys loved to collect war souvenirs. When the Americans were here they were forever pestering them for stuff.'

'Yes, I know. Dad often talked about the war – used to bore us with it, to be honest. He kept his identity card and his ration book, showed them to Scott when he was doing a project at school. But he never showed either of us this map. Don't you think that's odd?'

'Yes . . . I've never seen it either . . . But this is not your ordinary wartime souvenir – your dad should have handed it over to the authorities. I reckon he felt guilty about keeping it but couldn't bear to throw it away, something like that . . .'

'Surely he wouldn't have still felt guilty about it after all these years. I mean, nobody was going to come and arrest him now, were they?' Phil laughs ironically. 'He was a strange one, my dad . . .'

I pick up the map and run its smoothness between my hands. The lightness yet durability of the silk suggests secrecy, concealment. I scrunch it up and tuck it into my palm like a conjuror, then release my fingers, letting it spring open like the petals of a flower. There's a story here, I can sense it.

'This is what I'd like to have, if you don't mind . . . Would that be all right?'

'Of course, Ellen. Have what you like – most of it's only going to charity.'

I say my goodbyes to Phil and Tina, gesture a friendly wave across the garden to Scott to signal that there are no hard feelings between us, and make my way back to the house. As I clip in my good shoes down the tarmac lane, I slip my hand into my bag and rummage blindly for the map, finally trapping the soft silk between my fingers. It feels familiar, as if it belongs to me. As soon as I saw it I knew I was meant to have it.

What was the real reason why Jory never showed to anyone? He clearly didn't forget about it – Phil found the map in the mermaid book, marking a particular page, no doubt. So does that mean there's some connection between the map and Selina? I know you are hiding something from me, Jory, you sneaky bastard – you have taken a secret to your grave.

TWENTY-SEVEN

The village was eerily quiet now the Americans had gone. In the period leading up to D-Day we experienced several false farewells. The troops would be driven away in convoys, not knowing themselves whether this was a training exercise or the real thing, leaving behind a box of personal belongings they didn't want to take into combat and a letter for their families. But they had always returned after a couple of days – dirty, exhausted and starving hungry. This time, however, we knew for certain they would not be coming back. They packed everything in a couple of hours and stole out in the middle of the night without a word of goodbye to anybody. Everything had been dismantled and removed with all the wonder of a magician's disappearing trick: the only clues to their presence were the thick streaks of muddy tyre tracks snaking up the lane, and even those were soon washed away by the rain. Now it was as if they had never been here at all.

I had been ordered to keep my distance from the soldiers, but many of the locals – especially the children – had made particular friends, and one girl had even become engaged. There must have been a few tears shed that morning when we discovered they had gone for good. We all knew what their departure meant – the invasion must be imminent. The schoolboys were full of excitement: there was a fresh energy in their play as they charged around with sticks for guns, shooting imaginary Germans. But most people felt uneasy about the Americans leaving – soon they would be facing real conflict and many of them would never return to their home-land, let alone to Cornwall.

Some of our own servicemen were still billeted with families, radar operators working at Trevose Head and chaps from the St Merryn air fleet, but without the Yanks village life was almost 'back to normal'. It was over two months since Uncle Charles had been arrested and still there was no word. I started to dream that he was dead too, his body not yet found, drifting along the ocean floor, waiting to be washed up on the beach.

I kept myself busy so that I had no time to think, working so hard that I always fell straight to sleep with exhaustion. Clara was still very ill and appeared to have no interest in getting better. She resisted my efforts to encourage her to get up and face the day, usually going back to bed as soon as I'd left the house. I found her apathy frustrating and felt my patience running thin. She should have had somebody to look after her all the time but there was nobody else available. Sometimes Alice Nancarrow popped round with some freshly baked saffron buns or a few eggs, but I don't remember any other visitors. We needed Charles. I finally plucked up the courage to go to the police and begged them for news, but they said they had no idea what had happened to him. I was desperate.

I rarely saw Jory, and then only by chance. When he wasn't driving himself to exhaustion in the fields he could be found up the road in the White Horse, drinking the cheapest beer and bantering with the airmen. Sometimes I'd catch a glimpse of him in the upper field and wave as I cycled past, or I'd find him in the kitchen when I dropped by to return Alice's cake tin. As soon as I arrived he'd make some excuse to leave – it was very obvious that he didn't want to talk to me. He was behaving as if one of us had done something wrong and I racked my brains to work out whether it was me. Like so many men of that generation, he found it difficult to deal with strong emotions, but I badly needed him then and he let me down. On the surface we remained friends, but a gap opened up between us that would never be fully closed. True, we ended up leading very different lives, but it wasn't the differences in education, social mobility or material wealth that changed our relationship – it was Jack's death.

It was a Saturday in June, about a week after the D-Day landings, and the smell of victory was in the nation's nostrils. Everyone in the village was talking as if the war was about to end. The weather was warm and sunny and I'd managed to persuade my aunt to sit in a deckchair in the back garden. She was wearing a straw hat tied under her chin and had a blanket over her legs like a proper invalid. I was hanging out some washing – I remember I hadn't put it through the mangle enough times and it was wet and heavy. But there was a good dry, a hefty breeze coming off the sea, white puffy clouds chasing each other across the sky. I was trying to engage my aunt in some conversation to do with school, asking her what she knew about Cromwell, I believe – it didn't matter what the subject was, I just wanted to get her to talk. Suddenly Charles walked out of the conservatory doors and said, 'Ah, there you are . . .' I dropped the sheet on the grass and ran towards him, throwing myself into his arms.

'Steady on,' he whispered, stroking my back. 'Now, now, don't cry, everything's going to be all right . . .' He prised himself free and went to Clara, who was staring at him as if he were a stranger. Charles bent down and took her hands in his. 'I'm back, dearest . . .' She nodded slightly and the corners of her mouth almost rose upwards in the memory of a smile.

'Any news?' He looked up, mouthing Jack's name to me.

'They found him,' I said. 'Five weeks ago.'

Charles let out a deep moan and sank to the ground, his body crumpling in on itself. He took off his spectacles and rubbed his face with his hands. 'I kept telling myself he'd just run away,' he murmured. He broke down then, doubled over, shielding his face from me, his whole upper body shaking. It was as if I was hearing the news for the first time all over again, Charles's pain slicing into me.

I bent down next to him and put my arm gently round his shoulder. 'We so needed you.'

He finally lifted his head. 'I must have missed the funeral . . .' I nodded. 'I should have been there . . .' he groaned. 'Good God, I should have been there. They should have let me bury my own son.'

He rose to his feet and wiped the tears from his cheeks with the back of his hand. His face looked unfamiliar without his glasses on, tired and vulnerable. He stood there in the sunshine, blinking like a child. Clara just stared at him, saying nothing, failing to comprehend.

'How long has she been like this?' whispered Charles.

'Ever since they found Jack . . . I've done the best I can, but she's getting worse and worse. You can't imagine the strain . . . We didn't know whether you were alive or dead!'

'There, there, you must be brave.'

'I *have* been brave!' I shouted. 'I've been as brave as I can possibly be. But I've had enough of being brave now. I've had enough!'

'Yes, my dear, I know, you've been marvellous,' Charles replied, his voice trembling slightly. 'But it's over now. I'm back.'

'Did they let you go?' I stupidly thought for a moment that he might be on the run.

'Yes, Ellen, I am a free man. Totally innocent. I'm home for good, and I promise you, everything will be put to rights.'

Charles went upstairs to have a bath and change into some fresh clothes. He stayed in his room for a couple of hours, sleeping, while Clara sat in the garden staring at the sea, only dimly aware that he'd returned. That evening the three of us sat down to dinner, taking the places we had always done, the fourth side of the table where Jack used to sit occupied by a vase of wild flowers I'd picked from the garden. I did my best with a leg of mutton, which my uncle praised to the skies, and the two of us made polite but awkward conversation in front of Aunt Clara. She sat there in her usual trance, occasionally picking at her food and not saying a word. Charles said nothing about his imprisonment and made no mention of Jack. It was so close to normality it felt completely surreal.

But I couldn't behave as if nothing had happened. I wanted to talk. I needed to know exactly how everything was going to be 'put to rights'. We had lost friends, people were no longer talking to us, I couldn't walk outside the front door without being stared at suspiciously. How was everyone to know the truth? Was there to be some announcement in the local newspaper that Charles had been wrongfully arrested, some public declaration that he was not an evil traitor but a loyal servant of the crown? Would the vicar be standing up in church next Sunday to deliver an apology to the family? No, he would not.

I knew what was most likely to happen. The word would get around soon enough that Charles Rosewarne had been released, and there would be a flurry of hushed conversations in the pubs, the post office and the queue for the butcher's as to what it was he hadn't been charged for. A variety of opinions would be expressed as to whether he was a victim of injustice or had 'got away with it', most of them falling in on the side of the latter because it made for juicier gossip. Some would say he had used his high-up connections to secure his release, or that the authorities knew he was guilty but didn't have enough evidence to prove it – no smoke without fire. Then somebody would claim that they knew somebody who knew somebody who had inside information, and before long a generally accepted 'true story' would be created. This would quickly spread until it was reported as known fact, adding a splash of colour to local history – 'There was a German spy in our village during the war,' people would tell their grandchildren in the future. And what would my uncle's strategy be to combat this? Say nothing. 'Let the fools think what they like,' that's what he was going to tell me. 'Rise above it.' But he was not going to rise above it with me.

After dinner I waited for Charles while he helped Clara upstairs, pouring him a glass of whisky and placing it on the small table next to his favourite leather armchair. It was a mild evening, but I lit a small fire all the same – it was extravagant but I wanted to create a homely atmosphere. The curtains were drawn and the lamps turned on. The room looked cosy and welcoming, as little like an interrogation cell as I could make it, although an interrogation was precisely what I had in mind. Charles took what felt like for ever to put Clara to bed, so long in fact that I started to think he'd lain down beside her and gone to sleep. But eventually he came back downstairs and into the sitting room.

'I presume Dr Lewis has been visiting,' he said, picking up the glass and raising it to me in a silent toast. 'Thank you for this, most thoughtful.'

'Yes, once or twice. Only when she's been really bad. He says it's just nervous exhaustion.'

'I'm sure he's right,' Charles replied. 'I'll talk to him in the morning.' He sat down and took a large sip of his whisky, letting the taste linger in his mouth.

'Please, Uncle,' I began nervously, moving to the edge of my seat. 'Please would you explain why you were arrested?'

'I can't, I'm afraid, my dear,' he said solemnly. 'It's classified information. I had to swear an oath.'

'Yes, I'm sure you did, but you must be able to tell me *something*.' My eyes pleaded with him, every inch of me leaning forward in desperation. I was not going to give in easily.

'All you need to know is that I am innocent. I wasn't even charged with anything.'

'But innocent of what?'

'You must understand, Ellen, I can't tell you that.' He rose and poured himself another whisky.

I sighed with exasperation. 'People are saying you're a Nazi spy.'

'And you believe them?' Charles gave me a surprised and faintly reproving look.

'No, of course I don't!' It was time to deliver the argument that I had been rehearsing in my head. 'I'm aware that there are some things you don't wish me to know, personal things perhaps. You have a perfect right to your own privacy. But this is a different matter, a public matter: everyone in the village is gossiping about us and I am involved too. Surely I've a right to know the true story. We may not be blood-related but legally I am your daughter and therefore a member of your—'

'Hush, hush – there's no need for all this,' he interrupted, raising a hand in gentle protest. But I carried on.

'I want you to know that you can trust me absolutely, Uncle. I'm prepared to swear on the Bible that I'll never tell another soul for as long as I live. Even if I was tortured I wouldn't say.'

'Ellen, nobody is going to torture you!'

'And besides, what loyalty do you owe to people who locked you up and accused you of something you didn't do? They have destroyed your reputation, Uncle Charles. Do they care about that?'

Charles sat down again. 'Perhaps you're right . . . They knew I was innocent almost immediately but they still kept hold of me until after the D-Day landings – just in case. As for my reputation, well, that remains to be seen.'

'So, will you tell me the truth?' I demanded. There was a long pause while Charles stared into the fire, stuffing his pipe with tobacco. He was deliberating, weighing up the pros and cons, judging my strength of character, assessing my maturity, calculating whether I could be trusted with his secrets.

'Very well . . .' he said. 'I need to tell somebody and your aunt is – well, not at her best . . .'

I got up from my chair and sat at his feet, like a child eager to be told a bedtime story. Our faces glowed in the soft lamplight, the fire flickered and Charles lit his pipe. The familiar smell of his tobacco filled the room.

'In late nineteen forty I was approached by an old university friend who was recruiting for the newly formed Special

Operations Executive, known by its initials as the SOE. He knew I was half French and remembered I had a faint Breton accent picked up from my mother – it had given rise to a certain amount of mockery at Cambridge, you understand. Anyway, all this made me an ideal candidate for covert operations in northern France. I was delighted. I'd wanted to make a proper contribution since the day war was declared but was too old to volunteer. Clara didn't want me to go, but I insisted – it was what I'd been waiting for.'

'We never thought you were in London all that time,' I said. 'We knew something was going on.'

'Yes, well, I was sent to a secret camp in the south of England and threw myself into the intense training with great gusto.' He went quiet for a few seconds, remembering. 'But my first mission in France didn't go well. I was nervous, over-excited . . . I made a stupid, schoolboy error almost as soon as I arrived. It was pathetic – I can't tell you how ashamed I was.'

'What happened?' I gasped. 'Were you arrested?'

'No, but I knew a couple of people had noticed and there was a chance they'd report it. You don't know who you can trust. My contact decided there was no point in risking it and my mission was aborted before it had even begun. Two brave chaps set out across the Channel to pick me up . . . One of them was shot trying to land the boat, the other one was captured. I was hiding in the undergrowth and managed to escape. I blamed myself of course. When I eventually made it back to England I immediately resigned.' Charles helped himself to another whisky. 'Not much of a hero, eh?'

'I'm glad you resigned – it was too dangerous.'

'Well, they had another job in mind for me.' He looked at me carefully. 'You know I absolutely shouldn't be telling you any of this; even your aunt doesn't know exactly what I've been doing.'

'Please . . . I need to know.'

'I joined an auxiliary unit, ostensibly part of the Home Guard. We're all local men, specially trained, working in very small groups. The idea was that if the Germans invaded we would operate as resistance fighters and carry out acts of sabotage. We've a secret hideout near Mussel Cove – there's ammunition, food supplies, even explosives.'

'So that's why you had the Highworth's Fertilizers book,' I said slowly, 'with the bomb-making instructions . . .'

'Yes, that's right . . . Did you find it or did Jack?'

'It was my fault, I thought it was salvage. I tried to stop Violet taking it to her father but she wouldn't listen.' I decided not to say anything about Jack's involvement: there was no point now.

'You mustn't blame yourself – it was very stupid of me to hide it so badly,' Charles replied. 'The police handed the book over to the MoD and eventually it reached the hands of somebody who knew what it was. But it took some months. You see, our units are so secret that officially we don't exist. If the invasion happens we're on our own; if we're captured we have no protection. We're not even recognized by the Geneva Convention. You see how important it is that you don't breathe a word to anyone – not to your aunt, or even your closest friend.'

'I understand. So what happened? Did you get into trouble?'

'Yes, but no more than I deserved. I was paid a visit by my commanding officer, got hauled over the coals for being so careless. My card was marked, as they say: one more slip-up and I'd be for it.'

'But they let you carry on.'

'I begged them to. I liked all the cloak and-dagger stuff. It was rather glamorous, like being back in the SOE, only better. A damn sight less risky than going to France, anyway . . . But the reality was we were playing soldiers. As the war went on we knew there was virtually no chance of being invaded, but nobody seemed to want to disband us. We started to get a little carried away with the training exercises. I suppose we were turning it into a game.' Charles sighed then and took a long puff on his pipe.

'I started to believe that I was the dashing hero, carrying out important top-secret missions for my country, the fate of the nation lay in my hands – some such nonsense anyway. I wanted to lead a really successful mission, the more daring the better, something that would make my commanding officer sit up and take notice. I would wipe out the memory of my miserable failure in the SOE once and for all.'

'And did it go wrong?'

'Well, yes and no,' Charles replied. 'Every so often the auxiliary units would be tasked with testing the security at various military establishments, such as radar stations or army camps. We had to penetrate the defences, usually by cutting through the perimeter fence, and make our way to the guardhouse. We would leave some sign that we'd succeeded – a jocular note or sometimes even a dummy charge and detonator. Then we had to return to base without detection and phone our commanding officer.

'I requested that my unit undertake such an operation at St Mawgan airfield. The Americans are essentially in charge there so to penetrate their defences would have been especially pleasing – they consider themselves rather superior to us. It wasn't normal for units to suggest their own training targets but nobody thought it suspicious at the time and I was immediately granted permission.' He paused for a moment. 'The date I chose was Tuesday the fourteenth of March.'

'The day before Jack drowned,' I said quietly.

'Yes . . . My unit met here at midnight. You were already in bed and fast asleep; your aunt knew nothing about it. We blackened our faces and checked our equipment. I was very excited, couldn't wait to get going. I'd even composed a witty verse in German to leave at the guardhouse – I thought that would put the Yanks in a flap, give them something to think about.' He sighed. 'So foolish . . .

'We took my car and drove out of the village, following a twisting route of narrow back lanes to avoid being seen on the main road – we didn't really need to do that, but it all added to the sense of drama. I parked the car about a mile from the perimeter fence and we went the rest of the way on foot, through the trees and scrubland. It was totally black, you understand – we couldn't use torches or even a lighted match. It took about an hour to reach the airfield.

'We got down on our bellies and crawled towards the barbed-wire boundary fence, hiding behind a bunker to wait for the sentry to pass. The fence was more closely guarded than we'd expected; we only had a couple of minutes in which to get through. There wasn't time for us all to go at once, so as patrol leader, I volunteered.

'I edged forward, marching on my elbows. The ground was hard and stony, scraping the skin off my knees. My heart was racing with anticipation as I reached the fence. It was now or never. I took out my wirecutters and had made a hole just big enough to squeeze through when one of my men gave out a warning signal, a completely convincing hoot of an owl. Somebody was approaching. I had to withdraw straight away or I'd be caught. So I placed the German verse just inside the fence and crawled as fast and as quietly as I could back to safety.

'Two sentries walked by, chatting to each other, and neither of them noticed the gaping hole at the foot of the fence. Well, that was enough for us to call the mission a success. We drove back and spent the night in our hideout, drinking whisky and congratulating each other for getting one over the Yanks. I tried to get home at dawn the next morning but the place was swarming – at first I thought they were searching for Germans. We laid low, thinking ourselves very clever.'

'And that's what they arrested you for?' I asked in disbelief. 'For playing a stupid prank? Surely it was the Americans' fault for not guarding the fence properly.'

'It was more complicated than that,' Charles replied, pouring himself another glass. 'Remember the plane crash?'

'Of course.'

'It was a Warwick Mk One – took off from St Mawgan's at dawn that day. Judging from the questions in my interrogation – they were particularly interested in my knowledge of Arabic – I would hazard a guess that it was an intelligence mission, bound for North Africa.'

'So what did that have to do with you?' I interrupted.

'The Americans believed that the aircraft had been sabotaged – blown up.'

'And they suspected you of planting the bomb?' I was incredulous.

'Yes, that was more or less the gist of it.'

'But that doesn't make sense. Why would you draw attention to yourself by asking for permission to breach the security of the airfield?'

'I suppose they thought it was some kind of double bluff. I really don't know. Their case against me was extremely flimsy: they did a lot of digging into my past, used my knowledge of languages against me. And they knew I was trained in bomb-making. The theory was I'd been turned by the Nazis when I went to France in nineteen forty and had been operating as a double agent ever since. But they didn't have a shred of evidence. My little training exercise had caused a deal of embarrassment, you see. If they could have exposed me as a spy then all that would have been conveniently forgotten.'

'And do you believe the plane was deliberately blown up?'
I asked finally.

'I doubt it. It was probably just engine failure. Those
Warwicks are notorious.' Charles looked at his watch. 'It's
late . . .' He stood up and began to switch off the lamps. 'You
do realize, Ellen,' he said as we were about to climb the stairs,
'that we can never speak of this again. I have told you far too
much, certainly more than was necessary. But I must admit
it's helped to get things off my chest. The last couple of
months have been very lonely.'

'And for us too . . . Thank you for telling me, Uncle,' I
whispered. 'I promise I'll never breathe a word to anyone.' I
gave him a cautious kiss on his freshly shaven cheek. 'It's
good to have you home.'

'Yes. I just wish . . .' He hesitated, struggling to keep his
voice even. 'I just wish that Jack—' He stood at the foot of the
stairs. 'When I was in prison I kept asking for news – they
wouldn't tell me anything of course. But I convinced myself he
was still alive, that he'd run away with that girl – I swore to
myself that I'd find them, I'd even give them my blessing
to marry, if only he'd come back . . .'

'You were so good to him,' I said. 'To both of us.'

'He was my son,' replied Charles simply. 'My own dear
son.' And then he went upstairs to bed.

Charles was, as ever, true to his word, and the subject was
never mentioned by either of us again. He left his 'Home
Guard' unit, went back to his practice in Padstow and slowly

reintegrated himself into village life. There was some gossip, as I had predicted, but nobody dared to say anything openly to my face. We all missed Jack terribly, but as the Allies made their long arduous progress through France, there were so many deaths. We were nothing special, just another grieving family. With Charles there to care for her, Clara slowly recovered, but she could not cope with any mention of Jack. All his possessions – his clothes, his schoolbooks, his cigarette cards – were put into boxes and stored in the attic, all the photos of him put away. I found it very hard washing him out of our lives like a drawing on the sand, but that was how my uncle dealt with it. For Clara's sake, he kept insisting, but it was also for his own.

Charles was tired to the roots of his being. All that enthusiasm he'd shown us at the beginning, that desire to fill our heads with knowledge, to give us fresh experiences, impart his wisdom, tell us stories – it had all gone down with the *Louisa May*. After Jack's death he gave up trying to be a father – he wasn't unkind towards me, just not very interested. I returned to my studies, working furiously hard in the hope that I might make up for his disappointment and win him back. It almost worked. I passed with flying colours and my uncle began to talk of sending me to Cambridge. But I would have given up every bit of my success to have had my brother back.

TWENTY-EIGHT

Last night I put the silk map under my pillow and allowed myself to dream of Jory. We were sixteen again, together, just the two of us – exploring the sandy coves between our bay and the estuary, crunching across the shingle, our virgin foot-prints seeping into the drowned sand. The sky above us was a plain unmarked blue, as if God had laid a freshly washed and ironed tablecloth across the heavens, pristine and perfect. The afternoon sun was low, beaming a wide path of shimmering silver across the surface of the ocean, parting the waves for us, tempting us to walk on water. Nobody else was there: the world belonged to us.

We gathered yellow shells and rescued sodden lumps of driftwood, laying them out to dry. We picked up white gull feathers and flew them into the wind, poked at the clusters of baby mussels sparkling like necklaces of black jet on the glowing pink rocks. Jory searched for flat skimming stones and bounced them across the water, once, twice, as many as four times. He found a small grey pebble in the shape of a heart and, without saying a word, dropped it into my pocket. I stood next to him, caressing the cold smoothness of my pebble as it lay in the darkness of my coat, and wondered at its meaning.

Jory took my hand and guided me over a large muddle of rocks that stretched beyond the beach to the sea. I was his shadow, stepping across shallow puddles, jumping the crevices, slipping every so often on the slimy green weed coating the sides of the ponds. Then he stopped and beckoned me to his side, pointing to a small piece of white silk floating in the middle of a pool like a waterlily. He crouched down and reached out, grabbing a corner with the tips of his fingers and pulling it to shore. He squeezed the cloth in his strong farmer's hand, and the water splashed onto the granite. He laid it out flat on a dry piece of rock and we bent down, our heads close together, to study the strange treasure we'd found.

'It's a map,' he said. Then he turned his face and kissed me.

I didn't remember my dream until I was making my bed this morning and found the map, screwed up like a tissue. It wasn't a memory but a vaguely erotic fantasy, not the kind of dream a woman of my age should be having at all. Jory's hand in mine, the heart-shaped stone, the silent declaration of love, our long passionate kiss . . . It made me feel slightly uncomfortable, embarrassed in front of myself. At the moment I can picture what happened very clearly; in fact now it's come back to me it won't stop replaying in my head. But with a bit of luck the dream will soon start to fade and by lunch time I won't be able to recall the slightest detail.

The map, however, is real, a souvenir not just of Jory but of everything that has been wandering through my head these past weeks, encoding my memories in roads and coast-lines, names of foreign cities written in indelible ink. Maybe it's the silk that gives it this magic quality, like a conjuror's handkerchief flirting for my attention, drawing my gaze to the Past while the Present performs a sleight of hand. It is such a beautiful thing – fragile and yet unbreakable, I almost can't put it down.

What young man wouldn't have been thrilled to find such a mysterious object, a map minutely drawn on silk, revealing secret places he didn't know existed, beckoning him on a journey, promising heroism and adventure. Perhaps Jory imagined himself as a secret agent with a vital message to deliver, making his way through the deep Hungarian forests, crossing the snowy Balkan mountains, running down dirty cobbled streets, hiding in doorways, sheltering in dark churches, with only the silk map to lead him to safety. No wonder he didn't hand it in like a responsible citizen but greedily kept it to himself, hiding it from his son and grandson, his own little piece of history.

I'm sure that Jory found the map on a nearby beach shortly after the plane crash – it almost certainly belonged to one of the passengers, probably a British officer from the Intelligence Corps, travelling with false identity papers, emergency rations and a cyanide pill. Maybe he was sitting by the aircraft window with the map spread across his knees, memorizing road networks, the location of his first rendezvous, when the plane exploded and ripped open like a sardine tin, tossing his body into the sky. I can imagine the small piece of white silk flying free, dancing for a few seconds on the warm currents of air like a miniature kite, before dropping into the sea. As the plane was consumed in a ball of red and orange flames, the map floated calmly to the surface, bobbing on the waves effortlessly towards the shore.

I discovered the 'true story' of what happened decades later when an article appeared in our local paper – UNSOLVED MYSTERIES OF THE SECOND WORLD WAR. The Warwick, as my uncle rightly guessed, was on a top-secret mission to Algiers. Its passengers included two extremely high-ranking French officers on their way to join De Gaulle, a Russian-speaking agent going to meet Tito, and several SOE operatives taking crates of gold bullion to pay off the partisans in the Balkans. Only a few bodies were ever recovered, and despite an intensive search, the bullion was never found.

There were various conflicting theories about what had caused the crash – poor weather conditions, engine failure – but the more dramatic explanation of sabotage persisted. An atmospheric bomb had possibly been placed on board, designed to explode when the plane reached a certain altitude. Fortunately there was no mention of my uncle in the newspaper article, and anyway, by then he was long since dead and there was nobody left in the village to remember. Apart from Jory, that is. At the time it didn't cross my mind to talk to him about it, but now of course I wish I had. If he were still alive I would ask him what the map had to do with Selina. But then, if he were still alive, I wouldn't have the map at all . . .

There are very few tangible reminders of Charles and Clara left now, and even these are about to be taken away: the card table they used for bridge parties, the gramophone, a battered seaman's chest with sharp rusty clasps, boxes of French and German novels, the china shepherdess that used to sit on my aunt's dressing table – I'll be relieved when the house clearance chap stacks it all into the van and I don't have to think about it any more. Cassie has been very kind, helping me decide what to discard and what to keep, but there is a sentimental side to her. She doesn't want any of the family memorabilia herself but wants me to hang onto it. What is the point of keeping it? To anybody else it's just a pile of junk. When I am dead it will be thrown away by strangers, so it's better to do it now and save other people the bother.

I am impatient to get the sale over and done with, itching to leave. I feel as if I am living in a strange, suspended state, no longer measuring time in days, but by the number of viewers that have looked over the house. Spindrift seems to have become a local tourist attraction. Gone are the days when visitors would have been satisfied with wandering round the shops, choosing an illustrated tea towel or a trashy novel. Now they want to pretend to buy a house. I've told Gareth that I'm going back to London soon and he'll have to handle the sale himself, it's the only way.

Besides, I'm about to be on my own again. Cassie is leaving today to restart her travels, staying in my flat for a couple of weeks, then moving on to France and Spain. She said her main goodbyes last night – the staff at the beach café organized a barbecue on the beach in her honour: they built a bonfire, played the guitar and sang songs – including 'Waltzing Matilda', I gather – then everyone went for a swim at two o'clock in the morning. Scott didn't turn up to the party, which offended Cassie because she'd thought they'd agreed to part as friends.

'He's so immature,' she said to me this morning, over breakfast.

'Perhaps he was too upset to come,' I suggested lamely.

'Why should he be upset? He was the one that decided to stay.'

'I suppose he wants you to stay too.'

'But that's so unreasonable. Why should I change my plans just for him?'

'Because you love him?'

She shrugged and finished her bowl of cereal.

I have watched this brief affair from the sidelines, an unfamiliar modern game played according to rules I don't understand. Cassie has given all, yet seemingly lost so little – there is a brittleness about her, like a thin layer of ice on the surface of a pond. She gives the impression that she doesn't take things too seriously, that it's impossible to hurt her, but I can't work out whether this is all one big act or she genuinely doesn't care. *I* would care . . . I would be so frightened of not being loved that I would instantly drop all my plans and bend to my partner's will. I admire Cassie's emotional independence, her willingness to take risks and trust in the future. I am a little envious – no, *very* envious.

I have spent so much of my life in patient expectation, believing that if I was good – put others first, obeyed the rules and followed all the instructions – then the success and happiness I truly deserved would eventually come my way. For years I put myself last on the list or left my name off altogether, tucked my clothes at the bottom of the ironing pile, gave myself the burned scone or the smallest portion of pie, stood back and waved others before me in the queue.

To what end? God does not keep a tally of our dogged obedience, our moments of self-denial or deferred gratification. He doesn't add all our kind deeds together and dish out an appropriate dollop of good fortune in return. Virtue is supposedly its own reward, but I have come to wonder whether there is anything inherently virtuous about self-sacrifice. Nobody ever asked me to behave in this way and most of the time they haven't even noticed. I have done it all in the hope of being loved, and even when I found someone who said they loved me I was never fully satisfied, never quite trusted or believed it. Poor Richard . . . the things I felt but never had the courage to say, let alone act upon.

Cassie comes down the stairs, dragging a large rucksack behind her. She is wearing her khaki shorts and the skinny white top, her hair screwed up in a careless bun pinned by a fabric flower, tendrils escaping onto her neck and round her ears. She has decided to do the journey to London by train so I am taking her to the nearest station, fifteen miles or so away.

The station at Padstow closed a long time ago, although the ticket office still exists at the end of the quay. The disused tracks were lifted to make a cycle path, following the route my train to school used to take, following the snaking outline of the Camel estuary as it makes its way inland. I can remember standing on the platform on a chilly winter's morning, watching my breath curl out of my mouth, holding my nose so as not to inhale the stink of mackerel as men in rubber aprons and long boots piled up crates of freshly caught fish, waiting to be put on the next train to Billingsgate.

But why has all this suddenly come into my mind? It doesn't matter what it used to be like, or what I used to do. I am satiated with remembering. Please God, bring me back to the here and now.

'Say goodbye to Spindrift,' I say as Cassie gathers up the last of her things and checks for her passport and phone. 'You'll probably never see the inside again . . . unless you rent it, I suppose.'

'No, that would be too weird . . .' She looks out of the sitting-room window one last time and sighs wistfully. 'I wish you weren't selling.'

'We've been through all that.'

'I know, but . . . It's so like you want to end everything, to disappear and not leave any trace of your existence.'

'Yes,' I reply. 'That's exactly what I'd like to do.'

'Why?'

'Because I don't think I've made a very good job of my life, I suppose,' I say after a few moments' reflection.

'That's silly . . .'

'Is it? You're probably right. I've just been feeling a little maudlin recently . . . That's what happens when you get to my age – everyone around you starts dying and it sets you thinking. I have always thought too much, it's been my curse.'

'Thinking's very unhealthy. I'd avoid it if I were you,' laughs Cassie. 'Hadn't we better get going? I don't want to miss my train.'

We leave the village by the only road, rounding the bay and passing the beach café and shop. Cassie instinctively turns round to catch a last glimpse of the sea before we turn the corner and climb the hill. We pass the entrance to the farm and she peers down the track – for a last sight of Scott perhaps, but he's not there. The coast road is busy, and within a mile or two we are stuck behind a convoy of caravans.

'I should have realized, it's changeover day,' I sigh. My car doesn't have the acceleration to overtake while going uphill so we are forced to join the procession of gleaming white boxes on wheels. Cassie checks the time on her mobile. 'Don't worry, we'll make it,' I tell her. And we do, but with only a couple of minutes to spare.

The station is on the other side of Bodmin, in the middle of nowhere, but the platform is full of people – families on day trips, elderly couples with small suitcases, young people with bikes.

'I've never seen the place so crowded,' I remark. 'I do hope you get a seat.'

Neither Cassie nor I are keen on sentimental goodbyes, and there isn't time anyway. We hug each other briefly and promise to keep in touch.

'Take care, dear.'

'You too ... Thanks for everything!' She swings her rucksack onto her back and climbs aboard the train. And somehow I know that I'll never see my granddaughter again. But that's just being silly ...

It takes me an hour to get back to the house, trapped with the incoming holidaymakers this time. I feel hot and dusty, desperate for a breath of sea air and a gin and tonic. To my irritation, Gareth's car is parked in the courtyard – he must be showing some more viewers round. I don't remember him ringing to confirm the appointment – he's treating the house as if it is already empty. I make a mental note to talk to him about this later as I let myself in.

'Hello?' I call, listening for the sound of footsteps, murmurs of conversation, the creak of cupboard doors being opened, but there is nobody there. They must be looking round the garden. I make myself a drink and go out through the conservatory, deciding that I should at least appear polite and introduce myself. Gareth is showing off the views to what appears to be an elderly couple – they are standing at the very edge of the garden overlooking the rocks that separate the two bays, their backs turned from me as they gaze out to sea. I pause to observe them unnoticed, sipping my drink, feeling the hot burn of the gin slide satisfyingly down my throat.

The woman is slim and stands upright; her long silver hair falls down her back, shimmering like waves in the sun. It's unusual to see someone of her age wearing their hair so long she looks artistic. An ankle length dress gathers at her waist, the very same colour as the blue-green sea beyond, so that for a second she looks disembodied, hanging in the ocean like a surrealist painting. I can't see her face but I'm sure she must be beautiful.

The man seems older and is more crooked, leaning on a walking stick. He's wearing pale linen trousers and a short-sleeved checked shirt. They have an air of wealth about them, a composure and self-confidence; it makes me think that perhaps they're not English. Gareth is pointing towards the Round Hole and has obviously just said something amusing because all three of them burst into easy laughter. Even from this distance I can tell that they like the house, can imagine themselves living here, sleeping in the best bedroom, listening to the sound of the waves, sitting in their deckchairs in the garden, admiring the view. And with that thought, a weight rises from my shoulders – for I sense that these are the people who will buy.

I start to walk towards them when the man turns, suddenly sensing my presence. His face is tanned and craggy with wrinkles, his features obscured by a full grey beard.

Then I stop. Something about the way he's standing – his weight on the right foot, the left knee slightly bent – strikes a chill of recognition in my heart. He smiles gently, cautiously holding out his free hand to me.

'Nellie,' he says.

TWENTY-NINE

Spindrift. I guess I always knew at the back of my mind that the house would still be here, as much a part of the landscape as the rocks and sand, almost as old as the Round Hole on top of the cliffs. It's smaller than I recall – the hole, I mean. We walked up there this morning and looked down into the well below. I wanted to lie flat on my stomach and crawl right up to the edge, peer over like we used to when we were kids – remember, Nellie? But I decided not to risk it – at my age I'm not sure I could get up again.

I thought the village would have changed more than it has – more commercialization, especially round by the beach – I don't know, hotels or bars or something – but if anything there's less. More people of course, on the beach, surfing, a lot of cars parked up . . . I felt a little disorientated at first. Weren't there a couple of tennis courts somewhere, and a duck pond?

I see the farm's still there. We walked up the lane and called into that funny little shop, bought a tub of clotted cream. I haven't had that in years. Yeah, everything's pretty much as I remember it . . .

The house now, you know, I don't think that's changed one bit. I even recognized some of the furniture – Charles's leather chair that nobody else was allowed to sit on, that dresser they used to have all the china on and you had to be careful when you went past because the floorboards were creaky and the cups would wobble on their hooks. I broke a fancy plate once, running round the room kicking a cushion like it was a ball. Upstairs too, same layout, same bathtub even . . . Even a couple of pictures on the walls looked familiar; it was like going back in time, kind of spooked me.

The views from the bedrooms are just as amazing as I remember, of course – indelibly printed on my memory. So many colours in the ocean, clouds of spray as the waves hit the rocks, the way the sea surrounds the house on three sides. I never really appreciated it, you know, when I lived here. I never really understood its beauty, the wildness of the place.

When I realized you still owned the place I was totally shocked. It sounds stupid, but it never occurred to me that you would have stayed all this time. Soon as I got the e-mail from Cassie, I knew I had to come clean. I wanted to tell you straight away who I was, but I . . . I didn't know how to do it. I tried writing letters, e-mails, but it didn't feel right. I was scared, I guess, scared you'd be so mad at me you wouldn't want to see me. So I decided to come over and face the music. Cassie mentioned you were selling up so we knew there wasn't much time – we just had to get on a plane and go for it. I didn't want to lose you again . . .

She doesn't know, by the way – Cassie. I lied to her. I feel real bad about that, but there wasn't much choice . . . She's my great-niece – is that right? Which means you must have married, had kids. There's so much we don't know about each other . . . Is Cassie around? I'd like to meet her – she sounds like a terrific kid.

So many times over the years I wanted to get in touch. I thought of hiring an investigator to track you down, but then the whole truth would have had to come out – you know, about what I'd done. Maybe if I'd known just how easy it would have been to come right back here and knock on the door . . . maybe I would have done it sooner. To be honest, I was waiting for the Rosewarnes to – well, there's no delicate way to put this – I was waiting for them to die. I couldn't have them finding out I was still alive and I couldn't guarantee that you would keep the secret. They were healthy; they could easily have made it into their seventies or eighties, and that was a long time to wait. The decades went by and – I don't know, once I came to the conclusion that they must surely be dead by now it seemed too late – too late for us. I began to wonder if you were still alive. It didn't feel like you were dead, but – I kind of didn't want to find out.

I don't expect you to believe me. I know how it looks, like I had no intention of ever finding you, but that's not true. It's just one of those crazy, inexplicable things that it was you that found me first, and you weren't even looking. I mean, why would you have been looking? Jack is buried up in the cemetery – we went there yesterday, I saw my name on the grave, clear as could be. That was a really moving moment, I can tell you, brought it all home, the terrible thing I'd done to you. I broke down and wept like a baby . . . But you have to understand, Jack Morrison, or Rosewarne, whatever you want to call him, he's truly dead, Nellie. He's been dead just as long as you thought. In that respect, I don't feel I've deceived you at all. That's not just some kind of self-serving rationalization – it's a fact. It was Tom Penaluna and the Rosewarnes we had to escape from, not you, although at the time it felt like you'd become one of them.

The Rosewarnes were very weird people. Good manners and pleasant smiles on the surface but all kinds of dark stuff going on beneath. They tried to get their claws into me right from the start – it made my flesh creep.

When we first got to Spindrift it was so exciting, like we were on vacation. We'd never even seen the sea before and suddenly here we were in this fantastic place, right on the beach. We were given a whole bedroom to ourselves; mine was so big it frightened me and I wanted to share with you, Nellie, but they said it wasn't proper even though we were twins. At night the house would creak and I'd lie there in the darkness listening to the sea grinding on the shingle and the wind banging the loose slates on the roof. I couldn't fall asleep no matter how hard I tried. I'd close my eyes and do my own versions of counting sheep. I'd try to remember every cigarette card I owned, listing the butterfly species or the names of the cricketers. I'd imagine myself back home, running over the skinny bridge to Galleon's Reach, naming the brightly painted barges – *Lovely Lady*, *Clear Skies*, *Rambling Rose* . . .

But the real reason I wanted to fall asleep so bad was because I knew any second Clara would come in. She did it every night, about an hour after we'd been sent upstairs. She'd tiptoe into my room and stand at the side of the bed. I think she just stared at me – she never seemed to move much. I kept my eyes shut real tight, and I'd breathe a little heavier than normal so she'd think I was asleep. Then after a few minutes she'd get a little braver and sit on the edge of the bed and she'd start stroking my forehead, very lightly, pushing my hair back off my face, again and again in a kind of rhythm. Her hands always smelled of lavender soap and sometimes there'd be a faint whiff of alcohol on her breath – sweet sherry or port wine.

I'd put up with it for a while, then make out I was having a dream and turn over sharply. She'd let out a little gasp and snatch her hand away. She wouldn't leave though – she just sat there watching me, letting out the occasional long sigh. Eventually Charles would come in and whisper it was time to go to bed. She'd beg him to let her stay a few minutes longer, insisting she hadn't woken me – which she hadn't of course because I'd never been asleep in the first place. He'd lead her out of the room and the door would close with a quiet click. I didn't know what to make of it. I didn't like it, that's for sure.

Charles wasn't as weird as Clara, but he still tried too hard. I reckoned I already had a father – I didn't need another one, not even after Dad died. Charles was always taking me out places, on long walks along the cliffs, lecturing me about boring stuff I wasn't interested in – the names of flowers and birds, Neolithic cultures that used to live here, the roots of the English language, trying to shape me into someone new, like I was his Pinocchio . . . He made me go fishing with him for sea bass – do you remember that? We'd go to the next bay, I can't remember its name right now – where there's that heap of rocks that jut far out into the sea? He'd make me stand on the very edge, where it was all wet and slimy, and I'd be so scared I was going to slip off into the water. Within minutes we were soaked to the skin but he didn't seem to notice or care – he was so hell-bent on showing me how to cast a line into the waves. I could never do it . . . didn't want to do it . . .

I was jealous of you, Nellie, because they left you alone. I don't mean they ignored you, but I don't know, I just felt like all the pressure was on me. I was their favourite, their pet, and I wasn't doing anything to encourage it; quite the opposite. I tried everything to put them off, but it just didn't seem to make any difference. It felt like they were never going to let me go. This was never a holiday as far as they were concerned, it was a permanent arrangement. It didn't matter whether the war ended or our parents came to ask for us back, no way were they going to surrender us. So when Mum and Dad died it kind of seemed like they'd killed them – like Charles had gone to North Woolwich and painted a big cross on the roof of our house so the Nazis knew exactly where to drop their bombs.

I know now of course that it was stupid of me to think like that. I let my hatred of them get way out of hand. It was just the trauma of being orphaned, of losing everything and being so far from home. But I felt totally abandoned. None of our relatives stepped in, nobody came to rescue us . . . We were just stuck there, in their power. I couldn't understand it. You seemed happy with how things had turned out, like you preferred it; you didn't even seem to miss Mum and Dad. But I missed them real bad, you know . . . Especially Mum. I missed her so much and there was nobody I could talk to about it. Until I met Selina, that is.

Over the years I've tried to work out when it was I fell in love with her. Maybe it's simple – maybe it was the first time I saw her in the marsh collecting the withy. One time I tried to paint that scene. Overcast sky, diffuse light, dark bare branches, thin reeds sticking out of the muddy water, a few specks of white in the foreground for snowdrops . . . I put Selina in the distance, no more than a couple of brushstrokes – a twig of a girl bending over with a sack on her back, long wavy hair falling across her face. I never could do her hair justice – so many shades of red and yellow, woven with threads of pure gold . . .

I can't remember exactly what we said on that first meeting. I think I offered to carry her bag or something and she refused without even a thank you. I was scared of her then: her beauty was overwhelming – something unnatural in the symmetry of her features, the intensity of pigment in the eyes, the deathly paleness of her skin . . . I couldn't believe that thousands of years of random coupling could have resulted in a creature that was physically so perfect. It was like she'd been created by some god, not human, a divine work of art.

I guess it doesn't make a whole lot of sense, but that's how I thought of Selina way back then – before I really got to know her.

She had an effect on me that by-passed the intellect and went straight to the gut. I couldn't think when I was with her, couldn't form an argument or make deductions – I *felt* everything, I had to go on instinct. It was like dealing with a wild horse that was never going to let you break her in. Later on in our relationship she'd make me so mad I'd think I was going to kill her. She'd reach out to hit me and I'd grab her by the wrist, wouldn't let her go. But as I held onto her while she squirmed like a fish, I'd be struck by some little detail of her loveliness – the white softness of her inner forearm, the purple veins running up to the elbow just visible beneath her skin.

Or another time I'd be shouting angrily in her face, telling her that I couldn't go on, that it was all over, when I'd suddenly catch the colours dancing in her eyes – like the underside of a rainbow, blue, indigo, violet, the irises flecked with gold like sparks from a fire – and I'd be struck dumb, forget what I was saying. She always got the better of me, never with words, or the force of argument, just with a look or a gesture. She still gets the better of me, after all these years.

I used to draw her all the time – it was our big secret. They were just pencil portraits to begin with, head and shoulders, facing me or in profile. I must have drawn her face a hundred times but I couldn't capture her likeness – I'd get the nose just right but the eyes would be too far apart or the mouth too wide. Even when I'd managed to perfect each individual feature I couldn't put them together in one picture: there was always something missing, something I couldn't get hold of . . .

I'd bunk off school and she'd meet me in the sand dunes near her cottage. If Tom Penaluna had gone out fishing we'd go up to her room and I'd draw her, sitting on a chair by the window, gazing out across the estuary, or I'd get her to lie on the bed and I'd sketch her full-length. Selina couldn't keep still for long – she'd moan and complain and say she had pins and needles in her legs, and if she didn't like what I'd drawn she'd rip out the page and put it on the fire. I got better though, and learned to draw her real quick, which helped a lot in later life.

Other times we'd go down to one of the beaches that lay on the other side of the Point. I'd draw her sitting on a rock or paddling in the water. I did a really good watercolour of her once, sitting on an upturned punt, the wind blowing her hair, her body arched back, head upwards like she was looking for the sun behind the clouds, bare legs, feet buried in the sand. They were good times, before everything got more complicated . . . We were real close then. I felt we'd been put on this earth just for each other and would never need anybody else. I trusted her completely.

One day we climbed into this small cove. It wasn't easy to get to – there was no real path – but we liked it there because nobody else ever came down. There was a cave that very few people knew of; it looked like a narrow fissure but if you squeezed through there was quite a big space behind it and it was dry – even during the spring tides the water never came up that far. Tom had shown it to Selina years earlier; he'd told her it was a smuggler's cave. I always wanted to go in there and explore but she wasn't so keen, said the darkness scared her. So we roamed around the beach for a bit, picking up flotsam and jetsam, finding each other shells. Anyway, we were happy, really in harmony with each other that day, and I asked if I could draw her. She said yes, but she wanted me to draw her as a merrymaid. She never said 'mermaid', always used the Cornish name.

'I'll try,' I said, 'but I don't know how to draw the tail. I've never seen a real merrymaid.'

She had a yellow dress on that day, with buttons down the front and short sleeves, a faint pattern in the cloth, I think, and the hem was uneven. I got out my sketchbook and a piece of charcoal, found a rock to sit on. She started taking off her clothes, unbuttoning her dress and twisting her arms out of the sleeves so it hung round her hips. Then she pulled her undergarment over her head – it was like a vest, I guess; she didn't wear a bra. That was the first time I saw her breasts – quite small but perfectly round with beautiful brown nipples. I think I went very red and dropped my stick of charcoal in the sand. She lay down on her side, leaning on her elbow, and wrapped her dress round her legs, so they looked joined together, like a tail. And she arranged her hair so that some of it fell across her chest, just obscuring her right breast, but the other one she left bare. She wasn't at all nervous. It was like it felt totally natural to lie half naked in the open air.

'Go on,' she said. 'Draw me.'

I screwed up my eyes so her legs became a blur and I thought of the grey sheen on a salmon, the golds and greens that glitter on the back of a mackerel, the hard silver skin of whitebait, and then I just knew how she would look. I started the scales from the top of her thighs, layering them in rows, tapering the tail towards the bottom, then adding this beautiful, extravagant fin. She kept quite still the whole time, not saying a word, just thinking herself a mermaid, lying on the sand by the edge of the shore. She looked – what's the word I'm looking for? – she looked serene . . . It was the best picture I ever drew of her.

You knew about the mermaid thing, of course. A few people had told her when she was very little that she looked like one, on account of her hair, I guess. They liked to touch it, as if they weren't sure what it was made of, because it was too beautiful to be human hair somehow . . . I think it started out as an attention-seeking device, or some kind of escapism – you couldn't blame her for that: she had such a hard life. But as time went on, I don't know, sometimes I thought she actually believed it might happen.

She got it into her head that it was connected to losing her virginity, as if she would wake up the morning after and find herself transformed. Part of her wanted it to happen, was desperate for it to happen, and the other part was absolutely terrified – it was insane either way. I didn't know how to deal with it. She'd fly into a temper if you challenged her about it:

you couldn't reason with her, it was a waste of time. There was no choice but to humour her. You had to go along with it.

Now I realize that she had some serious emotional issues but I was only fifteen or sixteen then, and I was crazy about her. I couldn't bear to see her hanging around the GIs, flirting and kissing, letting them play with her like she was some novelty toy. I couldn't understand why anyone so beautiful could act so cheap. If Selina hadn't been so hung up about the virginity thing she would have become a whore, I'm sure of that. She didn't value herself; she didn't even feel she owned her own body.

But you know, there were good reasons for how she got into that state – in fact it was the trigger that led to us deciding to run away. She told me that Tom had been abusing her for years, sexually abusing her. It had started not long after her mother ran off with another man – he was lonely, I guess, felt angry and rejected – not that I'm excusing what he did, not for one moment. I'm just trying to paint a picture, you know, of how it must have been for the two of them, trapped in that tiny cottage, out at sea together for hours on end, working on that little fishing boat. They both had a really tough life. I don't think I realized at the time how bleak an existence it was.

The day you and I last saw each other, Nellie – that was the day I found out what had been going on. We'd got drenched in the rain so we went to the house to dry off. I suggested she borrowed one of your dresses, came into the room while she was getting changed and, well, inevitably we started fooling around on your bed. I suppose it was kind of what I had in mind . . . I wanted to make love to her so bad. Things were going good, then all of a sudden she got upset and backed off – I couldn't understand it: why did she keep doing this to me, leading me on and then pushing me away? We started yelling at each other and I got real angry. That was when she told me about Tom – it hit me like a ten-ton truck.

Can you imagine? The girl who I was crazy about, who I wanted to marry, telling me her own father had gone further with her than I had? It was unbearable. Once the truth was out, Selina just collapsed, cried and cried. She felt ashamed, guilty that she hadn't stopped him, thought she was somehow to blame – she went through all the classic things that victims of abuse are supposed to feel. But I was just furious; my male pride had just taken a hammer blow. I felt anger like I've never felt before or since. If I'd set eyes on Tom Penaluna that night I probably would have killed him.

I said that settled it, we were getting out of Cornwall. I was taking her away as far as possible, we'd get married, start a new life. I'd been trying to persuade Selina to come to London with me for months, but she'd always refused – she belonged here, she said, she needed to be by the sea – more stupid mermaid stuff. But I wasn't having any of that. I decided to take control . . . Take control of Selina? Some hope.

To my amazement, she agreed to elope – at least I thought that was what she meant when she said we'd always be together. Now I think that maybe she had no intention of leaving with me, that she was just telling me what I wanted to hear. Who's to know what was really going on in her head at that moment?

But we made our peace. I comforted her and calmed her down, took her in my arms, stroked her hair, told her that I loved her more than anything else in the world. And slowly she melted, she gave herself to me . . . That evening, as it was growing dark, we lay on your bed and finally lost our virginity to each other. But you know that, Nellie, you were there, you saw it happen. One of the most incredible, significant experiences of my life and you spoiled it.

I'm sorry. I know you didn't mean to do it, but it still took me a long time to forgive you for that.

After we'd made love and there'd been that ugly scene with you, we thought we'd better get out of the house right away, before Charles or Clara came home. I wanted us to spend the night in Jory's haybarn, then walk to Padstow and catch the early morning train to Billingsgate. We didn't have the money to pay our fare, but I thought maybe we could hide amongst the fish crates. Selina had other ideas. She wanted to go back to Cove, to say goodbye to the sea and the *Louisa May*, she said. I said no, I wasn't having it, she wasn't to spend even one more night with her father in the house, but she had to have her own way.

As we trudged up the cliff, the rain started up again. I told her we'd catch pneumonia if we walked all the way to Cove. I begged her to stop at the barn, but she wouldn't listen to me. It was dark and the wind was whipping up; out in the ocean the storm was beginning to take hold. Selina marched on, stumbling over the stones, slipping in the mud, even running when she could. Her hair was lashing her face, streaming wet with rain. Even in the darkness I could see that her eyes were wild. When I tried to grab her arm she shook me off and ran even faster. The wind was buffeting around us, tearing at our ears. A great gust took us by surprise and nearly threw us off the cliff. 'At least stay away from the edge!' I begged.

Eventually, after constant pleading, I persuaded her to leave the cliff path and take the short cut to Mussel Cove, across a field of cowering sheep and along the track that led to Langham's farm. From there it was only a short walk to her cottage but we were wet to the bone and freezing cold. I was so desperate for shelter I didn't care where we went, even if it meant confronting Penaluna.

We reached the top of the hill and the dark outline of the cove came into sight. I breathed a sigh of relief and stopped, bending over to release a stitch from my side. But Selina was already running ahead of me down the path. I stood up and started to chase after her but she hurtled on, straight past the front of the cottages and then up the hill again to the pig houses at the back.

'Where are you going?' I shouted, but either she couldn't hear me or she wasn't going to answer. She went down a side alley and disappeared round the corner, lost in the blackness. I ran after her through the alley, coming out on the narrow overgrown coastal path that hugged the estuary. I couldn't see her anywhere, so I carried on going forward, away from the cottages towards the sea again, the whole time screaming her name. She didn't seem to be ahead of me, so that meant there was only one place she could be: on one of the small beaches below. I looked for a gap in the hedge and began to feel my way down a muddy path, grabbing onto spiky bushes, skidding on the wet stones. The mud gave way to slippery rocks. I couldn't see well enough to climb over them, had to slide down on my butt. Selina was already on the sand, untying her father's punt from a mooring stump. Out in the channel, I could just make out the *Louisa May*, bobbing about in the darkness.

'What the hell do you think you're doing?' I said, trying to grab the rope off her.

'I 'ave to.' She turned to me, her violet eyes flashing like a cat's. 'I 'ave to go out there one last time.'

'In this weather? You can't. It's suicide!'

'I've got to fetch 'er,' Selina grunted, climbing into the punt. 'She'll be dashed to pieces if 'er lies 'ere all night. I 'ave to take 'er into harbour.'

'I won't let you, do you understand? I won't let you do it, Selina. Get out of the boat now!'

'Out of my way! 'Ee can't stop me!'

So what did I do? I got in too – I was really angry, but I couldn't let her go out there on her own. I had no choice. She sculled out to the *Louisa May*, released one of the anchors and climbed aboard, tying the punt behind us. I carried on protesting and pleading with her to turn back, but she wouldn't listen.

Selina took hold of the starting handle and cranked up the

engine. She ordered me to haul the bow anchor aboard, and like an idiot I obeyed her – I was shit-scared, didn't have a clue what I was doing, but I figured we'd have more chance if there were two of us. And I guess I still thought I could persuade her to give up and go back. We chugged forward for a few yards and then, to my horror, she turned the boat round and started heading away from town, out to sea. I couldn't believe what was happening.

'What the hell are you doing?' I screamed. 'You said you were taking her into harbour!'

'It's too shallow 'ere. We 'ave to go out first and cross the bar!' she called back. 'I'll bring her back on the other side of the channel.'

'Take us out there? You can't do that! You'll kill us!'

'There's no other way.'

'Please, Selina,' I begged, 'stop this now.' But she took no notice. I couldn't get through to her – it was like she was in a hypnotic trance. There was some other force far stronger than me pulling her out to sea.

The waves were mounting now, like towers of water, all white with froth, and the boat was bumping up and down like the scariest rollercoaster ride I've ever been on. The punt was still tied on at the back, but it kept banging against the boat: I couldn't see how it could last much longer. I didn't have a clue what to do. I felt so useless. Selina was struggling to control the wheel and called me over.

'Hold on tight,' she said. 'Keep pulling her to sta'boa'd!' I was in such a panic I couldn't even remember which way starboard was. The gale was roaring loudly, the rain squalling and there was so much spray we could barely see each other.

We'd reached the most dangerous part of our terrifying journey, crossing the mouth of the estuary. We were virtually out in the open sea and the waves were hitting us side on. The boat was lifting and dropping, lifting and dropping, my stomach was heaving and my legs were like jelly. I could barely stand up. Either the waves were rising like a wall on either side of us, trapping us in the middle – which was awesome, but terrifying – or they dragged us up onto their crest and then threw us back down so heavily they knocked us off our feet. The deck was swirling with water and we were sliding about, gripping the gunwale, trying to get back to the wheel.

'We're going to die!' I shouted. Selina didn't reply, just hurled herself at me, wrapped her wet slippery arms around my neck and kissed me hard on the lips. We clung to each other for a moment before a surge of water pushed the boat up, tearing us apart. Suddenly we saw an enormous wave rumbling and roaring towards us, bigger than I've ever seen in my whole life. It lifted us high into the air and for a moment the boat flew through the darkness, then it dashed us back down again and toppled right over us.

To be honest, I don't remember much about the *Louisa May* capsizing; all I know is that wave hit us full on and we just went under. I was flung out and disappeared under the water. I was being thrown about, kept banging into the side of the boat. I was gasping for breath, coughing and spluttering, gulping in water, and it was so cold – I can't tell you how cold that sea was. After a few seconds the waves abated and I managed to get my head up. I saw the punt – it had broken free and was tossing about in the waves, right next to me. I clung onto the side, but another wave came and threw me off, but then a few moments later I got close to it again and, with some kind of superhuman effort, don't ask me how I did it, I managed to fling myself in.

I looked around for the *Louisa May*, but it seemed to have vanished. I couldn't see or hear Selina – I was choking and vomiting, didn't have the strength to call out for her. It was very dark and there was a lot of spray, the swell heaving up and down, roaring in my ears, and I knew she could be many yards away by now. I wasn't going to last long in the little boat: another big wave was sure to break any time and I guessed that would be it for me, but there was nothing else I could do. I lay across the bench seat and wrapped my arms round it like I was strapping myself to a mast. The water washed over me a hundred times that night, but I just clung onto that little seat.

The punt was being hurled towards the shore and I knew any moment we were going hit the rocks and would surely break up. If I wasn't too badly injured by the impact I thought maybe I would have a chance to get onto the beach. You know, the strange thing is, I don't know exactly what happened next: I guess I must have lost consciousness. But by some miracle I woke up lying on the shingle, washed up like a piece of driftwood. I didn't know where I was at first, wasn't even sure if I was alive or dead. Everything hurt. It was like I'd been beaten up, could hardly move. It must have been about four or five in the morning. I saw the sun rise, like a huge pink ball – I'll never forget that.

After a while, don't ask me how long – it was probably just a couple of hours but it felt like days – I managed to sit up. I realized I was in some tiny cove shaped like a horseshoe, so small I don't even think it has a name. Selina and I had been there a few times, but had never found much there; it wasn't one of our regular haunts. I tried calling out for help, but there didn't seem to be anyone about – to have seen me at all you'd have had to lean right over the cliff edge. The longer I lay there waiting, the more I began to think that maybe I didn't want to be rescued after all. I didn't know what had happened to Selina but I started to think she could be dead. I couldn't face being on my own any more. Life had never made much sense with her, but without her it was completely point-less. I seriously considered crawling back into the sea and drowning myself.

But then I thought, what if Selina hadn't drowned? What if she'd managed to get control of the boat, or was lying on some beach somewhere, wondering if I were dead? What if this turned out to be some awful Romeo and Juliet kind of mix-up? I could go kill myself and then she'd be without me. I decided I had to find out for certain what had happened to her. But I was feeling so weak. I'd swallowed a lot of salt water and been badly sick. I needed a drink, desperately. I had to get off the beach. I don't know how I did it, but I gritted my teeth and edged my way up the rocky path inch by inch, setting myself a new target every couple of feet – that piece of slate, that clump of heather – until I finally made it to the top. Once I was up there I just collapsed on the grass, exhausted. I have no idea how long I lay there – could have been hours.

It was Jory who found me. He was on his way to Langham's farm to borrow some piece of equipment when he saw my legs poking out from behind the gorse bushes at the cliff edge. He couldn't understand what the hell I was doing lying on the ground, soaking wet, covered in bruises. My eyes were open and I was staring up at the sky, watching the moving clouds, and suddenly there was this face leaning over me, like an angel.

He bent down and I managed to get a few words out, told him what had happened. He instantly wanted to go fetch Charles, but I said no – I remember I grabbed his ankle to stop him running off. I couldn't bear the thought of going back to the house, to be put to bed and nursed by that woman, to have to listen to Charles reprimanding me for my gross stupidity in going out in the storm . . . It was a moment of pure thought, a revelation. I knew that if Selina was dead, there was no way I was ever going back to the Rosewarnes. I wanted them to believe that I had drowned too – it was the only way I was ever going to truly escape. Of course that meant deceiving you too, Nellie, and believe me, I didn't want to do that, but – well, at the time, there didn't seem to be any choice.

Jory said he'd carry me back to the farm, but I said no to

that too: it was too risky and I couldn't expect his mother to hide me. We thought about using one of the cowsheds or the haybarn, but Jory's dad had just taken on a couple of Italians and they were bound to find me. Then I remembered the smuggler's cave. It was perfect – not many people knew it existed, and though they might search the beaches they'd never imagine that I was hiding somewhere. So that's where Jory took me – lifted me onto his back and carried me to the beach, edged his way down the narrow path with me clinging round his neck like a baby. We found the cave and he laid me on the sand, in the darkness. I was shivering so he covered me with his jacket; later he brought me candles and firewood, blankets, pails of water and as much food as he could sneak out of the house without his mom noticing. I reckoned I could stay there until they'd given up looking for my corpse; then, as soon I was fit enough, I'd sneak out of town and make my own way to London.

It was a lot to ask of Jory. He'd find a way to bring me food and water every day and I'd ask him if they'd found Selina, but the answer was always no. No news. He told me that Clara had had some kind of breakdown, Charles had been arrested and some people in the village were saying he was a traitor . . . I wasn't surprised. I'd always had my suspicions about him, you know that. Jory kept telling me how upset you were and that he couldn't bear it, seeing you suffer when he knew I was still alive. He wanted to tell you the truth, but I pleaded with him not to. I promised him I would get in touch with you later, once I'd gotten away.

Those were the most wretched weeks of my entire life. Physically I was OK, but mentally I didn't know if I was alive or dead. Trapped in the cave I lost all sense of time: day slipped into night and back again without me knowing it. I was having nightmares, hallucinating, imagining that I was still out there in the middle of the storm, Selina and I flailing about in the water, calling for each other in the darkness . . . Or I'd dream she was with me, lying next to me on the ground under the blanket, holding me tight, kissing my face. I'd be running my fingers through her hair and stroking her naked back, and as my hands ran down below her waist I'd suddenly feel something cold and slimy and I'd pull away sharp. 'Don't worry,' she'd whisper, 'I'm a merrymaid now, it's just my tail . . .'

I began to venture out onto the beach. I'd stand at the edge of the shore and look for her, hoping to see her darting in and out of the sea like a flying fish. Sometimes I'd catch sight of something bobbing on the surface of the waves. My heart would leap and I'd start shouting her name, wading towards her – but it was only ever a gull or a piece of driftwood.

Or I imagined she was sitting on a rock just a few yards out to sea, warming her body in the sunshine, untangling her long tresses with a shell comb and singing a strange wistful song. She'd beckon me forward and I'd walk blindly into the water, not caring if I lived or drowned. As I reached her rock she'd slide effortlessly into the sea and wrap her arms around me and kiss me with her cold wet lips. And then she'd pull me down with her, underneath the water, and we'd sink to the bottom. At first I would splutter and try to reach the surface, but then I'd see that she was nodding and smiling, gesturing for me to follow her, and I'd realize that I could breathe. She'd take my hand and we'd swim through the underwater forests of kelp until we reached her cavern, nestling at the base of a rocky island in the middle of the sea. And a great tiredness would come over me and my eyes would close. Selina would lay me down on her bed of soft sand and gently sing me to sleep while the waves rumbled above us and the crabs scuttled round my feet. I was driving myself crazy.

I knew I couldn't stay in the cave for ever, relying on Jory to bring me food and water. A couple of weeks had gone by: they'd stopped searching for my corpse; it was time I left and went on my way. But I couldn't do it. Staying close to the sea was keeping me in touch with Selina, and I didn't want to leave her. I no longer thought of her as dead. I was sure she was out there, waiting for me.

Then one evening Jory came to see me. He looked bad, really shaken up. 'They found a body,' he said. 'Mrs Rosewarne identified it, said it was you.'

'I don't understand, how come?'

'Don't ask me. I'm just tellin' 'ee what I know. Ellen's up at our 'owse now, breakin' her heart; Mrs Rosewarne's collapsed, lost her mind. You've got to come clean, Jack.'

'I can't, not now . . .'

'I know that body's not yours – by rights I should tell the police.'

'It's OK, Jory, I'll leave tonight and you'll never see me or hear from me again. But you must never tell nobody I'm alive, not even your wife when you marry, or your closest friend.'

'You'm my closest friend, bastard.'

'And you can't tell Nellie neither, you understand?'

'It's not fair, Jack, you can't do this to 'er.'

'It's the only way, Jory. Promise me you'll keep this secret for the rest of your life.'

He went back to the farm, grabbed me what food he could and a few more clothes. We both cried when it came to saying goodbye. I wanted to give him something, as a token, a reminder of me . . .

That morning there was a plane crash, remember? A Warwick exploded and dropped into the sea out in the bay, and the boats were out searching and stuff. Well, Selina and I found one of the passengers: his body was washed up on the beach. I can still picture his face – all black and charred, not human . . . His clothes were ripped up, and he was wearing this body belt. I know it was wrong, but I took it. Selina was mad at me for it, but I just wanted it, I guess, as a wartime souvenir. Inside there was this tiny silk map, smaller than a man's handkerchief – I gave it to Jory. He was worried about taking it at first, but I said if he'd manage to hide me for three weeks then sure as hell he could find somewhere to keep a little piece of cloth. There were a few gold coins in the body belt too, but I kept those to sell later, and there were also some identity papers.

The dead man's name was Paul Blanchard.

THIRTY

I wake to find myself lying fully clothed on top of my bed. But the clock says 2 a.m. and the curtains have not been drawn. My head aches and my mouth is dry. I feel dizzy and disorientated, as if I've taken a tranquillizer. I stumble to the open window and breathe in the night air. The sky is intensely black, pierced with millions of stars, the sea calm and inky – the tide is at its height, and it feels as if the house is floating. It's only now that I remember why I am here in the middle of the night, in this strange, still-dressed state, like a child sent to her room before bed time, exhausted with anger, crying herself to sleep.

Yesterday my brother rose from the dead.

I was very angry, yes, I remember that now. But at first I was just shocked, dropped my glass and fell to the ground. Young Gareth had to pick me up and carry me to a seat. I think he thought I was having a heart attack and tried to call an ambulance. But I stopped him, said I was all right, not to bother anyone, I was fine, just a little shaken. I wasn't fine, of course: my heart was pounding and I could hardly breathe. I wondered if maybe I *was* having a heart attack.

Jack just stood there, not knowing what to do. His wife came up then and crouched down in front of me, told me to take some deep breaths, asked me if I needed a glass of water. That's when I got angry – I pushed her away – I think I even told her to fuck off. I've never said that to anybody before. The sun was shining straight into my eyes, I couldn't see her face properly; all I could see was this long, silvery white hair. I thought she was Selina.

'How dare you?' I shouted. 'How dare you?'

'I know, I'm sorry,' said Jack.

'Just go away, both of you! Go away and leave me be!'

'Maybe we should,' said his wife, but Jack shook his head. 'We should call a doctor, she's in shock.'

'You won't get a doctor to come out here,' said Gareth. 'But we could call an ambulance, or I could take her to Casualty . . .'

'I'm all right! Just leave me be!' I squawked. Jack's wife – I can't remember her name right now, not Selina, but something else ending in 'a' – took Gareth to one side and explained to him what was going on. I don't know what she said, but whatever she told him made him look taken aback and flustered.

'I'm really sorry, I didn't know,' he said, coming back to me. 'Are you OK? I mean, with these people here? Do you want me to ask them to leave?'

'Yes . . . I mean, no . . . No, it's all right. I'm feeling a little calmer now. Thanks, Gareth, you go. Honestly, I'll be fine.'

'If you're sure . . .' he said, still hovering, wanting to do the right thing.

'Yes, I'm sure. Thank you. I'll call you tomorrow.'

'OK then . . .' And the poor bewildered young man let himself out by the side gate. I closed my eyes and held onto the arm of the chair, trying to steady myself, slow down my heart rate. I felt hot and faint, suddenly thirsty.

'I'm sorry,' repeated Jack. 'But there was no easy way to do this.'

'I'll have that water now,' I replied, opening my eyes and swallowing the lump in my throat. 'No, make it a brandy . . . And then you'd better explain.'

We sat in the garden for a long time, watching the sun as it travelled westwards, a large circle of orange flame suspended above the sea. Jack did most of the talking. The words tumbled out with scarcely a pause for breath. Although I knew it was undeniably him, it was like listening to an actor playing the role of my brother, creating his character as he might have been had he not drowned more than sixty years ago. But there were features of the characterization that seemed wrong. This older Jack was too tanned and wealthy-looking, the grey beard was strange, he was too wrinkled and he spoke in totally the wrong voice, cracking halfway through sentences with a soft mid-Atlantic drawl. Nor could I believe that my Jack would have become a professional artist, living in California of all places. And then this wretched woman with the long silver hair kept getting his name wrong – why did she insist on calling my brother 'Paul'?

It was all so confusing and disturbing, like being in a

dream where unconnected incidents are thrown together; where bits of different people merge into someone else. You know who they are supposed to be even though it doesn't look anything like them. And I wanted to stop the dream and tell these strangers they'd got it all wrong, that this couldn't be my Jack because he was only sixteen years old, and anyway he was dead.

I cried through most of his story. Just sat there and let the tears roll uncontrollably down my face, sniffing them up noisily until the woman who wasn't Selina went indoors and found a box of tissues. Jack was crying too, releasing the emotion that had been trapped inside him for decades. I have listened to such confessions before in prison cells, watched the truth drain out of a man's face, the muscles round the mouth and eyes gradually relaxing. Once all the poison is out, they look twenty years younger.

'So, Selina did drown,' I said when he reached the end. 'She was lost in the storm, like the title of your painting.'

Jack looked across to his wife. For most of the time she had been listening, but when he started talking about Selina she had stood up and gone to look at the sea. She was still there now, walking idly back and forth, her hands behind her back, head bent in contemplation.

'She didn't know about Selina till around three weeks ago,' he said quietly. 'She didn't know anything about my early life, not my real name, not anything. She knew I'd been born in the UK – I had to account for the accent somehow – but I told her my parents were Americans. Basically I made up a whole pack of lies. When I confessed, well, she was almost as shocked as you. I thought we were going to split over it, after thirty-four years together . . . It's been a rough ride, but . . . I've a feeling it's going to be all right.'

'It was wicked, what you did,' I said, without any anger in my voice. 'A terrible thing to do, to both of us. And as for Jory . . .'

'I know . . .'

I rose stiffly from the chair and stretched my back. 'I've got a terrible headache. I need to go and lie down.'

'Of course, we must leave you in peace,' said Jack, getting up too. 'Can we meet tomorrow? Talk some more? There's so much we haven't said. You've hardly told me anything about yourself.'

'Yes,' I replied weakly. 'Let's meet.'

I wake again at dawn after a long dreamless sleep. Drawing back the curtains, I look out of the window at a mackerel sky, the sun just breaking through, edging the clouds in light. Below me the sea laps gently around the base of the house, the waves barely frothing; there is calm without and within. I don't feel anger any more, only liberation.

I've arranged to meet Jack and his wife at their hotel in Padstow. I decide to walk there the long way, following the coastal path all the way round the headland, even climbing to Stepper Point. I am not sure that I am up to the task physically, but like Jack I feel the need to retrace my steps, visit a few places – knowing it could be for the last time, but not feeling afraid any more to say goodbye.

I stoke myself up with a good breakfast, fill a flask with cold water, put on my straw hat and proper walking shoes. I feel strangely excited, like an explorer setting off on an expedition, although this is one of the routes I know best in the world; I could climb every slope, cross every stile, round every curve of the cliff edge in my head. Leaving the house, I turn left and walk round to the sandy bay, taking a short cut across the beach, then climb the few uneven steps to the narrow path that follows the headland, passing the huge round blow-hole to my right, the sandy beach way down to my left and the vast stretch of deep blue ocean ahead.

Once I pass the limits of Clifftop Farm the path dips down into a valley, a small dried-up stream running through it, now a river of pink heather. I step over at the narrowest point and climb the steep hill, digging my feet into boot-shaped indentations in the dusty earth, an unofficial path made by the constant tread of walkers. I'm feeling breathless but determined, knowing that I'll be rewarded when I reach the top. There is a stopping place there, where the grass has worn away to pale brown dust. I edge forward and look down into the cove below, a tumbling of black rocks, a small flat patch of washed sand, and remember that this was where I stood with my mother, when she came here on her one and only visit long ago. I felt angry with her then because she would not look properly, but carried on joking with Jack, prattling about the other girls who worked in the munitions factory.

I walk on past the gorse bushes, their yellow flowers

almost gone, until I come to what I think must be the cove where Jack hid. I want to climb down to the beach and find the narrow fissure that leads into the cave, but I know I'd never make it. Besides, there is a DANGER sign there now warning tourists of falling rocks. I peer over the edge to the small oval of sand below, just taking it all in, noting, recording, filming with a mental camera.

I imagine Jack shivering in the cave, smiling gratefully as Jory arrives, the pig bucket sloshing with water, a pasty stuffed into one pocket, the end of a loaf in the other. They sit together in the gloom of a single candle and share a cigarette. And when Jory leaves – to stay too long would arouse suspicion, and besides, there's too much work to do – Jack blows out the candle and lies down on the hard, pebbly sand. He pulls a blanket up to his chest and dreams of his beautiful merrymaid, Selina. Of course he does. How else could he cope with her death? And with that thought, astounding in its simplicity, I realize that I no longer hate her.

I carry on past the Daymark and round the Point, descending now as the path takes me inland along the side of the estuary. Soon I reach Mussel Cove, where Selina used to live with her disgusting father, the old boathouse where she sat to mend the pots in winter, the mooring stump where they tied up the *Louisa May*. The cottage sits in the middle of a row rising up at a right angle to the shore, its front garden steeply terraced – I can't remember which one it was they lived in: they have all been refurbished, painted in cheerful colours, their small, narrow windows double-glazed, the porches filled in. I have not been here for years, fearing, I suppose, that Selina's spirit haunted the place. Now I find myself hoping for a glimpse of her, sitting on her front step perhaps, or dangling her legs over the side of the slipway. The wooden jetty isn't there any more, but I can still see it in my mind's eye – Jack diving off the edge and Selina laughing at him, pushing the shock of bright hair off her face.

I should have known deep in my subconscious that my brother was alive – I should have felt his beating heart, even thousands of miles away. Where was the twinning of our souls? Even when I saw the photo of Paul Blanchard there was no recognition, no inner stirrings, no spiritual awakening. If I have any psychic energy at all I have diverted it all to Selina. I have kept her alive all these years, conjuring her spirit from the sea like a morning mist, letting her drift through the house, brush my face as I stood on the edge of the cliff. I spent all my fury on a poor beautiful girl who drowned before she could grow up, punished her for something she never did, punished myself too – all useless, destructive emotion.

The path is flat now, winding behind the sand dunes. Tall straggly hedges obscure my view of the estuary but I know exactly what it looks like, can picture the vast mound of sand where the gulls feed at low tide, the gentle rise and fall of the dunes where sea snails cling to the spiky grasses. The blackberries are just ripening. I stop to let a couple of walkers pass by and nod a greeting, but they stare right through me as if I'm not there. I quicken my pace, afraid that I have disappeared into the landscape. I head for 'up town' – busy, bustling, touristy Padstow where the cars jostle for spaces by the quayside and children lick ice cream in the rain, where a retired fisherman will take you out in his boat and teach you to catch mackerel, where small boutiques sell floral Wellington boots and jute laundry baskets woven in Bengal. I want the Present, long for the Present. I have done with the Past.

My brother and his wife – small and beautiful with silver hair, who I still have to tell myself isn't Selina – meet me in the foyer of the faded splendour that is the Metropole Hotel. Jack looks calm and rested, a reprieved man.

'I knew you would come,' he says. 'Maria thought you might wake up feeling angry, but I knew you'd come.'

'We haven't got time to be angry,' I reply. 'Not now.'

'Shall we have coffee? We can sit in the conservatory.' He gestures at the door.

'Yes, please. I've just had a long walk, I could do with a rest.'

'I'll leave you to it, if you don't mind,' says Maria. 'You have so much to talk about . . . I'll be up in our room, Paul – OK?' I still can't think of him as Paul, haven't asked him to call me Ellen instead of Nellie. Rosewarne, Morrison, Blanchard – the names don't matter any more.

The sun is blasting onto the conservatory windows, heating the room like a sauna, and although Jack wants to look at the fishing boats on the quay he agrees to take our drinks outside to the small patio garden round the back. The white-painted wrought-iron table wobbles on the paving slabs, spilling my coffee onto the saucer. Jack leans across and pours the hot liquid back into my cup. 'Remember how Mum used to do that?' he says. 'She never would waste a drop.'

'We couldn't afford real coffee,' I remind him. 'Only that disgusting Camp stuff.' There is a pause as we sip our hot drinks, our cups clinking noisily as we lift them up and down. Jack unwraps a brown wafer biscuit and nibbles un-enthusiastically at the edge.

'How are you?' he asks.

'Still in a state of shock probably, but actually fine.'

'Manage to sleep at all?'

'Yes, surprisingly. What about you?'

'Like a baby.' He lets out a faint breathy chuckle. 'I am so glad I did this . . . I don't know why I didn't come clean years ago; no – decades ago.'

We carry on talking, taking turns to relate snippets of history about our respective families, a whirlwind tour around our spouses, children, grandchildren – the weddings and divorces, the long careers and the retirements, the big holidays, the illnesses, the deaths . . . When I tell Jack that my two sons live on the other side of the world, one in South America and the other in Australia, that I haven't seen either of them for years and have lost touch with Peter's children completely, he seems very upset.

'So you have no family living here at all? That's terrible.'

'Since Richard died last year I've felt quite lonely,' I admit. 'Very lonely in fact.'

'Thank God we've found each other,' he says, reaching out and clasping my hand. 'Thank God.' It's the first time he's touched me since we met and I like the feel of his warm, soft skin, mottled with the liver spots of old age – it looks and feels so familiar it could be my own.

'I have something of yours,' I say, breaking the brief silence. 'I thought you might like it back.'

He frowns at me questioningly. I reach for my handbag and take out a large brown envelope.

'What is it? My birth certificate?' He laughs.

'No. Just look inside.'

Jack gasps as he takes out the escape map. He runs the soft silk between his fingers, holds it up to the light. I wait for him to say something, but he just sticks out his bottom lip in contemplation, lost with remembering.

'Did Jory give it to you?' he asks finally, the words catching for a moment in his throat.

'No, his son did. It was amongst his possessions.'

'I can't believe I only missed him by a week or two. I really wanted to see him again, tell him who I was.'

'He worked it out.'

'You think? I don't know . . . I lied to Cassie, told her I'd never even been to Cornwall. I felt so bad about that. If only Jory had contacted me directly, I could have – I think maybe I would have . . .' He falters. 'I should have told him myself; at least I could have written or given him a call. But I got it into my head that this time you should be the first to know.'

'I'm sure he knew it was you. But he kept your secret to the very last.'

'Jory was a good friend.' Jack nods to himself. 'After all these years I still think of him as my best friend, you know that?'

'To you, yes, he was . . .' I reply, a little sourly. 'But not to me. He stood by and watched us suffer. Clara went to pieces, Charles aged years overnight – it took us years to recover. It would have hurt to know that you had run away, but at least they could have hoped that you'd come back. Jory deceived me very badly. In a way I'm more angry with him than I am with you.'

'It wasn't his fault. I put him in an impossible situation.'

'I was his friend for over sixty years – at least, I thought I was. I deserved to be told the truth.'

'Don't be too hard on him, Nellie . . . After all, he was the one who recognized Selina. He brought you back to me.'

'Actually it was me who recognized her and showed Jory.'

'OK, so it's Selina we have to thank.' Jack smiles. But I don't reply to that.

'Would you like to visit the cemetery?' I ask him instead.

'Didn't I mention, we went there yesterday.'

'No, the big cemetery, near the airport. There's a grave there I really think you should visit.'

He looks up at me suddenly, a flicker of panic in his ageing brown eyes. 'You mean, Selina's?'

'No, Jack, dear . . . Her body was never found.'

After Selina's death, Jack tells me, he thought he could never fall in love again. He did a lot of travelling and had a series of casual relationships with women of various nationalities, but couldn't find anybody who made him feel as strongly as he had done for Selina. He couldn't get her out of his head, turning his grief into an obsession with mermaids – collecting images, visiting galleries, researching myths and legends across the world, reading any stories or poetry he could lay his hands on. And painting them of course – in oil, watercolour, pastels, charcoal, pencil. Jack – or rather Paul Blanchard, as he was by then – made his home in California and started selling his work on the beach, mainly to tourists. Time went on and he started exhibiting in proper galleries, sold a few big pieces; some of his work found its way onto table mats, posters, posh calendars, art books for the gift market. He became known as the Mermaid Man. The trouble was he didn't seem to be able to paint anything else.

Jack was in his forties when he met Maria. She was a student in one of his painting classes, they became lovers and she started modelling for him. The reason for his initial attraction to her was obvious, but the relationship turned out to be more durable than that. Maria was bright and intelligent and a talented sculptor herself. She gave him back his sanity. They married, had children and set up a gallery together with two other artists. Gradually the need to conjure up images of Selina subsided and Jack concentrated on impressionist seascapes instead.

Poor woman, this pilgrimage of atonement must be very

hard for her to take. She is about twenty years younger than Jack, but even so she wears her age very well. An attractive woman now, but in her twenties she must have been stunning, especially with the mermaid hair that so enchanted Jack. He admits he made her promise never to cut it short. But hers is a safe, pretty-pretty look. She lacks the wildness, the unearthly, almost animal quality of Selina. I wonder how Maria feels now she's discovered she was a substitute for the lost love of Jack's life – a good substitute, I grant you, but a substitute nonetheless.

To her credit, Maria agrees to come with us to the cemetery. We take their hire car and on the way I tell them the story behind the plane crash. I even reveal what happened to my uncle, finally breaking the promise I made when I was sixteen years old. But I don't think Charles would have objected on this occasion. Maria finds this area of conversation much easier to listen to and eagerly asks questions about Charles and Clara, teasing out my version of the story and comparing it with Jack's, like a judge balancing the scales of justice. When I tell them about young Henry's death, Jack looks shocked and embarrassed.

'But – but they never said . . .' he stutters. 'I mean, if I'd known they'd already lost a son—'

'You wouldn't have faked your own death?' My tone is slightly challenging.

'I don't know . . . Maybe, maybe not. I still would have left somehow. I had to get out of their clutches.'

'I don't think the Rosewarnes were as bad as you make

out,' declares Maria as we turn off the Atlantic Highway. 'They were doing their best in difficult circumstances. And they had a tragedy of their own to deal with.'

'Maybe you're right.' Jack shrugs. 'We've all got some forgiving to do, I guess.'

We arrive at the cemetery and park the car in the lay-by outside. It doesn't take long to find the war graves – the two neat rows of pale headstones stand out sharply amongst the crooked slabs of weather-beaten grey. There is a modesty in their even shape and regular size: the smooth sandy-white rock looks almost new, unsullied, youthful – glowing with immortality. As we pass from one grave to the other Maria reads aloud the simple inscriptions carved between their regimental emblem and a long thin cross.

'*Arthur Stanton, Lieutenant-Colonel, Intelligence Corps, died 15th March 1944, aged 54* . . . *Matthew Henry Trudgill, Flight Sergeant, Royal Air Force Volunteer Reserve, died 15th March 1944,* no age given. *Gordon Douglas McBride, Flying Officer, Royal Canadian Air Force, age 23* . . . *Unknown Merchant Seaman, died—*'

'U*nknown Merchant Seaman,*' says Jack. 'That must be Paul Blanchard.' His voice is quivering.

'It's OK, Paul.' Maria puts her hand on his arm.

'I never thought he'd be in some unmarked grave – *Unknown Merchant Seaman* – where's the honour, where's the dignity in that? He's not recognized, he's just some anonymous guy. His name should be there on that tombstone, like the others.' Jack's crying freely now, wiping his tears with the sleeve of his jacket. 'I took his papers, so they didn't know his name. I stole his identity. His family never knew he was lying here all this time; they couldn't come and pay their respects . . .'

'Do they sell flowers here?' says Maria. 'I'd like to lay some flowers.'

'It's impossible to know who this man really was,' I say gently. 'It was a secret mission, there were SOE agents on board, they would have been travelling under false names. Paul Blanchard probably never even existed.'

'But if I'd left the papers on the body they'd have been able to work out who he really was . . . This is just – appalling.'

Maria and I lead him to a bench and he sits down, weeping, railing against himself under his breath. 'And who's the guy lying in the Padstow cemetery, in the grave that's got my name on it? Another victim from this crash, I guess. What about his family? Oh God, this is too much . . .'

'I don't understand,' says Maria. 'Somebody must have identified Jack's body.'

'Yes, my aunt did,' I reply. 'But the corpse had been in the water for several weeks. I don't suppose it was in very good condition. It's not very pleasant – fish eat the flesh, it gets bashed against the rocks . . . And my aunt was in a terrible emotional state; she couldn't bear the waiting any more. She wanted it to be Jack's body – so that's what she saw.'

Maria walks back to the entrance and buys some roses to put on the Unknown Merchant Seaman's grave. 'I'm so sorry,'

Jack whispers, resting his hand gently on the top of the tombstone. 'So sorry . . .'

My brother's so upset that Maria has to drive the hired car back to Padstow – she tells me she's never driven on the left-hand side of the road before and I can believe it: we have several near misses at junctions and she nearly kills us at the large roundabout where the A roads converge just outside the town. When we get back to the hotel Maria insists that Jack takes a rest, but he refuses.

'I'll be OK,' he assures her. 'This is a necessary part of what I have to go through. A kind of expiation.'

We walk slowly through the narrow, crowded streets, trying to return to some feeling of normality – we have lunch in The Ship; Jack drinks a pint of bitter; Maria wanders in and out of the shops looking at pottery, buys some postcards to send back home. As far as the rest of the family knows, they're here on a spur-of-the-moment holiday – but he's promised to tell his children the truth when they get back.

'I've booked a short boat trip for this afternoon,' Jack tells me, taking my arm as we walk along the quayside, bobbing with leisure craft. 'I'd really appreciate it if you'd come with me. There's a chap over at Rock who has a shrimper – he's going to take me round Gull Island. You remember, Selina used to call it her island, where Tom Penaluna used to lay his pots.'

'Of course I remember,' I reply. 'But there's nothing there. It's just a lump of rock and a few nesting birds.'

'I know, I know. I just want to go, for old time's sake.'

'What about you, Maria?'

She shakes her head. 'I'm not too good on small boats,' she replies. 'And you know, I think this is probably one trip down memory lane I can do without.'

So we leave Maria to go back to the hotel, and take the short ferry journey across the estuary. Our chap is waiting for us in a pristine navy fisherman's smock and cream trousers, a jaunty red scarf tied round his neck and a sea-captain's cap on his head – not a local, it turns out, but a retired business-man with a love of sailing. Leslie welcomes us aboard his small, trim boat, with its polished wooden deck and graceful white sails, and we set off towards the mouth of the estuary. There is very little wind today so he reluctantly turns the engines on, apologizing for the smell and the noise. Even so, we seem to be travelling very slowly, away from Padstow, crossing the Doom Bar and out into the open sea.

'This must be roughly where the *Louisa May* foundered,' says Jack, shuddering. 'It was pitch dark so I can't be sure, but it was some place round here.'

'I wish they'd found Selina's body,' I reply. 'It would have been better for all of us. Without it, you can't have "closure", as you Americans call it.'

'I never wanted closure. I'm glad they didn't find her body. It means she could still be alive, out here somewhere, living the immortal life of a merrymaid. I like that thought; it's sus-tained me over the years.'

I sigh. 'You're seventy-seven – don't you think it's about time you stopped fantasizing about Selina?'

'I know, I know, you don't have to tell me, I'm a romantic old fool . . . But I can't help it, she still gets to me. Something reminds me of her almost every single day. I might be walking along the beach picking up shells with the grandchildren, or going for a midnight drive along the coast road, maybe just staring out to sea watching the sun go down. Sometimes when I'm on my own I have to say her name out loud, let the sounds wash round my mouth. Selina Penaluna . . I still play out scenes from our life together in my head, like it's a drama I've been performing for years and I know everybody's lines, can play all the parts.'

'How could you let a dead person have so much control over you?'

'Don't get me wrong, Nellie. I've had a great life, a happy marriage, wonderful family. I've done all kinds of things I never would have done if I'd stayed where I was. Things worked out OK, better than OK. My only regret is that you weren't part of it. Honest to God, that's my only regret.'

'Well, we're together now,' I say, a little limply.

'That's right.' He smiles. 'I'm going to pin a tag to our coats – *Twins. Not to be separated*, remember?'

'Yes, Jack. Not to be separated . . .'

The boat bounces over small, playful waves as it heads towards the island. Leslie shuts off the engine and re-hoists the sail, which flaps noisily in the breeze. Turning round, we study the coastline in the distance, a green-grey smudge of hills and pale beaches, outcrops of dark rocks. It has only taken half an hour to get here but I feel as if we could be a hundred miles away.

'I can take you right round if you wish,' Leslie offers.

'Please,' says Jack.

'It might get a bit choppy on the other side, so just hang on tight.' We slow down as we reach the rocks. A few coloured buoys bob about, marking out the lines of pots beneath. Jack sits back and absorbs the surroundings, taking in deep breaths of the atmosphere.

'This is where she said she'd live when she became a merrymaid. She said she'd lie on these rocks in the sunshine, swim with the crabs and lobsters, sleep in an underwater cavern.' He leans over and gazes down into the depths. 'I think she would have been very happy here, don't you?'

'It wouldn't have worked out, you know, Jack,' I venture. 'If you had eloped together. She would have hated London: she'd have run back here. Or gone off with some other man. It's just a fantasy. We all have fantasies about what might have been if things had turned out another way. I used to wonder what it would have been like if I had married Jory. I would have been a farmer's wife and lived here all my life. I wouldn't have gone to university or become a barrister, and I wouldn't have married somebody I didn't really love . . .'

'Don't say that, Nellie . . . You don't mean it.'

'But I do mean it. It's only when you get older that you realize the terrible truth of things, but by then it's far too late to do anything about it. Although not for you, as it turned out . . .'

But he's stopped listening to me. He's staring over the side, trailing his fingers gently through the water, holding his breath. He's thinking of Selina, imagining her swimming alongside the boat, her silver fish tail dipping in and out of the sea, for ever young, for ever beautiful . . .

Suddenly Jack lets out a small gasp and smiles.

'What is it? Are you all right?'

'I think I just felt her,' he whispers, laughing gently. 'She reached up and touched my fingers, held them for a moment, then let me go.'

'Oh, Jack, you're a hopeless case . . .' I smile back at him indulgently as the boat finishes its circle of the island and heads back to the shore.

THIRTY-ONE

The wave passes over us and I do find the *Louisa*'s still upright, though the deck's swimming with foam. I shout out for Jack but I can't see him. He's no longer in the boat, I can't see him anywhere. I call out his name and I think I can hear him shout back, but I can't tell where his voice is coming from – maybe from inside my own head. I lean over the gunwale and stare into the seething, boiling water. He's not there, but I keep screaming his name. I'm going out of my mind, my legs are giving way under me and I haven't the strength to hold the wheel.

The boat's tossing about, this way and that, catching the waves broadside, and another breaks over me and covers me in water. And I'm so despairing for losing Jack that I don't bother to hold on this time, just let myself break off like a piece of planking and be carried away from the boat. I'm swallowing water, choking; it's so cold I can't feel my hands or feet, and I'm still trying to see Jack but he's not there. The boat's moving away from me now, a black shape like a coffin, listing to one side, heading towards the rocks. I'm gasping and coughing, can't keep my head above the surface:

it's like something's dragging me under, claiming me . . .

Then I feel myself floating down and down, sinking further and further – everything's slowing up and I'm falling through the water, my hands drawing circles in front of my face. It feels as if somebody's there at the bottom, holding out invisible arms to catch me. No need to struggle for I feel no pain, just a warm, loving feeling as I come to rest on the sea floor. I close my eyes and breathe in the water; the sand's as soft as a mattress, the kelp lightly strokes its fingers across my face. It's like lying down after a hard day's fishing, all your limbs heavy as you sink into your bed, your eyes can't keep from closing. And I feel myself falling into the most beautiful, deep sleep. There's a great peace all around me, everything slow and calm. It all feels so right and natural I don't want to fight it, I want to be filled with the water, dissolve into the sea like grains of salt.

Now I'm leaving my own body and floating upwards again, towards the surface. I look down and see myself stretched out on the sea bed. It makes me smile for I do look some peaceful there, bubbles of air escaping from my mouth as I lie on my side, one hand to my head, the other across my chest, like I'm a small child fast asleep and no one must disturb me. I'm looking kindly on myself, not fretting, for I know I'm safe now and everything's as it should be.

But suddenly it all starts blurring and I can't see my body any more. I'm falling again, spinning round, colours are swirling all around me, bright greens and yellows, purples – it's like being thrown through a rainbow, so fast, so fast . . .

I'm falling through a tunnel, a tunnel of light, shining more and more bright the faster I spin. And now I can see clearly, but I'm inside a ball, a white ball of light, and everything is going on at once, all around me, like I'm watching it on a screen. Wherever I look I can see my life, every moment of everything that has ever happened to me, going forwards and backwards, one picture after another. I see zackly how my life was, all the things I ever did. I can feel just how it felt, smell every smell, taste everything I've ever ate. Round and round I spin, looking up and down and side to side, watching every moment of my life again.

I'm with Jack – oh, and he looks some 'ansum with his twinkling brown eyes and black hair. We're lying on the dunes looking up at the sky, laughing and kissing. His lips do taste of tobacco and pasties.

Now I'm in the boat, it's a cold morning and my fingers are numb. I take a lobster out of a pot – it nips me and I cry out, toss it back in the water. I'm sucking hard on my torn finger; it tastes of blood and fish and salt.

Years back and I'm in my seven or eight, running across the Doom Bar in my rubber boots, shouting at the top of my voice and nobody to hear me – the sand is hard and flat, rippled with waves. It's dawn, all pinks and lilacs, the moon a white coal burning itself out in the sky.

Back further still, I'm no more than a baby now. I'm in my room, tucked up all safe in my bed, and my mother is stroking my hair, wishing me sweet dreams. It's dark, late at night. I do reach up and touch her soft hair, see threads of gold in the candlelight.

I keep spinning, back and back so fast, to the very beginning of my life, to the moment I first saw my mother's face. It's like I've been thrown upwards, out of the water, and Morva's grabbing my wet slippery body, clasping me tight to her soft breast. She's so warm and sweet-smelling, her arms round me so strong, keeping me safe. She's crying and smiling and my tiny heart floods with joy, for never have I felt so loved and wanted.

Now the picture fills with light, bright white light like rays from the sun spreading all around me. I'm back in the water, looking down at my own body, still lying upon the sea bed. I know it's me there, but I do look some different. I'm naked, my clothes all gone and my legs too, for now I do have the most beautiful fish tail – shiny silver scales, flecked with green and gold. I'm gaking at my body full of wonder, for never have I seen a thing of such beauty. And it's me, me down there. I float downwards, gently back into my new-made self.

I start to stir, shifting a little. I do open my eyes and lift my head, looking around me. I can see everything so clear – a crayfish crawling between the clumps of black rocks, crushed shells, coloured stones, a shoal of small grey fish swimming through the quivering ore-weed. I reach out to touch them and the sand puffs up in my face, a cloud of pale pink dust. I smile, for I know there are new ways I must learn in this world under the water. I push myself off from the sand with my hands and float upwards, flick my tail from side to side as I start to swim – it feels so light and easy. I move slowly, gliding just above the rocks, weaving my way through the kelp, my soft hair floating behind me like a veil. And I never felt so happy, so at peace – for I've come back to my true home, a merrymaid at last.

ACKNOWLEDGEMENTS

This book is a work of fiction, a mixture of Cornish history and folklore. I have drawn on actual events that took place during the war – most notably the Warwick plane crash – but dates, names and locations have been altered. The story is set in a real place, but I hope locals will forgive the liberties I've taken with the coastal geography around Padstow. Selina Penaluna can be found in the Gothic tale, *A Mermaid's Vengeance*, by Robert Hunt, and inspired the creation of my character.

I am particularly indebted to the following authors and books: Neville Drury, *Seaborn*; Peter Hancock, *Cornwall at War*; K. C. Phillips, *A Glossary of the Cornish Dialect*; Les Merton, *Oall Rite Me Ansum!*; the people of Trevone, *Trevone 2000*; Barry Kinsmen, *Good Fellowship of Padstow*; Vic Acton and Derek Carter, *Operation Cornwall 1940–1944* and *Cornish War and Peace*; Edward Prynn, *A Boy in Hobnailed Boots*; Tor Mark Press Redruth, *Strange Tales of the Cornish Coast*; Craig Weatherhill and Paul Devereux, *Myths and Legends of Cornwall;* Ruth Inglis, *The Children's War*; Angus Calder, *The People's War*; and the *Cornish Guardian* (1939–45).

Many people have helped me with the writing of this book, but I would particularly like to thank the following: my father, Fred Page, for sharing his memories of East London and his experiences as an evacuee; my mother, Brenda Page, for her invaluable assistance with the research; Coroners Frank and Helen Warriner; former evacuee George Taylor; Tony Pawlyn at the National Maritime Museum; my literary agent, Caradoc King; my editor, Kelly Hurst; and of course David, my husband, for his enduring patience and support.

ABOUT THE AUTHOR

JAN PAGE is a novelist, screenwriter and television producer, whose experience ranges right across the age spectrum. Over the years she has written hundreds of episodes of television and thirteen of her plays have been professionally staged. Jan lives in London and is co-founder of Adastra, an independent production company specialising in the children's sector. This is her seventh book.